love will tear us apart

Holly Seddon is a full-time writer, living slap bang in the middle of Amsterdam with her husband James and a house full of children and pets. Holly has written for newspapers, websites and magazines since her early 20s after growing up in the English countryside, obsessed with music and books. Her first novel *Try Not to Breathe* was published worldwide in 2016 and became both a national and international bestseller. *Love Will Tear Us Apart* is her third novel.

love will tear us apart

HOLLY SEDDON

CORVUS

First published in hardback in Great Britain in 2018
by Corvus, an imprint of Atlantic Books Ltd.

Copyright © Holly Seddon, 2018

The moral right of Holly Seddon to be identified as the author
of this work has been asserted by her in accordance with the
Copyright, Designs and Patents Act of 1988.

1 2 3 4 5 6 7 8 9

A CIP catalogue record for this book is available
from the British Library.

Hardback: 978 178649 052 0
Export paperback: 978 178649 506 8
E-book: 978 178649 054 4

Printed and bound by CPI Group (UK) Ltd, Croydon, CR0 4YY

Corvus
An Imprint of Atlantic Books Ltd
Ormond House
26–27 Boswell Street
London
WC1N 3JZ

www.corvus-books.co.uk

For James, forever

PROLOGUE

'Are you sure?' I ask, my hollow laughter fading into a wavering smile.

'Deadly,' he says. 'Are you?'

I undo my jeans. I wriggle out of them and they fall to the floor. He holds his breath so I take off my T-shirt as well.

'Are you sure about *this*?' he asks, and I don't know if he hopes the answer is yes or no.

'If not you, then who?' I say, and unclasp my bra.

'Always you,' he says, and he pulls his T-shirt over his head. 'Always *you*.'

CHAPTER ONE

November 2012 – Sunday night

My husband used to get embarrassed by talk of how we got together. But once the story had been rolled around the dinner party table a few times to riotous appreciation, he seemed to flip position. He started to tell our story more often. He even added to it, ran his tongue over it, embellished and enlarged it. People are always fascinated the first time they hear it. 'I didn't know things like that really happened,' they say. Or they laughingly tell their own tales, adding, 'But I didn't really mean it!'

We're beyond that now. Even a story like ours can feel stale, and we don't have any new friends to tell.

Stories change over time, just like the rest of us. 'Time has a habit of ageing us,' as Paul's mum Viv used to say. And it's not just the dogged chronology of putting one day in front of another, it's the litter that those days scatter in our paths. The drip drip drip of post through the letterbox. The groaning repetition of school runs, after-school clubs and food shopping deliveries. The bittersweet climax that every holiday brings.

And then there's the big stuff.

Harry was surprisingly easy. We waited a couple of years, then decided it was the appropriate time to try for our first baby. We had the regulation sex every other day for two weeks a month.

By the end of the third month of 'trying', my breasts were tender and my belly was stirring with a gurgling nausea that *all television shows ever* had prepared me for. I knew even before I was 'late'.

Because conceiving Harry was so reassuringly textbook, and conceiving Izzy a few years later was so tortuous, there was even a brief time Paul worried that I'd conceived our son though an affair.

While doctors assured us that secondary infertility was 'very common', especially with my medical history, for a while Paul became so certain of my infidelity that he stopped mentioning it, as if he was frightened that one day I would throw my hands up and say, 'Yes, you cracked the case, he's not yours. Now what?'

When I look at my eight-year-old boy with his flutter of deep, dark eyelashes and a delicate stoop in his narrow shoulders, I know with absolute certainty that he is all Paul's. And Paul must know that too, now. Our son barely resembles me at all. In fact, neither of our children inherited my red hair and pale skin. But if I take an impassioned look, I can see why Paul would be suspicious. There were others, early on. Bodies that weren't his. And that's all they were, bodies. At the time, I had no idea he knew. Maybe I've underestimated how many of my secrets he's unearthed, while he's watched me so carefully and closely for the last ten years.

Perhaps he never really *knew.* Not the facts anyway: our one-time builder, fucking me dusty on the floor of the loft he'd just finished converting. A foreign exchange student I met on a doomed attempt to sign up for a master's degree. A woman in a swimming baths, just once. Paul may not know, but he knows me. He knows me to my bones.

Perhaps he knew it was an inevitability. But I stopped casting my net outside of our marriage as soon as we started to try for a baby. Then my body was Harry's. A vessel in which he could grow and twirl around, kicking me into funny shapes and swelling my flesh in a way I was scared it wasn't capable. Once he was born, I only had eyes for him. My body was more valuable than I'd known. It had higher purpose, not just something to be crushed against a near stranger.

Now, even if I had those passions, I wouldn't act on them. I would never give Paul a reason to cut me out of our family, to keep my kids from me, to start up anew with someone else. To do things that, until recently, I would have thought impossible.

CHAPTER TWO

1981

Last night, I dreamed about days I haven't thought about in years. I dreamed about the sticky, irritable summer of 1981. The summer we were eight and ten-twelfths. The summer Britain ran amok outside of the stifled air of Little Babcombe, our tiny Somerset village.

The riots that year outraged my father, causing him to ruffle his *Telegraph* so violently I imagined it would crumble in his hands. Between imagining the IRA bombing our car to the Toxteth youths smashing our windows, I spent weeks convinced of imminent, newsy danger.

When danger eventually came, it sounded like a whisper. I was sent out to play and barely heard it.

My parents were locked in their own cold war by then, both retreating into their private bunkers. My father in his office, when he wasn't flying to Eastern Europe, my mum dancing with friends at the Blitz Club and the Rainbow in her beloved London. There was a great deal of activity and quiet conversation about this going on among the staff at Greenfinch Manor, our family home, but I left it all behind to skim stones on the river, to make daisy chains or peel the cobweb layers of sunburn off my arms.

The air sagged, crickets rubbed their legs together in protest and pollen clung to my eyes and hair. The roads were carpeted with squashed frogs and slow worms, their innards dragged by cars and baked into the tarmac.

At the end of July, the whole country slipped inside to wave flags and wipe their eyes at the royal wedding. Most of their good cheer focused on Lady Diana Spencer, the doe-eyed nanny with impeccable credentials. Even my father joined my mother and the staff who were hovering in the lounge to watch the dress make its way into St Paul's Cathedral, while I made my way out of the side door and into my mother's abandoned studio to play with off-cuts of fabric and glue sequins to my fingernails.

By the beginning of August, I'd grown bored of skimming stones. I spent my days jumping from the climbing frame in the village recreation ground where the smell of the air was so strong you could taste the iron.

Or I lay on my belly by the stream, shielding my eyes from the orange sunlight with one hand, daisies tickling me through my dress, daring myself to take a running jump over the water.

One day, my gangly legs freed by summer shorts, I finally leaped. I cleared the stream easily, the water giggling below me. As I flew, I saw that the big rocks that had frightened me were just pebbles, magnified by the water. I saw tiny black minnows wriggling their bodies busily under mine, slipping downstream and out of view. I saw a reflection of my messy red hair fanning out from my crown like a cape.

I landed heavily, the perfumed grass rushing up to meet me. I sprang around and leaped again without a pause, back the other way, heart pounding. And again and again, daring my legs to stride out further each time, to stay in the air for longer. With every run-up, I took a step back, the momentum keeping me flying with cartoon whirly legs.

As I took my most daring jump, running up from the roadside to the stream, I felt my ankle twist under me, clicking like a cupboard door. I fell face first into the water, a slick black knob of a pebble bashing my cheek and narrowly missing my right eye. As I scrabbled out and crawled back up the bank, wet from chest to feet, I heard the thud of something in the grass behind me and rolled over to see two very thin legs coming into view.

'You okay?' Paul asked, squinting slightly as I got up onto my feet.

'I'm okay,' I said, wiping away my tears as if they were just stream water.

'Where did you come from?' I asked, suddenly angry and defensive in my embarrassment.

'I was up in that tree,' Paul said, lowering his eyes and pointing behind him with an arm that was more elbow than anything, drowning in a thin cotton polo shirt.

'And what were you doing up there, spying or something?' I'd cocked my hip to one side in a practised stance I'd seen on *Grange Hill*, watching it in secret with the sound down low.

'No,' Paul had huffed, turning to walk back to the tree.

'What *were* you doing then?'

'I was counting, if you must know.'

'Counting what?'

'Counting your jumps.'

Paul and I met every day after that. Never formally arranging it, but each leaving home straight after breakfast and spending the day together, only returning to our separate houses, briefly, to bolt down sandwiches that had been laid out for us, or to pick up our bikes or a pack of cards or a ball. At nearly nine, Paul was my first experience of habitual friendship, and I his.

Our children will never know the anxiety and pleasure of whole days and weeks yawning out to be filled, to be spent hiking through fields, making dens in hedgerows, swimming in the river. Parents with no idea or concern about where we might be.

We were wracked with fear almost constantly. Fear of the punks with their crunchy sugar-paste hair painted bright green or magenta. The ones we'd seen in town that loomed seven-foot tall in doorways, fingers pinching hand-rolled cigarettes burnt down to the nub. Fear of the IRA, who we were convinced had planted bombs across Little Babcombe. We threw whole days into terrorist hunts, inching under cars on our backs like tiny mechanics, checking for explosives. Fear of returning to school, of the daylight folding away into lessons. Fear of no longer being together.

Some time towards the end of the holidays, I was invited to have tea at Paul's house. Before I went, my mum called me into her room and I sat up on her bed as lightly as I could, knowing she was still feeling fragile from the weekend. She brushed my hair so slowly I thought she'd fallen asleep a couple of times. She scraped each half into bunches, grimacing slightly as she grappled with the hair bobbles and set it all into place.

'You look beautiful, Katie,' she told me as she patted down my fringe and straightened the thick straps of my gingham dress. 'Have fun on your date,' she said with a smile.

I scowled. 'Paul's my friend. That's all. I don't even like him that much.'

'Oh, I'm only teasing. Have fun.'

Paul's house was so different to mine. Most of the downstairs space at 4 Church Street was taken up with the living room, with a small kitchen behind it and a smaller bathroom and separate toilet behind that. In the corner of the kitchen was a wooden table with a floral-patterned Formica top. Great play was made of pulling it out and lifting up the drop-leaf extension to make it a four-seater. Paul was wearing a thick round-neck jumper and was sweating around his ears and forehead.

'I hope you like pizza sticks,' Paul's mum, Viv, said.

'I've always wanted to try them,' I answered honestly.

Paul's dad arrived home as the Findus French Bread Pizzas were being placed on the plates; a salad of dark green floppy lettuce, tomato wedges and egg slices sat in a bowl untouched, salad cream on standby.

'What's this in aid of, eh?' Paul's dad boomed as he came in, winking at Viv and ruffling Paul's hair as my friend shrank into his chair.

'I'm only joking,' he turned his wink to me. 'We've all been looking forward to meeting the guest of honour.'

'I can't remember the last time we had dinner in here,' Paul's Dad said, opening a can of Hofmeister as Paul looked close to tears. 'We'd usually be watching the telly, wouldn't we, Viv?'

'Stop it, Michael.'

'Let's put on some music, Viv.'

Paul swallowed and looked at his lap.

'Do you like The Quo, Katie?'

'I don't really know, what is it?'

Michael – Mick – found this hilarious. He crunched the sticky play button on the radio-cassette player. I heard the soon-to-be-familiar de-dun de-dun de-dun of every Status Quo song.

'Does your dad not like The Quo then, love?'

'I'm not sure, I've only heard him listen to music with no words.'

The adults laughed.

'It's really boring,' I added, enjoying the attention.

The pizza stick had gouged deep scratches into the roof of my mouth but I wished I could eat one every day. The little pieces of bright red meat like gems; the brittle cheese like a gold lattice. A nice change from the food that was made for us by Mrs Baker, our housekeeper.

I knew by then that Paul was ready for me to leave but every room held fascination. From the tiny WC and its sign, 'If you sprinkle when you tinkle, be neat and wipe the seat', to the beads hanging between the kitchen and living room. Photos of Paul coated every surface. I was fascinated by the videotape cases that had been made to look like old books. I wished my father's old books had Disney videos hidden in them. Viv and Mick were delighted. Paul told me later that they didn't even have a video player back then, they rented one for special events. They had recorded the royal wedding a few weeks before I visited. Mick had stood solemn-faced with his finger over the record button waiting for the exact moment the programme started as if it was his actual job.

Paul's dad was 'a jack of all trades' and his mum was a nurse. I only understood what one of those meant.

When it was time to go home, Mick drove us.

'It's okay, I can walk from here,' I said as his royal blue Austin Allegro reached the gates at the foot of my drive.

'Are you sure? That looks like a very long drive.'

'Oh, it's fine,' I said. 'My father doesn't like to open the gates to other cars.'

Paul looked wounded but his dad seemed amused.

'Thank you very much for having me,' I added.

CHAPTER THREE

November 2012 – Sunday night

I look across at my husband's locked jaw, his thin black glasses pushed back into the groove on his nose, his forehead bearing down on the road ahead. He's wearing a light woollen sweater and dark-blue jeans. I can't see his feet but I know he has tan brogues on. I'm wearing an oversize knitted T-shirt that I like to wear in the car as it's so comfy. My favourite jeans hug my legs and I've slipped off my knee-high boots so I can wriggle my socked feet in the fanned warmth of the footwell.

I watch Paul when he's driving, it's the most 'zen' he can be. He generally manages to tune out the bickering from the back, he doesn't hear the radio, he claims to only hear me on the third try. I try, and fail, to imagine what is running through his mind. What is he planning, while I study him discreetly?

His wrists are as slender as they ever were, the same wrists I see on Harry. Paul's are now covered in a thick, dark layer of hair that wasn't there when he was eight and isn't there on Harry's arms yet. The bones are the same though. I've grown to love those bones.

'Mum, Harry just said I was a himp-oh-pot-oh-mose.'

'You can't even say it!'

'Harry, why did you call your sister a hippopotamus?'

'I didn't.'

'You did!' Izzy trills. 'Liar!'

'I didn't!'

'You did!'

'MUM!'

'This is ridiculous,' I say, and I refold my cardigan in my lap. 'I'm not getting involved with this silliness.'

Izzy starts to sob, quietly. When this doesn't stir any kind of reaction, she grabs Harry's arm and bites it, quick as a flash. Her baby teeth carve grooves in what little flesh there is.

Harry yelps and Izzy smiles. Before I can say a word, Paul slams on the brakes and shouts, 'Harry!' at the top of his voice.

'She bit him,' I whisper to the side of Paul's head.

'He goaded her,' Paul says.

'It's been a long journey,' I say.

'There's no excuse for them going feral,' he says back, without lowering his voice.

'This is nothing.' I laugh but he doesn't. Holiday exposure to the kids is always a shock to his system, and we left Blackheath seven hours ago.

The tick-tock of the indicator is the only sound. The engine holds our breath for us and we pull back onto the road and roll into the blackness ahead.

We finally reach our holiday cottage. In the back, Izzy has fallen into a dribbly sleep while Harry is drooping, close to nodding off. Paul leans across and pats Harry's shoulder. 'We're here, time to wake up.' As Harry shakes himself awake, Paul opens the back door and scoops Izzy up into a curly bundle. His right hand is tucked under her bottom while the other strokes the mahogany hair out of her sweaty face. She's only four, but she's a solid little unit. I notice his knees buckle a bit.

Breathing in the tangy air, heavy with ozone and the promise of sea, I take Harry's hand. He's dozy enough not to fight me off – a devastating new habit that's taken effect over the last school year. We lean on each other as we walk up to the front door. The key is exactly where they said it would be. I'm giddy with relief.

'Come on, Kate, she's not getting any lighter,' Paul says, shifting Izzy onto his hip. I fumble my way in, and feel for a light switch on the unfamiliar wall.

'Oh, it's beautiful,' I say.

'This is nice,' says Harry, scratching his head.

'This girl is definitely growing,' says Paul, kicking his shoes off.

I know the layout of the cottage from the booking website, but it's always different in the flesh. You can feel the temperature of a place, smell the air freshener and the remnants of what the previous guests cooked for their last, melancholy dinner. The whole place seems entirely unknown, clandestine.

This cottage really is lovely. And it should be. I wrote off three whole days finding just the right place. One pyjama-ed leg tucked under me, clicking through galleries of pictures until my eyes stung. So many pretty cottages had sofas that looked a little hard, or an uninspiring white oven in the sea-facing kitchen. The lovelier we've made our own home, the more this stuff seems to matter. Avoiding disappointment to the point of mania. And it has to be right. No distractions, it has to be right.

Paul pads upstairs and I follow closely behind to click on more lights, while Harry sits heavily on the bottom step.

'Come on upstairs,' Paul whispers hard. 'Time for bed, Harry.'

Harry drags himself up to a wobbly stand and starts to plod up the stairs after us, before sitting back down to take his shoes off. I shouldn't have bought him lace-up trainers, it takes for ever to get him in and out of them, which drives Paul to distraction.

I know full well that they've not brushed their teeth as we tuck them in and kiss their sweet, sweaty heads. I didn't make them go for a wee either. I'll play dumb through any accidents.

I run back into the black cold to fetch a carrier bag of journey-mess from the car. For a brief, chilly moment I think about lowering myself into the driver's seat. I imagine moving my hands slowly around the soft curve of the steering wheel and gingerly feeling the smooth tip of the gear stick. But I don't sit down. Instead, I lock the car with a thick satisfying click and wonder what it would feel like to drive home alone.

CHAPTER FOUR

1981

In my memory, my mum's ill periods seemed more like long lie-ins. She'd be in bed but claiming that the rest was in preparation for going out to her studio. Theoretically, her studio was the place where she made jewellery and painted canvases or customised clothes.

Occasionally in the morning, I'd tip-toe into her bedroom to find the bed empty, and hear her throwing up in her bathroom. Once, I overheard Mrs Baker talking to her husband, who did the gardens for us. 'She's down with another bloody hangover.' One of my first thoughts after Mum died was, 'Hope you feel guilty now, Mrs Baker.' It's impossible to say how long Mum's illness was sneaking around her body, interfering like a malevolent version of *Beezer*'s Numskulls, planting little cartoon bombs. Maybe it all happened like a flash flood and all those earlier episodes were just commonplace hangovers – or come downs – but either way, I didn't appreciate Mrs Baker's constant, open judgement.

I don't entirely trust my recollections, though. My pace is off. Memories from several years can come in one big rush and neighbouring days can seem years apart. The past is a hall of mirrors and, besides, I've seen first hand how two children can have a totally different understanding of the same situation.

With all those caveats in place, I'll say that by Christmas after the first bout of illnesses, my mum seemed fine. She was back in her usual clothes, up and out of bed most days, sometimes before lunch. Her blonde hair was always a little bit wild, thick like a lion's mane and as shiny as shredded glass. She wore leather trousers and a lot of animal print. One time, she smeared a line under her eyes like Adam Ant but changed her mind when she saw me giggle. She was very young. Eighteen when she married my father, nineteen when she had me. My father, Roger Howarth, had been in his thirties. To her friends my mum was Suki, to my father she was Susannah. I think she'd also been Susannah to her own father but I never met that generation. Not on either side.

After the bout of sickness in '81, Mum emerged newly interested. Dressing me up and sometimes dropping me at the bus stop in her old Jaguar, so long as the weather wasn't too cold for the engine to start. My father hated that car, but my mother could never get to grips with the Alfa Romeo he bought her. And that never started in the cold either.

When I couldn't hold my mother's interest any longer, she returned to her London friends and I picked back up with Paul. At weekends, we peddled hard on our bikes to meet by the stream or cycle two abreast into Castle Cary, the nearby town. We'd whip by the crumbly orange Somerset-stone terraces, like cycling past rows and rows of LEGO.

We spent hours staring at the swans in the Castle Cary horse pond, daring each other to find out if they really could break a human's arm. The big white birds eyed us with contempt as we nudged each other and tried to calculate their wingspan. Most days, we bought a five-pence bag of sweets, inspecting them carefully through the semi-transparent paper before committing, trying to avoid any blackjacks.

In September 1981, Paul and I turned nine within days of each other and our adventures moved indoors as the temperature dropped. I visited Paul's house every weekend while my mum slept, shopped, or returned mothlike to the flame of London. My father stayed locked in his office. At Paul's, we watched *Grandstand* and the wrestling with his dad, ate fistfuls of lardy cake, wrote songs using Paul's tiny Casio keyboard and played card games like Rummy, Patience and Pontoon. We got really good at a game called Shit Head and I wish I could remember the rules. I certainly remember the giddy liberty of saying 'shit' without repercussion.

We briefly made up our own band. Naturally, Paul was the keyboardist because he owned the keyboard. We were heavily influenced by Sparks and Ultravox, whose megahit 'Vienna' we both loved. Our band was called The Captain and Kate, which I still can't say without laughing, although I took it very seriously for the three weeks we were in circulation. The best part was that Paul came up with the name, which means that for some reason nine-year-old, four-foot-tall Paul really did want to be known as 'The Captain'. He had a surprisingly emotional row with his mum when she asked if it was a word play on the Captain and Tennille and we disbanded soon after. *The Captain*. Even now, if a ship's captain appears on TV, Paul only has to raise one eyebrow and we're both in stitches.

In November that year, the tornadoes came, ripping holes in the country one Monday night. We convinced ourselves that they were coming back to hit Little Babcombe the next night and met after school to build a bunker in the disused coal shed in the Loxtons' garden. We spent ages sweeping it out and covering the walls with cardboard and masking tape. The sky was dark grey when we started and pitch black by the time we finished. Our hands were thick with coal dust that had mixed with frost to make a punishing paste. Paul had already changed into jeans and a jumper but I was still wearing my royal blue school uniform and what had been a crisp white shirt.

We took out tins of food squirrelled from the cupboard, torches, a pack of cards and a tin of biscuits. A haul we figured was all pretty tornado-proof. After six, I called my house from the chunky rotary dial phone in Paul's hallway. My mother answered, which caught me off guard. I asked to stay the night at Paul's and was given a breezy okay. That night, sleeping bags rolled at the ready, we lay on Paul's bed, topping and tailing. We were both wearing pairs of his pyjamas and our school shoes so we could act swiftly in case of emergency. The Z-bed was pushed against the window to protect us. We were prepared to run to the bunker when the winds came, and took it in turns to stay awake on tornado watch. We woke up on Paul's bed on Wednesday morning, curled into each other like baby animals, huddled for warmth. The freezing air outside the house was calm, the bunker untouched. Before I ran for my school bus, Viv made us locate and return all the stuff we'd stolen, although we were allowed a biscuit from the tin afterwards. Later that day, I was given ten strong swishes of the cane across my blackened bare legs for turning up at school thick with coal paste and wild-eyed through lack of sleep. I didn't go to Paul's that night, I lay in the bath, running my classmates' laughter and insults over and over in my head. I gradually let more and more scalding water into the tub until I couldn't feel my feet and my temples pulsed and the red welts on the backs of my thighs went numb.

My father spent most of Christmas 1981 in his London office, dealing with something happening somewhere in Poland that involved his money but that didn't concern me. My mum and I spent it in our pyjamas, Mr and Mrs Baker away visiting their grandchildren, the shelves gathering dust. We didn't manage to cook the dinner and ate beans on toast with cheese grated on top for Christmas lunch. We didn't watch the Queen's speech but agreed to tell my father that we had. It was the best Christmas I ever had.

On the morning of New Year's Eve, I came down in my nightdress to find breakfast laid out for the household. Grapefruit juice in a jug, tea in the pot, toast in the stand. Mrs Baker was back. My mother had called her so she could drive to London in the early hours for a very important party.

CHAPTER FIVE

November 2012 – Sunday night

'We must decide what to cook for Saturday night,' I say, as we inspect the kitchen, fiddling with the utensils and coffee machine, which is better than the one we have at home and is giving Paul stirrings for an upgrade. I want to lay the groundwork for Saturday night now, because if we leave it, we'll have left it until Saturday afternoon and it will become a problem. Our anniversary meal will become an emergency, we'll not know what we fancy, or where to get it, and the whole night will disintegrate into cold, unspoken nothing. My moment, my nerve, will be lost. Another ten years could trickle past.

'Let's have something local,' Paul says, half of his voice lost to the inside of a cupboard he's rooting through. He likes to have 'local' things. Cromer crabs in Norfolk, Welsh lamb in Wales, and Gloucester Old Spot in the Cotswolds. For a moment, I imagine him on these holidays without me. I wonder where he would go, if he could go anywhere.

'I'm not really sure what food Cornwall's famous for,' I say, lightly.

'Cornish pasties, do you think?'

'Yeah, yeah. Clotted cream and pasties. Yum, let's have a big bowl of clotted cream with a pasty on top,' I say with faux belligerence that makes him smile at last. I search online while he pours us a glass of wine from the complimentary basket.

'Seafood,' I say, 'and ale. Seafood floating in ale?'

'Ooh, ale,' he says, smiling easily now. 'That'll put hairs on your chest.'

I wish I could wrap this moment neatly and hide it away, among the boxes of baby clothes. I'm hoarding these fleeting moments even before they turn into memories.

In six days' time, we'll have been married for ten years. That's quite an achievement by modern standards. 'And they said it wouldn't last!' That's the joke people make, isn't it? No-one says that about us.

Ten years is tin, apparently, which I was at a total loss how to deal with. I can't imagine what gifts this would have encouraged even in the olden days. A tin hat? In the end, I just cheated. In my leather holdall, I have a pair of cufflinks in a beautiful box tucked into a new tin can that's been artistically 'distressed' to look like an old tin can. I also have a £500 first edition of *Under Milk Wood*.

Paul and I have always liked to make a quiet fuss over intimate events. Neither of us gets birthday or Christmas gifts from siblings, or parents. We don't have sprawling, extended families to make a big deal about anything, so it's down to us. It started a very long time ago, before we were 'together', even. With every pay rise and bonus, the prizes got bigger, the bar got winched up until the rope was so taut it squeaked.

Of course, I've not worked for a very long time so I suppose in the cold light of examination, Paul is buying both our presents. I don't think he sees it like that and I try not to. It's what he wanted and he never complains. Not to me. Lately I've wondered, when I've dared, if he's described our set-up to someone new. If he's allowed the corners of his mouth to turn down in symmetry with theirs, if he's rolled his eyes at the disparities and the sacrifices, things I never considered he might resent.

The cottage is relentlessly white, still bright this late in the evening. The walls are panelled with pale painted timber, the floorboards washed in a similar shade. An overstuffed sofa is the colour of clotted cream and the creamy grey rug tickles our feet like sea spray. It's white in a way only a holiday home can be.

The kitchen has huge suspended white pendant lights and the cream Aga makes my tummy flutter. Paul and I leave the curtains open and head into the living room. I place my glass on the windowsill and flop into a soft pale grey armchair next to a tiny window with just a slap of sea view. The deep dark blue is lit in peeps by the fat moon.

'Dylan Thomas honeymooned in this village, you know.' As I say it, I have my eyes closed but I know that an appreciative smile will be creeping across Paul's face. I glance over. He too has flopped onto a sofa, eyes closed, empty wine glass resting on the arm. His feet are bare and his toes wriggle this way and that, this way and that, in time to music I can't hear.

'You've picked well, Kate,' he says and I smile again. I walk over to top up his wine and he reaches for my other hand, stroking it just briefly.

'Let's take the kids to the beach tomorrow after breakfast,' I say. The hug of the underfloor heating leads me to make bold plans I probably won't fancy in the cold November morning.

I snuggle back down into the belly of the armchair, my head on a cushion that smells of cinnamon and nutmeg.

'I could fall asleep right here,' I say. And I hear the steady rhythmic breathing that tells me I've already lost Paul.

    I take a sip of my crisp, floral wine, and reach into my pocket. It's still there, of course. I don't want to see it again, not yet. But I need to check it's there.

CHAPTER SIX

1982

When it wasn't showing gloomy pictures of the dole offices and unemployment queues that year, the TV news was filled with the Falklands war. Mick was suddenly furnished with all sorts of opinions on and information about Argentina and its people. Like much of the UK, I think, Paul and I had never heard of the Falklands. When Mick tried to explain to us why 'we' owned an island eight thousand miles away, he grew quickly frustrated by our questions.

'I still don't get why it's ours,' Paul whispered to me as he made us a Kia-Ora in the kitchen.

'Maybe your dad doesn't really know either and that's why he's getting cross.'

Mick had a tendency towards tearful patriotism in certain circumstances, and blanket disapproval of the upper echelons of British society in the next breath. While Viv clucked and cooed over pictures of the new royal baby in the papers that August, Mick had rolled his eyes and made cutting remarks about another mouth on the teat.

'Dad's a republican,' Paul explained. 'He doesn't think we should have a queen.'

'Oh, hang on boy, I wouldn't go that far,' Mick spluttered. 'I just don't think we should be paying for them, not with all these new ones being born.'

'One new one,' Viv chided. 'Charles and Diana have had one little baby and it's a bloody blessing after the year this country's had.'

'That's how it starts, Viv.' Mick grew animated. 'You'll see, they'll have another one in a year or two, then another, then another. He looks like a randy bugger, that Charlie, and a nice young maid like her to get his hands on.'

'Mick!'

My own parents never talked like this. They barely talked at all. And my dad had nothing but respect for the royal family. But Viv and Mick seemed to enjoy play-fighting. Paul was used to it and rolled his eyes but I couldn't get enough, my face flushing with excitement.

'You're the only randy bugger around here, Mick Loxton,' Viv laughed as Mick chased her around, trying to slap her bum.

'Gave you one royal prince, didn't I? Fancy another?'

'Mick!'

Mostly, we had our eyes on September, and turning ten.

Ten was the big one. We started talking about turning ten almost as soon as we turned nine. Ten meant something back then. Nowadays, we'd no more allow our kids out on their own at ten or eleven than at five. They're shuttled between playdates and wholesome activities and extra tuition with their feet barely touching the pavement.

But when our tenth birthdays finally came, we got jobs sticking up skittles at the local pub, The Swan. Paul had to beg his mum to let him do it. It meant a late night on a Tuesday – a school night. Paul's dad Mick was all for it.

'It'll put hairs on his chest, Viv. A bit of work's no bad thing for a boy and he'll have our Katie with him.'

I was treated like one of the family by then. A fixture, so confident of my place in their world that I could let myself in the back door without knocking. I could touch the TV and the new record player with its built-in tape deck.

Mick collected us at the end of our 'skittling shifts' and dropped me at the bottom of my drive. His car smelled of warm ale and cigarettes and I was allowed to sit in the front because I was taller than Paul. My arms and feet ached from the night's work: stop-start, stop-start, yank the skittles into position as fast as possible or get a wooden ball in the shins. The journey home was only ten minutes but my head would droop over the seat belt. There were no seat belts in the back. Imagine that now.

My mother's attentions had increasingly turned to London by then. She talked vaguely about some fashion project or other with her art school friends, but the black marks under her eyes when she occasionally reappeared told a different story. I prided myself on being less gullible once I hit the lofty age of double figures. My father's business was experiencing some 'bumps', whatever that meant, and Mrs Baker was called upon to stay past supper and babysit, which she did only nominally. In the end, we all just did our separate things.

I didn't have to beg or plead with my parents to go sticking up skittles, I just left through the front door and let myself back in afterwards.

'You're so lucky,' Paul would say, and he'd roll his eyes behind his mum's back when she fussed and worried.

Sticking up skittles was hard work and poorly paid, but we were desperate to do it because it seemed so undeniably grown up. We each got a quid, a bottle of pop and a bag of crisps from Lorraine behind the bar. Lorraine was the landlord's eldest daughter, the closest thing the village had to a glamour puss. Her clothes were bright and thin. I used to see her getting off the bus from Yeovil on a Saturday, arms hung with bags from Chelsea Girl, Etam and Topshop. Of course, looking back I realise how much more glamorous my mother was, how Lorraine would have killed for a wardrobe like the one that my mum left behind.

Back then, Paul and I never let on to each other how much we despised those wooden skittles and the sweaty red-faced skittle players who yelled at us for not sticking them up quickly enough. We never acknowledged the splinters in our hands. I often dropped my pound's wages in the car on the way home, it was never about that.

Paul stockpiled his earnings, making a careful note of his running total in a little book from WHSmith. Any chips or sweets he bought were deducted from the running total in the front. Written neatly in the back was a list of things he was saving for.

After a few months, the sticking-up job ended abruptly. Letting myself in to 4 Church Street to wait for Paul one day, I found myself eye to eye with Lorraine from The Swan. She was at the foot of the stairs, struggling into her boots, make-up harsher in the hall daylight. Mick was sitting, skinny and shirtless, a few steps up from her. I was so surprised that I just turned and left, all of us wordless. He never mentioned it to me, or I to him.

I wasn't an idiot, I may not have understood it all but I knew she wouldn't have been there if Viv hadn't been at work. I knew something must have happened, something adult. It sat in my gut, wriggling and ever present, and I was distracted by that when we played. After a few days, I blurted it out to Paul. Even then, he barely reacted on the surface. His lip quivered and he balled his hands up into little fists but he didn't say anything.

'So your mum's right,' I said, trying to lighten the mood. 'Your dad is a randy bugger.'

Paul said nothing.

CHAPTER SEVEN

November 2012 – Sunday night

I wake up sometime after 4 a.m., alone in the lounge. I have the thick blanket tangled in my legs and my neck is cricked. For a moment, I don't know where I am or why I'm folded instead of flat and I blink helplessly into the dark. Paul must have turned the lights off when he woke up and took himself to bed. I wonder if he watched me a while before leaving and flush at the thought. I tip-toe upstairs and try to remember which child is in which room, check their breathing and sniff the air for accidents.

I creep down the hall, the floor squeaking under foot. The master bedroom is the whitest of all. Chalky white walls, thick cream carpet, white curtains, white bedding, white lamps. Even in the deep of the night, it glows like a harvest moon. I discard my clothes in a heap and shiver into my pyjamas.

I lift the covers as carefully as I can, trying not to let the cold nip at Paul's bare arms and feet. I shuffle in sideways and turn my back to him and am asleep seconds later. When I open my eyes again, Izzy is between us. Her whirligig legs work their way up and down my back as she burrows, snoring, into her father's ribs.

'How long has she been in here?'

'Not sure,' Paul whispers back. 'I woke up and she was already here.'

I turn over slowly and kiss her puffed-up pink cheeks, smelling the sweet perfume of sleep. Paul smiles and kisses the top of her head, her dark hair tangled but shining. She's one of those kids you just can't keep your hands off. Even though she's past toddler age, we're always carrying her, cuddling her, kissing her and getting in the way of her busy work with our pleas for attention and affection. Since Harry turned a corner and immediately found all affection abhorrent, Izzy has borne the brunt even more.

I cuddle up to her solid little back and fall back asleep until the sun streams in and she's sitting up demanding breakfast.

In the kitchen, I fumble around finding mugs and filling the kettle from a surprisingly feisty tap that sprays up my arms and jolts me awake.

'Did you bring anything for breakfast?' Paul asks without looking up.

'No, why?'

'The kids need to eat something.'

'Isn't there anything in the hamper? The website said they'd provide breakfast for the first day.'

'They don't like it, it's all adult stuff.'

'What constitutes "adult stuff"?' I lower my voice. 'Crack cocaine and dildos?'

Paul lifts his head and stifles a grin. 'It's granary bread and marmalade.'

I turn to look at the two panicky faces. 'Oh guys, marmalade on toast won't kill you.'

'Dad!' Izzy protests and Harry looks on the brink of tears.

'Oh, for goodness' sake. I'll go out and get something.'

I look back from the hall and catch Paul watching me as I leave. He looks down quickly like he's been caught out and I push outside, blinking into winter sun as the cold takes my breath away.

CHAPTER EIGHT

Viv and Mick

Viv had come from a Romany family originally, a background that was entirely alien to me. She had surprising blue eyes, very dark hair and skin that had faded from dark almond to tired beige. Her Romany background was not something spoken about, or explored. It only came out in arguments, when Mick would yell that she was nothing but a 'domesticated gyppo', and Paul would nod sagely and tell me, 'Mother has some Romany blood in her lineage.'

'So do you then,' I'd say every time. And every time he would look at me quizzically and then shake his head, like I'd said something so silly he couldn't even respond to it, he just had to scoot over it to save my blushes.

Considering that Viv's history made my children a quarter Romany, I wish I knew more. Their heritage is hinted at in their glossy near-black hair, if nothing else.

Viv loosened up about her past in later years, telling me the occasional story about her family's squeaky-clean caravan, her mother's jewellery collection, the money-making schemes her father came up with at the expense of idiot 'gorgias'. *Gorgia*, she told me, was a Romany word for a non-Romany person, too arrogant to think they might ever be taken in by a gypsy.

Although I found out about the big Romany secret early on into my friendship with Paul, I had no idea then how that little Romany girl had become a house-owning nurse with a *gorgia* husband. I only heard the real background story from Viv herself years later.

Viv had been one of four children, her father Fennix an important man in the traveller community and her mother, Bidi, something of a prized catch. Bidi had been whip-smart, fierce and creative. She'd demanded the best at all times, and that included from her children. All four kids had been educated by Bidi from what sounds like a curious and patchy mixed bag. Glamorous interpretations of history and English, absolutely no mathematics or geography and a very home-based version of science. Beyond this, Viv and her sister were exceptional seamstresses and her brothers were dangerously charming.

The family had lived on a semi-permanent camp just outside of Shepton Mallet, a few miles from Castle Cary.

At thirteen, Viv had met Mick while she was out blackberry picking and he was pinching copper pipes to sell. For a smart girl with a trickster father, she was surprisingly taken in by Mick's patter and the two started a clandestine relationship, kissing under the shade of trees outside of the camp, or cycling into Shepton Mallet for milkshakes.

Some time when she was fourteen, Viv's older brother Robbie had followed her to a dusk rendezvous, suspecting she was up to something when she had rejected the insistent attention of a visiting boy of fifteen, one ideal for courting and likely marriage.

Robbie saw his sister kissing and holding hands with an outsider and returned a short while later with their younger brother Dukey and two cousins. Mick was beaten badly, his eye socket smashed and a rib cracked. The next week, after being given camp-wide silent treatment, Viv was driven to the house in which Mick and his father lived. The house in which Viv, Mick and Paul eventually lived. She was dropped at the door of 4 Church Street with two bags of clothes. The brothers dropping her off had intended to extract a dowry from Mick and his father but took one look at the house and decided not to bother.

They all left the county the day that Viv moved out. The whole camp, ten families in all, upped and left for good.

CHAPTER NINE

November 2012 – Monday morning

I'm underdressed in a pyjama top, cardigan and jeans. The urge to fix the breakfast problem, to make everything perfect, has taken the place of common sense. The kids could have waited while I got dressed properly.

The sea rages metres away and I fight my way through the wind as I lurch along the harbour. Eventually I shove my way into a shop, which doesn't feel much warmer and doesn't sell a great deal of anything. I panic-buy and return back to howls of delight as I tip the bag upside down and watch the packets of biscuits, currant buns and long-life muffins tumble out.

Paul frowns at the sugary haul and bites into his adult marmalade on toast while I reveal my offering for him: a local newspaper with a humorously naive headline.

SEAGULLS CAUSE £60 DAMAGE TO BUS STOP

'Can't believe I turned my back on the glamorous world of journalism,' he snorts. 'Pulitzer for the seagull scoop, for sure.'

'Well, if you'd stayed in the high-octane world of B2B publishing,' I test, cautiously, 'we'd not be celebrating ten years of marriage.'

He smiles thinly then takes another bite of toast, swallowing noisily.

'Hey,' he says, as I pour us both more coffee, 'what are you having for breakfast?'

I push my hand into my jeans pocket and feel the fold of the letter, pushing its edge under my fingernails until it hurts.

'I'm not hungry,' I say.

CHAPTER TEN

Mick and Viv

Mick was seventeen when he acquired a wife. After years living without his mother, at first a woman's domestic touch was a bit like a holiday. Within hours of Viv's arrival, the house was being cleaned – a full-scale operation that required the mouldering carpet to be pulled up and burned in the garden, the floor underneath mopped and polished like a skittle alley. Within her first few days she'd darned socks and seams, bagged up their washing and rearranged the kitchen.

With very few words, she'd extracted money for the laundrette from Mick's belligerent father and cycled to the town three miles away, bags strapped to the handlebars and back of the bike, balancing like a circus act. She came back hours later with dried clothes ready for pressing. She did that every week but after the first few times Mick and his dad had stopped watching agog, and had started to complain that washing day was too infrequent.

Three years after she first moved in, Mick bought Viv a washing machine for her birthday – a big display of affection to apologise for a slip-up with a local girl – and she used the time it freed up to sign up for nursing college.

She'd wanted to be a doctor, but needed to earn money. She'd learned fast that both Mick and his dad earned sporadically and spent unwisely. Besides, she didn't even have CSEs let alone O-levels. People like her didn't do medicine degrees.

It wasn't an unhappy marriage. In fact, it wasn't a marriage at all, not legally. But ex-communicated from her family and her community, Viv's name was no longer hers to use so she took Mick's. Mr and Mrs Michael and Vivian Loxton.

I also took the name Loxton when we married. Taking my husband's name felt like a nice thing to do, the ritualistic satisfaction of a new signature. The unusually ceremonious and celebratory feeling to something as mundane as picking up new bankcards, the smile of the cashier when I asked for them.

For me there was no wrist wringing. Howarth meant nothing good to me, and 'Kate Howarth' had been dragged through slime and was ready for the bin.

Besides, while I never grew up coveting a husband's name (or a husband, for that matter), there were many years I wanted nothing more than to be a Loxton. To be truly one of the family.

CHAPTER ELEVEN

November 2012 – Monday morning

For our fortieth birthdays in September, we stayed in Whitstable in Kent. The dying summer air was thick with fish guts and ozone and we soon got sick of walking up and down the same little strip of jelly bean beach huts or the short sliver of cutesy shops before bursting back out into the pound shop territory at either end. The kids were miserable the whole time, real little whinge-bags. Harry bore the brunt of it. As the oldest, he's often charged with dragging Izzy down with him, or – if they're having a good time – getting her overexcited.

Paul and I were both only children: Harry and Izzy's dynamics are a mystery on some level, and curiously familiar on others.

I remember one childhood Saturday when Paul and I had been driving Viv to distraction with 'I Know a Song That'll Get on Your Nerves'. We'd both been singing it, I may have even started it, but it was Paul who got clobbered because I was 'a guest'. Worse still, Viv made Paul apologise to me because I had to watch him get a hiding. Paul fumed all night and into the next day, eyes pink with rage. I gloated a bit and then said he could give me a dead leg to even things up. He made a fist, but never struck.

Anyway, Paul hated Whitstable's pebble beach and seemed almost affronted, as if someone sneaky had designed it to mess with him. I took the blame because I'd made the booking. I felt sick with regret by the third day and probably took it out on the children. They were already miserable, they couldn't run around on stones and they wouldn't eat the seafood. I secretly didn't blame them. I couldn't swallow oysters for years after a university friend joked that that's what performing cunnilingus is like.

After living on chips and trudging around miserably for three days, we cut our Whitstable stay short. It had been a write-off from the moment Paul saw the stones.

After Whitstable's Big Birthday let down, it was even more important to get the Big Anniversary stay just right.

All eyes on Cornwall.

Harry and Izzy are wedged into opposing ends of the big sofa, staring at the television screen. The cottage came with a basket of assorted DVDs, all of which could have been grabbed en masse from a petrol station, and so far the kids have been mutually delighted by the exploits of a cartoon rat who works in a commercial kitchen.

The chill of the outside still sits stiffly in my bones so I go to the bathroom to shower. There is a beautiful roll-top bath – white, of course – standing in the middle of the room. Before Paul and I were together, he once sat beside me for ages cheering me up while I wept into the bath. It felt like a watery rock bottom at the time, but there were so many more depths to plunge.

I slip into the shower and crank it up as hot as I can get it.

Back in the kitchen, I spring the kettle on for a cup of tea and ruffle my damp hair with the towel. The underfloor heating is heaven-sent and my joints have stopped aching with cold. Right now, I'd be happy spending the whole week just tucked up in this little cottage, hiding. In truth, I know it's only a matter of time before the kids go stir crazy and we have to get out before we kill them.

It's obvious as I step back into the lounge that the kids' pact has already broken down and they're fractious and in need of fresh air.

'Where have you been?' Paul asks, his eyes narrow. In a laser like beam of sunshine I see the wrinkles around his eyes, just like his mum had at his age. For all his expensive grooming products and his £80 haircut, he's still his mother's son.

'I just had a shower and made a cup of tea.'

Paul says nothing.

'Do you want a coffee?' I add, avoiding his gaze.

'I think we should get moving.'

Paul, of course, showered earlier so he's ready to go. The kids are dressed in numerous brightly coloured layers under their thick winter coats. Izzy has her toy cat hanging from the top of her coat like a papoosed infant.

'I'm not sure that's a good idea,' I whisper to Paul, who doesn't respond.

I don't press the point but the number of daring rescues that have had to be staged for that stuffed animal is beyond a joke. Not to mention return visits to restaurants, shops, friends' houses. She's only spent one night without it in her four years, crying herself to sleep on our pillows as the morning light bled in. Paul had his PA arrange a courier to collect it from a 'glamping' farm in Suffolk the next day.

Before we leave for the beach, I tuck the handwritten letter carefully into the inner lining of my holdall, pushed up against the anniversary card. I pull on my welly socks and Hunters, give up looking for my gloves, and join the family on the front step.

'C'mon, Kate,' Paul chivvies.

'C'mon, Mum!' Harry yells loudly, joining in.

Izzy opens her mouth but closes it again. Her daddy ruffles her hair and pulls her coat up, stuffing her curls in so that her hood is bulging.

The beach at Mousehole is an almost perfect circle. The harbour with a protective arm around the gold sand and cerulean blue water.

Little fishing boats dot the beach in various states of undress. Some without sails, others with nets tossed over their sides like stockings. Paul breathes deep and talks about the 'working beach' and the 'noble lifestyle'. Paul is a lousy swimmer and an even worse fisherman. As kids we used to go stick fishing and the only thing he ever speared was a dog shit bobbing downstream.

Izzy and Harry busy themselves making a frozen sand castle, alternately blowing on their sandy gloved hands and moving closer to each other for warmth. I feel Paul's tentative arm around my shoulders and let it stay there.

I take about thirty rapid-fire photos on my phone while Paul tries to capture that one perfect shot.

'Thank you for finding this place,' he says, without looking over. His jaw is looser.

'You deserve a break,' I say, gently. 'You work so hard.'

He smiles, doesn't disagree.

'We still need to think about Saturday's dinner, though,' I say as we trudge along the harbour wall.

'Let's get lunch out of the way first, Kate,' Paul says.

'I just want Saturday to be perfect,' I say, surprised by the swell in my throat.

Paul looks at me quizzically.

'Fish and chips?' he asks the kids.

'Yeah!'

Sometimes, Paul will reminisce about the days that he and I would combine our coins and split a bag of chips. We'd walk around Little Babcombe, taking it in turns to carry the bag while planning our careers as a great writer and a great fashion designer. We'd shovel smooshy potato into our mouths, vinegar clearing our noses, grateful for the heat in our bellies. He was going to be a poet, a whiskey-soaked wordsmith. Me, fashion's new wunderkind and a regular on *The Clothes Show*.

Paul romanticises these moments more than I do. For him, they underline a certain ragged-trouser background that doesn't tell my story in the slightest. My family was undeniably rich. But Paul hardly came from Dickensian poverty. His family was aspirational working class, they had a tumble-dryer and used sheets of Bounce. Their house was always warmer than mine and his mum was kind and gentle. And there.

Perhaps pitching his start lower in the soil helps take the heat off the middling years where – not that I'd dare say it – Paul's fortunes were redirected by me. The rest, he did himself.

I've not been totally idle all these years, but it's been an unsatisfying and vague kind of busy. Every itch I've had, Paul's scratched it. The Indian head massage classes, the pottery, the Open University applications. He's tried to keep me busy, supporting my every whim, presumably to stop me sinking into inertia. *Back* into inertia.

As a result, I've gone three-quarters of the way to starting a fitness class for new mums, a dog-grooming business, a video yoga website. . . every project and plan, Paul has listened patiently, written the cheque, and never asked for a progress report. We've never discussed why the master's degree didn't go ahead in our early days of marriage, but he was unexpectedly home the afternoon I was walked back from the open day by another prospective student, a beautiful feckless French guy called Baptiste. As we stood too close and swapped numbers in the street, Baptiste's kiss fresh on both my cheeks and my lips, Paul watched from the window. I pulled out of that course and Paul and I spoke with only stilted, polite words for days.

The simple truth is that my grand plans are rarely my own ideas. Often I'll overhear someone in a coffee shop talking about returning to uni or starting a kitchen table enterprise. Or I'll read about someone in the *Sunday Times Magazine*, how they changed course in middle age to great fanfare and self-fulfilment. It's the result that appeals, but I tend to fall on the journey. I've always been this way. Years and years ago I watched *How To Get Ahead In Advertising* a few days before the careers event at my uni and signed up to the TMC agency's graduate scheme. Just like that. If my flatmates had wanted to see *Indiana Jones* instead, I'd have been on an archaeology course within days.

It's been a while since I started one of my projects but I fill my days. I drop the kids at school and walk on Blackheath or out through Greenwich and beyond, along the Thames. For hours, sometimes. I can spend a good while just picking up five items for dinner, and when I get home, I can spend another forty-five minutes rearranging the spice pots or fussing around the slow-cooker. My cleaner comes while I'm out, I don't need to make small talk. And I spend an ungodly amount of time doing laundry. I luxuriate over it. I love the way the utility room smells when the tumble is at full tilt and the washing machine hits forty degrees. It's so warm. It smells like mothers.

———

Izzy is picking at her cod like it's alien faecal matter and Harry has bolted his sausage and chips and is up on his knees, staring out the window. The chippy is surprisingly busy for a cold Monday in November. The only free table was right by the door. With every customer that comes in, we pull our coats tighter around us with pantomime shivers.

I take one of Paul's chips, catch his eye and smile. He's negotiating with Izzy. 'Just finish this little bit, c'mon Iz, you said you wanted what Daddy was having.' Harry is rocking the back of his chair in boredom and I put my hand on his shoulder to stop him.

Izzy still isn't eating any of her cod and big fat tears have started to tumble down to her chin.

'Can I have her chips?' Harry asks and Paul grinds his jaw, glaring. 'Go on then,' he says.

I couldn't face a whole meal and I knew that Paul would have questions about a full plate untouched, so I said I'd pick at theirs instead as the portions looked large. He's stopped arguing, but if he thinks he's being subtle when he mentally tots up what I've eaten and gently offers more, he's wrong.

I nibble at a bit of Izzy's cod batter. It's nearly cold and feels tacky and thick between my finger and my thumb. It's still delicious, but I can understand why a four-year-old wouldn't enjoy it.

The cod upset has put her off eating anything here but I know it's only a matter of time before she pesters for a snack. We're on holiday rules now so we'll probably give her two.

'Steady on, Harry,' Paul says, the sides of his mouth turned down. 'You'll make yourself sick.'

'I think he must be growing,' I say. 'He'll be bigger than us soon.'

I realise my mistake too late. Paul is sensitive about his height. Or, I suppose, about my height. He's of average height and I'm the same height as him in flats – which I exclusively wear now – and many inches taller in heels.

'Right, let's get going,' Paul says, standing up so his chair squawks on the tiled floor. 'Don't be a piglet, Harry.'

Harry shovels as many chips into his mouth as he can, one-handed, while he stands up.

'Harry!'

'Come on, Harry,' I say, peacekeeping. 'Daddy said we were going.'

Paul picks Izzy up and she cuddles into his chest and sniffs her fluffy cat deeply as if recovering from a significant trauma.

'What are we doing now?' Harry asks.

'I want to go home,' Izzy says.

'Well, we can't go *home* home,' I say. 'But we can go back to the cottage and warm up.'

'That sounds like a good idea, Mummy,' Paul says. I hunch over a little and walk behind him, Harry at my side. He is definitely looking taller.

I fumble with the keys to open up the cottage. The white light bursts out as we pile in and I yell pointlessly for the children to take their shoes off when all they want to do is get warm. I push the heavy cottage keys back into my pocket. The whole set is on one ring. Every window, the back door, patio and front. Two for the front. The weight pulls the waistband of my jeans down my hips. I could lock up everything I own and slip away. Instead, I pull the set back out, drop them noisily onto the hallway table, and take a deep breath. Five days to go.

CHAPTER TWELVE

1983

My room at Greenfinch Manor was on the corner near my mother's and next to a guest bedroom that was kept permanently made and very rarely used. My room was large and sunny, with a huge wardrobe that ran across one wall and a basin in the corner that I wasn't allowed to touch until I was old enough. No-one told me when that was, but at eleven I decided enough was enough and I moved my toothbrush from the peach-coloured bathroom down the hall to the green basin in my room without complaint.

My room was very pleasant, but the room I remember most fondly was the guest room. A part of me would like to try to recreate it in our home in Blackheath but I can't articulate exactly why that makes me nervous.

I always called it the sunshine room, I'm not sure if that was a name handed to me or my own creation. My mother decorated it – or rather, she designed it and instructed some local tradesmen on how to decorate it. It had pale lemon walls, deep gold curtains and thick, black carpet. To me, it looked like sunshine over soil, although I now know it was in the Art Deco style. My mother had found a huge black antique traveller's trunk with bright brass hinges, which sat at the foot of the bed like a blanket box. To the side of the bed stood a large, brass photographer's lamp on three legs.

The bed was tall and, in my memory's eye, it was a good ten-foot wide, although of course it wasn't.

Sometimes, I would go to read in the middle of the bed, lying carefully so I wouldn't leave a trace. I'd always loved the opening scene of *Jane Eyre*, although I've never finished the book despite trying several times. In the opening pages, Jane, ever so slightly grumpy with her dislike of long walks and being kept at a distance by the Reed family, tucks up in the window seat of the drawing room, shrouded by a curtain and snuggles into solitary reading in her red den. When I look back at myself, lying quietly in the sunshine room, reading *The Secret Garden* or *The Ghost of Thomas Kempe*, I romanticise it the way I did *Jane Eyre*. A lonely girl finding peace in a beautiful, private place. But that isn't how it felt.

As far back as I can remember, my family – my immediate unit of three – were like points on a triangle. Connected, part of the same shape, but kept at arm's length from each other. My father, I guess he'd be the point at the top, my mother and I on opposing ends of the bottom. I adored my mother but I'm not entirely sure why. Perhaps that's just the way we're programmed. She was fun, full of laughter and naughty words, she was beautiful and kind. But no more kind to me than to her friends, probably less, really. She certainly dropped everything when they called. I never risked calling for her.

My father, on the other hand, I saw as more part of the house than connected to a living, breathing group of people. I don't know if this has just become an apocryphal tale that I tell myself, but I swear on my eleventh birthday, my father shook my hand.

When it came to the actual logistics, the nuts and bolts of family life, we had a guy for that. Or to be more exact, we had a few guys and a woman. Mrs Baker ran the kitchen, cleaned the house and handled laundry. If all of us were home – which was rare – she sometimes got her husband to come and help. I would hear her chastising him from another floor, and imagine his gardener's hands trying to fold sheets to her exacting standards. Ordinarily, Mr Baker would just take care of the grounds.

I liked to imagine that Mr Baker was like old Ben Weatherstaff from *The Secret Garden* and that I was sour-faced Mary. That we would bond over the pruned bushes and he would teach me the names of the flowers as we mutually defrosted each other's outer shells. Then he would introduce me to my very own Dickon. In reality, Mr Baker wasn't a bit icy, he was very polite. But he had no interest in teaching me the names of the flowers and after bidding me hello in the garden, would patiently wait for me to go and play somewhere else so he could just get on with it.

The Bakers lived in the Manor Lodge, an old gatehouse the shape of a fifty-pence piece at the edge of the estate. The drive no longer ran past their window, so the gatehouse was a toothless tiger, its many backs to the road, to the Manor itself and to the village. The front door faced towards the old disused gate and the church in the distance.

When I was very little, I used to stay with Mrs Baker sometimes. I'd go for my tea and stay in the spare bedroom with a crocheted blanket and a clay hot water bottle in winter. The room had a little window seat, and I'd curl up with the Bakers' unpredictable cat, Tabitha, and look back towards the Manor. I quite liked staying with Mr and Mrs Baker. I imagined that's what staying with grandparents is like. My own grandparents were dead on my father's side, and bitterly estranged on my mother's. While the Bakers tired easily and put me to bed early, I also felt fussed over.

As soon as I got old enough, Mrs Baker would babysit from the comfort of her cosy living room. She'd do a final bedtime check on me, her torchlight bouncing around on the drive as she trekked up to the big building.

My father also had an occasional driver, Ted, and then there was Sid who lived in the village and could be called upon day or night for any kind of maintenance. Sid had been the maintenance man before my father bought the Manor so he seemed to come with the place. All of the staff were polite to me, polite in the way they waited patiently for me to leave them alone.

Sometimes, if Ted was at a loose end waiting for my father, he would drop me to school in the big black car. As we crunched out of the drive and onto the village roads, he would ask me about the day ahead, the lessons I had and whether I liked my teachers (my answer, always, 'no, they're all mean'). Then he would smile and nod in the mirror and wait for me to finish before sliding up the driver's screen. Then I would hear the muffled sound of the radio.

Sometimes, my mum would take me to school in her old light-blue E Type Jag, the top down revealing the glorious navy-blue leather seats, slightly pockmarked from cigarette burns. She always drove too fast into corners and would laugh manically, buoyed on by my excitement. The car was a right-hand drive, which my mother never seemed fully prepared for. It was incredibly dangerous and I loved it. Despite the high speed, I would always be late because we didn't leave the house until gone nine o'clock. My mother was not a morning person. Years later, even when she was ill and her whole body would itch from the medicine, making sleep almost impossible, she would still be unconscious in the morning.

Generally though, I caught the private minibus sent around the villages by my school, included in the fees and no doubt a selling point in a rural area. Knees knocking together at the bus stop in winter, feet sticking to the tarmac in summer.

I sometimes wondered what happened to the house while I was out at school. Such a big place, and it felt like I was the only bit of life in it. Did it sleep while I was out? A stone giant lying in wait, eyes closed. My father, if he was home, would sit so still at his desk he was like a corpse, propped up and painted, like a practical joke. My mother, for most of the day, would lie in bed, either sleeping or clunking the buttons on the big remote control to scan through the four channels of her boxy television on loop or flick through magazines until her eyelids were heavy again. I wondered if they ate lunch together; it seemed unlikely.

Occasionally in summer, my mum and I would eat lunch outside on the table, laid out by Mrs Baker. My father would be offered a plate but would stay in his office and pick from a tray. Even his eating was terse. In poor weather, a lunch would be laid out on the side in the kitchen and we could come in turn to take our food in safety, unwatched and alone.

So much is made these days of 'date nights' and dinners as a couple. If ever the children are away or a babysitter is offered, the automatic thing to do is dinner. Increasingly fractious text messages relay back and forward as a restaurant is negotiated and an available table found, legs are shaved above the knee, good shirts are ironed. Paul and I do it, dragging ourselves out and struggling to hear each other over the roar of other diners, when really we'd both prefer to fall asleep in contented silence on the sofa after a take-away.

But eating out is almost sacrosanct, protected by law. I heard about a pre-nuptial agreement in the upper echelons of our social circle that included both a date night once a week and a guarantee of sitting down to dinner as a couple and later a family, at least two nights a week. It had been knocked down from three, and was a sore spot. But back then, back in my childhood, the idea of my family eating together as a pleasurable, special thing was alien. Formal dinners were torture. And the thought of my mother and father *choosing* to dine together was laughable.

I mean really, God knows why my parents got together in the first place. I struggled to imagine my mother – her long limbs, mane of hair, nervous energy and wild laugh – even sitting down to have a conversation with my father, much less falling madly in love with him. And yet they appeared to have had a wild passionate encounter that burned brightly enough for them to rush down the aisle.

My mum, I can almost understand. Impulsive, even reckless. I could see her falling in love with the excitement of a whirlwind romance. And now to marry! And to fall pregnant on honeymoon! A love child! But not my father.

While she had been a teenager on their wedding day, he was thirty-three. A success already. A self-made man from a working-class background he'd long since rejected. A staid and steady hand. A man of property and means.

Suki didn't want him for his money. The thought would not have crossed her mind. She came from nobility that was born rather than earned, she thought nothing of the world my father had created for himself. She didn't need it or want it, because it was just air, just water, she knew no different. She wasn't grateful or ungrateful, she just didn't really notice. I think my father might have liked that because at least it was honest. I'd heard him talk to Ted about other businessmen, vain fools with young brassy wives only there for the cash.

Yes, my mother was far younger than my father. And she was golden and beautiful. But she was no gold-digger. Her interests in life extended far beyond being bought things because being bought things was just par for the course.

My mother had gone to art college in London for a bit, until I came along. She dallied with jewellery design, fashion, painting, sculpture. The huge studio on our grounds was set aside for her, but she rarely went in.

She'd mostly gone to art college for the social scene, she once told me. And her friends were wild. While I was still small and portable enough to be taken with her, there were picnics and bottles of champagne in lush gardens. I remember clambering around sleeping adults and wobbly drives home.

Mum was nineteen when I was born. She was still a girl and she remained girlish her whole life. Her art friends, as I remember them, loved me like a mascot. I was dressed up, and had my face painted. I was carried on knobbly shoulders, thrown in the air and petted. It was all very good fun. Looking back, it wasn't really *my* fun, I was just the recipient of fun being had anyway, but I didn't care.

When I started prep school, at nearly four, their fun carried on but I wasn't privy to it any more. Instead, I was in a huge classroom with fifteen or so other children and a strict woman in a blue dress. All the children at my school came from money, but they had all been more properly turned out than me. There were some patches in my etiquette and I never really recovered from being on the back foot. A girl from a very rich family, in one of the best private schools in the country, somehow I managed to be the hick.

Private-school kids attend from three until eighteen and their memories are long. And it's easy to stand out for the wrong reasons.

At eleven, I was taller than most of the girls, with no boy pupils to balance things out. I stood out just by standing up. And then of course there was the red hair. In a sea of golden pigtails and mahogany French plaits, my red hair pulled back into a ponytail did nothing to increase my social standing.

At home, I would read my mother's discarded copies of *Vogue*. I would look at the leggy, alien-looking women staring out from the pages. They looked more like me than the girls in my school did. That didn't really help me day-to-day, but it did draw me into daydreams. Those models and Mum's David Bowie records – which became my David Bowie records. Aladdin Sane and Ziggy Stardust looked back at me knowingly and I felt okay.

Sometimes, my mum's friends would post down copies of trendier magazines for her, like *I-D* and *The Face*. I'd plead with my mum to hurry up and finish them. She would savour them because they were so hard to find in Somerset. The waiting just enhanced my excitement. There was an almost animal tribalism, a war-paint feeling to the looks and the poses. I cut out my favourite pictures and stuck them in my scrapbook and then I tucked my scrapbook and magazines back under my bed, pulled on my jeans and carefully selected top and went out to find Paul.

For a boy, Paul was into clothes too. He was very particular about the colours he wore, and even more so the textures. Refusing jeans Viv had bought him because the waistband irritated him or he only wanted zips and no buttons. He's still like that now. If anyone ever asks if I buy his clothes, something I'm astonished so many wives do, we laugh and slap the table like that scene in *Goodfellas*.

In the end, when he was thirteen or so, Viv stopped bringing clothes home for Paul and just went along to monitor and pay as Paul and I traipsed around Yeovil looking for the perfect yellow polo shirt or new pair of drainpipes. I brought my own cash, rolled up in a velvet handbag that I loved, but mostly I was there in an advisory capacity.

Jeans were always the uniform, but we were both fussy about which type and Paul would petition and petition for Wranglers, back and forthing with Viv until they settled on a pair from C&A or BHS. When I was with them, I'd buy one or two things, off the shoulder sweaters (which would actually be very en vogue now) or leg warmers (which wouldn't). I once snapped at my mum for bringing back some miniature Guess jeans from London that matched her own. 'Why can't you get me some Clockhouse jeans from C&A?' I pouted, and she nearly spat out her drink in surprise.

CHAPTER THIRTEEN

November 2012 – Monday afternoon

In the quiet of our temporary bedroom I strip off to get changed into some comfier clothes, and catch sight of my pinkness in the long mirror I'd been trying not to notice. It isn't a bad body, fair to middling. Everything is a bit droopier, the wrong things are flatter. But it could have been worse. It has been worse.

Mine was once a tangled knot of a body, angular and dwarfed by T-shirts and sweatpants. Once you've experienced your own body disappearing, scrunched up like a Coke can, it's hard to shake it. The memory lurks in the mirror like a phantom.

I'm a tall woman. When you're slim and curvy, that makes you willowy. When you're thin, it makes you frightening, like some kind of spiky tree. Like the bent and bumpy old trees that my parents should now be. Of course, my mother died with her green leaves in place and I don't think my father ever had them, but I like the idea of it. I imagine them stooping to fuss over my children. It's wishful thinking to the point of delirium.

Anyway, I was pretty gaunt on our wedding day. My skin pale and dry, my eyes sinking into their holes. A few years ago, I floated the idea of renewing our vows. I could replace those long-hidden photos. I could grow my hair long for one last time. Our children could be pageboy and flower girl. How adorable and restorative.

Paul wasn't keen. 'I married you then, not now. It's not healthy to rewrite the past.' I argued that it was a celebration, a triumphant declaration. He argued it was vanity.

How simple that argument seems now. To think, I was able to huff and puff about his accusation of vanity, but I've had to keep something far deeper, and darker, inside for weeks now. Boiling me from the inside while I smile like a statue on the surface.

I perch on the bed, my stomach skin collapsing like a lopsided smile, my breasts frowning downwards. The letter feels endangered in my lap, although I know it back to front and could recite it in my sleep. I cannot recite it in my sleep, for all our sakes.

I was born slight, my limbs were long like my mother's and my appetite was twitchy like my father's. If I don't pay proper attention to it, I can become raw-boned. Losing my curves to a desert flatness, a constant chill settling on my skin.

Luckily, I went into advertising after university with its steady stream of client lunches, brunch meetings, biscuits on the boardroom table and booze on tap – literally.

My agency had a bar in the basement where the whole company would descend after work. Evenings would often turn into group dinners or swaying in a queue for a take-away if things had gone sideways. Even us grad-schemers took part, making the most of the free provisions and then peeling off for junk food on the way to the tube.

I started there at twenty-two, just after graduating. The agency, TMC, had visited my faculty during a careers fair and I'd made a beeline for the stand.

TV advertising had been such a constant element of my formative years that I almost didn't realise that it was a construct.

I found it a revelation that it was an industry with a set of jobs. As kids, Paul and I would play the ad game, where we had to race to name the product as soon as a jingle started on the box. Or we'd take it in turns to point to something in the local shop and the other had to yell out the tagline.

'We all adore a Kia-Ora!'

'A home's not home without Homewheat!'

'Hands up if you use Right Guard!'

I didn't realise at the time quite how much I soaked up, but whenever I was involved with brainstorming any TV campaigns at TMC, I would always think to myself, 'Would we have sung along with that?'

Of course, in those early days, most of what I did was grunt work. And I certainly wasn't coming up with any jingles.

In 1994, I started working on a bank of desks that had a fax machine at one end and a huge printer at the other. We each had computers, great big boxes with bulging screens. And we had phones with headsets and three thousand buttons. It looked like a typing pool.

I was a trainee account executive so I sat with junior account executives. Which sounds like almost the same thing but I was perched precariously on a significantly lower ladder rung.

For the first three months of the scheme, the ten of us grad-schemers had rotated through five different departments: account management, planning, project management, TV production and development. I'd imagined that TV production would be the sweet spot. Glamorous and creative. Making good use of all the artistic sentiment I'd carefully constructed throughout my three years at university. I hated it. And not only that, I was terrible at it. Project management was my second doomed assignment. In short, my projects were badly managed. I started to wonder if I was for the chop. And then I wondered what the hell else I could do. College hadn't really prepared me for much outside of creating impractical clothing that would disintegrate in most everyday situations and/or weather.

Don't get me wrong, I enjoyed college. It wasn't the free-for-all party time that my dad had worried about, but it was fun. Free from Somerset and new to everything, I felt scrubbed clean. A fresh canvas that could be splattered with any colours. I could try anything, safe in the knowledge there was always someone else trying something worse, wearing something brighter or saying something louder. I drank a bit, smoked a bit, took ecstasy and did not act cool. After swallowing my first pill, I convinced myself I was having a heart attack and told anyone who'd listen. Ecstasy was strong then, not the chocolate buttons you get now. For a while I went out with a Doors fan who was studying fine art. One night, we ate magic mushrooms while painting. It wasn't the mind-expanding experience that he'd billed. I ended up with five brown canvases, severely bitten nails and an anxious headache.

University is supposed to be transitional, that's the point. Three years is significant but not for ever. The years after university, *that* was my for ever and I wanted to make them count. Anyway, by the time I'd cycled through the other departments at TMC and arrived at account management, I was in last-chance saloon. Thankfully, through luck or design, it clicked.

If you watch *Mad Men*, you see Don Draper owning the room with his charm, laying out breath-taking ad campaigns that the whole fictional country will talk about, everyone hanging off his every word. Well, that is *not* account management. Account management is what Pete Campbell does.

So I finally found my calling – my work home – in the account management department.

CHAPTER FOURTEEN

1984

Because of our September birthdays, Paul and I were nearly twelve when we started secondary school. Albeit my secondary school was the same school as my primary school, I just moved into a different building.

Mick seemed to be absolutely loaded the summer holiday running up to secondary school. He also seemed to finish work at lunchtime most days and we were often taken to a beer garden for ginger beer and crisps. Sometimes we just strolled over to The Swan and bobbed between the beer garden, Paul's house and the recreation ground.

Other times, some of Mick's friends would be in other village pubs and we'd be brought along in the back of the Allegro, sliding across the seats as we careened around narrow lanes.

With characteristic melodrama, Paul and I considered it to be our last summer as children. We played the fruit machines in the pubs or sat on the grass and talked, sometimes stringing a blade of grass between our fingers and blowing solemn reedy tunes like we were blind old blues men.

Paul had always complained about his primary school, but I knew he was nervous about his first day at Big School – Ansell Secondary School. 'It'll be alright,' I said, not really knowing what else to offer.

'Dad says I need to find the biggest boy in my class and hit him in the face,' Paul said.

'What? Why?'

'He says if I do that, I'll get left alone,' Paul said, nervously.

'I don't think that's a very good idea.'

'I know.'

'You'll be left alone anyway, why wouldn't you be?'

I started back at Sunnygrove the same day Paul started at Ansell Secondary School.

By then, I had spent nearly nine years getting used to a school I hated. Nine years with people who left me, at best, cold and, at worse, in tears. School had always been something I had to get through, not something I could enjoy.

Before Ansell, Paul had attended a primary school where the mums took it in turns to watch the kids on the playground at break time, where the dinner ladies cuddled you and gave you an extra pudding on your birthday and there was a sleepy corner in the classroom if you wanted a lie down or felt poorly. He rolled his eyes about the lads playing football with a tennis ball and the girls stretching elastic to jump over while they sang 'stupid' songs. But when I told him what it was like at Sunnygrove, he stopped complaining quite so much.

For all my vague reassurances and Mick's bad advice over the summer, Paul wasn't left alone when he started at Ansell. From day one, he was a target. He wasn't allowed to just *be* like he was at his old school. In his first week, his choice to sit on a wall reading a book had led to his book and bag being thrown over the wall and into a neighbouring field, guarded by a line of thistles and stingers. His lunch was frequently ruined by kids tipping water into it.

So we banded together tighter than ever that year, our time outside of school a kind of salvation. It just felt easy. Unlike at school, we could breathe and just be still. We trusted each other to be kind, and felt safe to be ourselves.

At Sunnygrove, the emphasis was on learning the classics. Classic literature, art, history, language, philosophy. Even now I can reel off titbits of Latin as party tricks. Did *you* know that *'nihil taurus crappus'* means 'no bullshit'? As impressively useless as my residual Dog Latin is, the only things that really started to stick for me were literature and art. I'd always enjoyed a story, but as I started my later prep years, I began to read like a fever. And after years of him devouring books like most kids eat sweets, Paul was delighted. Finally we could talk about books the way some kids talked about Panini stickers or pop trivia. Paul's own school library was patchy and was largely used by Ansell's pupils as a quiet space in which to heavy pet. By contrast, my school library groaned with the weight of words. Its huge bookcases needed slide-along stairs to access the top shelves and you could get lost in its wooden corridors for hours, the perfume of the old paper other-worldly. I knew Paul would have loved to spend just a day in there. A field trip for one. But an Ansell boy would never have been allowed in the library. A boy, in fact, would never have been allowed through the front gate of the school. But I could check books out for him under my name. Every week Paul gave me a list. And the following week, he'd give the books back with a new list on top. We did that for years. He read far more of my school's books than I did.

It may not have offered many books but Ansell did furnish Paul with one wondrous gift, which he generously shared. An outright bottom-of-the-barrel vocabulary that covered every disgusting sexual indiscretion or toilet situation two pre-teens could ever hope to describe – never mind if they understood it. We practised the new words in whispers, laughing hysterically and trying them out in different contexts. One day, when I had come back into the school changing rooms from P.E. to find my clothes had been taken from my gym bag and hoisted up on a flagpole on the school front lawn, I let rip at the giggling perpetrators with such a stream of filth that my father was called into school.

Ted drove us home in silence. My father had, of course, smoothed things over behind the thick mahogany door of the headmistress's office. Without needing to be told, I went to my room for the rest of the day and night, and left the next morning before I could be noticed. Or not noticed. Alongside books, we started to pay more attention to music. Rifling through Viv's record collection and putting her seven-inch singles in order of our preference. 'Fire' by the Crazy World of Arthur Brown was our favourite and we loved '(If Paradise Is) Half As Nice' by Amen Corner, 'Pretty Flamingo' by Manfred Mann and everything by The Small Faces.

We put 'Flowers in the Rain' by The Move on the turntable repeatedly and took bets on how long it would take Mick to tell us – again – that this was the first full record ever played on Radio 1. If Viv was home, she'd always say 'yes, Mick' the moment he opened his mouth and we'd snort with laughter.

It wasn't just that we liked the old music, it was about abundance: there were hundreds and hundreds of shiny black singles, all lined up in proper record boxes.

Years before, Viv had arrived at Mick's with only her clothes. Buying records was a treat that Viv had allowed herself when she started to earn nursing wages at the end of the sixties. It took Paul and me holding a handle on each side to shift the boxes into the living room ready for a rummage.

But we were also becoming interested in the music of the time too. We were obsessed with Frankie Goes To Hollywood because there was so much outrage about their song 'Relax'. We liked Bronski Beat, loved 'Small Town Boy', and felt that it reflected us, even though it really didn't. I loved songs like 'Dr Beat' by Miami Sound System and Madonna's 'Like a Virgin'. We loved 'When Doves Cry' by Prince and Paul liked Howard Jones and Nik Kershaw. We both loved David Bowie. Always, and to this day. We have a Ziggy Stardust telephone box painted in our study in Blackheath; it was one of the first things I did when we moved in, dragging paints out that hadn't been prised open since college but had been moved from home to home.

And so we both turned twelve that September – old for our year group. Paul was given a Sony Walkman and I was given an electric typewriter and a party dress from Miss Selfridge that my mum had picked up in London. I opened that present before breakfast, perched on the edge of my mum's bed as she smiled and watched me from the pillow. She seemed nervous that I would like it, which was a new thing, possibly caused by my jeans outburst the year before. Mr Baker had already placed the typewriter in my room the night before, without ceremony. It was heavy and grey. I liked the fact that I had it more than I liked using it. Paul was the real writer and I was desperate to show him.

Mrs Baker gave me a birthday cake that she'd baked in the pantry, and a little bag with Miners make-up from Boots in it. 'Don't tell your dad,' she said and I hid it under my bed and wore it later that evening when I pedalled out to see Paul.

'You look like a clown,' he laughed.

'Well, you look like a fucking gaylord,' I said, fists in balls at my side.

'I'm sorry,' he'd muttered, looking down. 'I'm not used to you wearing make-up.'

'It's my fucking birthday,' I said, and I started to cry a bit, despite myself, bright blues and purples trickling down to my chin.

'I know. I'm sorry.' He shuffled around and watched me until I finished sobbing, something he had only rarely seen. He gave me an awkward pat on the back and then handed me a small parcel wrapped in a Londis bag and sellotaped neatly.

'I made it,' he said. 'I have to go.' And he ran off full pelt without looking back.

I listened to the mix C60 tape inside until the black ribbon spooled out, snagged on the workings of my Alba tape player.

Three years after we first met, I finally took Paul to my house. He was the first friend to ever step inside the gates. I waited until both my parents were away and Mrs Baker was out shopping. I'd promised to let him use the typewriter.

His house wasn't far from mine, but it had seemed to take a long time to snake our way out of the centre of the small village. I fumbled with our wrought-iron gates and suggested we should just scramble over the wall, like I often did, but Paul was worried that he'd be seen and people would think the worst. No matter who he was as a person, he was still Mick Loxton's boy; Mick was no angel and assumptions would be made. Eventually we got the metal moving and trudged up the drive.

Paul was sombre and weirdly deferential at first. He asked politely about the large paintings in the formal dining room, and the black-and-white photos of my mother, taken by a photographer friend. He followed me up the stairs like it was a walk to the gallows. I hadn't noticed quite how big the landing was until I saw it through his eyes. The downstairs of Paul's house could have slotted neatly into it. I almost apologised.

Paul's bedroom at the Loxtons' was the bigger of the two, a hangover from his childhood when his big bright boxy toys took up more space than Mick and Viv's chest of drawers and bedside lamps. In his room, there was space for a desk, a single bed, a wide, flat record player and a sagging bookcase that left enough space for a Z-bed and a holdall. My holdall. After a while, I saw it as 'our' room. A space I could describe in intimate detail with my eyes closed. It smelled of whatever was being cooked downstairs, and when the heating was on, the windows dripped with condensation that slipped over the sills and down the walls. I loved it.

My room was on a corner of the manor, with two sash windows along the longer wall and a smaller window on the other side. Each window had double curtains with a pelmet, dark purple velvet. Just looking at them with him by my side made me want to bundle him back out.

I pointed to the typewriter, sitting on its writer's bureau near the window but Paul was distracted by my wardrobe which ran the length of one wall, full of velvet dresses I didn't need, pretty little broderie anglaise blouses and fine cord skirts. At the nearest end, were several pairs of Levi, Wrangler and Guess jeans. I hoped he wouldn't look in, and notice brands he coveted that I never wore in front of him. Behind the jeans were some Chelsea Girl tops and a stripy tight dress I'd never worn outside of the manor but looked at a lot. At the back of the shelf along the bottom, I'd hidden my make-up bag even though the only person to clean in my room was Mrs Baker, and she was the one to buy most of the contents of the bag for me. Probably because she realised no-one else would think to, my mum certainly didn't.

I watched Paul scanning the room. The *Wired for Sound* poster from Athena. Framed. The David Bowie Serious Moonlight tour poster. Framed. Paul's posters were pinned to the wall with thumbtacks. His mum didn't allow Blu-tack because it took the paint off, but *framed*?

The thing that seemed to catch Paul's eye the most was the basin in the corner of the room, with my toothbrush in its pot. My own toothpaste! He looked at the basin, and he looked back and me with his head to one side, like he was waiting for an explanation. And then he shook his head a little.

'I'll put some music on while we do our homework if you want?' I offered. 'You can use the typewriter.'

'Sure, thanks.'

I wavered over the turntable, unsure what to play. I picked up *Let's Dance* by Bowie, turned it over like I was looking at it for the first time. Put it down. I picked up *Rip It Up* by Orange Juice and looked to Paul for approval. He nodded but then a door had slammed downstairs, jolting us into a panic. We rushed onto the landing and, once we could see the coast was clear, thundered down the stairs and into a corridor. I showed Paul out of a side door and leaned against the wall, breathing hard. I went upstairs before Mrs Baker could ask questions and did my homework lying on the black carpet of the sunshine room, heart still racing.

CHAPTER FIFTEEN

November 2012 – Tuesday morning

'Have you given any more thought to Saturday?' I ask in my lightest voice as I realise Paul is awake next to me.

'What about Saturday?'

'Dinner, about Saturday's dinner.'

'I've not even had breakfast yet. And it's only Tuesday.'

'I just don't want a nice thing to turn into a problem.'

'Well, right now you're the only one doing that.'

I bite the inside of my cheek and feel a gush of something in my chest.

Paul has one hairy leg hooked over the starched white duvet, his arms up against the headrest either side of his face like chevrons. I can smell his morning smell, the musty, slightly sharp scent I've woken up to for all these years.

He curls away from me and picks up his phone, glancing at it and replacing it on the side in one practised move.

'Work?' I ask but he's staring at the ceiling and doesn't answer.

I breathe deeply and glance sideways at the sliver of sea framed by the dove grey curtains. It's a bright winter day, golden sunshine plays on the cream carpet and the bed is as warm as buttered toast.

'I love it here,' I say, and I flip onto my side and look up at Paul.

'It's lovely,' he says, 'though I definitely think a week will be enough.'

He looks at me for a long time, and then pecks me quickly on the nose.

'I should get in the shower,' he says.

Seconds later, I can hear the furious blast of the water and I push my head back into the pillow.

When I open my eyes again, Paul is at the foot of the bed, watching me.

'I forgot to take the towel in,' he says, avoiding my eye. 'You should go back to sleep, Kate, I'll tackle the troops for a bit.'

'You sure?' I know he's sure.

After his shower, Paul dries in the bathroom and dresses quietly. I keep my eyes screwed shut and pretend I'm already asleep.

Paul's visibly uncomfortable under my glare so I never watch him drying or getting changed. Even after all this time, it still feels like a forbidden act. Like watching how a teacher behaves when they don't realise you're still in the classroom. And Paul prefers to get undressed in the dark. Like the first time.

I always dry and dress in front of him without a moment's thought. He has seen me beyond naked. He has seen me beaded with sweat, crouching on all fours, giving birth to a huge and hairy baby's head. Twice. After that, covering up after a shower seems almost insulting. But perhaps I should retain an allure, perhaps I was wrong to feel confident in a skin I thought he wanted above any other.

The first time we slept together in the light, my nakedness was raw and brittle. I heard him suck his breath in surprise, and pretended I hadn't. He'd made love to me the way you might handle a leaf skeleton or ancient piece of glass.

We'd expected to know each other's bodies but I too was surprised that his chest had thick hair on it, that his skinniness had rolled out into something more like 'lithe' or 'athletic'. I'd run my hands over his shoulders, measuring them silently, while he'd avoided doing any such thing to mine.

Ours is not the most adventurous sex life, or the most regular. It has been months since the last time, a lethargic near miss late at night leading to an almost panicked burst of activity the following morning. But our sex life is still probably more varied than some outsiders might imagine. We try new things occasionally. We make an effort. I buy new underwear every few months and try it on when he's in the room. That's a staple in our routine. Admittedly, we rarely kiss. We peck goodbye, hello, good night. But we rarely *kiss*. I don't recall ever pushing my mouth, hot and searching, onto his. In turn, his mouth is almost always somewhere near my ear. Only when he's had an awful lot to drink – an *awful lot* – will he whisper things into it. Things I'd never repeat. And then, the morning after, he dresses behind the door of the en suite.

I'm surprised to feel my eyes prickle when it strikes me that I might never experience these filthy whispered words again.

I want to stay under these warm covers all day. I find it harder and harder to get up these days. But throughout my childhood and right through to my twenties I'd sprung out of bed like a baby rabbit. It almost chokes me how heavy I feel in the mornings now. From Izzy's age, I was collected by the school bus at barely seven in the morning, early starts were in-built. Very few children outside of town attended my prep school, and we were scattered across the tiny villages so the bus took a good hour to gather us all up. I was one of the first, socks pulled up to my knees against the cold. My red hair in bunches, satchel, shiny patent shoes.

I would stand and wait, shivering and frightened of the words scratched on the old wooden bus shelter.

When I stayed at Paul's for the weekend as a teenager, I'd wake up as soon as I heard the click of Viv's kettle downstairs. Paul's mouth would be slightly open like a fish, his arm hanging off the bed and his scrappy chest rising and falling. I'd ease myself off the Z-bed quietly but he never stirred. Viv and I would have had at least five cups of tea, have covered all sorts of topics and be sitting tucked into the corners of the sofa by the time he'd appear.

Even at university I relished being up early enough to catch the rush-hour tube. I threw my arms up and let the tide take me, happy to be swimming downstream with a thousand faceless people, professionals I hoped to join soon. I drank in the sweat, the tapping feet, the sheets of newspaper smudging into nothing on the floor. Everything a blend of grey and neon. God, I miss having it all in front of me.

And then, after graduation, I was a part of it. I was up and at 'em. Glassy-eyed, fully made up and intensely caffeinated, bouncing into the office before 8 a.m. Sometimes I needed to be in the office earlier, summoned to a breakfast meeting or to prepare for an event. I was always on time, enthusiasm pulling me out from my warm covers. I can't even imagine it now.

At home in Blackheath, our household is alive by seven but I conduct the chaos from my bed for a good hour, yelling instructions. Finally, when the need for caffeine is too great, I slope downstairs. School is a five-minute walk, but we generally leave with three minutes to go. At the last minute, front door wide open, one of the children will thunder back up to their bedroom –

shoes on – to collect some urgent bit of paper or collectible card to swap. I stand there and shriek that they will *genuinely give me a bloody coronary one of these days*, but really I should just get up earlier. Every Sunday night, as I'm lying in bed running through the week ahead in excruciating detail, I promise over and over to myself that I will slow the mornings down, give myself more time, not blame the children.

Sometimes, when I've dropped the kids at school and my heart rate has returned to normal, I turn left at the last minute and keep Greenwich on my right. I follow the Thames all the way through the dust of Deptford and the hum of Bermondsey – so cosmopolitan compared with a decade ago. I plod on towards Southwark, my feet starting to sting from the repeated slap of the pavement. I stride out onto Tower Bridge and then wedge myself into one of the little triangle cut outs in the belly of the bridge. Time dissolves as I stare down at the old brown river. The boats stream underneath. HMS *Plymouth* sits like a beached whale in the distance, the square mile within shooting distance.

Sometimes that's enough and I walk home on gritty feet, arriving back with enough time to throw myself into the laundry and pick at a bit of toast before the school run gobbles up the afternoon.

On emptier days, I creep on up and over the bridge, eventually flopping down into St Katharine Docks, all cobbles and coffee places, gleaming glass buildings blocking out the sky. I tread lightly over the footbridge by the moneyed marina and count the little boats. So many names remain the same: *Mia, The Sheemaun, Pride of England*. . . I walk past the enormous anachronistic Dickens Inn, its big mock Tudor face gussied up with flowers. And then I'm there. Right outside the first home I ever bought, and the last home I bought alone.

I stare at the windows of my old flat like a jilted lover. I worry whether the new owners look after it. It always looks so tiny, pushed at from above, below, left and right – the middle block in a sea of LEGO. The little flat could fit inside our current home's kitchen–diner extension. Back then, all those British clichés about homes and castles. . . but it *did* feel like a tiny palace. A shrine to *me* and my adulthood. A sanctuary. But of course it made sense to sell it. It became the deposit on our married home, the real start of our new life.

CHAPTER SIXTEEN

1985

I loved Viv and Mick. I loved the smell of their soap. I loved the feeling of the rough doormat under my feet, the sofa that perfectly fitted the four of us and our lap trays.

All day at school, I would sit quietly and watch the other girls play-acting. Hours of pirouetting and pouting, hair-flicking and bragging. Underwired bras had spread like poppies that year, but Mrs Baker still bought me soft cups from Marks and Sparks.

At school, it was a race to the tallest tale. They all – *we* all – had so much already, and they'd still plump it up. Telling exaggerated tales about holidays, gifts, boyfriends, celebrity playmates. Yachting with Jagger's nephew or polo with a minor royal.

Viv and Mick were not dirt poor. But what they had was smaller and more cherished. One television, in the sitting room. One sofa. Two bedrooms because they only needed two bedrooms.

'Moving's for them's that have,' Mick once prophesied, when Viv tutted about the leaking tap and the bit of the kitchen known as 'mildew corner'.

'They're building new houses up near the hospital,' she said. 'And I bet those new houses don't have a doorbell that shorts the lights.'

'Fancy that then, Queen Viv!' Mick said.

They never moved. The house had been Mick's dad's. Maybe I'm making it sound like their reluctance to move was out of nostalgia or obligation. It wasn't, they'd both disliked Mick's dad a lot. When he died of a heart attack a few years after Viv moved in, they celebrated with a Party Seven and new living-room curtains that hung until the nineties. But even in the housing boom, as they watched their neighbours selling up for increasingly soaring prices, the Loxtons rolled their eyes like they were watching an entertaining farce.

The house at 4 Church Street was always warm and always vacuumed and polished, no matter how many shifts Viv had at the hospital.

By 1985, I stayed over on weeknights more often than not, catching the school bus from a different stop to my own. My dad was rarely home and Mrs Baker had known the Loxtons for years and trusted Viv. Knowing I was safe under Viv's gaze saved her the trudge up the drive with a torch to perform her cursory version of babysitting.

Most evenings, Paul and I would read our respective books by a nightlight and sometimes listen to Radio 1 or Paul's tapes or records. He was obsessed with the Smiths. I liked them a fair bit but he would listen to their records like a gambler listens to the horse tips, writing down the names of playwrights, poets and writers. Morrissey was his cultural curator.

So only once did we flout the trust we were given, and it felt like a very good reason.

It was all last minute. We saw the Meat Is Murder tour dates in the NME the day before, checked that Viv had a shift on the calendar in the kitchen and casually asked Mick what his plans were for the next night.

'Arrows,' he said, without looking up from the pools form he was deliberating over.

Darts at the pub while Viv worked invariably meant Mick would be installed in The Swan's snug until kicking out time, or staying for a lock-in, arriving back with no mind to check that we were sensibly sleeping (which we usually were).

The plan was set and Paul and I figured we'd get to Bristol, find the Hippodrome and buy tickets when we arrived.

I went home after school, did my hair and make-up, changed my clothes and grabbed a fistful of money left for 'food, or school things or what have you' by my dad before he left for Czechoslovakia a few days before.

I'd essentially dressed like Pete Burns from Dead or Alive, who were big at the time, my hair crimped *and* back-combed, a satin shirt I'd swiped from my mum's wardrobe and a denim skirt. When Paul opened his door to me, he was wearing his mum's blouse unbuttoned to the waist, black Morrissey-style glasses and drainpipe jeans. We looked at each other approvingly.

Paul's glasses were actually varifocals that he'd found in the Save the Children in Castle Cary. He couldn't get to grips with them, walking like a man on the moon as the ground seemed to rush up to him, and grabbing hold of my arm for support every few steps. In the end I took them from his nose and popped the lenses out before giving them back.

'Thanks,' he said, and we ran the rest of the way.

'What are you two dressed as?' The old man in the ticket office at Castle Cary station asked. We looked at each other as if for the first time. Paul with his little pigeon chest on display, my ludicrous hairstyle and daytime satin.

'Two child returns to Bristol Temple Meads,' I said, with less conviction than intended.

The old man passed the tickets over, laughing. 'Carnival's not 'til October,' he added.

'Thank you, sir,' Paul said, solemnly.

'Thank you, sir!' This made us laugh again and again as the afternoon train wheezed along towards Taunton.

'I don't look stupid, do I?' I asked, tugging my crinkled hair.

'No, you look ace,' Paul answered emphatically.

'*You* look ace,' I replied.

We arrived in Bristol at gone six. A group of older teenagers with Smiths T-shirts hopped off the train in front of us so we tracked them like shoddily conspicuous spies until one of them stopped and turned back.

'You going to the Hippodrome?' he asked, the start of a bum-fluff beard impressing us.

'Yeah,' Paul said, flicking his hair out of his eyes. I noticed with affection that he tried to make his voice sound gruffer when even now it's gentle.

'Wanna walk with us?'

We trudged in excited silence, bellies rumbling as we were used to having the tea that Viv had left for us by now. A big bottle of Coke was being passed around among the group, whose names we never learned. They seemed like a serious bunch, aged sixteen or so. When the drink came to me, I took a big thirsty swig only to cough it all back up. It'd been boosted with cheap vodka. Paul took a more cautious sip and passed it on, quickly.

'What time are they on?' Paul, emboldened, asked the bum-fluff guy.

'Who, the support?'

'Er, yeah.'

'Half seven. It says on your ticket.'

Paul and I looked at each other.

'You've got tickets, haven't you?' We looked at each other and blushed.

The plan, as devised by our new gig-going 'mentors', was to find a 'tout' outside the venue. This was a shady kind of character we'd not heard of before, naively believing that we'd be able to stroll up to the box office and buy a pair of tickets, though the gig had been long sold out. As we approached the building, a snake of flower-holding, weedy-looking poets shuffled around on the pavement out front. Some of them were stooped, others were sitting on the floor with their sprawling Doctor Martens littering the path. I felt foolish in my off-genre outfit and guilty that Paul had to be seen with me after he'd done a much better job of dressing for the occasion.

As the crowd made its way inside, we spotted some scruffy older guys looking shifty. A couple of the group we'd latched on to went over with my money to check if they were selling weed or tickets and came back with both. The former being some kind of commission that had not been pre-agreed but we pretended to be fine with that.

We lost the older group as soon as we were inside the Hippodrome, pushing our way through the smoky crowd and claiming a little spot somewhere in the middle just after James – the support act – had left the stage.

When Johnny Marr jangled those opening chords to 'William It Was Nothing', Paul grabbed my hand, kissed my cheek and jumped on the spot.

When I remember that night now, it's in black and white. For a first gig, we could not have asked for more. At forty years old, I still feel a surge of teenage pride for going.

Days later Viv had called through to us from the kitchen where she was doing laundry. 'Why is my good blouse in your basket, Paul?'

'I'm sorry,' I answered loudly for him, my volume still scrambled from the ringing in my ears. 'That was me, I borrowed it to try on and—'

'Why does it smell of smoke?' she interrupted. Paul and I looked at each other in a panic.

'I took 'em to the pub with me,' Mick said from the sofa, without looking up from his *Daily Star*.

'I don't want to know,' he said quietly to us, trying not to smile.

The funny thing, looking back, is how many times the girls at my school would brag about doing things with boys and having secret rendezvous and here I was, sleeping in a boy's room almost every night and sneaking out to go to concerts. But I never said a word to my classmates. I couldn't bring myself to shape it like that.

I think Viv and Mick might have worried more about us fooling around had they not been convinced that Paul was gay. Viv's childhood experiences of her male relatives left no room for foppish, soft-handed boys who were also heterosexual. And Mick didn't understand Paul at all. However, he never pushed his son to change or to 'man up', and he must have taken flack for it at the pub, especially when Paul started to affect a fey walk around the village, confusing camp for poetic.

Viv didn't seem to care if Paul was gay or not, even in those clumsy days of stereotypical sitcom characters and mean-spirited jokes. She just adored him.

And Paul adored his mum back. He tried to play it down but I knew. One time, when Paul was little and before we were friends,

Mick had done some work for a cash-rich 'it fell off the back of a lorry' type, called Bob. And one day, after dropping Mick off, Bob had given Paul a fiver, sloughing it from a stack.

Armed with his fiver, Paul walked into town all by himself at the age of seven. He spent the money on a gold-plated necklace for Viv. She wore it with pride every single day.

When Viv spoke about things that mattered to her, she put her hand flat on the top of her chest so the little gold necklace was pressed against her palm. When she talked about Paul and me, about our futures or our talents, the things that made her proud, her hand would creep up unconsciously. Many years later, when she watched us get married, she made this gesture. And then her eyes had sprung with tears and a strange rictus smile had ground her to the spot.

CHAPTER SEVENTEEN

November 2012 – Tuesday morning

I wake up again. I think an hour or more has passed. Downstairs, I can hear wails from Izzy and muffled protests from Harry. As I tug my jeans on, I notice the waistband is looser than I realised. It's not a surprise, my appetite slid to the gutter as soon as I found the letter. It's been almost as hard to hide that as to hide the letter itself.

I hear footsteps crashing upstairs followed by Paul bellowing, 'Go and cool off!'

I stumble out and pause by Harry's room, poised to knock. But I don't knock. I can hear his breathing from my side of the door, steaming, fast breaths, like a charging bull in slow motion. Like his father. It's best to just stay out of the way when they're like this.

Izzy's sing-song giggles flutter out from the lounge and I head towards them, hoping to get in on the act but the laughing stops when I walk in.

'Sounds like you're having fun,' I say.

'Yeah,' says Izzy, and flops onto her belly in front of the television. 'Harry was being really naughty though.'

'What did he do?' I ask Paul, in the same insipid and cautious tone I've been talking to Izzy.

Paul groans a little as he gets up and goes into the kitchen, asks if I want a tea without looking back.

I'm rarely privy to their fun. Izzy is the very definition of a daddy's girl. She belongs to him and he to her. She mimics him, does everything she can to get and hold his attention. He seeks her approval like a lovesick teenager. Like *him* when he was a teenager.

She was hard-won. After the first six months of negative tests and unwanted periods that increasingly felt like taunts, we ramped up the sex. Daily bouts of angry, defensive love-making 'just in case ovulation is out of whack'. Paul blamed me, though he never explicitly said so. I blamed me. We could only bring ourselves to fight that fight for a few more months after which we stumped up for our first round of IVF. We did everything they told us but it didn't work. Sometimes, it just doesn't work. The stupid thing, though, is that you always believe, on some level, that it will.

The second time, because we had a failed attempt under our belts, they punctured the outer shell of the two embryos to give them a better chance of implanting. I imagined the doctors scratching at our babies, and struggled to sleep for the images. All of the injections, seasickness, spots, excruciating extraction of the eggs and even the previous failure had been building up to that second IVF cycle. Despite the damp squib of round one, it felt like momentum would somehow carry us through this time. It felt like fair's fair, it had to happen.

During the two-week wait to find out if they'd 'taken', we even started to worry about handling twins. We started to write lists of all the double items we'd need, talked bedtime logistics and night nurses.

I took the pregnancy test in our en suite, getting up at five in the morning to use that hallowed first piss of the day. Afterwards,

I sat on the loo with the negative test in my hand for twenty-five minutes before waking Paul. Breaking it to him. Holding his head to my chest.

By the third round, I was a tight knot of hormones, emotions and spots. Our whole lives had started to revolve around injections, clinic appointments and small, sturdy sample pots. I worked myself up into an exhausting frenzy watching Harry sleep every night, suddenly all the more aware of how precious he was.

If the third round hadn't worked, I wanted to stop. To draw a line in the sand. A circle around the three of us.

Harry would have been enough for me. He was the love of my life. Unlike Paul, I was still so in awe of that rowdy little article that I didn't see an insurmountable loss in sticking with what we had. We'd have had to write off the thousands of pounds that we – Paul – had already ploughed into the endeavour, but it was hardly a good use of savings to keep throwing money into a black, scarred pit. As much as I liked the idea of giving Harry a sibling, that territory also felt uncharted, unreal and suddenly unlikely.

A few days before test day, I tried to tell Paul that I was ready to stop. He looked so horrified by the opening bars of the conversation that I back pedalled wildly. And then, of course, that cycle worked. One of the embryos didn't make it but Izzy did. And she's been making herself known ever since.

I had a tricky pregnancy – 'high risk' – needing weeks and weeks of bed rest. I lay on our bed like a big fat hen on top of the most precious golden egg. Harry and his little elbows and his excitement were kept from me at all costs. A nanny was brought in to look after him, while I lay upstairs too scared to move in case I shook the precious pearl free too soon. Like the cows and calves in the cruel Somerset summer, I could hear Harry cry for me as I lay murmuring for him. At thirty-six weeks, it became too much and I edged out of bed to go down to him, my waters breaking before I reached the doorknob.

CHAPTER EIGHTEEN

1985

After a year of extended absences that Viv had started to ask me about in increasingly concerned tones, my mum came home. Unfortunately, most of her time in Somerset was then spent being ill.

The lie-ins seemed to last longer and longer until they overlapped and she wasn't getting up for days on end by the summer. She had a constant cold and needed thick bedding even in July, but complained that she felt grotesque from night sweats. She wasn't really complaining to me, as such. She was just complaining in general and I was the only person who tended to hover near her bed long enough to hear it.

Sometimes she would tell me stories from college, or talk about the boys at the Blitz Club, muddling up years and months, sometimes, I suspect, confusing me for someone else in her feverish confusion.

We'd planned to watch the Live Aid concerts together that summer, using an extension lead to wheel the large television out onto the patio area. But when she didn't come downstairs that Saturday as planned, I crept up into her room. I was wearing a bikini top and shorts, my shoulders pink from sitting outside for just a few moments, trying to work out where best to put the TV.

As I approached the bed, I realised how thin and pale my mum's arms were. I saw a thick purple mark on her chest, peeping out from her nightdress. I knew not to ask.

'Hello, you,' she said softly, panting a little as she propped herself up with a pile of white pillows.

'Can we watch it in here, Mum?' I asked.

'The concert? Is that today already?'

She crunched the remote control to get BBC 1 up on the screen and I scrambled up onto the bed.

As Richard Skinner came on the screen to introduce the event, I lay down on my belly with my feet up near the pillow, chin resting on my hands at the foot of the bed.

About half an hour in, I looked around to smile at Mum as Style Council walked onstage, not that either of us liked them, but her eyes were rolling back and her mouth was slack.

The blistering day outside eventually cooled in the hours that we lay there, while my calves swayed in the air in a mimic of the crowd's arms.

I stayed on her bed until Phil Collins reappeared on the screen, nudging my mum to try to tell her that Concorde had flown him from London to Philadelphia to play again. She either didn't wake or didn't care so I flopped off the bed and went downstairs to make myself some toast before going to my room.

She slept until the early hours, when I was woken up by her shuffling slowly along the hall. I considered going to see if she was okay, until I heard her pass my room and head towards my father's. That was when I really started to worry.

After the strange, shadowy summer that year, I was almost relieved to get back to the routines of September. Almost. School started later for me than Paul that year so for his first week, I waited outside Ansell's gates to walk home with him. Every day we were trailed by a group of boys from his class yelling sexual suggestions and asking Paul repeatedly if my pubes were red like my hair. They hadn't put it quite like that.

'Oi short arse, do 'er collars match 'er cuffs?' was the politest version.

'Sorry,' Paul would say repeatedly, as if he was in any way responsible.

'I don't give a shit,' I lied, my heart thumping as they yelled and stamped along behind us.

On the final day that I walked home with him, they threw a small rock which sailed over Paul's head and hit my cheek. I spun around, tears in my eyes and a dotted red line on my cheek. The boys ran off at the sight of blood and trouble, and Paul angrily threw the stone back at them, hitting one of their duffle bags.

'You shouldn't have done that, they'll give you hell next week,' I said, although I was tremendously grateful.

'If I wasn't such a short arse, it would've hit me,' he said, apologetically.

'Don't say that,' I said, and remembered to stoop a little for the rest of the walk.

Paul was always waiting for a growth spurt that never came. He felt it had been promised to him.

'You'll catch Katie up soon, Paul,' Viv always said. 'It'll happen when you hit your teens, you'll see. That's when the boys take over.' Because Viv was a nurse and had worked on the children's ward before intensive care, Paul took her words as gospel truth.

When he reached thirteen that September and I was still an inch taller, he was furious.

Paul's dad Mick was tall. Tallish, anyway. Five foot ten, maybe. Viv was small, just a little over five foot. Paul held her largely responsible for his stature, even though he eventually reached average height. He didn't thank her for the intelligence, the creativity, the fierce eyes he'd inherited. He also didn't thank her for the adoration or the sacrifices or the encouragement. Kids don't thank, do they. Not if they've always been given these things without question.

I thanked her. She adored me, made sacrifices for me and encouraged me. And I thanked her. Because she didn't have to do any of those things.

'I think Mum always wanted a girl,' Paul had once huffed in a way that I think was intended to be light-hearted but didn't land like that. He was sore because Viv had used the Focus Points she'd saved from Mick's fag packets to buy me a little art set as a gift.

'Don't be a dick, Paul.'

'You're the dick.'

'No, you're the dick.'

And so on.

We'd never really fallen out before, but I noticed that we were bickering more and more that year. I felt like Paul was seeing me for the first time, fully seeing me and all my differences. And he seemed to hold me accountable. That my family had money, that I was tall.

We scrapped and bickered and tussled and I would sometimes catch Paul glaring at my long legs. And he sometimes caught me narrowing my eyes at him as he rolled his eyes at his mum. We started to do this a lot. Perhaps it was catching, because while we bickered upstairs, Paul's mum and dad bickered downstairs.

Mostly it was just sniping, the kind of argument that simmered and then cooled without ever really boiling. The kind that comes from tiredness or low blood sugar or a red bill that needs to be paid.

I learned about red bills in that house, having never seen a bill in my own.

But sometimes they were big, boiling rows. Sometimes they were the kind of rows where Paul would say things like 'Dad'll be on the sofa tonight'.

The idea was alien to me. Back home, no-one needed to sleep on the sofa. My dad had his own bedroom and an office next door to that, which overlooked the small pond and a fountain where water trickled from horses' heads onto grey stone roses. My mum had her own bedroom with an adjoining dressing room and bathroom. Mum's bedroom was becoming her room for dying in.

The more she died, the less my father went in to see her.

The summer cold had never left her. Instead of any respite, diarrhoea had started, hollowing her figure from the inside out. She'd stopped going to London altogether by then. Soon after, she stopped leaving the house. Then the bed. At first, it had seemed like all the other times she'd stayed in bed long into the day. Mrs Baker would take trays of food up and return with them untouched an hour later.

The local doctor came out to see her and diagnosed flu but my father and Ted helped her out to the car one day, and they drove up to London to see a specialist. When they returned, my mum was helped back into bed without meeting my eyes.

I was told by my father that evening that she had cancer. The conversation went something like this:

'I'm afraid your mother is very ill, Kate. She has cancer and is going to need strong medicines and a lot of rest.'

No more, no less.

My father patted me on the shoulder and then walked slowly to his room. I lingered outside my mum's bedroom for what felt like a full hour before I could force myself inside. The sky darkened outside the landing window while I stood, in passive panic. My right leg had pins and needles and I remember feeling guilty because my mum's pain must have been so much worse but I had still allowed myself to notice the pins and needles.

Eventually I crept inside and stood next to the bed, scared to look even though I'd only seen her a couple of days earlier. I knew that cancer was bad. Everyone knows cancer is bad, it's like knowledge we're just born with. I looked at her face and noticed how much thinner it had got. She had little white dots around her mouth that she later told me were 'stress spots' and whispered that she was scared. I told her I was scared too and that I was sorry she was ill. I wanted to tell her that I loved her and would look after her – the kind of words people said on TV – but I was too embarrassed.

She was so thin by then. Not the kind of thin you mention, not the 'how did you shift those last seven pounds?' variety. The kind of thin that isn't acknowledged. The kind where bones rattle with the cold when everyone else is warm. The kind where my mum's eyes became like fish eyes, bulging out on each side of her razor-sharp nose bone.

The more she died, the more I hid at Paul's.

I would get off my school minibus in the village and rush around to let myself in the back of the Loxtons' house. I'd find Viv in the kitchen and let her make me a cup of tea. She had made me more and more tea as those weeks went on.

'Your father came into the hospital today, Katie,' she said one day. And then she'd put her hands around my hands, which were already wrapped around my mug of tea.

'Because of my mum?' I asked, quietly.

'Yes, darlin'.'

'But I thought she'd be going to the private hospital in London, I heard my dad telling Mrs Baker.'

'I don't think they have the facilities she needs, m'love. And I think the journey would be too much.'

'She only went up there to see a doctor a few weeks ago though?'

'These things—' Viv had stopped for a moment and cleared her throat, taken a small breath. 'These things can develop very quickly,' she'd said quietly but firmly.

My hands burned from the heat of the mug, but I didn't want to lose her touch by moving them. We stayed like that, silent, until the tea was cold.

My mum was admitted in mid-December while I was in school. It was Viv who took me to the hospital for a visit. My only visit, as it turned out.

In the weeks leading up to Mum moving into hospital, I had run through every possibility in my head. She would wake up and call for me, and I would spend the last of her days holding her hand and soothing her, promising her I'd be okay once she was gone. Light would stream in through the window and she'd look more beautiful than ever, and we'd feel an unspoken connection that would stay with me my whole life, like a butterfly on my shoulder.

Or that I would write her a letter telling her all of the ways I would make her proud, that I would look after my dad and live up to her legacy, even though I really didn't know what legacy she was leaving. I would slip it to her as she was carried out of the manor and she would die with it clasped in her hand.

Or right at the last minute, she would desperately want me with her and I would be called out of my lessons at school and whizzed through the countryside to make it to her bedside for her last moments.

None of those things happened. I said goodbye to her sleeping head at home, on the morning of her move into hospital. Then she was whisked away, but still *there* just a few miles up the road. Breathing and sleeping and dying, just in a different room.

As usual, I hovered on the outside of the situation and let things happen behind closed doors. It was Viv who decided for me. I'd regret it if I didn't go to see her and say goodbye properly, she said. It didn't matter that she'd not always been a great mum, she was still my mum, Viv said, and I wouldn't get another.

So Mick drove us to the hospital one afternoon. Viv, still in her nurse's uniform from her earlier shift, sat in the passenger seat, my long legs scrunched into the back.

It was raining but sticky warm from the radiator and the Allegro's windows ran with condensation. Mick was quiet, driving carefully in a way that had all the hallmarks of Viv giving him a talking to and a warning about behaviour. About not Micking the whole time, blabbering on and saying the wrong thing.

'Would you like me to come in with you?' Viv asked when we got near to the ward, her soft eyes searching my face for something.

'No, it's okay. I think it's okay.'

I continued to whisper 'it's okay, it's okay' to myself like a mantra as Viv showed me down the squeaky corridor and I stepped into the cool of my mum's room. I left Viv in her uniform outside, like some kind of guard. I wasn't supposed to visit. I was forbidden from visiting by my father. Quietly, totally, forbidden.

I was wearing a blue angora sweater, matching blue leg warmers and tight pale blue jeans. My black pixie boots had a slight heel on them and I felt like an overdressed Hammer Horror monster looming over the tiny body in the bed.

'You look very pretty, Katie,' Mum had whispered.

'So do you,' I lied. She had a piece of red tinsel wrapped around the bed frame and a fake red plant with gold berries on the bedside table. I was taken aback by its ugliness.

Mum had wrinkled her nose just slightly when she saw me looking. I wondered if she was thinking of the Christmas we spent alone together, or about all the Christmases we'd barely seen each other.

I lay my hand on top of hers and when that wasn't shooed away I squeezed her hand ever so slightly.

'I'm sorry this has happened to you, Mum.'

'I'm sorry too, Katie. I'm really sorry.'

I poured some water from the plastic jug into the plastic beaker, even though she had a hydration drip going into her left arm like limp spaghetti. I straightened the top sheet a little and sat down again, trying to think of something to say.

I wasn't sure if she was sleeping or resting so I put my hand on hers again and her eyes opened quickly like a doll, with the same clicky, sticky sound.

'Do something for me, Katie,' she said with a fast puff of breath.

'What?' My heart raced, I wanted to back out of the room, afraid that something weighty was about to happen and I wouldn't handle it in the right way.

'Don't be scared to live the life you want, and please don't settle,' she rasped.

I nodded, looking down at my lap.

'I love you so much, Katie. I'm sorry I didn't know what I was doing. You're all I think about in here.'

I stayed there with her until she fell asleep again. I kissed her hand and crept out of the room, not looking back. Viv had wrapped her arms around me and walked in silence until we reached the Allegro, Mick stony-faced inside.

CHAPTER NINETEEN

November 2012 – Tuesday afternoon

We're back from our lunch, the kids' bellies full of crisps and sandwiches. Paul and I are full of Ploughman's, which two Somerset kids can never resist. As I'd bitten into a huge slab of bread with salty butter laid thickly on top, Paul watched me approvingly. I ate the lot. Eye-watering mature cheddar, chunks of pickled onion, ham as thick as gammon steak. Now Paul is lying down on the sofa with the top button of his jeans undone. He thinks I haven't noticed. I've come up to get changed into my jeans from yesterday with the looser waist but I couldn't help but head for my overnight bag.

The tips of my fingers root around but don't connect with anything. They should be feeling folded paper, the edge ridged and prematurely aged from frequent handling. But instead, all my fingertips can feel is the grit of an empty section of my bag.

I feel the uniquely catatonic panic of a cornered animal. Rigid with fear, heart thundering. Fight and flight making my wheels spin pointlessly. *Who the hell has the letter? Where the fuck is the letter?*

If Paul has it, wouldn't he have said something by now? Wouldn't he have marched to find me, grabbed my shoulders? Asked me where I'd got it from at least? Could he have sat opposite me, shovelling Ploughman's into his mouth if he knew what I knew? There would be a confrontation, surely? But then, *I* found it and *I* didn't march to him, or grab his shoulders. I didn't ask where he got it from. I just went for a really long walk and tried to make sense of what I'd seen and what it meant for us all.

I sit back on my heels and think, think, think. Who would have gone through my bag, besides me? Izzy had barely left Paul's side and she isn't allowed in our room without us. Not since she'd got into my make-up a year ago and scrawled all over her face and the wall with a red lipstick I daren't have worn any more but was still devastated to see used for graffiti. It was the closest I'd ever come to smacking either of them, and Paul had thrown himself in front of her like a royal bodyguard.

Harry.

Harry had asked to fetch his Nintendo DS from our room. He'd called down to ask where it was and I'd shouted back that it was next to our bed. Paul had rolled his eyes a little bit. 'I wish we didn't yell,' he said. Meaning all of us except him, because he only yells when he's angry with Harry and apparently that's different. But how long had Harry been up here rummaging before he called down to ask? Long enough to unearth the letter, to tuck it into his pocket for secret spying. Maybe he wanted to use it to leverage something out of us. Out of me.

Oh God, I think, *I'm acting like a crazy person*. Harry's a little boy, not a hijacker. But he isn't an angel. It might not be beyond him to try to force my hand. Nothing serious, maybe some extra gaming time or a McDonald's.

I tuck my bag away and step lightly down the hall to Harry's bedroom. Inside, he's playing with some Match Attax cards that have spread like wildfire through his class this year. I don't think he really cares about the footballers on them, it's more about collecting and joining in with classmates. Paul and I used to collect the cards from sweet cigarettes. Always more from Airdrie than any other team. Paul and I got quite obsessed despite a mutual distrust of organised sports.

'Hey, Mum,' Harry says as I walk in to his room, looking up at me with those beautiful deer eyes. Mum. The shortening of Mummy still stings. He sees it. 'Mummy,' he adds with a smile.

'Hello, Harry Hair Pot,' I say. We like to give them both ten million nicknames for no reason.

He starts to tell me about the cards he has and the order he's putting them in. Not really for my benefit, more a chant of enjoyment as he contentedly sorts.

'Harry,' I say, cutting him off as he's talking about the shinies he swapped with a boy whose name I vaguely recognise from the year above him.

'Yeah?' he asks, without looking away from the face of a Congolese footballer.

'Did you go in my bag, Harry?'

'What bag?'

'My overnight bag, the leather one.'

He furrows his brow but looks down. 'No.'

My heart sinks until I realise he's not avoiding my eye but has already finished with our conversation and returned to organising the world's football players.

'Are you sure you didn't take anything out while you were looking for your DS?'

'DS?'

I'm getting frustrated but it's obvious he doesn't have a clue what I'm talking about. I grab his wrist and whisper hard, 'Look, Harry, did you take a piece of folded paper out of my bag?'

He looks at our skins scrunching together under my pressure.

'It's really important, Harry.'

His eyes well up a bit and he shakes his wrist free. 'I don't know what you mean, Mummy.'

I stand up and survey him. Paul is always telling me that I give our son the benefit of the doubt too easily – and I probably do – but right now he just looks upset, not guilty. I grab him into a hug. 'I love you,' I say into his hair as he squeezes his bony arms around me.

'Love you too,' he says and then breaks free to attend to his cards again.

The guilt washes over me and I want to go back and insert big fat lumps of benefit of the doubt into the last five minutes. 'I really love you,' I say. 'Sorry for being mental.'

He smiles with the side of his mouth. 'S'alright, Mummy,' he says, without looking up.

As I turn to go, I put my hand into my back pocket and realise with a start that the letter is wedged in there, soft and warm from my body heat.

There are gaps in my parenting. I often don't know what they are until it's too late.

I learned a lot from television. Which sounds awful, but is true.

Harry's baby years were largely instinctive, and I was incredibly relieved and proud about that. But with both our children, I wavered around the age of three. Never in my love for them, but in my understanding.

Potty-training and all those generic milestones I gauged from leaflets, Mumsnet and half-conversations at playgroups. It wasn't the practicalities that let me down. I just didn't know how to be a mother. When to soothe, when to chide. How much to explain, how often to say 'love' and how to show it without words.

I didn't have a deep bench to draw from. When I thought about myself at three, what little I remember had revolved around shoulder rides on drunk hippies or being dressed up and often forgotten. I think of egg and chips at Mrs Baker's house, of drawing endless pictures of my mum's yellow hair and red smile.

It got easier again when Harry got older and I could draw on memories of Viv.

I know Paul worried about my patchy CV, my poor parental education. I know he thought he'd have to jump in and commandeer things with Harry. That he was surprised and maybe affronted when he remained an understudy. He certainly stuck his stake into Izzy early on.

But I think he struggled the most when he saw a familiar competence in me, those echoes of his mum, rather than gaps in experience. He had adored his mum but not her background and lack of scope. And here I was, his wife, aping everything that he had rejected. And, of course, if I was playing Viv, what would that make him? Mick? A role he shied from his whole life. A buffoon. A philanderer.

I stand in the doorway of Izzy's room and watch her with curiosity. I look at her and wonder if that's what I looked like at her age. A dimpled smile that drops into a deep, dark frown when she concentrates. She still looks and behaves a lot like she did as a baby. All squidginess and endless demands. I don't think I made endless demands.

At least as neither of them has my colouring, they don't burn at the hint of summer like I do. I would have liked at least one of them to look a little like me though. Sometimes, I forget that I contributed anything into Izzy's creation. The IVF process probably didn't help. At times, I felt like a vessel. A birthing unit for something belonging to Paul, which had been placed inside me for safe-keeping.

As a kid, I remember Judith Hann on *Tomorrow's World* talking about IVF – or 'test-tube babies'. It was proper science-fiction stuff, but I never thought it would play a role in my life. When I was young, I never really imagined myself having kids, beyond that vague silhouette that childhood storybooks implant in all of us when we picture ourselves as grown-ups. Funny how things can change.

In my storybooks, children were children and adults were 'mummies and daddies'. I remember reading *The Tiger Who Came To Tea* when I was really little, fantasising about having a mum who'd feed buns and beer to a tiger, and a father that'd take us out for bangers and chips at a cafe. A daddy, rather than a father. Paul is definitely daddy *and* father to our children.

Paul was more established at work when Izzy came along, Creative Director – respected and admired throughout London's AdLand. He was important enough to be allowed to take a month of leave and then work from home for the next month. He was also important enough to know that he was hugely missed at the office and to take plenty of 'crucial' calls throughout that time. Huffing at the lit-up screen but answering anyway.

We were co-parents for those two months. Sharing the job, me nursing Izzy and then Paul whisking her off for cuddles and slow walks around the garden with her cradled in his arms, leaving me to curl up to Harry and reassure him over and over that he was still so special to me.

When I think about the fathers we grew up with, the idea of them co-parenting is almost funny. Mick loved Paul, I know he did, but change a nappy? Take a role in his weaning? Know what weaning *is*? Not on your life. And as for my father. . . Saying that,

I really can't imagine my mother doing any of that stuff either. I know there were night nurses and nannies, I vaguely remember cuddling up to starchy uniforms, and that was probably for the best.

When I was on my bed rest while pregnant with Izzy, our nanny was a bouncy Antipodean with golden hair and a face-splitting smile. She wore workout clothes all day. She got up early to run on the heath or do yoga in the garden. She was our very own kids' TV presenter, irritating as shit and brilliant with children. Harry loved having her to stay and I hated her to her core for that.

Paul liked her, as much as Paul likes anyone. I caught him watching her stretching on the grass as I lay round and heavy on the bed. 'She's great with Harry and his behaviour has really improved,' he said one time as I inched carefully into a new position, my back aching from lying, bored and grounded by the memory-foam mattress. 'And she's so trustworthy for a twenty-three-year-old, don't you think?'

I wished he'd just fuck her and get it over with, that's what I thought. But Paul may well have imagined himself tugging those yoga pants down, but he never would have. Back then, I thought that was because he only had eyes for me. The truth is simpler: it would be the wrong thing to do. And Paul's whole adult life has been about 'doing the right thing', whatever the consequences.

1995

When I was twenty-three, I wanted much more than a nannying job. My one-year graduate placement had flown by and in 1995

I was no longer just a junior at TMC, in part because I craved mentors and asked them lots of questions.

The best advice I got was from John Silver, then an account director who had gone through the grad-scheme himself years before. 'You want to stay on here after this scheme?' he'd asked in the bar one Thursday night in 1994.

'God, yeah.'

'Make yourself indispensable.'

This isn't unique advice, I've heard this exact line on numerous TV shows and read it in numerous books since, but it was the first time I'd heard it. I took it on board, wholesale. I inserted myself into every cross-department project. I made sure I introduced myself by name to every client I ever answered the phone to, regardless of who managed their account. I got to the office earlier than any other junior, stayed in the bar until the last important person left and always got the drinks. That was the biggest joke: the drinks were free but they seemed to appreciate the effort of me collecting them and bringing them to the table.

That year, I became a junior account executive and then an account executive when two execs were poached in quick succession by Saatchi, just up the road.

Saatchi & Saatchi was the mortal enemy, so much so that the name was banned from our office. They were simply known as 'them'.

At night, I returned to my magnolia room in a shared house in zone three, set the alarm for 6 a.m. and then crashed out. I loved it.

CHAPTER TWENTY

1986

Mum continued to die throughout Christmas in the intensive-care unit that had a thin piece of tinsel over the door leading to the ward and large cardboard Christmas bells taped to the walls. I spent Christmas eating toast and Mrs Baker's Christmas cake, watching the Christmas telly and looking away when adverts of smiling, healthy families bubbled onto the screen. My father hovered around the house, never really settling. He gave me £100 of Topshop vouchers, a king's ransom that had Mrs Baker's influence written all over them. I gave him a coffee pot for one.

When she actually died for good, Mum was on her own. It was three days after Christmas. My father had visited her the day before and was due to visit that afternoon when the call came. Mrs Baker passed the receiver to my father in the hall. I listened from a hiding space behind an antique chest on the landing.

'Yes, I see, I understand. Thank you. And do I need to—? Okay, thank you.'

He put the phone on its cradle as though it was made of ultra-thin glass and stood motionless. I hid in my room until Mrs Baker knocked softly. I opened it a crack but didn't look at her face. 'It's okay,' I said. 'I know.' I shut the door with more of a bang than I'd intended and heard the weight shift on the floorboards outside of my door as she walked away. I sat on my bed and thought, 'What am I supposed to do?' I willed tears, but they didn't come, not then.

Mum's funeral was arranged for the third of January, a Friday. Party day. I asked my father if I could help to plan the funeral. I thought I could look for ideas in whatever fashion magazines Mum had been reading recently for ideas. I thought I could help choose the colour scheme. I just thought I could help. He looked at me like I was a terrorist.

'It's not a wedding, Kate. There's no colour scheme.' And he walked away, head bowed. More grey than before.

I didn't know. This was going to be my first funeral, I'd had no warm-up.

On the day of the funeral, I wore a black skirt, black tights and a black top with lace panels that I found in my mum's wardrobe. It had taken a long time to build up the courage to go in, but once inside her room, I started to sift through the treasure trove. A collection I'd barely peeked in before, let alone touched. Colours and patterns folded and slumped where they had once been a part of my mum, her look. Her leather trousers hung like an animal carcass. Her Russian fur hats peered down from a special shelf that ran above the rails.

For the service, I wore a dark pewter bracelet removed carefully from her jewellery box, and a black feather fascinator – very Siouxie and the Banshees – in my hair. I had tried on some black patent shoes with tiny pinprick heels but my feet slipped around in them too much. Just before Ted arrived to take us to the church, I painted my face carefully using her colours.

My father and I were the only family there. My mother had an older brother – Wilbur – who she'd mentioned, disparagingly, from time to time. I suppose I should say I had an *uncle* that my mother had disparaged. But he wasn't invited. I'll never know the circumstances that led to my mum's life being so full in one way, and utterly barren in others.

'No, no other family,' my father had said to an inquisitive older mourner from the village who may not have been officially invited. 'Those were Susannah's wishes,' my father was forced to insist. 'The only family members she wanted were Kate and myself.'

My whole life, my father's communication tended to be via the ruffle of a newspaper, a raising of an eyebrow or a polite cough. When speech was unavoidable, he spoke sparingly. And it was fucking unbearable if you actually needed him to say something that mattered. Speaking to villagers, making small talk, was visibly painful to him.

It had been mild in the run up to Christmas that year, clear blue skies and crisp nothingness that showed no sign of snow. Then Mum died and the temperature dropped overnight. From mild to minus degrees in hours. The *Nine O'clock News* showed footage of northern towns covered in piles of snow. On the day of the funeral, the wind buffeted the local church and the threat of ice hung from the clouds.

During the service, I sat as still as I could. My eyes were dry, and my chest felt light and giddy. I tried to hold my breath – not to suppress tears but to quell an inexplicable urge to laugh. I could feel it, the bubbles of it, tickling at my chest. The corners of my eyes twitched, heavy with far too much of my mum's make-up. My mouth wobbled. My father was sitting next to me, his mouth a grim straight line. He saw me looking at him, saw my wobbling lips and reached for my hand with his much larger hand. And then the unwanted laugh popped and turned into a strangled cry. People looked. I would have looked. The twitches in my eyes turned to scratches and I felt my eyelids scrunch into scribbles and soon black-dyed tears were running down my cheeks. And while I cried, I remember thinking how lucky I was. How lucky that I hadn't laughed and that instead I was crying and that everyone could see me cry. That I was doing the right thing, behaving in the right way.

My father's hand felt heavy, almost crushing mine into the dark, dusty wood of the pew. I couldn't remember ever feeling his skin on mine like that. I concentrated on the weight and the softness of his palm, the sharp hair on his fingers.

Throughout the service, the local vicar talked emphatically about a woman no-one in that church would have recognised. Not the few villagers who only glimpsed my mother as she flew past along the country roads, nor my father who had watched her from hallways, or through windows or across large tables the way a cat eyes another cat sitting on the edge of its territory. And the vicar's description was definitely unrecognisable to the Londoners who had come down by train and looked at the ground with its lack of pavements like they had never seen anything like it. To them, Susannah was Suki. And Suki in the mud didn't make sense.

Afterwards, I saw Mum's friends huddled from the wind next to the church porch, all cigarette thin and turned in on themselves.

'Oh my God, is that Katie?'

One of the men I remembered visiting with a big group years before started to shuffle towards me, a pained look on his face. A woman I didn't recognise pulled him back by his too-big shirt. The man had a bleached flop of curls that fell from the top of his head to the side, like a breaking wave. He carried his shoulders in a limp, sloping style. His fingers curled around a cigarette and he allowed himself to be pulled back into a hug by his friend. The woman hugging him smiled at me apologetically, her tight dress almost swallowed up by a white fur coat.

Behind them, several other Londoners shuffled and studiously avoided looking at me. The women wore high heels that sank into the mud, which they pretended not to notice or mind, instead taking fresh cigarettes from the packs offered by the men. All of them were thin and dramatic, like my mum. I recognised some of their faces as more hollow versions of the ones that had smiled at me during drunken picnics when I was little. In fact, all the women resembled my mum. Ghoulish versions of her.

My knees knocked together in the biting cold, the thin tights bagging at my ankles as my chunky shoes crunched the frost. I took a step toward the Londoners and my father appeared at my side. 'No,' he said. I wasn't sure if it was aimed at me or the thin people but my father put his hand lightly on my shoulder and swivelled me away.

My father's attention took my breath away and I started to sob again, but before I could turn in to him for a hug he had strolled away purposefully, shaking an older man's hand. Mr and Mrs Baker came towards me and led me away from the church and I heard the strangled sounds of the friends crying behind me as the skinny man in the baggy shirt called, 'I'm so sorry, little Katie!'

After the funeral, mourners filed into the formal lounge at my house. We'd lost half of the congregation by then, including the thin friends who had headed off to The Swan. I wished Viv and Mick had been invited, even though I would have been embarrassed at them seeing the house, the ridiculous scale of it. The way their house could have fitted inside one of the outbuildings like a Russian doll.

After wandering from room to room for a bit, trying to see them as if for the first time, I slipped through the shoulders of the adults and almost laughed as I ran, skidding, down the drive and out through the gate.

The village was deserted. The wind so fierce it picked up fistfuls of gravel and hurled them all around. Sludgy, lazy snow had started to dollop onto the ground, fizzling away to nothing. It was late afternoon and the only light by then was from the pub. I could hear murmurs of laughter inside and clinking of glasses as I passed.

By the time I reached the Loxtons', my hands were red raw and my damp black skirt as heavy as bricks.

Viv opened the front door in her housecoat with wet dye on her hair, which was piled on her head.

'Katie?' At first I thought she was annoyed that I'd turned up without warning. Stomach dropping, I turned to go when she grabbed me and pulled me in to her. I stood shivering and let her hug me until drips of purple-black dye landed on my shoulders.

'You should have come round the back out of the cold, you never need to knock,' she said.

We didn't talk about Mum.

'Let me rinse my mop off and I'll make up the Z-bed. Paul and Mick will be back in a minute, they're out getting chips.'

Paul stepped through first and took off his new Doc Martens, his main Christmas present. He looked up self-consciously as he heard me and Viv talking on the sofa. I realised how dramatic I must have looked. Black clothes, damp hair, bedraggled feather fascinator and drops of his mum's black hair dye on my skin. I looked like Robert Smith from The Cure.

He looked embarrassed. His nose was red from the cold and his hair was wet. Mick had barrelled through just after him, carrying the newspaper-wrapped fish and chips. Their scent escaped from the thin, stripy carrier bag that swung like a thurible.

'Glad you two are back, it's terrible out there,' said Viv. 'Say hello to Katie then, Paul!'

'Hi.'

'Paul, fetch Katie some PJs would you? She's too tall to get into mine and no-one in their right mind would want to wear Mick's.'

'Hey, they're antiques, they are,' Mick called back from the kitchen.

As they divided three portions into four, I realised I hadn't eaten since the previous day. And that had been toast. Always toast. That's still my default today. If Paul has to stay away for work, I'll exist on toast the whole time he's gone.

We sat in near silence that evening, plates on trays on laps, drinking ginger beer and watching TV. The Christmas programming had given way to January's slim pickings. We watched some of *The Machine Gunners*, but it was all about dreary wartime bombing so Viv turned the channel to BBC2 for some show Paul wanted to watch about aliens that invaded earth and froze everyone to death. I didn't fancy it after watching my mum's coffin being lowered into the frozen ground earlier that day, so I drained the last of my ginger beer and asked Viv quietly if I could have a bath.

When I came out of the bathroom, peach towel around my head and pyjamas back on, Mick had switched to *Match of the Day*. Paul and I played cards in his room. He seemed cross, barely making eye contact and grunting when I won. Viv later said he just didn't know how to act given everything I'd been through and the best thing he could do for me was to treat me normally.

No-one called from home, not that night or the next morning, so I stayed for the whole weekend, playing cards, watching *Ghostbusters* on the new video player over and over, drinking tea. That film is forever bound up with that time; I haven't watched it since.

Paul was due to return to school on the Monday, but my school had longer Christmas holidays and wasn't open for another week. I waved Paul off on the first morning, his shoulders slumping as he hoisted his black duffel bag up onto his shoulder and trudged towards the town. I helped Viv clear the breakfast things away and tidy up. Mick's work had been cancelled due to the weather, so after some verbal and non-verbal discussion between them, he drove Viv to run some errands.

While they were gone, I drifted from room to room. I lingered in the doorway of Viv and Mick's bedroom, still wearing Paul's pyjamas, which skimmed my ankles. I'd seen this room so many times, the door was rarely closed and I'd often go in to take Viv a cup of tea or help her carry laundry to sort on the bed. But Viv and Mick's bedroom in an empty house felt different.

The bed was made, the tight curls of the crocheted blanket spread as smooth as possible. One pillow each side, a bedside table apiece. Mick's side had a black John Player Special ashtray on it, polished to a shine. Viv's had a stack of books. *Riders* by Jilly Cooper was at the bottom. I sat on the floor, leaning against the divan and opened it carefully so I didn't crack the spine. The inside cover had a message from one of Viv's friends, another nurse. A Christmas present.

I started to read, turning the untouched pages silently like they could set off an alarm. As I read further and further, I wondered if Viv yet knew that Jake Lovell, the handsome hero, was a gypsy. Whether Viv's friend was in the loop on the whole Romany secret.

But the more I read, the more I forgot about that until I was nearly a hundred pages deep and heard a car pull up outside. I scrambled to my feet, slipped the book back under the pile, and tried to act normally as I padded back down the stairs and into the kitchen to put the kettle on.

'She's only a young girl, and she's just lost her mum,' I heard Viv hissing, as she came through the front door.

'I know, darlin', it's not right,' Mick said.

I swished through the bead curtain as if I hadn't heard and said, 'Oh hi, you're back! Would you like a cup of tea?'

Viv had my holdall in her hand and she placed it at her feet.

'Hello, love,' Mick said, before he was shooed back out to grit the front step.

'I thought you might want some bits from home,' Viv said, walking towards me and putting her hands on my shoulders. 'And I got you a pad and some pencils for drawing. I know you like to doodle.'

She smelled of Comfort fabric conditioner and Anaïs Anaïs perfume. She'd dressed up carefully to visit my house. I stood before her in her son's pyjamas, limply holding the drawing pad and pencils.

'I wanted to speak to your dad and see how he's doing. We met at the hospital a couple of times and he. . .' She hesitated and gently pushed my growing-out fringe behind my ears. 'He seemed like a decent man. I thought I could let him know how you were and arrange for you to stay for a while to give you both a bit of space. People deal with grief differently. . .' She trailed off.

It was incredibly thoughtful and kind but I remember feeling embarrassment above all else. Embarrassment that Viv had wasted all that time thinking about my father's feelings and thinking she had to ask his permission to let me stay.

'What did he say?'

'Well, he wasn't there m'love. I spoke to Joan, Mrs Baker, she said he'd had to go off to East Germany of all places.' Viv took a breath, softened her voice again. 'She doesn't know how long he's going for so Joan and I agreed that you'd stay here for a bit, until your dad was back and you felt like you wanted to go home. If that's okay?'

'That's fine,' I smiled. I didn't know what to say, so I hugged her. And she hugged me back so tightly I gasped for air and nearly dropped the pencils.

'Will Paul mind?' I asked.

'Of course not, darling. You're one of the family.'

I smiled into her shoulder, burrowed into her neck. Breathing in the smell of the Comfort and the Anaïs Anaïs, clean washing, warmth.

CHAPTER TWENTY-ONE

November 2012 – Wednesday morning

On the first day of this holiday, Paul's phone had mostly stayed in his pocket as agreed, emails unchecked. In front of me, at least.

He'd even left it charging in the bedroom on Monday evening, like it was no big thing – although he did do this small thing very visibly in front of me, waiting until I was going in to the bedroom to get something. I wanted to ask him, 'What point are you trying to prove?' I also wondered if I could work out his pin code when he went back downstairs but didn't dare try.

Yesterday, he started to stare at the screen more and more, thumb twitching, watching the number in his inbox climb.

Today he's been climbing the walls and furrowing his brow and staring at the screen all morning, so I say, 'Maybe you should check it, it's stopping you from relaxing.'

He glares at me, like I'm forcing his hand. Then he softens a bit. 'Cheers,' he says, already in work mode, like he's signing off an email.

'Just work stuff?' I ask softly, ten minutes into his busy thumb activity.

'Mmn?' he murmurs. 'Of course.'

When we're at home in London, he glowers into his phone all evening. Occasionally huffing, the odd snort of laughter or derision. Foolishly I sometimes ask what's so funny or raise my eyebrows to be included. 'It's just work stuff,' he'll say.

I was lucky, I suppose. I left – ha, *left* sounds so decisive, like a choice – I left this world just as BlackBerrys were arriving. Little more than pagers, really, pagers telling you that you had an email. I didn't see the appeal. Only the very top bods had one then and although it was a status symbol, I resisted. I always worked late in my time, we all did, but once I left the office I was gone. It took a phone call to pull me back in, and back then plenty of mobiles needed to be switched off to charge at night, including mine. There was a clear separation of work and home. For most people, anyway.

Now, Paul's working day starts with emails in bed. It fills both commutes, bleeds through most of the evening and trickles along until bedtime when he'll huff and grab his phone on and off until he passes out. I read a book and worry about the effects of radiation from his phone. If it gives us both brain tumours, as absurd as that panic might be, who would take care of the children?

Paul doesn't read any more because he doesn't have time. Now he collects books instead.

I also have a mobile, obviously. I use it in a way that makes Paul cringe. I don't update apps, I let unwanted emails from online shops rack up. I crack screens, I leave phones to go dead. And every time a new iPhone comes out I snap it up. I like shiny, new things.

When I daydream about going back to work, picking up where I left off – or, ideally, about six months before where I left off – it's often the mobile phones that stop the whimsy dead. The thought of being permanently on call, of being accountable twenty-four seven, chills me. Paul never relaxes. Ever. Even on holiday, he's ticking off a bulleted list of relaxation goals. Lie in, check. Fall asleep on sofa, check. Long walk along the beach, check. All the while, his phone sits in his pocket like an anchor, tethering him to work. Even when he's not checking his emails or making notes or talking on conference calls with blah blah blah from so-and-so or you-know-who from God-knows-where, it's there, connecting him silently to that other place. To that other Paul.

So much of Paul's job I still feel, I still own it in my head a bit. I have never forgotten the lingo, the processes, the feeling of a winning pitch, although my job was very different to his. But I don't understand this new way of working. I don't understand how it delivers results when there's no time to think. Cortisol just surging through data packets and decisions always made on the hoof, agreed or dissolved with a tap of the thumb. How can that be a job well done? And that way of thinking makes me a dinosaur. It makes me a laughing stock. It means I can never go back, even now that people have forgotten me and moved on. Even now that I could call my gap in service a career break to raise kids and try to inch my way back, a few rungs below. I just wouldn't be able to work that way. Maybe I'm making excuses, or I've just listened to Paul for too long.

I once asked him, 'Would TMC take me back on do you think, if I applied?' He stopped in his tracks and stared at me, his mouth wavering, I guessed, between a laugh and a scream. He was peeling sweet potatoes at the time, jagged strokes, a frustrating vegetable to work with. 'I only meant theoretically,' I blurted out, to save myself from his answer.

I was good at something once. I've not found anything I'm good at since, not truly. Not purely. Not 'good but. . .' just good.

Even drawing and working with textiles at uni felt partial. It was more of a hobby, like wine-tasting.

As a result, I have a permanent itch, trying to find something else that I can truly own. Knowing there isn't anything else. Knowing I can't go back.

And make no mistake, motherhood is not the thing. Motherhood is death by a thousand cuts. Nature's cruellest curse. To make you love something so furiously, while at the same time telling you – through the billions of animals that have done it before you – that you've already lost them, you're just killing time before they realise it.

We can see Mousehole's harbour from our bathroom window here. It sits grey and blue like a little watercolour, framed in white wood. Earlier, we went to collect seashells and find the 'best pebble on the beach'.

The best pebble on the beach was a game Viv started when Paul was little, and they shared it with me the first time we went to the beach together. We'd been maybe ten or eleven, and I knew Paul wanted to fight it and declare the game babyish but he couldn't quite do it. It wasn't complicated, it literally was a competition to find the best pebble on the beach. And after feeling the weight of hundreds of pebbles in our hands, touching the round edges, softened by the bashing of the sea, holding them up in the sunlight, squinting like we were on the *Antiques Roadshow*, we'd finally settle on one each. Our own perfect pebble, to remind us of the day. I took my collection of pebbles with me when I went to university but lost them somewhere in a later house move.

I went to the beach with the Loxtons at least once each summer. Either Weston-Super-Mare or Weymouth, both equidistant from Little Babcombe. A lot of industry went into the day trips. Sandwiches made and packed first thing, bottles of Kia-Ora mixed in advance, packs of crisps from the multipack, pickled onions wrapped in cling film, Scotch eggs, Ski yoghurts and picnic spoons. The food was always tucked in the same old green coolbox, the blue ice blocks frozen for days in advance. We'd pack the Allegro's boot with sun hats, towels, sun cream (factor two or factor four – it's a miracle we weren't cremated) a ball, a frisbee and a woven papery-plastic striped windbreaker. Paul and I would be in the back, Viv in the passenger seat with her feet up on the coolbox in the footwell, Mick driving and singing along to his Barron Knights tape or whatever was playing on Radio 2.

I'd wear jelly shoes and a swimsuit under my dress, so I didn't have to take my knickers off on the beach. Paul would wear his usual jeans and T-shirt, refusing to bring shorts and then regretting it and rolling his trouser legs up until they were rolled so tight he'd get deep wrinkly grooves in his skin.

The smell of ozone would slap us as soon as we got out of the car and walked along the front. We'd stand still for a moment in the frenzied colourful blur of amusement arcades, with buckets, spades and lilos dangling from every shop. Every summer, one twenty-four shot roll of film would be slotted into Viv's old Instamatic and she always got them back with twenty-three grinning pictures, plus one photo of the dashboard and Viv's thumb as she was loading the film.

I imagine unwrapping sandwiches and pickled onions from home for our kids. Our artisan loaf kids. Our brasserie kids. Our farmers' market kids. Our spoilt little kids.

Sometimes, I think we had more fun than they do.

I walk into the lounge and find the rest of my family in a state of catatonia. 'Come on, let's go for another walk on the beach,' I say, with a manic jollity even though it's spitting with rain.

'Oh, Mum,' Harry moans plaintively, Izzy bucking her body silently like she's about to launch into a huge moaning session.

'No,' I say to them both, more sharply than I mean. I soften my voice. 'You can sit at home all day watching television in London. It's such a waste to do the same thing here.'

'Mummy's right,' Paul says from the armchair, keeping his eyes on the screen of his phone. 'We're by the beach, on holiday, it's ridiculous to just lie around in front of a screen.'

'Says you,' I say and he looks up, opens his mouth like he's about to rebuke me and then stops. 'Sorry,' he says. 'I shouldn't still be using it but they're fu—' He looks at the kids and softens his voice. 'They're screwing up the Amnesty pitch and it's the only one I bloody care about.'

I shrug. What can I say? We're on holiday, but it's a holiday his job pays for.

'Sorry to hear that,' I offer eventually.

It's really not so rainy now we're out and the puddles are shimmering with rainbows. I'm glad I pushed us back out of the house. The place is deserted, the fish all caught and sold for the day and no holidaymakers with bright buckets and spades. It's November, I remind myself, hardly a peak season.

The boats are tied up like dogs on leads, sitting at the edge of the water, waiting for the tide. I look around furtively, then get Harry and Izzy to perch on the edge of a particularly pretty white-boarded boat and take a rapid round of bad pictures.

'Get in this one too,' I say to Paul, who stuffs his phone guiltily in his pocket and strides over to stand awkwardly next to the kids, leaning on a boat that belongs to someone else.

'Come on, Captain, smile!' I laugh, and he laughs then too, despite himself.

We carry on walking, the kids skittering like crabs, running in front, behind, to the side. Harry takes delight in daring the shallow water to get him.

'Don't get your socks wet, Harry,' I shout.

'Maybe it'll stop him dicking about,' Paul says to me, lifting an eyebrow.

'Yeah, right,' I laugh. 'He'll just dick about with wet socks on.'

We look back just as Izzy tries to similarly goad the sea and ends up ankles-deep.

'For God's sake,' I say.

As I start to walk over, Harry helps his sister back to dry land and they laugh together and run behind us again.

'Well, that was a freebie,' I say to Paul but he doesn't look my way or answer.

'Amnesty?' I ask.

'Hmm? Oh, yeah. Bloody Amnesty,' he says.

'What's the problem?'

He doesn't generally talk to me about work and for years I actually couldn't talk about his work. I just couldn't let myself. But I think he's at the end of his rope because he starts talking cautiously and soon it's a tidal wave. I let him get on with it, chipping in occasionally, but mostly just acting as a sounding board. As we talk, I notice his shoulders drop and he looks looser. I want to ask who else is on the account, any new (female) creatives. But there's no subtle way to segue into the subject.

'Mum!'

I spin around. Harry is running towards me at full pelt, his jeans soaking.

'Mum!'

'What is it?'

We both start to run to him.

'Izzy!' he says, bending over like he's going to be sick.

'What? Where is she?' I'm looking around as I ask, a montage of terrible images rushing through my head. Kidnappers. News reports. Graveyards.

'Where is she, Harry?' Paul shouts angrily now.

'I think she fell in!' Harry says, and he bursts into tears.

Paul starts to run to the water's edge, but he doesn't know where to look and runs around uselessly.

'Where was she when you last saw her?' I ask, my heart pumping panic around my body so hard I can hardly see straight.

'We were playing hide and seek,' Harry says through his wild tears, the kind I've barely ever seen from him.

'Where?'

'In the boats,' he wails.

'Paul!' I shout, running to him. 'Check the boats.'

He doesn't argue, just starts to frantically look under tarpaulins and around the ropes tethering them in place.

The boats are bobbing about now. When did the tide start to come in?

'Why do you think she fell in, Harry?'

Even as I'm asking, I'm aware of time ticking past. Images of little lungs, bubbles, I rub my eyes to make them go away.

'I heard a big splash.'

I feel sick. I leave him crying on the beach and wade in and start to check the freezing water around each boat. I'm looking for a flash of her coat under the surface, berating myself for not starting swimming classes yet. Harry was in the water as a newborn.

'I've got her!' Paul cries and suddenly I'm too scared to look. If I see her, limp, grey, I'll never see her any other way.

'I won!' I hear her shout and I finally look at them, shaking all the worst-case scenarios away.

She's holding Paul's hand and marching triumphantly towards us. Harry and I look at each other. Embarrassment sweeps his face. I reach to squeeze his hand but he's already storming off to her.

'Where were you?' Harry demands of his sister. 'I thought you fell in.'

'Hey,' says Paul, looking about a hundred years old. 'That's enough.'

They start to run off again but I stop them.

'Daddy and I are soaked,' I say. 'We need to go and get dried off.'

They complain a little as we leave the beach and we waddle like wet cowboys, looking at each other with wild eyes, teeth chattering.

'Jesus,' Paul says.

As we leave the harbour, Izzy comes up and holds my hand. 'I threw a big stone in the water,' she says proudly. 'I distracted Harry so I won.'

I don't know whether to laugh or berate her but in the end, I just enjoy the fact that she's confided in me. I kiss her on her head and tell her quietly to keep that a secret.

'Okay,' she whispers.

Just as we reach the front door, the rain starts to come down in wild sheets.

We get in and race upstairs to shower and get into our comfy clothes: joggers and age-softened T-shirts. My legs are so cold from the seawater that they glow pink, smarting when the shower strikes.

Back in the lounge, the kids rummage through the DVD and video basket while Paul and I make coffee and tea. My hair is still damp, I pull it up into a hair band and think about how used to it I am, but how strange it actually is to be the only person who looks like me in my family.

We sit heavily on the sofa, collapsing into it with a happy weariness that could have been so different. A weariness from which we'd never recover. I pull the fluffiest blanket over me, tossing it so it covers Paul's feet too.

I look across at him. He wriggles his feet further under the blanket and blows on his coffee, both hands on the mug, phone nowhere to be seen. He hasn't mentioned the Amnesty pitch or work in general or even what happened on the beach. No dissection of what we did wrong, of how we could have prevented it. Of whose fault it is. There's no need. But how differently this day could have ended. I think guiltily of the mad zoetrope of worst-case scenarios that had spun unbidden through my head, and wonder if Paul experienced the same thing. I think too, of all those terrible family tragedies played out in the national press that serve as safety reminders and touchstones of relief for those of us lucky enough not to get caught in fate's storm. I think of the epilogues we often hear third hand, years later.

'Did you hear about that little girl's father?'

'That poor mother killed herself afterwards.'

'They broke up, you know, very soon after.'

I wonder what our epilogue would have been. How big our buffer is. Whether we have any buffer at all, and if there's any hope of it covering us on Saturday. I wonder if Paul has been slowly rubbing the buffer away right under my nose. And then I stop myself, focus on the screen and gasp a little as I realise the kids have chosen *Ghostbusters*. I haven't seen this film in such a long time. A very long time. I sit up and reach for Paul's hand and find his fingers are already reaching for mine.

CHAPTER TWENTY-TWO

1986

With Paul at school, I spent the rest of that January week after the funeral curled up on the green sofa in the Loxtons' watching daytime TV and eating toast.

When it was just me, and the TV had been taken over by schools programming or *Take the High Road*, I'd often get the sketchpad out that Viv had got me. I drew everything, and nothing. Crinkled packets from the cupboard, bottles, pictures of Paul in his school uniform from the cardboard framed photos.

Viv worked split shifts that week so sometimes sat with me to watch TV and I lay with my feet across her knees and she'd rest her hands on my ankles. We took it in turns to make tea or switch the channel over.

A couple of times, I almost started to talk about my mum. I would open my mouth a little, and try to think of the first word, the first sound, that would let it out. I thought about the Christmas I spent with her alone. Both of us in our pyjamas, eating toast and giggling at the naughtiness of not doing the proper thing. The hysteria when the Queen's speech came and went and we hadn't watched a word of it. I wanted to tell Viv about that, I wanted to say out loud how much it meant that my mum had let me see her like that, just for a bit. Totally relaxed. That I knew she didn't know how to be with me. She didn't know how to be an adult at all, let alone a mum. That she would swing from acting like a wild babysitter to an older sister to a casual acquaintance. But despite that, I knew she loved me. I opened my mouth to say something like that but never found that first sound.

A couple of times, I was taken aback by a ball of tears that welled up in seconds and splashed all down my face. I would reach up and touch my face in surprise, finding it wet and contorted. When that happened, I would sometimes see Viv in the corner of my eye, her own mouth barely open, trying to find the first sound. Generally, tears happened alone. I cried a lot on the toilet. The sudden silence of the bathroom slapping me.

Paul got home from school at just gone four o'clock and we'd go straight upstairs to play music while he did his homework and I read a copy of *Jackie* that Viv had brought home for me, folding the corners of the pages with hairstyles or clothes I liked.

The Z-bed sagged perfectly like a memory mattress and sometimes I dozed while I waited for him to finish his schoolwork, the sound of his Parker pen swiping across the pages soothing me like a lullaby. I'd half offer to help him, but he didn't need my input. He was always smarter than me, and more dedicated to perfecting his work. His penmanship was beautiful, it still is. Though all he ever writes these days is cheques, or 'Daddy' in birthday cards to the children. He still has a fountain pen, a beautiful Graf Von Faber-Castell with a discreet herringbone pattern along the shaft of it. It was a gift from our old CEO when Paul was promoted to Creative Director.

On the Sunday before I started school again, as Paul and I finished washing up and drying the plates from that afternoon's roast dinner, my father knocked on the door. I heard his voice as he was invited in, the tautness of it unsuited to a house used to chatter.

'Katie,' Viv called. 'Your dad's here.'

I walked out of the kitchen carrying a tea towel. I did this for show, I'll admit now, because I wanted him to see me taking part in the domesticity of family life – another family's life.

'Hello,' I said solemnly. Although it had only been a week and a bit, he looked older and thinner. He was approaching fifty then, but he could easily have been past sixty. His neck was scrawny with a spray of new grey hairs creeping down from his nape. It made me think of the roast chicken carcass that was being boiled for stock and stinking out the kitchen.

'Hello, Kate. Are you ready to come home now?'

It was an odd question, and an odd sensation – being given the power of veto to something that really should have been enforced.

I shrugged. I had hoped that one of the Loxtons might have vetoed for me. 'Oh, please let her stay' or 'She's one of us now' or just 'Would you like to stay a bit longer, Katie?' but my father took my shrug as a sign of readiness and told me to go and get my things together.

Paul and I went upstairs in silence and he sat on the bed watching as I stuffed my clothes into my bag.

As I went out to the narrow landing, I could hear my father downstairs offering Viv and Mick money for my keep. In her rebuttal, Viv's voice had a haughtiness to it that I hadn't heard before.

'I'm sorry if I offended you,' my father said in his crisp manner. 'I didn't ask for any of this but I appreciate your support to Kate.'

'I think you should go and wait in the car now, mate,' Mick said. He was topless, shaving foam on his neck with drag marks through it, the final strokes left to go. 'We don't need your money,' he added. 'We're happy to do this for the girl, we're not after anything.'

'No, I, I'm sorry. I'll wait in the car.'

When I left, I hugged Mick and Viv in turn and thanked them for having me, even though I stayed several times a week without such fanfare. I started to go through the front door but looked back to wave to Paul. 'Thanks for sharing your room with me, Paul,' I said.

'You're alright,' he said, half-smiling.

'See you after school tomorrow?' I asked.

'Yeah. See you. Good luck with the bitches.'

I returned to school a celebrity. Somebody, possibly Mrs Baker, had called the school office to tell them about my mum.

I think my form tutor had spoken to the girls in my class before I got there. On my return, girls that I had been in school with for ten years, who had never acknowledged me unless forced, were putting their arms around me. I was offered sweets, asked to be their partner in science. At lunch I was even invited to sit with the boarders – cool, aloof kids who I realise now were sad as hell. I was even given uneasy smiles from teachers for forgotten homework. It was bewildering.

The Wednesday after I returned, Harriet Blythe, the reigning queen bee in my class, had asked me to her house for dinner and I had to bite my lip to slow my giddy acceptance down. Ten years, and that was my first invite to a classmate's home.

Her father worked away in the Emirates ('It's an emerging marketplace,' Harriet had told me confidently) but her mother and two younger sisters were home. We were collected in a green, mud-splattered Range Rover Classic that bounced over cattle grids like an armoured tank.

They lived in a huge converted farmhouse, with a long drive through fields that belonged to their estate. Harriet, her mother and her sisters, Rebecca and Rosie, all had golden hair and round blue eyes. Like Hayley Mills in *Pollyanna*, but without her chutzpah.

Harriet and I dropped our bags by the front door and we all ate Chelsea buns and drank orange juice that had been laid out for us like a TV commercial. Harriet showed me to her room. 'Let's put make-up on and take pictures. Mummy gave me her old camera and I've got loads of film,' she trilled in a rehearsed and earnest voice. Then she opened a small trunk full of make-up, laid out in a rainbow with professional-looking brushes.

I painted her face first, carefully brushing her cheeks upwards as instructed. I applied green and gold eyeshadow, like a kingfisher, and two coats of mascara. She looked in the mirror afterwards. 'Oh,' she said. 'I don't think you've done this before, have you?' I'd actually practised that exact look myself, copied from a photoshoot with Grace Jones that I'd seen in one of my mother's old fashion mags. But I didn't argue. I watched as she 'fixed' the look into something more akin to Shirlie from Pepsi and Shirlie.

Eventually, she turned to face me. 'Now, let's do you.'

I'd never had a problem with my red hair. Despite it giving classmates yet more ammunition (it's so easy to boost an insult just by adding 'ginger' as a prefix), I liked the way it looked. This was the era of Molly Ringwald in *The Breakfast Club*, Kate Bush and Cyndi Lauper. I still like my red hair, still boosting it to a brighter red, rather than adding gold as hairdressers are always keen for me to do.

But back then, Harriet seemed embarrassed for me. 'Let's call you. . . strawberry blonde,' she consoled.

I know, and have always known, that I have a relatively limited make-up palette that works for me. That palette doesn't involve pink. But Harriet insisted on adding magenta, baby pink and flicks of purple to my eyes, hot pink cheeks and a kind of lemony-pink lipstick. I looked like I'd had an allergic reaction.

Nonetheless, still desperate not to destabilise the burgeoning friendship, I posed for all the pictures as instructed, pulled every face, and kept the make-up on for the rest of the afternoon. 'You have such a. . . striking look,' Harriet had said and I tried to hide my huge smile.

Their place was more lived-in than my home and a bit smaller. I asked to use the bathroom and noticed all the toothbrushes in the holder, even though there must have been several bathrooms, probably an en suite or two.

I hitched up my skirt, tugged my tights and knickers down and sat on the loo, looking at a hodge-podge of books on the windowsill. I didn't notice it at first, the smear of dark brown blood lying dormant on my underwear. I'd been prepped for this moment for years, hearing all the other girls bragging about their periods and their tampons and their this and their that. We even had a special lesson on it in science, although that was far more theoretical than practical. I cleaned up as best I could with toilet roll and looked around for something I could use. Nothing. I washed my hands and looked inside the mirrored medicine cabinet over the cream-coloured basin. Nothing useful, just a lot of pill tubs and a bottle of TCP.

Harriet was waiting for me outside when I opened the door. 'You've been ages. Are you okay?'

'Um, I need some towels or something,' I whispered.

Her brow furrowed. 'Towels? Have you made a mess?' she asked, eyes widening as she tried to peer around me and into the bathroom behind.

'No, not those sort of towels, like, y'know, tampon towels. Or tampons. Or, y'know, whatever you use.'

Harriet lifted her head back and made an exaggerated 'hawww hawww' sound. Eventually she stopped, but not before attracting the attendance of her younger sisters in their matching Sunnygrove uniforms and golden pigtails.

'You don't call them tampon towels, Kate.'

'No, I know that, I was just—'

'Don't you have any with you?'

'No, I, this is my first—'

'Oh, Kate.'

I didn't say how suspicious I found it that Harriet, the great period expert, laughed at me for being a 'late starter' but didn't have any sanitary products of her own to share. Instead, Harriet's mother, stifling a laugh at my makeover, gave me a brick-thick wedge with strings hanging out of it to attach to stockings I didn't have. I stuffed it into my knickers, pulled my tights up and hoped for the best.

Later, when the Blythe females had dropped me home, I took a deep breath and ventured into my mum's abandoned bathroom, gathering up everything I needed and tucking them into my wardrobe.

The next day, I went to Paul's after school as usual. My belly aching with a new pain, trying to forget how quickly it had spread around school that I'd had a 'giant period' all over Harriet's house.

'Where were you yesterday?' he asked.

'A friend's house.'

'What friend? I thought you didn't have any friends?' He wasn't being unkind, I had told him this many times.

'Well, I won't be going back.'

'How come?'

'Because she's a bitch, just like the rest of them.'

'What happened?'

'It's embarrassing.'

'I won't tell.'

'Who would you tell?' I sniped, and then felt bad. 'Sorry,' I said, 'it's just. . . Something happened at her house, she said she wouldn't tell and then it was all over the school today. I just hate that fucking place so much.'

'Fuck them,' he said. 'Let's get some chips.'

We played 'who would you have on your celebrity list' at a dinner party once, a couple of years ago, While I reeled off five famous men I'd happily sleep with, and then switched one of those for another, Paul ran out at two: Nicole Kidman and Molly Ringwald, for which he was roundly abused.

'You been to see the latest Molly Ringwald film then, Paul? Or doesn't your time machine work?'

'Certainly got a type, haven't you, mate?'

I knew full well who his celebrity crushes were way before that game, because if Paul has a crush, he angles the conversation their way or inserts the object of his affection into situations. This is why we went to the cinema to watch *Eyes Wide Shut* despite the reviews, and how I knew, over two decades before, that Paul like *liked* a girl called Anna in his class.

'Oh,' he said out of nowhere one day, 'Anna told me that they're opening a Burger King in Yeovil. Wimpy won't like that!'

'What are you talking about? Who is Anna?'

'You know, Anna from my class. I sit with her in science. . .

sometimes. I sat with her today and she said that they're opening a—'

'Burger King in Yeovil, yeah, I heard, but. . . so?'

'I'm bored of Wimpy, aren't you?'

'I've hardly ever had one.'

'Yeah, I know, but—'

I sighed. 'Tell me more about Anna.'

The Anna project rumbled on over the weeks, with Paul bringing home titbits of conversation to dissect. 'I think she likes you too,' I said finally, although something irritated me about that. I guess I'd spent so long with Paul that I felt a private sense of ownership. That she, this 'Anna' who Paul had proudly pointed out from his class photo, with her shiny chestnut hair and brown doe eyes, was swooping in to take over from the careful friendship he and I had built.

I would never in a million years have admitted to Paul that I was jealous, I didn't admit it to myself at the time. Instead I rolled my sleeves up and approached the situation with fervour.

'Let's write her a letter,' I said, thinking about the mating rituals of my classmates. 'Girls love getting notes from boys.'

We crafted it carefully, scrapping several drafts and eventually reaching the point where it wasn't going to get any better.

'Spray it in aftershave,' I suggested but obviously, being a smooth-faced thirteen-year-old, Paul didn't have any. In the end, we dabbed our fingers in Mick's Old Spice and smeared a couple of greasy print marks across the Basildon Bond paper we'd swiped from Viv's treasures box.

The next day, I rushed to Paul's after school, desperate to hear what went down, at the same time nauseous at the thought of it. I imagined Paul strutting home, a girl on each arm, somehow sporting a moustache and a foot of extra height. Moustachioed imaginary Paul would look down at me as he glided past with his harem.

'Who's she?' the girls would chirrup.

'Her?' Paul would laugh. 'Oh, she's nobody.'

I waited outside the front door, chewing my nails. Paul was the same height when he came into view by The Swan. His face was still smooth. There were no dolly birds on either arm. And, far from laughing, he looked thunderous.

'Don't ask,' he snapped, as he fumbled with his key to open the door.

The relief ran through me like cold water.

'Sorry,' I said.

'She's got a boyfriend,' he mumbled. 'And she's not going to sit next to me any more.'

I took a big breath because I didn't have a clue what to say. 'Ah,' I said, awkwardly. 'You've still got me.'

CHAPTER TWENTY-THREE

November 2012 – Wednesday evening

Paul once said that he knew deep down that I could fade away like my mother. He was drunk, I wasn't. I was still nursing Izzy and barely awake most evenings. At the time, I argued that I would never do that to my children. I could never retreat from them, never leave them to pick their own way haphazardly like I had.

And yet.

Sometimes, like right now this afternoon, I imagine I'm watching myself from above.

I drift higher and higher, my body becoming smaller and smaller below until it's barely a pin prick. And that feeling of disappearance feels just slightly right. As if the whole world might be smoother without my little dot disrupting its surface. But I've never said this to Paul. Instead, when he measures me with his eyes, probes me about my health, I smile as naturally as I can and thank him for caring.

Did my mother choose to fade away? Did she even know what was happening to her? I didn't know at the time and could never ask her. Only Viv offered a breadcrumb trail of revelation too many years too late, when the damage was long done.

———

The kids are in bed and Paul is asleep on the sofa, half a glass of amber-coloured wine losing its chill on the side table.

I'm the only one awake in this house. I could slip out of the door and no-one would know until morning. I love the kids so painfully but I sometimes explore, in exhaustive detail, the other lives I might have had. The life I could be living now if I'd followed colleagues to New York in the nineties. The Kate I'd be if I worked in fashion. The life I could have lived back in Somerset, facing my mother and father's memories down and creating an actual life there. But I know I'd have ended up here anyway. This is the bed I made. And if I feel like that, the rescued, the grateful. . . how does Paul feel? Does he imagine the other wives he could have had? The journalism career he walked away from? To think I believed I'd rescued him, once upon a time. I shudder at the naivety.

The evening has long given way to black night and I check in on the kids casually, walking in to their rooms just far enough to hear their breathing and smell their sweetness. When Harry was a new baby, I could never have imagined such a flippant whistle-stop. For months, he slept in a cot by my side while I barely slept. Instead, I stared at the little, pink, wobbly creature in disbelief.

I'd heard people talk about 'new baby smell' and assumed it was in the same spectrum as 'new car smell'. Something along the lines of fabric conditioner and milk. But there's no describing it, that perfume that's like a thumbprint, unique to them. That you don't just learn to recognise your baby's unique squawk, but you could pick them out of a line-up blindfolded, just by sniffing the top of their head. I lost hours sniffing Harry's scalp, nuzzling him like something tending its young on the Serengeti. Sometimes, I'd sit in the chair in his nursery, curl him up in my arms like a little prawn, and just rock and hum. It wasn't for him, he was asleep already. Sometimes I would catch Paul watching me, hovering nervously in the doorway like he had many years ago. I felt momentarily strong, curled around my little prawn baby, basking in my own ability to fall in love.

Paul always wanted to be a very hands-on father with Harry. But there's not a lot of space for a father's hands early on, and he was back at work so soon. He changed his fair share of nappies, he was very capable and solid. He would take the baby downstairs on weekend mornings, curl him in his nook while he made coffee and read the paper or made notes on upcoming campaigns. It would feel like barely a blink, a morsel of sleep before I would hear the door creak open quietly and the snuffling of a baby preparing to yell for milk, Paul passing him to me apologetically. I was grateful for every minute of sleep I got, but I also wanted to grab Harry from Paul the second I saw them.

The weekdays were just me and Harry and, with some surprise, I looked forward to them. He consumed my days the way my job had, and I needed him and loved him all the more for it.

Maybe I didn't make enough space for Paul. I fed Harry constantly. Curled up in front of the TV or in bed, stopping to feed on park benches on the Heath. His hunger was my hunger, his pain was my pain. When he had his baby jabs and his squidgy little legs were injected with vaccines, and his eyes looked at me with sudden despair, it was more than I could handle. In pain and disbelief, he clawed at me, with desperate wet eyes as if the whole world was ending. I was so upset and felt so guilty that I welcomed the pain of his hands scratching at me. I welcomed too his furious and frenzied chomping when he fed on me through his teething. That willingness to be hurt because he was hurt, that was a whole new dimension. Who knew? Paul didn't know. Paul didn't love him like that, he didn't get the chance, and he knew it too.

Harry grew, unfurled and became a little person. We went out to cafes and walked in the park, or went to see the animals in Mudchute City Farm. His tiny little hand in mine, or drowsy-eyed, listing out of the side of the buggy on the way home like a drunken sailor. Harry was my platonic date, my constant companion, the love of my life.

It was a kind of furious intimacy. Everything was heightened, especially panic. We'd emerged from the maternity ward on his second day of life with the world's heaviest car seat, newly concerned by everything. My domestic world shrank, circling Harry and me like cling film. The world outside seemed bigger and swollen with danger.

One of the couples from our NCT group lost their baby at a few weeks old. I horrified myself and the rest of the group with the visceral and frenzied reaction to get as far away from them as possible. I deleted their phone number from my mobile phone. As if their grief was catching in some way. Their reality left the door open for more, brought those distant fears closer. Those poor people, abandoned like they carried a deadly disease.

But my boy was everything to me, and that was all that mattered. A blind, wild, prehistoric love. I loved him so much that I wanted to trash the world, burn it to the ground before it could burn him. I sound mad, I know, but it was a thunderbolt and brand new to me. Other people probably have more of a hint of what's to come when they have a child. But while I loved him with every fibre, I also learned two things.

One: I despised my parents, suddenly and totally, for their inability to love me like that.

Two: I had never, ever loved anyone so completely before.

During the pregnancy, I'd been too scared to think about life after pregnancy – life with the baby. To imagine a little wrinkled face, tiny toes, romper suits and baby giggles felt like tempting fate. For months, the pregnancy felt like a held breath. When I finally saw him on the screen at our first scan, when he was really there, where he should be, oblivious to the world outside, I burst into shuddering tears.

1995

At first, I'd worked on low-level clients during my early years at TMC. Eventually I moved on to women's fast-moving consumer goods. Tampons, face wipes, pantyliners and such. Lucrative accounts, but after I'd put in the minimum time with blue liquid pseudo-science, I made myself more and more available to broader accounts. Staying late to help brainstorm for pitches, doing research at the weekends and offering it on Monday without strings. Eventually it paid off, and I was part of a winning pitch team for a new alcoholic drink aimed at women. Aimed, really, at the grey area between teenagers and women. Alcopops, as they were known by the tabloids. A slur we were strictly forbidden from using.

Our client wanted a slice of the new Bacardi Breezer market, and was coming from behind with a sweeter, more 'refreshing' taste. It actually tasted like lollipops and car sickness tablets. Part of the reason I was awarded the work was the sheer quantity I was willing to drink, even though the smell made me gag.

In my early twenties, I was the perfect age to work on an alcopops account. Soon I was the go-to girl for all things sticky, sweet and intoxicating.

I'd go back to my shared house lugging coolbags full of single-serving bottles in watermelon, cherry or grape flavours. My flatmates would pull faces through the taste but drink them down. They weren't in a position to turn down free booze, and I needed the extra insight.

'Why would you buy these?' I'd ask as they gagged.

'I wouldn't.'

My disinterested flatmates were fair-weather uni friends who I had nothing in common with by then. One day I told my work friend Lucy that I wanted to move and she smiled broadly. 'Why don't we move in together?'

It was a flippant comment at lunchtime and a full-blown plan by the time we left the work bar that night.

We moved into a converted flat in Stratford; East London prices suited our salaries.

Our flat was on the first floor of a converted house in Bluebell Road. It was technically a three-bedroom but was really a two-bedroom plus box room. We talked about using the extra room as a spare bedroom, but in reality it was a de facto extra wardrobe and dumping ground. We did keep a sleeping bag in there though.

An old lady lived downstairs, a Haitian ex-nurse whose husband had recently died. She wore huge hoop earrings and bright colours, looked exceptionally glamorous and hated our guts.

Lucy came from a large and cheerful family. We weren't wrong to imagine people coming to stay. Our living-room sofa was a temporary bed for – at various times – her two brothers, numerous cousins and Lucy herself, who gave her own bed up for her parents. Her father was one of the first black bus drivers in Bristol after the famous Bristol Bus Boycott in the 1960s. I'd been too embarrassed to admit I hadn't heard of this, and treated him like he was a minor celebrity. Her mother was a small blonde hairdresser who'd met her husband riding his bus home after a job interview at a city salon. Which she didn't get, and still had opinions on. They were funny and relaxed. Lucy's whole family were sweet and kind. And living with Lucy was fun.

We were both account executives but on different teams so we weren't in each other's pockets and there was no pecking order between us. I'd started to formally specialise in booze. Alongside the teeny-bopper drinks, we looked after high-end spirits that looked like perfumes in fancy bottles. Lucy was more on the bread-and-bakery side of 'fast-moving consumer goods', more family favourites and nostalgic adverts. And that suited her, really. She *was* a cuddly, cosy kind of a person. Living with Lucy was fun.

We were in our early twenties, living in London by ourselves and working somewhere with a free bar. There would have been something deeply wrong with us if we *weren't* having fun.

1996

I'd been working on alcohols for a year when we won the cider account. It was a departure from my usual work. Some brave souls were trying to make an upmarket scrumpy – a traditional south-west cider – to package up and sell as a slice of country cool to urban daydreamers. Never mind that real scrumpy tastes like rocket fuel and is twice as deadly, we were going to help sell this as some kind of nuclear apple juice.

During the early tastings of Apple Rock, which most of my team bailed on after a couple of sips, I found myself transported straight back to 4 Church Street, and watching the *Generation Game* through woozy headaches with the Loxtons. I'd not spoken to Viv in so long by the time I tasted that sour drink but I imagined her pottering around that same little living room, ironing her nurse's uniform in front of *Casualty* and *The Bill*, overlooked by clusters of photos of Paul and maybe still a few of me. I later learned that she'd never taken down the collage she and I made from pictures on the beach, her thumb carefully cut out and added on top, which still makes me laugh.

I got back home from work after the tasting, edges rounded off by the Apple Rock, and found our flat empty. Lucy must have been visiting her brother or out at step aerobics so I picked up the phone and called a number that was permanently etched in my brain.

Viv was so pleased to hear from me that she let out a little squeak, like a chick. We spent the next hour catching up. I told her all about London and my job, about Lucy and the flat. Viv told me about her work, the big extension on the hospital and the changes in the village. She told me that my dad had driven past her a few days before our call but he hadn't recognised her.

I asked about Paul. Viv drew a breath.

'He got a first in his degree, Katie, he did really well. I had to beg him to go to his ceremony but he gave in,' she laughed. 'I've got a picture of him bloody furious in his cap'n'gown.'

'What's he up to now?'

'He's working in a bookshop.'

'Oh?'

'He's applying for writing jobs all the time though, he's got an interview at a magazine next week.'

'Is he still living in Bristol?'

'He lives in a shared house with a few other lads but I don't think he's too keen on them. I worry he never leaves this room except to go to work.'

'He never did like spending time with other people,' I said.

'Except you,' said Viv, and I left that where it lay.

We had barely spoken since our first year of university, no-one had mobile phones then. I never went back to my dad's house in the holidays, choosing to spend summer in the city. Months turned into years but I couldn't shake the idea of Paul fading away in a bookshop, his big brain straining at the leash. That September, I sent him a birthday card. I'd had to call Viv to get his address in Bristol and I heard Viv speaking through her smile as she read it out. The card was made to look like an old mixtape and it had reminded me of him when I saw it in the WHSmith at the station. He didn't send anything in reply, but years later that card was among the few belongings he brought with him when he moved into my flat.

CHAPTER TWENTY-FOUR

1987

That cheesy thing about not needing to speak? Paul and I had that. The funny thing is, now, I often panic. Try to fill a silence. The gaps loom too large. But back then, we could spend hours without words. We even got to the stage where one of us would put on a tape, knowing it was the one the other wanted to hear. We'd listen to each side and then the other would put on the next perfect tape, all without conferring. Sometimes, the one listening rather than DJing would just give a little nod. Or a slight smile. The peace would only be broken when Viv called up for dinner or I realised it was time to go home. If I was going home.

When it was warm and bright, I walked back, scuffing grit into the stream. But on dark days, I'd get a lift from Mick. I sat in the front, in Viv's seat. Once I hit my teens, every car journey with Mick began with me reaching under the seat for the lever and sliding back to give my legs enough room. For Mick, it was a handy excuse to get out of the house, which meant he could pop into The Swan for a pint and a bag of nuts before going home.

Mick would fill the quiet with blather, or put the radio on. There was a swollen feeling in the car, like there was the potential to talk about anything. Eventually, I started to ask questions. About Mick. About his childhood, growing up in the same village I'd grown up in but in very different circumstances. He told me the prices of things in the shop when he was my age, about the headmaster with a fondness for the cane, about his own father's fondness for fists.

Mick was a teenager in the sixties. But sixties Somerset was not swinging London and Mick and his friends had to hitchhike to Bristol if they wanted to experience anything close to those scenes.

'I was there when the Beatles played Colston Hall,' he would say. 'I was fifteen and it was November sixty-three. And if you add up the number of people who *say* they were in Colston Hall that night, you'll have twice the population of Bristol. But –' he'd smile and raise his finger '– I really was there.' And then he'd whistle 'Twist and Shout'. 'You couldn't hear the fab four for the screaming. Brilliant night.'

As I got older, those short drives gave me a snapshot into the young man who emerged as Mick. The capers, the swindles, the girls he chased and the scraps he had. He was sixteen when he met Viv and in his stories she would alternate between 'her indoors' and a queen. Even then, in 1987 – nearly twenty years after they first met – he was both pinching himself that he'd snagged her, and scrabbling to free himself.

We never mentioned Lorraine, the barmaid. The casualness of the scene I'd walked into on that day years earlier had told me, with hindsight, that there was a degree of comfort with the deceit, that it came easy. That I hadn't seen the first or the last indiscretion, I just happened to see *an* indiscretion.

Over the years, I saw the tenderness between Mick and Viv. I also saw how she looked down at him. I wasn't surprised that he'd struggled to say no to flattery. Plus, I think he was bored; I think they were all bored in that village. *We* were all bored. But it always surprised me that only a few of us dreamed of escaping. Of hitchhiking to see the Beatles, or making it to London to buy the magazines I loved first hand.

One of Mick's friends died suddenly of lung cancer that spring. A breakneck circuit from late diagnosis to funeral. He got sad and angry, and talked about death a lot. I didn't think it at the time, but looking back I realise that, as a nurse, Viv was constantly surrounded by death so she seemed to see it in more philosophic terms. Sure, her bit of the hospital looked after people in their final days. But other parts had babies being born in them, lives being saved, children being cared back to health. Death slotted in. But Mick didn't have access to death in his day-to-day life and his brief obsession bled into Paul and me.

Nobody had told me where the cancer had been in my mum. I'd focused on the big picture of it, and never dared ask the details but I wondered if I should. I overheard some *TVAM* segment about breast cancer one morning after I'd stayed over, and for the first time wondered if I had ticking time bombs up my school jumper.

'No,' Viv said when I asked her. 'But you must get yourself checked when you're grown up. Everyone needs to get themselves checked but I want you to be extra careful.'

I took this to mean that I had extra risk and dared not ask any more, it was just too much. I wonder now if she'd meant that I was extra-special, to her.

Anyway, that morning in the kitchen she told me about new tests called smear tests, where they swab your bits to see if your cervix is at risk. She described it in jolly terms, but the squint she did suggested she hadn't much enjoyed her first smear. And she told me about checking my breasts for lumps. Immediately after our conversation, I pretended to need the toilet and scurried off to squeeze my growing boobs in the bathroom until they were sore, panicking at how decidedly unsmooth and, dare I say, lumpy they were.

'I have lumps,' I said, quietly and forlornly as I re-joined her in the kitchen.

'Oh,' Viv said, putting the teaspoon down mid-mash of a teabag. 'Oh, love. I shouldn't have worried you. That sounds fine, Katie. Every boob is a bit lumpy and bumpy, but when you're older you just need to check for *new* lumps. Okay?'

'Okay,' I said.

'Every month, okay?'

'Yes.'

Paul had flopped down the stairs, running late for school.

'What do boys have to check?' I mused.

'Just their balls,' Viv answered, without taking her eyes off the mug.

'Oh God, I'm going to school,' Paul wailed, practically running for the door.

CHAPTER TWENTY-FIVE

November 2012 – Thursday morning

I go for Well Woman screenings every year and when they ask me for details of my mum's condition, the treatment they tried, I just shrug and say, 'I don't know.' If pushed, I say, 'Whatever they tried didn't work because she died,' which tends to draw the questions to a close. I plain don't want to discuss it. Paul never asks about the specifics of my mother's death. He barely mentioned it at the time, even though my mother died on his mother's ward and I did my grieving in his pyjamas.

It wasn't something you talked about. Not in a family like mine. Besides, *everyone* was more reserved back then. If someone was terribly ill, the old ladies in the village shop would ask relatives, 'How is he in himself?' Or if someone was at death's door, they'd say that 'Mrs Such-and-Such is poorly.'

'Poorly' covered everything from the common cold to renal failure. I'm not sure if anyone knew my mum was 'poorly' until she died, anyone outside of my family and the Loxtons. No-one in the shop ever asked me how she was in herself, that was for sure.

1997

It was spring of 1997 that I met Steven Miller at a conference about alcohol regulation and advertising in Victoria. He wore a pinstripe suit and was mostly handsome, with dark auburn hair. When he approached the bit of the bar I was drinking in, he made a crack about us being in 'the ginger corner'.

I was used to being propositioned back then. I'd taken to wearing very high kitten heels that accentuated my height, had invested in a lot of good-quality black clothes and dyed my hair a brighter red. In short, I decided to stand out. I wanted to make a name for myself and planned to use everything at my disposal.

Steven certainly wasn't the first guy to approach me in a hotel bar after a seminar or conference. Not interested in a boyfriend, my main source of dates were industry functions. Charismatic men who would flatter me, feed me and screw me a couple of times. I'd already clocked Stephen before he came over, and had made a decision to say yes.

'Kate Howarth?' he asked, although our name tags had made the question pointless.

'Stephen Miller,' I smiled, looking down at his badge from my heels.

'I was hoping you'd be here today,' he said.

'Oh really?' I smiled brightly.

'Yeah, your name's crossed my desk a couple of times recently and I'd like a chance to talk. Do you have dinner plans tonight?'

He didn't want to screw me. Or, if he did, he wanted to do something else first. He wanted to sound me out about a job.

I was flattered, and more importantly I knew this gave me

leverage at TMC. A vodka brand whose pitch we'd nearly won had apparently been impressed by me and dropped my name to the winning agency – Steven's company, Elliot & Finch.

Steven asked me to come in to meet the team the following day, which I did. I wore my new MaxMara coat – the most expensive item I'd ever used my own money to buy – over a black Donna Karan dress and Patrick Cox shoes. I regretted my tiny Fendi Baguette bag as soon as I arrived and was handed a file on the company, which I couldn't conceal on my way back to TMC and had to dump in a bin.

I walked in to Elliot & Finch with my head held high, flame hair shining. I wanted the office to seem dull once I had left.

It worked. On the way back to TMC's offices in Charlotte Street, my Motorola StarTAC rang with a central London number. Senior account executive, 30 per cent pay rise, bigger bonuses and a better expense allowance.

I considered it, of course I did.

That night, I brought home three bottles of rosé and told Lucy.

'What should I do?' I asked, not giving her a moment for the news to sink in.

'Hmph,' she said, and pulled a glossy strand of black hair taut before letting it snap back to a curl.

'Hmph indeed,' I said.

We talked it through, although it was apparent that Lucy felt a bit sour about the offer, sour it had happened to me, and sour that I could even consider leaving her. 'Perhaps I'm not doing a good job noisily enough,' she said when we were into our second bottle.

I wasn't ready to burn any bridges but I took it to John Silver, then a senior on my team, nonetheless.

'I'm not going to take it,' I said. 'My heart lies with TMC but it has made me think.'

'Go on,' he said, giving me a half-smile.

'Well, I'm ambitious, as you know, and I don't want to stagnate anywhere. I know I still have plenty to learn and I want to learn it here.'

'Atta girl,' he said, 'that's how you use a job offer. You *have* been paying attention.'

I smiled, knowing he'd speak to Andy, the head of client services – our boss.

I was promoted to account manager, a big leap and a significant salary bump. I let Steven Miller take me out on a couple of dates as a consolation. By the third date, we called each other Red as a nickname. It was fun, but we were too busy to go further with it. To be honest, I forgot to call him.

Every month throughout university, my father had paid £500 into my bank account for living expenses. He hadn't stopped when I graduated. When I first got accepted onto the graduate scheme, I thought about calling him and telling him to stop paying it, that I didn't need it. I was all set to one Sunday night, as I laid my Kookai blouse and River Island skirt out for the next day. And then it dawned on me. *He didn't even know I had a job.*

Fuck it, I thought. Let him pay money into my account and tell himself he's being a father. Let him salve his guilt that way, and I'd use the money my way. My salary paid my rent, bills and food, my father did not prop me up that way. So that £500 went on clothes and make-up, shoes, handbags. My uniform.

As I earned more money and bigger bonuses, I started to add my own cash into this clothing allowance I awarded myself. I started to buy more strategically. I bought myself a subscription to *Vogue* and already bought *I-D* and *The Face* every month from

Charlotte Street News. When I remembered how I'd pored over months-old copies back in my childhood bedroom, I felt a soaring pride from being at the epicentre of something, living in a city where stuff came out *first*.

I'd gone from trainee to a leading account manager in four years. It felt meteoric. I'd earned it, hustled for it, watching and learning from the best. And I didn't hide my light under a bushel either. I'd like to think I didn't brag or rub anyone's nose in it, but I wore it. I wore my success and I dressed for more.

In advertising, you grab every nugget of gold and you sell it as bullion. I took this to heart.

I was not the best ideas person, I wasn't the most attractive woman, no longer the youngest. I had *no* family ties of any use in the industry. What I had was height, hair and confidence. I exaggerated them all.

I was slim but shapely. And although I joined in with the tugging of waistbands and inspecting of split ends in the work mirror, really I enjoyed the way I looked. I'd gradually stopped being skinny and become more 'willowy'. I dressed to look statuesque. I needed to stand out, be remembered. It was a professional strategy.

But I was also a very hard worker. I still turned up first, left last, and paid attention. I didn't play politics, I didn't get sucked into the passive-aggressive blind copying on emails and throwing people under the bus, but I put myself forward time and again. I was hungry.

Lucy was a hard worker too but work wasn't her life, her life was her life. She wouldn't put herself forward, out of self-consciousness, she said, but I started to think, privately, that she just didn't care as much as I did. She would make barbed comments, and I would think barbed thoughts. That just doing a job well isn't enough to stand out. Just doing a job well means you don't get sacked. That's the bare minimum. That I shouldn't feel guilty for getting ahead.

When I got promoted to account manager, it was the final straw. I asked her to come out to celebrate with other colleagues but she went home instead. When I got in that night, she was on the sofa in her pyjamas, scowling at the TV.

I woke up before her the next day, a Saturday. I bought a bacon sandwich and a mug of builder's tea from Ozzie's cafe a few doors down, got a mortgage offer from my bank a couple of streets away, and started to hit the estate agents.

CHAPTER TWENTY-SIX

1987

Drink had always been around Paul and me. My mum generally had a glass in her hand if she was out of bed and her hangovers were one of the only constants in my childhood. Perhaps I'm naive but I didn't – I don't – think she was an alcoholic, I just think she didn't have much else to do.

Mick had a few beers most nights and their kitchen often contained a huge plastic bottle of cloudy scrumpy donated from one friend or another. Back then, almost anyone around those parts knew how to make scrumpy. And proper scrumpy was strong, like Snow White's poisoned apple in juice format. Apple Rock would have held nothing to this.

At the Loxtons', we were allowed a few beers or a small glass of something. When I spent New Year's Eve there – the first New Year's since the year my mum died – we drank Asti Spumante and they called it 'champers'. That drove Paul to distraction. He's still a pedant, refusing to lump prosecco in as champagne, even if it embarrasses whoever is offering it. On the anniversary of my mum's death just a few days before, I'd drunk at home. A first for me. My father and I had eaten dinner together, the room so quiet I could hear the food squeak on his teeth. We ate salmon, green beans and new potatoes with butter, cooked for us by Mrs Baker.

My father spent several minutes checking his fish for tiny bones, and teasing them out with his knife and fork while I stared. He found three, and had laid them gently side-by-side on the edge of the plate like bodies dragged from a lake. I barely touched my food but I accepted my father's offer of some La Scolca Gavi dei Gavi Black Label. I think it was offered on autopilot, but I seized the chance. It probably cost nearly as much as Mick would earn for a winter morning's work but I didn't really care, I just pretended to give a shit when I sighed my way through the story the next day, to Paul.

I drank most of my father's bottle that night, after he'd finished his food efficiently and gone back to his office. I'd staggered upstairs and tried to fall asleep, somewhat indulgently, on my mum's bed. I wanted to be found there. I wanted someone to know that I'd tried. But I couldn't do it. I lay wild-eyed, my thoughts swarming. Eventually I sloped off to my own room around midnight.

Viv didn't really like us drinking – she'd known real drinkers in her family – but she turned a blind eye. You wouldn't know it to look at him, but Paul can handle a drink. He can remain fairly stable and sound of mind several drinks past most people.

As the piles of homework we had to do grew taller each week, we started to reward ourselves more and more with a tin here, and a glass there. No different to the middle-class 'just opening a bottle of wine' adult habit. Who doesn't indulge in the commiseration bottle, the celebration bottle, the 'happy hump day' middle-of-the-week bottle, the weekend bottle. . .? It's no different. We blamed the 'stress' of schoolwork and nurtured the idea that we were alcohol-dependent because most of our heroes were creative drunks. Neither of us has ever been alcohol-dependent.

But things were ramping up at school, even if we were overegging the stress to justify the booze. We were to be the first year to take GCSEs rather than O-levels and CSEs. No adults seemed to really understand the new exam system. We tried to explain it to Viv and Mick numerous times but ended up in fits of giggles at Mick's glazed-over expression whenever the subject of school came up. Viv really wanted to understand, but she hadn't taken part in formal schooling herself until she was in nursing college, it wasn't her world.

What was so hard to understand? we'd say. Instead of two different types of exams, there was just one. Just one general qualification for everyone our age. So Paul and I could both take the same exam and stand the same chance of getting the same grade as each other.

'Your dad could've saved all that money, Katie, seeing as you're doing the same bloody exams our Paul's doing,' Mick would say, as if he was genuinely concerned for my father's financial affairs. Paul saw it differently. He thought Mick was claiming some kind of good sense on his own part by not sending Paul to private school.

'I really don't think it's that, Paul,' I'd laughed.

By then, Paul's affection for his parents had been tainted by an increased level of scoffing and eye rolling. After years of his mum praising him for being smarter than everyone else, and his dad playing up his part as family clown, it had gone to Paul's head. He would recite the lyrics from 'Nowhere Fast' by The Smiths, declaring it the best description of his own adolescence. He would quietly sing the lyrics about banal consumer excitement whenever Viv got animated discussing an advert she'd seen on TV.

Teenagers are always insufferable but, God, we were *awful*. We weren't just awful, and sneering, we were embarrassingly late too. Most of our school peers had already done the teen rebellion thing by the time we discovered it. We'd spent our teens with noses in a book. To this day that's a running joke we have in response to anything edgy. 'Heroin? Oh, I know lots about heroin, I've read William Burroughs.' 'Travelling? You don't need to tell me about travelling. I've read *On the Road* and *The Motorcycle Diaries*.' And so on.

It had been a subdued summer in 1987. It felt like everything was conspiring to scare the country. The darkness started with Ian Brady, that same shadowy photo staring out from every paper. He'd confessed to two murders and then when that got everyone jumping, he'd confessed to five more. Just two decades too late. The Hungerford Massacre, a few counties up the road from us, had split the heart of the summer wide open. An unassuming little town peppered with bullets, sixteen dead at the hands of Michael Ryan, a gun-nut mummy's boy who had the newspapers pumped with excitement when it turned out he was also a fan of *Rambo*. And then, like the blackest spectre of all: AIDS. Sticky summer headlines warned that one person a day was dying of AIDS in Britain. One person a day. In a country of 57 million. The maths didn't matter, we were straight-up petrified.

The spring had been dominated with documentaries on disease prevention and condom use (we took these as a sign of the certain death that awaited us, before we'd even got to experience the mindless sex available to every other generation).

We watched agog as the first AIDS public service advert rang out. Paul still refers to the power of that campaign when he works on charity accounts, something he'd love to do more. I can still remember it perfectly. John Hurt's voice silencing us with: 'There is now a danger that has become a threat to us all,' while nightmarish scenes of pneumatic drills chiselling a huge tombstone took over the telly.

'Put 'em on an island,' Mick said and Paul's glare had hardened.

'Oh don't give me that, Paul. I don't care what poofters do behind closed doors so long as it don't affect the rest of us.'

'Give over, Mick,' Viv had snapped, taking him by surprise.

'No, I won't, I won't give over.' Mick became more animated as he warmed to his own outrage. 'I'm all for live and let live but they're risking us all now with this bloody. . . this bloody gay plague.'

'You're quoting the *Sun*, Dad!'

'I'm quoting what we've just seen and heard! "It's a danger to us all."'

Paul threw his hands up in the air.

'It said not to die of *ignorance*,' I said quietly. 'Everyone's at risk of AIDS, not just gay men.'

'Are you calling me ignorant, Kate?' I saw a twist of anger in Mick's face that I'd only ever seen aimed at Viv before.

'Don't talk to Katie like that,' said Viv sharply. 'Anyway, she's right. It's not just gays and you are being ignorant.'

'I don't know what's bloody wrong with you lot – it's a gay disease, and now it's spreading to normal people like a bloody cold. You can't touch anything they touch, can't use public loos in case they've been in them, we're probably going to have to boil all our drinking water—'

I was still stinging from the sparks of friction with Mick when Viv spoke up.

'I think we'll let the nurse of the family field this one, Mick.'

'You nurses have refused to treat homos, so you can pipe down, Vivian.'

'Oh shut up, Mick. A handful of ignorant cows said they wouldn't treat AIDS patients and they were slapped back for it. The rest of us'll care for anyone that needs us, AIDS or not.'

She shook her head at her husband, who was rolling his eyes.

'It is bollocks, isn't it, Mum? You can't really get it from a toilet seat?' Paul asked.

'You can't catch anything from a toilet seat, Paul, unless you're planning on licking it. And no, you can't get AIDS from touching things, but you can get other things so wash your bloody hands more often, all of you.'

I avoided Mick's gaze after that but when I was about to follow Paul up to bed, Mick had grabbed me and given me a wrestling-style bear hug. 'Don't mind me, lovey,' he said. 'I just got worked up before.'

By the spring, no matter how calming Viv's reassurances were or how many times she changed the subject, we were still convinced AIDS was weeks away from becoming airborne and wiping out all human life.

Throughout the summer we talked about the time we had left, and our urgent ambitions. 'Is it even worth bothering with school? Let's just go travelling.'

Paul had never gone further than Bristol. I'd been to London and had holidayed in southern France when I was little. Despite this, we felt oddly equipped for a life on the road; less odd was our failure to actually go anywhere.

The one bullet point on our to-do list far more pressing than travelling the world was losing our virginities. We moped about our lack of love, gloomily listening to 'How Soon Is Now?'.

We turned sixteen in September, a pair of melancholy, melodramatic virgins. For Paul's birthday, I spent a good bit of time drawing a pen-and-ink illustrated collage. It had the 'Smiths to Split' *NME* headline reproduced, black and white versions of the album covers, stencilling with Paul's favourite songs and snippets of lyrics.

When he opened it and saw it was something handmade, Paul looked flustered. 'Cheers,' he said, and put it down carefully on his chest of drawers and then changed the subject. I was hurt, and resolved not to bother next time. The next day when I went to visit, still smarting but having nowhere else to go and missing his company, I saw that the picture had been put in one of those 'frameless' clip frames and was hanging above his bed. Neither of us mentioned it, but he's kept that picture with him his whole life. It's hanging in our en suite.

For my birthday that year, the Loxtons gave me a present from all of them. A bracelet chosen by Paul, according to Viv, and wrapped in a little black box from Elizabeth Duke at Argos. I still have it in my jewellery box, I always did, although Paul didn't believe me until I showed him just before our wedding. 'My something old?' I asked.

'Don't wear it,' he said. 'I can get you something nicer now. Let me get you something nicer.'

So yes, we were a pair of virgins at sixteen and it was getting us down. At school, the talk was all about bases reached, boyfriends and gifts. I thought about wearing my bracelet into school, acting coy about which boy gave it to me, but I couldn't bear the piss-taking over something precious.

I was called frigid and I didn't argue. What could I say? I wasn't frigid, I was frozen out. There was a difference.

The kids at Paul's school didn't call him frigid, they called him gay. The poet-heart in Paul wanted to embrace that, given how many of his heroes *were* gay. But mostly he was mortified under their spotlight and hurt under their feet. The violence at my school was only dished out by teachers. And that came in the form of teeth-gritted punishments that you only got if you broke the rules. At Paul's school, violence was just part of daily life, part of the big lumpy organism that the school's community formed. You got a punch for standing in the wrong place, you got your lunch wrecked for looking like 'a bummer' and you got tripped up just for walking in the corridor. Those who swung their fists back then probably look back on all that now as good-natured rough-and-tumble. Paul's angry to this day. He felt utterly humiliated and he finds humiliation impossible to move past.

There was a rising tide of anger all around us that autumn. Maybe there always was and we just started to see it, or the adults ceased to hide it. When my dad was home, he would hiss angrily into his office phone, chastise his staff for the smallest of indiscretions and stalk the halls, rubbing his temples. Luckily, he barely spoke to me. Business was bad, that's all I knew. I didn't even understand what his business involved, but I knew the high tide had passed on it. His company made its money from countries in the Eastern Bloc. Looking back, the upward march towards German unification and McDonald's in Moscow must have been visible on my father's horizon then, although his business didn't fully implode until years later, after I'd gone.

The Loxtons' house also felt smaller and more pressurised than before. Paul and I learned when to scurry out of the way and when to turn the music up. Mick was flush from building work, which had also made many of his friends richer than they would ever have expected to be. Mick was frequently taking wedges of notes to the pub after work, coming back later and later. I remember agreeing with Viv, a little reluctantly, that it was unseemly at his age. He was younger then than we are now! Viv started referring to it as 'Mick's midlife crisis' but it soon stopped being funny. She started to cry a lot, and openly. He started to be cruel.

It unravelled so quickly, it was dizzying. One day a family, the next day lots of broken bits. I wish I hadn't played a part in that. To paraphrase a Polish saying that my father once told me: it was not my circus and those were not my monkeys.

The incident occurred during the massive October storms that had thrown trees across our village roads and slashed roofs with lightning.

Paul and I had spent the evening drinking. Our childhood preparedness for extreme weather, with our canned goods and torches, had given way to drinking beer and moving Paul's bed away from the window. We half-heartedly propped the Z-bed in front of the curtains like a barricade. The electricity had gone out. The only sound was our lips and tongues on the glass, the hard swallows and the clink of each finished bottle joining the others.

I'd had a horrible day at school and was determined to get drunk to forget it.

I'd arrived at school in the morning to find every girl from my year on the front lawn in hysterics, pointing at a huge image being projected onto the school clock tower with one of those overhead projectors on wheels, an extension cord trailing into a nearby classroom.

It said 'virgin 4 life' across the top in pen and 'who would fuck that?' across the bottom.

Me.

Me with pig-pink eyes, yellow lips, dirty freckles. My red hair clashing and garish.

The photos Harriet had taken of me after my mother died, blasted across the pale bricks of the tower, eight foot high.

I didn't say a word. I shifted my bag onto the other shoulder, forced myself to lift my head high. I marched away from the lawn, back out of the gate and walked several miles to Greenfinch Manor.

Back home, I watched daytime TV and ate toast in silence, waiting for the afternoon to roll around so I could meet Paul. No tears, strangely, just a resolute acceptance. Mrs Baker had watched me walk past her window and chosen to leave me to it. I wasn't her circus or her monkey.

When I went to meet Paul, I left my house swinging a bag of booze from the larder. Bottles of continental beer, some half-finished whiskey.

So that night we had plenty of booze and drank most of it, right through the storms and into the power cut. Mick was nowhere to be seen and Viv had gone to bed as soon as the power went and the TV stopped working.

Around midnight, I'd popped downstairs to the loo. My mind was still churning angrily about the photos, my body was swaying with the booze. If I hadn't known the house so well, I'd have tumbled over in the dark. I was about to climb back up the stairs when I felt a hand grab my arm. I inhaled ready to scream and another hand clamped over my mouth.

'Sshhh, shhh,' a voice said in my ear, breath hot and wet from drink. 'It's okay Katie, it's only me.'

Mick, himself three sheets to the wind, making his way home from a lock-in at the pub.

He took his hand off my mouth and I turned to face him, squinting to see the outline of his face. I felt his breath mingle with mine.

'What time do you call this?' I whispered, giggling.

'Don't tell Viv, will you?' he asked in that very loud shouty whisper that only the very drunk can achieve.

'Okay!' I whispered back, louder than intended, and started to amble up the stairs. I tripped, probably on Mick's foot and landed on the floor.

Just as Mick foraged around for me and grabbed my arms, pulling me up to him, a thin light flooded the hall and there was Viv, standing at the top of the stairs with a torch. She ran down the stairs towards us and hit Mick hard on the head with the torch, so the light bounced all around the small area, highlighting the family coats, the shoes, the pile of newspapers to be used on the fire.

'No, Viv!' Mick said, and as he lifted his hands to protect himself, I lost my balance and fell over again all Bambi-legged.

'It's not what it looks like!' he yelled. He couldn't have chosen his words more poorly, more stereotypically. Mick was pushed back to the front door that he'd just come through and Viv slumped next to me. She found the torch, and shone it on me, running it from my head to my toes as I shielded my eyes.

'Katie, are you okay?' she asked, her voice strangled.

'I'm fine,' I said unconvincingly.

'What was he doing to you?' she asked quietly.

'Nothing,' I said. 'He was just pulling me up from the floor.'

She swung the torchlight onto Mick's face, and he threw his hands up to his eyes.

'What's wrong with you, woman?'

'What's wrong with me?!' she growled and then started to cry. I put my arm around her, instinctively and heard Mick step away.

'How could you?' she said into the dark.

'I didn't bloody do anything,' he said.

'I'm fine,' I added. 'I'm fine.'

'Is that what you think of me, Viv? Eh?'

Viv swung the torch back into his face.

'You've never been able to keep it in your trousers,' she spat. 'I don't know what to think any more.'

Mick swung the front door open and stormed outside, slamming it behind him. We stayed in the dark, me swaying, until eventually Viv led us into the kitchen and I went to the loo while she boiled water for tea on the old gas hob. She looked so much older in the torchlight, her shoulders hanging heavily with deep shadows tugging at her face. We drank in near silence and after I had sobered up a bit, she helped me upstairs. She must have known we'd been drinking, but I think she was too preoccupied to care. I went back inside Paul's room and stumbled around. The Z-bed was still in front of the window, the wind still whipping at the glass. Paul's bed was against the opposite wall and I stubbed my toe and swore loudly.

'What happened?' Paul asked and I heard him sit up in bed, his mattress creaking.

'Nothing,' I said. 'Nothing happened.'

'I heard Mum shouting. Did Dad come home?'

'Yeah,' I said. 'He was drunk and he'd been out late and he—' I stopped myself. 'Paul?'

'Yeah?'

'Your mum thought he'd tried it on with me.'

'What?'

'He didn't. I promise. No-one ever has and no-one ever will.' I started to cry. Horrible drunk indulgent tears.

'All those girls are getting boyfriends and having sex and they'll go on to fall in love and get married and what about me? Will anyone ever love me?' I sobbed, surprised by what I was saying, the drama of it.

'Of course you'll get a boyfriend and have sex and get married. Look at you. What about me? I've never had a girlfriend, never even had anyone interested in me.'

'Your time will come,' I said.

'Will it? Because what if it doesn't?'

'What if it doesn't for me?' I asked, sitting down next to him on the bed, trying to get things back to my own little slice of drama.

Paul reached down to the floor and fumbled to find his half-finished bottle of beer.

'Alright then,' Paul said as he raised his drink in mock toast. 'Here it is: if we're not married by the time we're thirty, let's just marry each other.'

I snorted and found an empty bottle to knock into his. 'Yeah, right,' I said. 'Let's do it.'

He stayed silent for a moment. 'I mean it, Kate. Let's just do it. Let's make a vow, right here.'

'Really? Are you sure?' I asked as my hollow laughter faded into a wavering smile.

I heard him move. 'Deadly. Are you?'

I thought for a few moments, the blackness in the room somehow swirling. 'Yeah,' I said. 'Yeah, why not?'

For a moment we said nothing.

'You know,' I said, 'if we're going to end up together anyway. . . maybe we should just get it over with?'

'It?'

'Yeah, *it*.'

Paul didn't say anything for several long seconds. Eventually he took a huge gulp of his beer.

I undid my jeans. I wriggled out of them and tripped over slightly as they fell to the floor. I heard him hold his breath but he didn't move so I took off my T-shirt as well.

'Are you sure about *this*?' he asked, and I didn't know if he hoped the answer was yes or no.

'If not you, then who?' I said, and unclasped my bra.

'Always you,' he said, and he pulled his T-shirt over his head. 'Always *you*.'

The next day, after having sex with the best and only friend I'd ever had, I left at first light without saying goodbye. Trees lay across roads like they'd been ripped apart by giant hands. The stream, churned black with mud, lay flat and still. The bodies of fish dotted the surface.

I walked home, stomach lurching, overflowing with liquid. I climbed between the starched sheets of my double bed and stayed there, occasionally shuffling over to my basin to throw up.

I didn't visit the Loxtons' house for a week. I knocked on the door, unsure how Viv would view me. Paul opened up and immediately coloured red, right through to the tips of his ears.

'Hi,' I said.

'Alright?' he asked, looking at his socked feet.

'Yeah, you?'

'Yeah. Want to come in?'

Paul told me Mick had gone for good. He was staying with a woman in Taunton. 'What choice do I have, Vivian?' he'd apparently said.

'Did your mum tell you what she—?'

'Yeah,' Paul grimaced. 'He didn't really try it on, did he?'

'No, he really didn't. I fell over, that's all.'

'I don't think that really mattered to Mum. She says she's been in denial about his "womanising ways",' Paul used air quotes. 'But when she actually thought that he could have done that, with you, she was like, God, if I think he's capable of that, I can't do this any more.'

'Fuck. I can't believe it.'

Paul shrugged. 'I guess it was always on the cards, but she's never actually booted him out before so. . .'

'Yeah,' I said, rerunning the stupid mishap in my mind. 'He really didn't do anything. He was drunk but. . .'

'And you? How drunk were you?'

I paused. 'Not too drunk to remember what happened.'

He looked at me, just quickly. 'I wasn't sure when you'd come back.'

'Sorry. I just—'

'Felt really fucking weird?'

'Felt really fucking weird!'

Paul and I did not repeat the activities of that stormy night. Whether Viv knew what had happened between us, or just recognised me as a growing young woman thanks to the confusion in the hall, she no longer thought it was appropriate for me to stay on the Z-bed. And this was fine with me. It had taken time for Paul and me to find our feet on the new ground. It had taken time for me to stop seeing him in a painfully naked light, to forget how he looked with no clothes on in the dawn light as I crept out.

CHAPTER TWENTY-SEVEN

November 2012 – Thursday afternoon

We have the heating on full but the wind whipping around outside makes me shiver. Earlier we went for lunch by the harbour, sheltering from an angry, churning sea, foaming and frothing and spitting so hard it hit our feet. I'm glad to be tucked away inside now, back in my lounging-around clothes.

Paul comes in and stands watching me in the kitchen as I grab our local bits and bobs out of the fridge and rummage for knives and chopping boards. He doesn't say a word or make a sound, but the air shifts slightly. A twig scratches at the window and I shudder, imagining a chill despite my socked toes grinding down onto the heated floor as I reach up to the highest shelves. I know he's still there. I move self-consciously, awkward under his gaze. I try to imagine his thoughts as he looks at me, his wife of nearly ten years.

Paul has always been a watcher. He has incredible stamina for just waiting it out. I had to have an operation under general anaesthetic years ago. The nurses told me gleefully that he had sat and watched me the whole time. From the moment they brought me back up from theatre, to the second I woke up. They said he didn't move.

'I don't think he even blinked!' one of them had laughed.

'You've got a good one there,' another said, overstepping a mark that I was too foggy to care about.

At the time, I doubted he did blink.

I can still sense the silent shape behind me, but it's only the increasing volume from the kids in another room that gives away the fact he's no longer watching them. By the time I've turned around, unsure what I want to see on his face, he's gone again. And the distant hum of a bollocking bubbles through the walls.

'But she—!'

'Daddy! He—!'

'Dad! She said—'

'Izzy, you're not a baby any more, you can't—'

I bend down to get another chopping board out of the cupboard. Paul comes back in and hovers just behind me as I stand up. I hear him take a breath before he places his hands on my hips and moves close to me. He murmurs into my hair and I can't make out what he's saying.

'Hmn?' I breathe, turning my head just slightly.

His lips touch my ear as he whispers, 'This weather reminds me of The Big Storm.'

I close my ears, lean back into him just a little. I'm not quite sure what to do because he never normally initiates anything like this when he's sober. It's always me. It's always been me, even when it's his idea. The thought catches me, the thought that maybe it wasn't like that, and he was just going along with it. But he seems to mean it now. I wonder if someone else has awoken this in him. I don't know what to believe, the handwritten letter scrolling through my mind like unwanted subtitles.

His breath feels hot even through my shoulder-length hair. I push back against him again ever so slightly, surprised by how much I don't want him to move away from me. It's been a long time and it could be the last time. His hands move up from my hips and I hold my breath. I can't help but wonder if it makes it easier for him that I'm facing away. My eyes cloud with tears, just as he moves one hand up under my top and traces my bra.

Just then, an explosion of noise comes down the hall and bursts into the kitchen. Paul pulls his hands back and jumps away from me as Izzy tears in and leaps up at him. He catches her, bewildered.

'Dad,' pants Harry.

'What did you do?' Paul snaps at Harry.

Izzy's smile drops.

'Nothing,' Harry says, furrowing his brow just like his father and looking down at his feet. 'There's a seagull,' he almost whispers. 'It landed on the windowsill and we thought you'd like to see it.'

'Oh sh—, I'm sorry Harry,' Paul says, following the kids back out of the kitchen without saying a word.

I exhale and stand still for a minute or two, catching my breath before I start to slice pieces of cheese and arrange them on the slate board I found.

1999

It was a kitchen encounter that changed things between me and John Silver, by then my boss. I'd worked at TMC for six years at that point, moving from eager junior to trusted senior. He'd replaced Andy Dowell as head of client services after the former left to spend more time with his family, i.e., was fired following an argument with the CEO.

Our team had been working late on a pitch, but the others had gone home as nothing useful was being suggested by then and we were just getting steadily drunk on company booze.

I went into the kitchen to make a coffee and sober up for the journey home. Then I saw him in the doorway with *that* look on his face. A kind of hunger. A look I saw many times over the next year or so.

John was handsome, late thirties, slightly greying at the temples, married. He was thickening around the middle but gym fit with big shoulders, big arms. He was taller than me, and many men weren't. Aren't.

He'd mentored me early on in my career and I'd always enjoyed his attention and guidance. I know, it doesn't take Freud to unpick that one.

Well, anyway, that was how our affair started, in the kitchen at the office while working late. Never feels like a cliché when you're in it. From there it was winks in the foyer and fabricated client meetings in a hotel an expensed cab ride away. Sex in the office kitchen and the disabled toilets. Kissing in the lift. And the best part was, he expected nothing more from me and could give nothing more to me.

When I got the call to say my father had died, I told John because I needed to take leave. He looked uneasy – was I asking for emotional support? I wasn't. John was my boss and he was my lover but he was not my boyfriend. To prove it, I arranged a fabricated client meeting in the hotel next to Paddington station, and we fucked each other stupid for a few hours before I left for Somerset.

Afterwards, I lay curled in the crook of his arm, afternoon sun seeping through the crack between the curtains. He looked at me for a while, and then got up and filled the small kettle from the bathroom basin tap. I wondered if he judged me for not crying about my father; I hoped he thought I was strong and mature. I was always looking for his praise.

'Take as long as you need, yeah?' he said, bare arse to me as he stirred hot water into the coffee granules.

'I won't be long,' I said, 'and I'll forward my direct line to my mobile.'

He fiddled with the lid of the long-life milk tub but couldn't get it off and brought it over to me. I pierced it with my nail.

'Don't do that,' he said. 'You need to take time off, even if you don't realise it. No-one will steal your accounts.'

'Promise? Look, I'll just stay long enough for the funeral and then come back.'

'Well, I want you back as soon as possible but you need time to grieve,' John said, and passed me a cup without a saucer.

'I really don't,' I said, and blew on the thin coffee.

I met my father's second wife at his funeral. She was pleasant, a bit bland and very attractive. I'd have guessed she was in her late forties.

'Nice to meet you. I'm your step-daughter,' I smiled, hoping she'd appreciate humour in the absurdity.

'Oh,' she said. 'You must call me Joanna.'

Joanna, not Jo.

I hadn't been invited to their wedding, no-one had. It had taken place somewhere in the Caribbean. I'd asked Janet, our team's PA, to send flowers.

The funeral took place in Little Babcombe's church, just like my mum's had years earlier. I kept expecting to go back to Greenfinch Manor afterwards, just like in 1987, but my father had long sold the house to prop up his shrinking business. Drinks and sandwiches were served in The Swan, in the old skittle alley that was by then a private function room. I crouched down when no-one was looking and ran the tips of my fingers along the old floor that had given me so many splinters when I was ten.

As mourners arrived, Joanna and I stood next to each other and thanked people who had come. Almost all of the guests were business associates and their wives, most of whom looked a lot like Joanna.

'I didn't realise Roger had a daughter!' one of the women said to my father's wife, clutching her hands to her chest as if a little joke had been played on her.

'Yet here I am!' I said, my cheeks pink from a couple of glasses of wine.

Lorraine brought in the trays of food, teetering on heels. Quartered baguettes and crisps, sausage rolls. I wondered if my father ever had a single drink in this pub, I couldn't picture it.

Lorraine was still striking but her big bosom had slid halfway down her chest and her bottom was wider. A solid, smiling Somerset woman in a leopard-print dress. No wedding ring. I wondered how many other women's husbands she'd slept with, and shrugged off the hypocrisy.

The house in which my father had his heart attack was on the edge of the village. Large, red brick, double-fronted but nothing like the manor. In her call about the funeral arrangements days before, Joanna hadn't invited me to stay at their home. Instead, I called Viv from London and asked to stay at 4 Church Street. She agreed immediately, and told me she'd make up Paul's old room.

I slipped away after a couple more glasses of wine, slightly tipsy. I had sat next to Joanna, stifling yawns from the wine and feeling more of an intruder and less of a daughter with every conversation. I had no idea what the people around me were talking about. My father's business was a mystery. He'd imported bits of things, and exported bits of other things. Whatever these things were, people had started to want them less and less. Maybe some of those people were at the funeral, maybe he blamed them. Joanna's blank look was no comfort, she was dazed and grieving. Maybe she often looked blank, I didn't know.

It would be a lie to say I wasn't moved and sad that my last living parent had died. I wasn't sad that Roger Howarth had died, because I didn't really know him, but I felt flattened that my father had died and any chance to feel anything for him had died too.

The pub was almost opposite Viv's house, and I saw her watching for me through the curtains. As I crossed the road, slightly wobbly, I was caught by a memory of Mum's funeral, and for the first time since the call about my dad, my lip trembled.

Viv threw open the door. 'Katie!'

I had to stoop down to hug her, lower than I remembered. Her hair was still dyed jet black, her eyes sparkling, deep smile lines and deeper creases criss-crossing her face.

'It's so good to see you,' I said.

I slipped my shoes off in the hall, Viv still holding one of my hands. 'I have a surprise for you,' she said. And then her sympathetic smile slipped just briefly and she said, 'Oh, maybe I should have checked, I hope you don't mind.'

'Mind what?'

We walked into the tiny sitting room and there was Paul, sitting on the edge of a new blue three-seater sofa, one I didn't recognise.

The sight of an unfamiliar sofa threw me more than he did.

'Hey, Kate,' he said, without smiling. 'I'm so sorry about your dad.'

He stood, looking a bit taller, a bit broader. I felt a sense of betrayal that I couldn't fully articulate – he'd turned into a man behind my back. We hugged clumsily.

'You've come to see the twenty-seven-year-old orphan then?'

That night, we drank tins of beer and ate fish and chips with curry sauce, mushy peas and buttered doorsteps of dense white bread. The three of us talked over each other, reminiscing and taking the mickey. Paul and I laughed at Viv's 'Vivisms', her mangled memories and funny phrases. We even talked about Mick. According to Viv, Mick was in touch quite often, popping in for cups of tea and asking after Paul. I found out that he'd been to see Paul a couple of times while he was at uni and called him every now and then to tell him about funny things he'd seen. That he'd occasionally, mistakenly, tried to offer life advice. 'If you get a good bird, son, never let her go.'

'*I* wouldn't,' Paul had apparently retorted but when he recounted the story, it was with laughter.

Paul was different that night, new. Easier, honest, open. His life in Bristol was stagnant and dull, he said, but he told its stories with a sense of humour. His job at a low-circulation magazine was at risk, and he wasn't sure if he hoped to keep it or lose it. Later I found out that he'd played this all down considerably. He'd had his hours cut to part-time and been applying for bar work to make up the money. His credit card – something he always said he'd never get – was at its limit and he thought he might have to move back to Little Babcombe, which would have crushed his ego.

Viv turned in before us that night and Paul and I took mugs of tea to bed. I had the Tetley Tea Folk mug that I'd always loved, instinctively feeling for it in the cupboard above the kettle.

I took the Z-bed and, despite Paul's protestations, he had his childhood divan. It was everything I needed right then. He wore some blue cotton pyjama bottoms and a white T-shirt and I wore a black Agent Provocateur chemise that looked fucking ridiculous in his little bedroom. I wished I could borrow some PJs like old times.

'So, do you want to stay in Bristol?' I asked, trying to get comfortable as the Z-bed creaked. 'I mean, would you be conflicted about leaving if the chance arose?'

'I never wanted to go to Bristol in the first place and I've definitely got no love for it now,' he snorted, with the first bitter edge I'd heard all night. 'Why do you ask?'

'Well, I know a junior copywriting job is coming up at my agency,' I said, shifting onto my side as the coils twanged under me. 'But obviously that's in London so. . .'

'Really?' he asked, and his uncharacteristic enthusiasm broke my heart.

'Yeah, one of our art directors is a nice guy called Colm and his copywriter left suddenly last week so they're looking for a new writer to join up with him.'

Paul was trying not to smile and I worried that I might have made it seem like too much of a sure thing. I didn't even know if Paul was any good. He always had been good but teenage poetry and schoolboy essays aren't exactly the same as pitch-winning campaign lines.

'I mean, those jobs are very sought after and we always get hundreds of CVs,' I started to fumble. 'So I can't promise anything but I could definitely try. If you think you could handle the ignoble art of advertising?'

'I'm too skint for ideals, Kate.'

I laughed, and so did he. Still smiling, I lay back on the creaking Z-bed and looked up at the ceiling, its wrinkles in the paint like the creases of an old palm. The same paper globe lampshade hung over us and when I heard Viv use the loo, the chain rattled in a way I instantly recognised. For the first time in a very long time, I felt a sense of home. Home with a capital H. Not my flat, not my personal space, but the soil that I'd come from. I turned over to ask Paul how often he came back to visit but his arm had flopped out of the bed he was too big for and his chip-shop-and-beer breath caught in his open mouth.

That night, I slept better than I had in years.

10 Morrison House
St Katharine Docks
London
E1W

August, 1999

Dear Viv,

I just wanted to write and thank you again for having me to stay after Dad died. I'm sorry it took so long – and such horrible circumstances – for me to visit. It was lovely to stay with you, though. It turned a crap experience into a nice thing. And you always make the best tea.

Paul's settled in really well at work. He's paired with an art director called Colm and they've made an excellent team. Colm's previous copywriter was a girl called Toni and she'd left under less-than-great circumstances (drink was involved) so Colm was a little bit bruised and nervous. Paul has completely set him at ease. Their ideas are brilliant and I've heard plenty of people requesting P for their accounts. I'm so pleased he applied. I've never recommended anyone before but he's not dragged my name through the mud – quite the opposite.

It's nice having him to stay as well, like old times. Unfortunately, I know it wouldn't work long term because it's not a big flat, and I'm sure Paul wants his own masculine space!

Did I tell you that my dad left his house to Joanna in his will? I didn't think he had much left after that but his solicitor got in touch the other day and I've been sent just over £200,000! I can't believe it. I paid off my mortgage and credit cards. And I bought a take-away curry home for Paul!

It's such a relief to know that I have my place paid for, that I'll always have that. And it means I don't need to ask Paul for any rent. I know how badly TMC pays junior copywriters, after all.

I would love to come to stay again soon.

All my love,
Katie xxx

CHAPTER TWENTY-EIGHT

1988

We found a new normal. And Viv and I were closer than ever. With Mick gone and Paul so insular, I think I became a confidante, a sort of peer at times, other times a compliant de facto daughter.

I've often wondered how she could have been so black and white about what she saw in the hall that October night. So many times I thought about asking her, checking that she hadn't thrown away her marriage because she thought I was covering something up.

In the end, she said it to me. It was the anniversary of my mother's death and I spent it curled up on the Loxtons' sofa. I was wearing a new dressing gown that was nominally from my dad, and found that I could cry easier that year and at the same time, felt lighter about it all. I think it was because my father was away, I didn't need to pretend that time spending the day with him showed some kind of honour to my mum. Instead, Viv told me about her mum and I told her about mine. Paul made us cups of tea, read in his room, stayed out of the way.

Viv told me about the boy her mum wanted her to marry. Laughed at how, really, he wasn't all that different from Mick, a ladies' man, always a wink and nudge away from a bad idea.

'I know nothing happened on the night of the storm, love.'

I sat up. 'Do you?'

'Yeah. I know you told the truth and Mick's a lot of things but he's not a perve, he thinks of you as a daughter.'

'Thank you,' I said.

'I was just at the end of my rope, that's all. So don't think about it, alright?'

'Alright.'

Mick had been coming back to see Paul every week or so, drinking a cup of tea and asking awkward questions about school. I hadn't been there.

And then, in the first hours of New Year's Day, Mick was back at the front door.

Outside, a newly minted 1988 was still black, the ground slick and shiny in the occasional street light. The pub was silent, but a light on in the flat above it suggested a lock-in had rung in the new year, and Mick had probably been a key player.

'Vivian!' he shouted through the letterbox. 'Vivian!'

I pushed the living-room curtains to the side as carefully as I could but suddenly his face was there, staring into mine with wild dark eyes. I snapped the curtains back as I jumped out of the way but it was too late.

'Katie!' he shouted. 'Little Katie, it's me! It's Mick! I've forgotten my keys!'

In the hall, I heard the top step sigh underfoot and crept out to the hall to see Viv sitting on the stairs in her maroon dressing gown and slippers, head in her hands.

Mick must have seen my shadow move across the hall as I made my way up to her.

'Katie! Let me in, I know you can see me!' He paused to regroup. 'I won the meat raffle, I've got some chops for Viv.'

I held my breath and wedged in on the step below Viv, leaning my head on her legs.

'I know you've seen me,' he yelled, his chipper shouts turning to more of a growl. 'Let me in, you little cow.'

Paul's door creaked open and Viv and I craned our necks to look up at him.

'Dad's here, is he?' Paul said.

Viv and I moved single file to one side of the stairs as Paul made his way down to the front door. He crouched down, pushed the letterbox flap open and out with his finger and said firmly: 'That's enough, Dad. Go home.'

'This *is* my home, boy!'

'Dad, you're pissed. Go home.'

'This was *my* dad's house, Paul. This is *my* house. Let me in, you little sod.'

'Go home, Dad,' Paul continued in his measured tone as I reached back to put my arm around Viv. 'That's enough now,' he said, evenly.

'I'm not going anywhere,' Mick said, and the sound of smashed terracotta scudded across the path as he kicked a plant pot.

'Dad, there's nothing for you here. You need to go and sober up. It's cold out there,' Paul started.

'So let me in,' Mick said, his voice trembling a little, bravado slipping. 'It's bloody cold, Paul,' he said quieter than before, 'so please let me in.'

Viv opened her mouth to say something but before she could, Paul had opened the door and was standing inches from his father, who was swaying and shivering.

'Dad.' It was more of a statement than a name. 'You don't live here any more. Mum doesn't want to see you and I don't want to see you like this. Get the fuck away from this house or I'll call the police.'

The door slammed and Paul marched back up to his room, squeezing past Viv and me. As Mick walked away down the street, we heard more terracotta scudding across the icy ground.

'The neighbours'll kill me if he's smashed another pot.' Viv sighed, squeezing my hand and easing to her feet to go back to bed.

CHAPTER TWENTY-NINE

November 2012 – Thursday afternoon

Izzy has just lost her first tooth. When I came into the living room and saw her outstretched, shaking hand covered in spit and blood, my first thought was *Harry*. Because Paul's first thought, if he came in and saw the scene, would be that it must be Harry's fault. 'He gets so carried away, he's so boisterous,' he says, astonished as ever by the physicality of our little boy.

Most boys are, I think and rarely say.

Izzy isn't crying, but her eyes are wide and her flashes of pink smile are uneasy.

'What happened, baby?' I ask her, as I rub her shoulders and walk her like a drunk to the bathroom, her dripping hand still outstretched.

'I was wobbling it,' she says, through her wet mouth.

'Did you pull it?'

'A bit,' she confesses. 'But not that much.'

'Where's Harry?' I ask.

'I don't know,' she says, and then brightly: 'Can I show him?'

'Of course you can, but let's clean you up first.'

After showing Harry, to his delight and disgust, we wrap the tooth in toilet roll and tuck it under her pillow. Paul watches from the doorway, looking dejected that Izzy has shared this moment with me. She looks so strange with her little gap, her broken bit of mouth. 'She's growing up so fast,' Paul says when we go back into the kitchen. But she isn't. They're babies for years these days. Far longer than we were. And I'm glad of it too.

I set my phone alarm for 11 p.m., just in case I fall asleep on the sofa after a couple of glasses of wine. I can't send an IOU for her first tooth.

It can all be measured in teeth, of course. From birth to death. The tiny little dots sprouting from red cheeks and gnawed knuckles, growing all those baby teeth so violently and then losing them like petals. Then come the big chunky adult teeth that twist their faces into new expressions. And eventually, decades later, they'll lose most of those and be left pulpy-mouthed and old.

I don't like teeth. The crunch of them when people eat, the way people pick food from between them, and even the way my children's teeth – teeth I should love unconditionally – look like fractures of skull dripping in their hands.

Our kids are all about the tooth fairy. I think it's a fairly revolting idea but I go along with it for them. They find it charming, the idea of a little fluttering Tinkerbell building her palace out of teeth. It turns my stomach. I can almost smell the decay when I imagine that outsider-art palace made from stolen enamel, its walls covered in yellow stains and left-over crumbs.

I didn't have the tooth fairy growing up. I didn't need the money but I'm pretty sure it was more that my parents didn't need the hassle. Because it *is* a hassle. Fumbling around for the right coin (who has cash any more?), staying awake and remembering to tuck the money under their sleeping heads, extracting the carefully wrapped tooth, disposing of it.

On the other hand, I really like Father Christmas. It's a role I enjoy. The Dutch have an untranslatable word: *Gezelligheid.* It roughly means cosy, convivial, the kind of feeling when you go 'hmn' and snuggle into a cushion and feel affection for the people around you. I think this word applies to the Father Christmas myth. And I definitely remember stockings when I was little, pillowcases with chocolates, oranges, bracelets and little toys. The idea-cum-memory makes me feel cosy. I didn't know who put them there and certainly didn't give my parents the credit at the time. By the time the myth burst for other kids at school, Christmas stockings had long stopped for me.

It's different now. Father Christmas, the Tooth Fairy, the *Easter Bunny*, for fuck's sake.

It's non-stop gift-o-rama, non-stop delight and surprise and myth. While I'm sure the kids don't believe it for as long as they used to, they expect the presents nonetheless. It's an almost joyless transaction by the time they reach Harry's age.

Do I sound jealous? Perhaps I am a little bit, but I don't begrudge my children. Perhaps the better a parent I am, the more of the list I manage to tick for them, the angrier I feel for the girl I once was. Perhaps that's it.

With dinner done and the kids in bed, after two glasses of wine I do fall asleep on the sofa and wake up at 11 p.m. to the calypso trill of my alarm. Paul is sitting on the armchair facing me, a second bottle of wine sits finished next to him. He has his head in his hands and doesn't flinch at the sound of my phone. For a moment, I think he must have nodded off too but then he looks up, tugs his fingers through his greying hair and pinches the bridge of his nose.

'What's that noise?' he says slowly, feeling for the words with his tongue.

'Alarm for tooth-fairy duties,' I say. 'Want to do the honours?'

'How about I pay the money and you do the parenting?'

'Just like usual then,' I say, smiling but he doesn't smile back.

'Oh God, I thought you were joking,' I say. He ignores me.

'I didn't imagine myself like this,' he says.

'Paul?'

He staggers a little as he stands up and reaches into his pocket, scattering loose change as he pulls his hand back out.

'What's the going rate?' he slurs.

I'm surprised that he's drunk, and feel alarmed and left out all at once.

'How much?' he says, sharply.

'A pound.'

'Here you go.' He passes me the coin and then drops to his knees to pick up the rest.

'Are you sure you don't want to do it?' I say gently, even though he'd probably tip her out of bed if he even attempted to find the tooth under Izzy's pillow. He doesn't reply.

'Paul,' I say, a rising sense of panic in my chest. 'I'm sorry she showed me first, I should have thought, I should have—'

'Should have what? You're her mother, it's normal.'

'But—'

'Just be a fucking tooth fairy,' he spits, and then throws a handful of coins into the far corner.

CHAPTER THIRTY

1989

Paul and I had prepared for our GCSE exams together, so it seemed strange that we weren't actually taking them in the same school hall.

My father had stopped coming home for weeks on end by 1989 and Viv's house could sometimes feel scrunched up with bitterness so Paul started to come to mine that spring and summer.

From May onwards, we didn't have to go to school as we were expected to revise at home. Most of Paul's schoolmates had already peeled away from classes long before that. We'd sometimes spot them on the swings in Castle Cary, smoking and jumping off onto the tarmac while little kids looked on. Or eating chips as they swaggered around town.

Most of my classmates from Sunnygrove were taking extended holidays in the south of France or America, some of them with a tutor in tow. Paul and I didn't aspire to joining either group. We liked the solitude, the long days stretching out in front of us. We liked being together.

In some ways, 1989 felt like that very first summer eight years before, transplanted to my domain. I would wear shorts and sit on the grass by the horse-head fountain, enjoying the fresh smell and the tickle of the bright-green turf on my legs. Paul would sit under a big sun umbrella, pasty arms sticking out of his Talking Heads T-shirt, thick jeans boiling his legs. We'd revise, while Mrs Baker brought us drinks of lemonade and sometimes, bizarrely, boiling hot cups of sweet Camp coffee – at our request. Even now the smell of chicory will zoom me back there so that I almost remember Pythagoras' theorem or the exact process of photosynthesis.

Paul never slept at my house, though. It wasn't just that Mrs Baker would report back to my dad, who, even while absent, was very old-fashioned. It was also that Paul had never slept at my house in the years before, so it would be a new thing, an almost exotic thing. A thing that would have to be acknowledged. Rules that would have to be established, unmentionables that might have to be mentioned.

That summer, we revised like revising was our job. We studied every day, for the whole day. And only at the end of the working day would we 'play'. And our play was mostly drinking a few Italian beers from my dad's cellar and reading until Paul bid me goodnight. Italian beers and reading! I look back and just think, *God, we were so old.*

All the revising was worth it. Paul did better than me in his GCSEs, the best in his school by far. He scored six A stars, two As and a B in French. We have the local paper clipping somewhere from when we went to collect his results together, though he hates to see it. Me, smiling at the camera and holding up *his* results. Him out of shot, refusing to take part because of that B.

After the bell went at the end of my last exam, I never stepped foot inside Sunnygrove School again. I even waited the extra day to receive my results by post instead of collecting them in person like we had with Paul's.

My father was packing for a flight to Poland the morning my results arrived. I hovered by the door to his bedroom as he opened his suitcase and lay it on the bed. I read my grades to him as he moved slowly and deliberately between drawers, wardrobes and case.

He nodded and 'mmned'.

'Well,' he said finally, 'that's a relief. Well done.'

'Thanks,' I said, picking at a knot on the doorframe and avoiding his eye. 'So anyway, I'd like to go to Yeovil College.'

'College? Why not sixth form at Sunnygrove?'

'I really don't want to go back to that school. I want to do proper modern art and textiles but they only do fine art at Sunnygrove.'

'But it's a much better school, and you'll need more than art to do well in your life, you need to think about the wider picture.'

'I'd rather not do A-Levels at all if it means going back to *that* school.'

'I beg your pardon?'

'I won't go back to Sunnygrove, no matter what.'

My father placed the last of his starched shirts into the case and clipped it closed. The clicks were rhythmic and controlled. I balanced on one foot and then the other, unsure whether to storm off or apologise.

'Do you know how old I was when I left school?' he said, eventually.

'No,' I said. *I should know that*, I thought.

'Fourteen.'

'Oh.' I moved my weight back to the other foot but that one didn't feel right either so I swapped again.

'And do you know what qualifications I left with?' he asked, as he went into his en suite bathroom.

'None?'

'None,' he said, as he returned holding a toothbrush in a travel case and then reopened the suitcase slowly, all the clicks in reverse.

'And I've worked hard to overcome that deficiency ever since.' He paused and looked at me. 'I've worked this hard so that you don't have to overcome that kind of handicap, Kate.'

I paused a moment, drinking in the sound of his voice saying my name. Dancing, just briefly, in his parental gaze. He'd never said anything like this to me before and I, unfortunately, was about to burst the bubble by arguing. 'But I've got GCSEs now, I've already done better than you did at school. I did well.'

'I heard what you said. You got three As and six Bs, you think that's enough to take your foot off the pedal?'

'I got six As and three Bs.'

'It's not about these exams, it's not even about the next ones. It's about university, who you know, which circles you mix in.'

'Mum went to art college, so why can't I?'

He stopped clicking his case shut again and looked up. Not at me, at the wall in front of him. I saw his shirt tighten as he took a deep breath.

'She did,' he said. 'And look how that ended.'

Autumn 1989

My father never relented and I never backed down. Instead, when I was home, we slid around the house avoiding each other or made polite small talk in communal spaces. Like colleagues. He left for the Eastern Bloc during the week when my college enrolment was due. I took that as implicit permission and the subject was never raised again. I realised this was a glimpse into my parents' marriage. When difficult decisions arose, one or both of them left.

So I got my way and made my very first life choice. I went to the local college to do A-level art and textiles. But I also took business studies and English literature, my love of books still strong. Business was a compromise no-one had argued for, but I thought my dad would be relieved. Maybe even proud of me, on some level. And I was saving him eight grand a year in school fees too, which must have been good timing given the late-night hissing I heard from his office.

Paul also applied to Yeovil College to do English literature, English language and history. We filled in the forms together, me making a mess of my first copy. I still struggle with forms, the pressure of the neat little boxes sending my handwriting sprawling. Paul says I have Form Dyslexia and we laugh, but I'm actually quite embarrassed about this specific brain fart. But we made it, the forms were filled in, handed in and accepted.

We talked about what we'd wear on the first day. Just the idea of wearing 'own clothes' rather than – in my case – a royal blue blazer and ridiculous boater hat was intoxicating. I felt like I could reinvent myself, paint myself in new colours. The only sticking point was Paul. He had borne witness to exactly who I was. Even without my uniform he could still place me in it. I wondered if he felt the same, as I'd suggested a full outfit for him that he said he agreed with, but then showed up at the bus stop on the first day, wearing the same old Smiths T-shirt and jeans.

We'd gone to Yeovil on the morning bus together for the first registration, coughing through the cigarette smoke that thickened as we approached the back seats. I looked at the cool kids with their Embassy fags and their peroxide hair and their acid-house smiley face T-shirts. I looked at Paul with his fey gestures and eye rolls and for a split second, I wished he'd go away. Just for a beat, swaying as we found seats, I wished I could sit with those cool kids and turn away from Paul for the rest of the journey.

CHAPTER THIRTY-ONE

November 2012 – Friday morning

I leave Paul sleeping. He has a silvery sheen on his skin that he only gets when he's hungover. His throat rattles as he snores, his mouth wide open.

After my cat-nap yesterday evening, I ended up awake for much of last night, running over the strange spat we had just before bed. Each time telling myself that Paul was just drunk and it meant nothing, then starting the cycle again.

'I didn't imagine myself like this.'

Well who did? Whoever does? I tried to brush it off and file it away last night but instead I kept working at it, chewing it like a jagged fingernail.

I was still weaving in and out of sleep when Izzy screamed with delight at 6.30 a.m. this morning.

'The tooth fairy came!'

Now she and I are downstairs as Izzy sits tonguing her gap and staring at the TV screen, nightie stretched over her knees. Harry is still asleep. He used to be up with the birds but just recently there has been some teenage foreshadowing. Grumpiness, hormonal spikes, sleeping in. I miss little Harry.

I make another pot of coffee, my senses sludgy. I briefly consider taking Paul a cup, sitting on the bed and asking him to explain himself. But I won't. I doubt he even remembers. In the grand scheme of things, it's less than nothing.

Ten years tomorrow.

Despite everything I have to say tomorrow, everything that might happen, I still hope Paul likes his presents. Especially the Dylan Thomas book. I know he doesn't have it already, I checked and checked again before I bought it.

He started his collection when he was still at university. Tucking the books into their protective covers, squirrelling them under his bed, away from his flatmates. Those books numbered significantly among the few belongings he brought up on the train from Bristol when he moved. They were lumped into the back of a taxi at Paddington and then carefully positioned in his small room in my flat.

That first night together again, he'd unwrapped them, gingerly but deftly. Told me about their backgrounds, how to keep them dry and not snap their delicate spines. I remember the smell of their protective perfumes. So unique then, and so familiar now.

His growing collection now has its own little room, which we grandly and only half-jokingly call The Library. I'd narrowed the anniversary gift options down to three other books but then I stumbled across a brief article about Dylan Thomas's Mousehole connection in a *Time Out* guide to Cornwall. It felt too serendipitous to ignore.

So I opted for *Under Milk Wood*. I've always loved the name but never really took to the play inside. The beauty of The Library, of course, is that there is no expectation that I should read through it. In fact, touching the contents is positively discouraged.

I checked so many times to be sure Paul doesn't already have this book, because it seems like one he would have prioritised. He's always loved the dark romance of Dylan Thomas.

Of course, not all of the titles in The Library are rare or even particularly old, but I can't help feel they're all chosen, the whole collection curated and guided by some private part of Paul that I'm not privy to. Every one of those books is there because they mean something.

Ten years tomorrow. Ten years of quiet, solid marriage. But really, it's been so much longer.

1999

Paul's rise at TMC throughout 1999 and into 2001 didn't bring out the best in me. And I'm not proud of what it stirred, a kind of sibling agitation. I was proud of him and how well he did, which was patronising. And I was jealous of how easily it came to him, which was petty. I felt like I'd handed it to him, which I had and I hadn't. And I secretly smarted that I hadn't been given constant thanks and recognition, which would have been ridiculous and uncomfortable for both of us. If I'd been accused of any of that at the time, I'd have denied it to my grave, seething at the accuser but it weighed on me, the realisation a little too late that I wanted to keep this part of my life, this new life, to myself.

Back then, at the turn of the millennium, my own career at TMC was at its peak. To be rattled by someone so junior to me was beyond silly but it wasn't just anyone, and it was clear early on that Paul would not stay in the little leagues. The month that

Paul was boosted to copywriter, shedding his junior stripes, I became group account director. I celebrated with other execs at the top of the Oxo Tower. The following week Paul was taken to the Fitzrovia pub in Goodge Street after work by Colm and the rest of the creative team to celebrate his own promotion. When I heard his key in my lock late that night, I made a point of flouncing into my room and banging the door just as he arrived to hear it. Had I actually wanted to be invited? Looming over the creative team like some unwanted dark apparition from the 'other side'? God knows. We never mentioned it the next day or beyond but I think of it often, when I'm struggling to sleep and spending the time berating myself for a catalogue of past fuck-ups.

When Paul had first arrived in London, with his small collection of neatly packed belongings, it had been fun. For the first few weeks we'd slipped into an intensity much like our old summer holidays. Playing each other CDs from the intervening years, remembering old jokes and Vivisms, talking about university, all the stuff we'd missed.

Neither of us had stayed in contact with any of our college friends and neither of us had any school friends to keep in touch with, so we talked a lot about ourselves. We played with young Kate and Paul like they were little marionettes we were watching, controlling with our remembered and partly constructed narratives. *Remember when? And then you? And then your mum said. . . and then, oh I can't breathe, I can't stop laughing.*

For those early weeks, I'd been happy to spend all my evenings with Paul because we had so much to catch up on, and because he wasn't going to be staying for long. And he really wasn't.

My flat had two bedrooms, but the second was barely a double and had been partly co-opted by the creep of my clothes and shoes. I had one bathroom. En suites weren't so de rigeur in those days. The kitchen was designed for someone who always ate out. I loved that flat, loved the feeling of being snuggled up to by other flats on all sides, my own little cube suspended and propped up by other people in their own little safety deposit boxes.

I had a flat-screen TV, which was quite something in 1999. Twenty-four inches of shiny, black luxury. There for me to watch whatever I wanted at weekends, to fall asleep in front of in the evenings, an almost empty glass of wine flopping to the side as my wrist dipped. I was giving up a lot of myself just to share that remote control and I hadn't wanted to relinquish control for long.

Paul's life in Bristol had been very different to my London life on a material level. He'd had no disposable income at all, he certainly didn't have the trappings of a free bar or an expense account. He'd lived in a shared house that had turned a little sour with time. He'd dedicated himself to his job, trying to pour every drop into proving his abilities, for all the good it did him. But there were some silver linings to his poverty too, for me at least. Because while I'd been in London dining out, Paul had learned to cook. He was pretty accomplished at following recipes like a scientist but also had a little handwritten book of his own creations.

While he stayed, he cooked for me if I came home early enough, which was a couple of nights a week. I figured it was a good way to accept his unspoken thanks without making a fuss about it. One time, I'd planned to be home for eight o'clock and told Paul so but then John had caught my eye just as I was tugging my coat sleeves into place and zipping up my bag. Without saying anything, we'd left the office and walked briskly to a nearby hotel and checked in hurriedly. Him sliding his corporate card over the reception desk with one hand, pushing the other down the back of my work trousers and tugging at the top of my knickers.

After a few lost hotel room hours, I eventually got home to the flat a little wobbly on my heels just after 1 a.m. As I slipped off my shoes and walked into the kitchen, I saw the cold dinner on a plate for me, covered in taut cling film. It felt wrong and mean to throw it away so I tucked it in the fridge for the next day but when I woke up, Paul had already binned it and left for work. I apologised when I passed his bank of desks that morning, but he'd waved me away with a smile, saying it didn't matter.

When Paul passed his three-month appraisal and was given a permanent contract, I offered to help him flat hunt. I bought home a copy of *Loot* and two bottles of red wine.

I'd poured two large glasses, spread the yellow paper out across my lounge table and asked, 'So, where do you want to live?'

For a moment, Paul had looked at me wide-eyed, like the enormity of London had just spread out in front of him and knocked him off balance.

'Where could I afford?' he said. 'Where's nice?'

'Well, you probably can't afford nice,' I said. 'Not yet.'

I suggested further out in the East End, doing his time in the cheap seats like I had, maybe in a shared house with other young professionals. I pointed to one in Stamford Hill.

'Jesus Christ, that room's three times what I paid in Bristol!'

'Really?'

'Literally, to the penny, three times the amount of money I paid for a large room near Clifton.'

I must have looked blank.

'Clifton's the nice bit, Kate.'

I wondered if Paul knew that my inheritance had paid off my mortgage, whether he felt cheated that life hadn't given him that kind of leg up. I wasn't asking for any rent from him because that would have been profit, hand over fist, and that didn't sit right when I already earned so much more than him. He didn't exactly ask to stay longer, but we didn't circle any ads that night in Loot and I silently decided to give him a few more weeks before I'd mention it again.

I hoped that he'd find a work friend like I once had in Lucy, and move in with them. Funnily enough he found a work friend exactly like Lucy: he found Lucy.

I didn't know they'd started seeing each other at first. I came home late one night and heard the sing-song sound of a woman's voice and saw two dirty plates next to the sink. I'd poked my head around the living-room door, planning to bid a pantomime mumsy good night, only to see Lucy hide a smirk and Paul's ears go red.

'Oh, hi.'

'Hi, Kate,' Paul said, scrambling to his feet. 'We've just been working on ideas for a campaign.'

'Which campaign?'

'The um, the one with the—'

Lucy tugged his sleeve to sit back down. 'Why are you being weird?' she laughed. 'Paul invited me round for dinner, we didn't think you'd be here. Hope that's not a problem?'

'No of course not, Luce, it's nice to see you out of work. I've missed hanging out with you.'

She left that dangling in the air and they patiently waited for me to leave. I went to bed stung and trying not to acknowledge it.

Lucy and Paul saw each other on and off for a while. Their sweet sunny normality in contrast to the shadows in which John and I hid. The clandestine hotel meetings, winks and late-night text messages hadn't seemed sleazy until I'd seen them up next to the tinkle of text messages Paul would get to wish him good night. The way he'd smile when he said Lucy's name.

Their relationship had a potential trajectory, painted out in front of them. They might move in together, get engaged, buy a flat, have a kid. John's and my 'relationship' would only ever remain a series of less and less exciting bunk-ups. Grinding out a nil–nil draw in hotel rooms that shook when express trains thundered nearby. Ending the nights with tiny measures of minibar drinks in plastic beakers.

I'd been able to ignore the gnawing shallowness of my own situation when I had nothing to compare it to. When it felt like some kind of 'express' arrangement, slotted into my busy life like a minimart in zone one.

I stopped instigating the meetings with John, going to the hotel rooms only when he pursued me enough and convinced me. Then he told me that his wife was pregnant. That she'd been 'off sex' for months, long past the end of morning sickness. That he wanted me more than ever. I asked him not to tell me any more about it and then cried on the Tube ride home.

Paul started to sleep over at Lucy's flat, the one she and I had once shared and that she now lived in with one of her cousins. After months of my flat feeling stuffed and over-occupied, it then felt quiet and abandoned. The cold kitchen seemed sadder without the smell of cooking when I walked in. And on the nights when I wasn't out with clients or pretending to laugh at shit jokes at industry events, I ate toast and felt sorry for myself. I imagined Lucy laughing and opening wine in our old kitchen in Bluebell Road. I could imagine in minute detail the utensil pot from which Paul would fetch the spatula, what the handle of the fridge would feel like in his palm. I wasn't sure which one of them I was more jealous of but either way it made me tetchy and unkind.

After that first night when I'd seen them together, Lucy rarely came around to my flat to see Paul. She certainly didn't come round when I was there, anyway. I saw her at work, of course, but I had my own office in a corner of the building and she was still on the same bank of desks she'd occupied when we lived together. We didn't cross paths deliberately.

I remembered the giddiness Lucy and I had when we got the keys to Bluebell Road. How we would get drunk and watch films like *Dirty Dancing* and sob that we were like sisters and even as I remember it, I'm mangling into a kind of pink glittery chick-flick montage. In reality, if I force myself to be dispassionate, we had a good few months' honeymoon period. Then there were a few more months when things started to grate a little, but nothing serious. She was messier than me and I was more turbulent than her, but we broadly got along well for a long time. It was only really work that caused the problems.

Rather than deal with any issues, I just moved out. Back then, that was my go-to approach. I'd never known another way of working. Every adult I'd ever witnessed left when things were difficult: my mother, my father, even Mick.

Even though it was me who flounced out of our flat and our friendship, I missed her. I still miss her friendship now, actually.

I'm not proud of what I said to Paul about Lucy. It had been a rough day. I'd seen John's wife waiting in the foyer of our office after work and recognised her from previous Christmas dos. She was round in the middle and looked pink-cheeked and healthy, all golden bouncy hair and big pregnant boobs. I smiled and made small talk, and was just saying goodbye when John appeared. He looked horrified for a split second and I scuttled off like a shamed woman, his oblivious wife waving me goodbye.

I wanted company and distraction from my guilt. I went down to the office bar but the only people drinking there were juniors, no Paul and no-one I really knew. I left to make my way home. Paul had a mobile phone at that point, his first. A big boxy Nokia that he hadn't answered when I tried to call to offer to pick up a take-away and some wine on the way back.

He eventually arrived home hours after me, by which time I was slightly drunk, tired and very emotional.

With little preamble, I made a smart-alec remark about him being under the thumb, spending all his time with his 'boring little girlfriend'. He'd balled up his fists by his sides, but said nothing and instead faffed about unloading the dishwasher in a manner I found to be condescending and passive-aggressive. Because, frankly, I would have found anything he did right then condescending and passive-aggressive.

'So is this it then?' I jabbed again, as I watched his back hunch over to reach the last of the cutlery.

'What?' he said, wearily.

'You're going to move in with Lucy and get married and have boring little babies?'

Paul shoved the forks into their place and slammed the drawer shut with the loud metallic whoosh that made me jump.

'What is your problem with Lucy, Kate? She was your best friend once.'

'So were you,' I bit back, regretting it.

'What? Look, I know you and Lucy had some silly tiff about—'

'It wasn't silly,' I said, getting upset and hating it. 'She was horrible to me.'

'That's not the way she tells it.' My eyes widened at that. 'Look,' he said, holding his hands up to placate me. 'I know it's weird for you, I'm sorry. I didn't realise it would be a problem but I'm trying to be discreet.'

'So what's the appeal then?' I said. 'She's not got much going in the personality stakes, so is it her body? Her arse? That big pair of tits?'

'What the hell are you talking about?' Paul rubbed his hand over his face and gritted his teeth. 'Look, you're obviously tired and emotional, why don't we—'

'Is it just that she took an interest, and no-one else has? You must have been desperate to sink that low,' I snapped, instantly regretting it but too drunk to back down.

For a moment, Paul said nothing. All I could hear was my own idiot heartbeat. I opened my mouth, to take it back or make it worse, I wasn't sure.

'Firstly,' Paul suddenly raged, yanking on his index finger so it looked like a bent reed, 'she's *not* the first woman at TMC to take an interest but your head's too far up your arse to notice that.'

I felt a wave of nausea as I realised just what a disastrous cul-de-sac I'd swerved down.

'Oh, I'm going to bed,' I tried.

'No, Kate. Secondly, I appreciate the assumption that I spent the last decade celibate but you're not the only person I've ever had sex with, you know.'

'Sure,' I started. 'I bet you've slept with tonnes of women, that's why you resorted to stealing *my* friend.'

'You need to go to bed, Kate.'

'I want you gone in the morning,' I said.

'Okay, Kate.' He used the same soothing tones he now reserves for Izzy.

I tried to slip out before him the next day but he'd beaten me to it. When I got to the office, he was already in a shut-door with Colm, their heads together, a big flip board covered in the scribbles of 'brainstorming' in front of them. At lunchtime, I noticed Lucy hovering by the creative team but leaving alone; Paul and Colm sharing a big bag of crisps while they stayed locked away for most of the afternoon.

That night, I came home to find Paul using his new favourite toy – a pasta machine. We ate pesto tagliatelle in silence and as I cleared the bowls, my back to him, I said, 'I'm so fucking sorry.'

'You were a real arsehole,' he said, softly.

'I know.'

He and Lucy broke up a few weeks later. 'She was a bit boring,' he shrugged as he told me over a Chinese take-away. 'I felt like I had to be nice all the time,' he grimaced. 'If I ever said anything a bit spicy she'd look horrified.'

'A bit spicy?' I laughed.

'Yeah,' he smiled, affecting Mick's voice. 'A bit blue. A bit rough around the edges.'

'I went to the university of life, son,' I joined in.

'I got a degree in hard knocks, mate,' Paul added.

He never did move out and neither of us mentioned it again but I still feel sick remembering. I didn't mean any of it. Not a word.

CHAPTER THIRTY-TWO

1989

Although Paul and I had one A-level subject in common, we were in different classes at college and our timetables rarely synched up. We travelled in on the bus together, at first comparing our experiences, slightly giddily dropping the names of new friends. But it was only a small college and before long, many of those friends were the same and we were both on the fringes of the same loose social group.

I'd never been in a group before. Moving as a homogenous lump through the corridors, bunking en masse to go to the crappy nearby pub where they never asked for ID, working on projects together, failing projects together.

We called the teachers by their first names. This was *mind-blowing*. Not only did the teachers wear jeans and sit on desks, but we used their first names! And none of my classmates grilled me on my virginity or my sexuality or where I'd last holidayed. We just chewed the cud and mucked about and enjoyed each other's company. It was easy, and light, and I wondered what the catch was.

Sometimes, I felt like Paul was trying to create a little silo of two. He'd whisper private jokes or reference things from Little Babcombe that made no sense in the Yeovil air. But I resisted.

Not to be cruel, or difficult, but because I liked the social element of college and I didn't want to be saved from it, or left behind by the others.

Paul and I passed our driving tests in quick succession, him taught by Mick, and me by a driving instructor with strong body odour. I credit that body odour with giving me the extra incentive to pass quickly.

My father bought me a car. A brand-new Ford Fiesta, with a tape deck and a radio and not much else. I loved it. As Paul didn't have his own car, I gave him a lift in the mornings, missing the raucousness of the college bus a little.

For Paul, the college experience wasn't all that different to school, but for me, it was like landing on another planet. No school uniform, no cane, a patchy timetable with hours to spare each day. And everyone, for the first time in my life, treated me as one of the gang. There was no pecking order. While there were cliques and tribes, there was something for everyone.

My group of friends was not the cool group. We were probably, if I look at us in a cold light, the nerds. Bookish and earnest, fans of indie music and alternative comedy. We used quotes in conversation endlessly, soaking up *KYTV* and *Blackadder* and spewing out the best lines the next day, yelling them over each other. We wore band T-shirts and talked about making trips to Bristol to watch gigs, which never happened, although Paul and I did dine out on our feted trip to see The Smiths some years earlier.

My closest friends were Gemma, Kirstin and Sammy. Gemma was a tiny little brunette who wore Morrissey-style glasses and thick eyeliner. She was a vegetarian, which I considered pretty avant-garde, and drank pints of cider like they were water. Kirstin and Sammy were non-identical twins, one blonde with blue eyes (Kirstin) and one mousy brown with green eyes (Sammy). You would never have known they were related. Kirstin wore slogan T-shirts and slashed stone-washed jeans; Sammy wore tie-dyed dresses and old hippie stuff bought for pennies at the Save the Children and Spastic Society shops.

A big difference between Sunnygrove and Yeovil College were the boys. In that there were some. The one I had my eye on, almost from day one, was called Will. He had shaggy dark-blond hair and rode a Yamaha DT 50cc motorbike, the kind anyone's allowed to drive with just a provisional licence and a helmet. I thought he was James Dean in *Rebel Without a Cause*. Will was in my English literature class and because he was also taking drama, I very nearly asked to take that as well, just so I could watch him more closely.

Sometimes Will would come to the pub with us, his bike helmet under his arm. He often had a book of poetry in his pocket, Ginsberg or Ferlinghetti. I would watch Paul as he eyeballed Will. Paul's head was filled with Ginsberg and Ferlinghetti, *and* Ezra Pound *not to mention* Sylvia Plath, Ted Hughes and Philip Larkin. But pockets trumped heads and Will was known as the poet. I'm sure it made Paul want to spit.

Is there anything more powerful than teenage lust? I would have crawled over dead bodies to get close to Will.

Despite the biker jacket and the poetry, he was pretty much the most cheerful person I'd ever met. Smiling, unpretentious. He asked questions about everything, unbothered about seeming stupid. He asked big basic questions. And he was tactile with everyone. If Paul had touched other guys' arms or other guys' girls they way Will did, he'd have been slugged in the guts.

After working together in English, deciphering a chunk of Chaucerian filth from the 'Wife of Bath's Tale', Will asked me out. Just like that. I'd been thinking of hints to drop, ways to trick him into spending time with me, lies to tell to seem interesting, and he just came out with it. 'Fancy going out sometime?' *Did I?!*

We went to the Cannon Cinema in Yeovil, an old cinema from the 1930s tucked down a little side street. Going in felt like slipping between decades. He picked me up on the back of his skinny bike and I wrapped my arms around his abdomen and breathed in the leather smell as deeply as I could. We went no faster than 30mph the whole way but I was exhilarated. This was it. What it was all about. We watched *Rain Man* at the pictures and Will cried. To this day, I couldn't tell you what happened in that film, I didn't take in a second of it. Afterwards, we got burgers from Wimpy and I had to chew each bite about ten million times before I could gag it down. I was smitten.

We went out three more times. On the last time, instead of the planned trip to a pub he came to my empty house. 'This is a great house!' he said. No playing it cool, and no grumbling about my family's money either. We had sex. My second-ever time. It was more comfortable, or perhaps *less uncomfortable*, than the first. Almost fun in a way I figured would become progressively more fun with practice. Afterwards, he kissed me and got dressed in no rush, uninhibited as I huddled smiling on the bed with my covers like a cocoon.

After he left, I sashayed around my room like I was Marilyn Monroe, bathing for hours and reshaving the whole length of my legs for the next day. Just in case.

I didn't stop smiling all night. I can say that with one 100 per cent certainty because I stayed awake, literally, all night. Too keyed up to sleep.

I forgot to pick Paul up the next morning and arrived at college late with wrinkly eyelids, my face continually contorting between yawns and smiles. I tried to be neutral but as soon as

I saw my friend Gemma my smile broke loose again and I ran over to her.

'Guess what?' I said.

'Will's dead,' she said. And then she clapped her hand over her mouth and burst into tears. 'Sorry,' she spluttered. 'He came off his bike—' she tried to say.

'We had sex,' I said, 'that's what I was going to say. We had sex and I really like him.' She stared at me. 'Liked him,' I said quietly and then I sat at the edge of the college corridor and cried.

I probably cried more over Will than I did my mum. Maybe it was emotional maturity, maybe it was drama. It felt genuine. It felt like being burned with ice, twenty-four hours a day.

All the talk at college was about Will's accident. The conspiracy theories, the lies. I knew he wouldn't have been speeding, especially through the village. Because it *was* in my village. And yes, it was just after he left my house. Perfect, isn't it?

Paul thought so. Paul thought I was wallowing and that it was distasteful. Every time I talked about Will, Paul would change the subject, or try to jolly me into the person I was before. But I didn't want to do a fucking Baldrick impression, I wanted to have had more than a few weeks of being a teenager in love. Happy, untainted love.

I didn't care what Paul thought. I didn't care about his rules for how to behave, his judgement, his impatience for me to forget. I hadn't exactly loved Will, not yet, but I could have. I really could have. I still get tearful when I think about him now. And I hide that more carefully than I would an illicit lover.

I read everything in the paper about Will back then. I read about his grieving mother, a woman I would have hoped to be introduced to as 'Kate, my girlfriend'. A woman to whom I remained a stranger and always would be.

I read about the unfortunate coincidence, the freak accident, that it was no-one's fault. Something in the road, just by The Swan, debris from a storm. The drinkers had run out to help and he'd died with his head in Lorraine's lap, of all people. Sometimes, when I couldn't sleep or I just wanted to dwell in my own anger, I would bitterly imagine her stroking his hair, talking to him and congratulating herself on her humanity.

He wouldn't have been there if it wasn't for me. His mother wouldn't have lost her only son if it wasn't for me. I wailed into my bedcovers at night for weeks.

But I was seventeen, and guilt soon gave way to baby nihilism.

By July, I stopped going to the pub so much and started talking to other people in my classes rather than Gemma, Sarah or Kirstin. I avoided anyone that I associated with Will. I started to gravitate to the ravers, 'the druggies', as Paul called them. The ones who didn't ask big complicated things of me, didn't need me to be fucking clever all the time. I started to crave easy fun.

There was a dive club in Yeovil but I'd never been. A girl called Anna who occasionally turned up to my business class invited me. Or more to the point, one day she lifted her hungover head up from the table next to me and growled, 'You going to Vipers on Friday?'

'Yeah, 'course,' I said as nonchalantly as possible with a racing heart.

That Friday, I got to the peeling door of the club at 9 p.m., tired already and trying to hide it. I'd spent a chunk of my allowance getting a taxi all the way from the village because I couldn't drive in the high heels I'd chosen. My mother's. I slipped inside easily, paying my £1 entry fee without any questions about my age.

I lurked at the side, scanning the smoky dark. My heels stuck to the floor and my eyes stung and I accepted a strong and filthy cigarette from a guy I barely recognised from college. I was relieved to burn it down far enough to be able to drop it, stub it out, the taste filling my throat and wrapping around my tonsils.

I bought a Bacardi and Coke, the first drink that came to mind. I sipped it slowly and thought about leaving. Eventually, Anna and some other faces I vaguely recognised from college and the pub came in. The music seemed to pulse a little bit harder, the crowd looked a little bit hotter.

Anna herself was just a peripheral character, the queen bee was a girl called Jax (short, I'm pretty sure, for the less streetwise Jacqueline). Jax was in her early twenties, a perennial further education student who re-enrolled every year so she could claim the dole and housing benefit. I say this without judgement, I'm merely reporting it. She was proud of her approach. She lived in a large bedsit over a pub where she sometimes worked behind the bar for cash. She was poor enough to be thin, and savvy enough to look amazing. I look back now and I wonder what sad end awaited her, given that this was her peak. And it really was her peak.

Jax entered the club that night wearing fake fur and Debbie Harry hair. She was flanked by a gaggle of seventeen- and eighteen-year-olds she'd picked up on her various and occasional college attendances. She was our Jerry Hall. Or maybe our Brigitte Nielsen. Nearing six foot in heels, hair bleached so translucent you could see the lights of the DJ booth through it. She was obsessed with Nico, who'd died in Ibiza the previous year. She was well-practised at being cool and the illusion worked, we all looked up to her.

That first night in the club, as I danced awkwardly to 'Ride On Time' by Black Box, I stole little glances at her.

It didn't take long to manoeuvre myself into the inner sanctum. It was mostly a case of just always being there. I spent that summer drinking in parks, flicking through magazines (that I always had to buy because Jax and her crew were permanently brassic) and dying my hair bright red in Jax's flat. I smoked half-heartedly, fags and joints. It was the sort of fun that you looked forward to remembering, rather than truly enjoyed at the time.

Every Friday and Saturday night was spent at Vipers with Jax, Anna and a rotating bunch of heavily made-up faces with black-rimmed eyes. I soon learned that girls like us got in free and that in exchange bouncers were allowed to touch your arse. I learned that drinking other people's drinks or accepting free drinks from older guys were the best ways to keep costs down and that no-one respected an expensive outfit. I learned that nobody minded if you asked stupid questions so long as you had cash. I learned that there was an unspoken camaraderie, that even near-strangers will hold each other's hair back or talk someone down if they're freaking out. I learned that acid doesn't agree with me. At all.

I toyed with the idea of tattooing 'don't settle' on my thigh, from my mother's last words. I couldn't do it. Thank God, the thought of the kids running their fingertips along it questioningly as I get dressed or take them swimming. . . not that I thought about that back in 1989.

It was the first summer I'd spent without Paul since we were kids. I didn't even see Viv. I would sometimes drive past Paul at the bus stop and pretend not to see him. I wanted to be rudderless and unaccountable. It's funny looking back, but I never considered my dad's feelings or concerns. Never thought about letting him down or keeping out of his eyes so I could do what I wanted. I finally did not give a shit.

I did wonder what my mum would have thought, though. Would she have been pleased to see me hurtling around with wild abandon, finally? Or worry about history repeating?

I was approaching the age she'd married my dad and that was confusing me more than ever. I've never got to the bottom of that strange brew. I doubt I ever will.

I went back to college in September but I struggled to stay motivated. I didn't really want to see Anna and Jax by then, their painted schtick got boring fast. I was tired of their need for attention at all cost, their draining of my money. I tried to re-engage with Gemma, Kirstin and Sarah but they seemed so desperately naive and young. And they were still talking endlessly about Will.

In the end, as I always have, I made my way back to Paul.

We never mentioned the summer, but Viv nearly popped my lungs hugging me the first day I drove Paul home after college.

'I don't know what happened between you two,' she said quietly into my ear, 'but you know you're always welcome here.' I felt my shoulders slacken and we stood like that for some time.

'Come on then,' she said, giving my arms a final vigorous rub. 'Let's put a brew on.'

Paul and I did our English coursework together, but he despised anything I read out about business and I couldn't help but yawn over his spoutings on the Russian Revolution. We read our respective books; he'd spent his summer mining through the

Beats and out the other side. By autumn, he'd become obsessed with Percy Shelley and William Blake. I had nothing to offer, I'd spent the summer reading *Cosmopolitan,* so I was still on the same copy of *London Fields* by Martin Amis that I'd been on when Will died.

At college, I did my art in private, letting myself into the classroom at lunchtime to carry on working on canvases, or sitting at the sewing machine in the textiles room enjoying the quiet. I put my portfolio together painstakingly, only showing Viv and never showing Paul.

At home, I crept into my mother's long-abandoned studio and set up camp. It had been locked for years, *Secret Garden* style, and most of the paints and glues had seized up and frozen like some terrible accident had happened, Chernobyl or a modern-day Pompeii. A part of me had wanted to feel some kind of connected shiver, some kind of ghostly connection to my mother through our art. Ugh, I was so pretentious. Once I'd cleared myself a space, opened the doors and put music on, I found I was able to sketch, stitch or paint without feeling haunted. And having actually looked around, sizing up the few bits of painting and silversmithing my mum had toyed with, I realised something a bit flattening. She wasn't very good.

It took a few weeks for me to actually spend a night at the Loxtons' again. On the sofa, as before, but not *before* before. It was different but the same, in that uniquely late-teens way. One foot in childhood, one foot out the door. But it was the only place I had that felt anything like home, and I was glad to be back.

CHAPTER THIRTY-THREE

November 2012 – Friday night

Downstairs, Paul is cooking chilli crab linguine. I can smell garlic and fresh red chilli sizzling in olive oil. He's restored now, but was tender for most of the day, quiet and contemplative. I let him nurse his hangover discreetly, offering to take the kids out by myself and tip-toeing around him. He insisted on coming out to the beach with us, blowing away the funk. And then said nothing and stared out to sea, or fiddled with his phone.

I don't know how he can stand to but right now he's dismantling a big fat crab that he bought on the seafront earlier today, the kids' eyes bulging at its monstrous, dead snippers. I couldn't bear to watch him digging the flesh out of every nook and cranny, scraping into the tip of each claw, so I've come upstairs to fuss over the presents again. To check the letter is still here, where I left it. My idiot, irrational fear on Tuesday has stayed with me, as has the guilt over interrogating Harry about a letter he had never even seen.

The letter feels so potent that I half expect it to have leaked into my things, staining them poison green.

I've been rehearsing tomorrow's dinner in my head. Trying to work out the order of things: the gifts, the food and the letter. The food, the gifts and the letter. I've revised mental cue cards, like I used to for big pitches, but when I think about speaking, my mouth feels like it's been sealed up. The delicate skin of my lips knitted together.

It will hurt to open them.

I found the letter tucked inside a paperback edition of E. M. Delafield's *Diary of a Provincial Lady* in Paul's library, while looking for gift ideas. I read that book years ago when I was too young to enjoy it or get the point.

I hadn't even meant to pick that particular book up, I pulled it out by accident and felt something bulging under the cover.

And now I've read this letter so many times that I don't need my copy any more. And it is a copy, whizzed off on our printer-cum-scanner-cum-photocopier grey box in the study, usually reserved solely for printing out the flurries of permission slips emailed like a meteor shower from the school each week.

After making my copy, I slipped the original back between Delafield's covers. Luckily when I found it, it sat just inside the front page and hadn't been positioned strategically next to a specific page number that I hadn't noted when plucking it out, heavy-handed and curious. I wondered if he'd read the letter over and over like I did. Whether he tucked it inside years ago and left it to grow there like an abscess. Or whether he lashed himself with it every day in a grand act of self-flagellation.

My copy is floppy and soft from my constant pawing at it. The edges are dyed denim blue from my pocket, the copied handwriting faded grey. The three looping, tightly packed letters of the name are barely there. A ghost name. Viv.

2002

I backed away from John even more after meeting his pregnant wife in the normal office light. Before that, it had been easy to think of her as a caricature: 'her indoors'.

I'd first met her years before at a very boozy work function. At that point, I had yet to see her husband's naked body in the sunlight streaming under hotel roller blinds.

When I met her again in the office – in my territory – it made her, and her baby, seem more real.

So I backed away more, but that seemed to make John hungrier. He started to come into my office for spurious reasons. Making a wink-wink play of closing the internal blinds, only for me to reopen them.

After a few weeks of this extra attention, I was in my office working late. My eyes were swimming. Numbers floating and colours trickling into my vision. It was just past nine and I was openly yawning, wriggling in my seat to stay awake.

I had no intention of doing anything that involved any effort, except dragging my bones out onto the street to hail a cab.

But when John knocked on my door, there was something about the look on his face. Something about the urgency with which he kissed me. I could lie and say I was too tired to resist, or that I was lonely and vulnerable. But the truth is more pedestrian: after the relentless chew of work, it just felt really good to be held. So I went with it. Looking back now, it was obvious. This was his last hurrah. A kid on the way, *man of principles*, time to close that chapter. *That* was the source of his hunger, not me.

We finished still wearing our clothes and as I buttoned up my blouse, he said: 'I'm going to miss this.'

And even though I'd been trying to back away from the affair, when I realised afterwards that my most consistent romantic relationship – if you can call it that – had just ended, I was surprised by the dent it left in me. John wasn't my husband or my boyfriend. He was my boss and my lover. And then he was just my boss again. I wasn't an idiot either, I knew I had to behave carefully or I would be inching myself onto the ledge ready for him to kick me off. No-one wants their ex-mistress making herself heard, not at work.

So I cried on the way home after that doomed desk fuck, sitting in the back of a black cab that smelled of someone else's perfume. The cabbie had made small talk about his daughters while I started to sob, feeling stupid and small and disposable. Eventually the driver noticed and said, 'Alright, love, it'll be alright', and then he stopped talking. Maybe he was thinking about his girls, how they'd never be caught sobbing in the back of a cab over some bloke.

When I got inside my flat, I said a quick hello to Paul who was working on a chunky TMC laptop at the table, and then sat in the bath adding more and more hot water until my head whistled.

I could hear Paul outside, shuffling up to the bathroom and then walking away again. Eventually, he knocked.

'I'm in the bath!' I called, covering my breasts with my hands even though he was the other side of the door.

'I know,' came the reply. 'I just wondered if you wanted a glass of wine? I've got my eyes closed.'

'I'd love one,' I managed through fresh tears.

He fumbled his way in, and, true to his word, his eyes were closed. He held a large glass out for me to take in my slippery hand.

'Can I sit on the loo?' he asked.

'I'd like that.'

He sat there for over an hour, making me laugh through my snivels, talking about nothing, his eyes screwed shut the whole time.

The environment at work was more toxic than ever, or maybe I just noticed it because it touched me at last. The politics were more pronounced, the double crosses more ruthless. But while I wasn't the one that set Lucy up a few weeks after that, I can see why she thought I was.

I don't know who else she'd told her secrets to but she *had* told those secrets to me, back in the first flush of our friendship years before. And when those secrets were papered all over the boardroom and the kitchen and the lift and both sets of toilets, it didn't look great. Worst of all, it happened just after a spat between us. The regrettable pictures had been stuck up with angry lengths of thick brown parcel tape. Eye level everywhere you looked. Not that she'd have believed me, you always mentally imbue 'enemies' with extra cunning abilities, but I wouldn't have known where to find them. I guess the internet, but I've never been inclined to check.

She'd posed for them when she was still at university, briefly hoping to be an actress. She'd been paid £20, cash in hand. She and another friend from college had gone in to the back room in Denmark Street to pay for head-and-shoulder shots but they'd come out with cash in their pockets and a sinking feeling.

When she told me one night over vodka and orange, confessing our worst secrets, I'd consoled her and joked about it. Reassuring her that any copies must be long-lost by now. 'Oh, I still have them,' she said. But I didn't ask to see them.

The worst part of it all was seeing her young face in the shots, beaming down from our office walls. Her eager smile and her eyes wide open like a doll. The girl in the pictures looked like my Lucy from back then. My fun, trusting Lucy. With her hair glossy and full the way she wore it when we first met.

There were only three pictures, but they had been copied and printed out many times. Lucy as a schoolgirl in stockings, her bright red underwear showing through her blouse. Lucy in a black nylon lace teddy, the type that had been considered risqué and fashionable in the late eighties. And, finally, Lucy lying on a sheet, in black silk knickers and nothing else.

Despite everything, my heart broke for her.

Our spat before the photos-on-the-wall incident had been so outwardly minor that it probably would have been forgotten had it not been for the pictures. We had both found ourselves in the office kitchen at the same time. I smiled at her. I didn't mean to, not after her snubbing of me, but I couldn't help myself. And she rolled her eyes. It was a step too far, impossible to ignore.

'There's no need to be rude, Lucy, I've not done anything wrong here,' I said.

'Yeah, sure you haven't.' She cocked her hip in a way that I thought was studied and deliberate.

'Excuse me?' my voice had been haughty, more shrill than I'd intended.

She rolled her eyes again and tried to push her way out of the small room.

'Hey,' I said, catching her arm as she tried to wriggle away from me. 'I really haven't done anything wrong. And you may not want to be my friend, but here at work, I'm your fucking superior and I deserve some damn respect.'

'And there it is!' she hissed at me.

I leaned down so we were nose to nose. 'Go fuck yourself,' I growled.

Then I marched into the toilet, heart thumping. I splashed water on my pink cheeks and rubbed my eyes until they were black with mascara. It took so long to clean myself up and reapply my make-up afterwards that I was late to a meeting.

What I should have said to her, then and long before then, was that I missed her and I was sorry. That I just wanted to be friends again.

So the next day, when the pictures were papered everywhere, it was all too clear why she thought it was me. And why she came and threw a scrunched-up pile of the photocopies on my desk and stormed out of the office for the last time.

A few days later, I and two other account directors had been called into a meeting with the head of human resources and the head of client services. Lucy's performance had been stagnant for a while, and no-one but me seemed upset at the loss but there needed to be a post-mortem to make sure everyone's arse was covered and nobody had done anything 'non-compliant' that could have left TMC exposed to a lawsuit of any kind.

'Could you just get us a top up on these coffees, please, Marian?' Deborah, our head of HR had asked her PA about half an hour into the meeting. Marian had stopped taking the minutes for a moment and walked out holding the empty coffee jug.

'Okay,' Deborah had said quietly. 'We should be alright here. Yes, she hadn't been given any warnings and she wasn't the subject of any current reviews, but on the other hand, she left us without fulfilling her obligation of notice. As a nod to her long service, we're going to pay her an extra month's salary and call it gardening leave, but if there is anything else we need to know, make it known now.'

Maybe I was paranoid, I'd certainly not had enough sleep for weeks, but I could swear Deborah looked at me a little longer than the others.

After silent consideration, a murmur of acceptance spread around the table.

That creeping feeling of paranoia grew. I started to notice little lingering looks from Lucy's old team, especially from the juniors who had followed her around like little ducklings.

There was something combative about a three-second-too-long stare from someone on a fraction of your wage, but if I'd actually drawn attention to it or questioned it, I would have sounded mental. 'I'm sorry, Kate? She what? She looked at you for a little bit longer than you think she needed to? Okay, yeah, that's definitely grounds for dismissal.'

If I didn't have client lunches, I stayed in my office and drank coffee all day. I drank so much coffee that I started to feel nauseous.

'You're going to waste away,' my PA Janet said one day as she placed a tuna sandwich in front of me that I hadn't asked for. Before I could thank her, the smell caught my throat and I threw up in my waste-paper bin.

'Oh God, Kate, are you okay?'

I wiped my mouth and stared at the bin in horror and surprise.

'I don't know, I think so. I'm just feeling a bit peaky.'

Janet fetched me a tall glass of water, whisked the sandwich and the bin away and did God knows what with them. She didn't bring me any more unwanted sandwiches.

If you'd asked me then, I would have guessed that the Lucy situation had hit me harder than I thought.

I was supposed to be going down to the company bar a few nights after Lucy left. I was supposed to toast a new childrenswear account and give a little rousing speech to the troops at seven o'clock. When I walked into the bar after the quiet calm of my corner office, the noise and laughter hit me like a swinging door.

I heard my name bubbling up from several corners. As I walked further into the basement room, I heard hyena-like laughing screeching to a halt. And then silence. I looked around wildly until I saw Paul gesturing me over. As I reached him, winding through other people's shoulders as they looked away, he hooked his hand around my arm and pulled me close. 'You should go,' he said, his eyebrows knitted together in a frown.

'What?'

'Come on, let's go together.' He tugged me lightly but I stayed rooted.

'What are you talking about, Paul? I need to get up in a sec and talk about winning George & Lili.'

Chatter started up again, a slower rumble than before. Bemused, I struggled to release my arm from Paul's grip just as one of the grad-schemers came staggering up to me. This new crop really couldn't handle their drink. She was nearly a foot shorter than me. Looking up, little nose pointing in the air, she said, 'I didn't know that's how we get ahead here.'

'Huh?' I looked down at her in shock. Lingering looks and raised eyebrows were one thing, but a grad-schemer talking to a director like that would have been unconscionable in my day. I felt so harassed that I didn't really take in what she was saying.

'I really looked up to you,' she said, suddenly seeming on the brink of tears. 'All of the girls thought you deserved respect for climbing so far up the ladder so young.'

'Okay, thanks,' I said, confused.

'We didn't know you'd got there by shagging the boss. What a total fucking disappointment.'

My mouth had dropped open slightly and the silence that had descended felt like a darkness wrapping itself around my head, seeping into my eyes and down my throat.

'Who the hell do you think you are?' Paul said to her, while I stood open-mouthed. 'We'll have your fucking job for this,' he said. 'And good luck getting another one.'

The girl's bravado slipped away and she sagged on the spot, just as another group of grad-schemers had come to sweep her away. One of the guys called back over his shoulder, 'She's really sorry, she's just had too much to drink.'

'Get her out of here,' Paul hissed after him.

'Don't pay any attention,' he added. 'It's bollocks, isn't it? I don't know where this has come from.'

'Yeah,' I puffed, mind whirring. 'Lucy must have made up something spiteful before she left.'

My knees were shaking slightly as I made my way to the bar and stood up on a chair, the standard makeshift speaker's corner.

'If I could have a bit of hush,' I started, trying to smooth the quiver out of my voice.

The silence was instant. Another collective held breath.

'I just wanted to say a big well done to the team that worked on the George & Lili pitch. It took a lot of hard, hard work –' a titter went through the crowd '– plenty of early mornings and late nights but the grind paid off.'

A grunting, sleazy murmur rose through the rabble and burped itself out at me.

'Well,' I said, forgetting everything else I'd planned to say. 'Enjoy your celebration drinks.'

A few polite hands clapped arhythmically and I walked towards the door as fast as I could without running, Paul struggling to keep up. As I pushed out of the bar and into the stairwell, I saw John's familiar shoes tapping down the stairs, light gleaming off them.

'Kate!' he said with matey swagger. 'Great news on G an' L, eh?'

Paul was standing next to me, our shoulders touching.

'It's great,' I said, forcing a flat smile. 'I've congratulated the team but I've got a migraine coming so I need to go.'

I started up the stairs but thought again and grabbed John's arm. He flinched and looked down at my hand. 'Could I have a quick word, actually?' I said. He dipped his brow.

'I'll wait outside,' Paul said quietly and jogged up the steps.

I waited to hear the click of the upstairs door.

'I don't know how but I think it's got out,' I whispered.

'What do you mean?'

'About us. One of the grad-schemers was drunk and she made some crack about sleeping with the boss.'

'What?'

'Yeah, and then there were giggles and double-entendres when I was talking. I think maybe Lucy guessed and said something.'

He frowned for a moment and then shook his head. 'Nah, you're being paranoid. That's what it's always like in there. It's just high spirits.'

'But—'

'Forget it. Anyway, it's not like there's anything happening anyway, is it? It's old news.' I stared.

'Okay, but if it's just high spirits—' I started.

He didn't wait to hear any more and walked into the bar without saying goodbye. I stood there in the stairwell until Paul started to come back down, his steps tentative.

'Let's go home,' he said, poking his head down. 'I'll make you some dinner.'

The altercation in the bar had stayed with me all the next day. Not just the feeling of being undermined, but the feeling of being *less than*. I was rocked by the idea that maybe I didn't deserve to sit on the pedestal I'd built for myself. As if John had lifted me up and held me there like he'd done against hotel room walls so many times. As soon as his hands moved, I slumped to the floor.

I look back now and I know this wasn't the case. I'd proven myself and climbed steadily before anything happened with him. And my rise, I'm sure, was on merit but also buoyed by the fiery ambition that can only be sustained by twenty-something energy. If anything, I'd plateaued by the time I first slept with John.

But at the time, I kicked myself for everything: trying to stand out, trying to climb, thinking I could separate emotion from sex and ambition. I kicked myself for that most 1990s of crimes: claiming all the boom and not seeing the potential for bust.

For the first time in my career I felt jaded with advertising. Jaded with the person advertising had turned me into. And more than that, I felt tired, disillusioned and paranoid. I thought John and I were a cast-iron secret, but if people knew about that, what must they really have thought of me? A flicker of fear grew into a flame: was I finished?

I spent that weekend snapping at Paul or pulling him into endless circles of scrutiny about who was spreading rumours and whether I should grab that loose-lipped junior and find out why she'd said what she had.

But Paul was advising me blind because, without knowing the truth about John, he didn't know I had any real reason to worry. Until the Sunday night when I told him about everything that had happened. The whole sordid mess.

It was probably a mistake. No, it was *definitely* a mistake, but it didn't feel like it then. It felt like opening a blister and letting all the badness soak into a tissue.

Paul poured me my wine with the same steady concern with which Viv used to hand out tea. He put his hands on mine as I held the chunky stem of the glass and he smiled ever so slightly. 'Don't worry,' he said, 'they'll all have moved on soon.'

The wine finally slowed the endless chatter of my brain. That night, after a weekend of fitful sleeping, I lay down on the sofa and passed into a deep burgundy-assisted sleep.

I woke up suddenly some hours later with a blinding pain in my shoulder. Cramps radiated from the pit of my belly and across my abdomen, taking my breath away. I swung my legs around, panting to cope with the pain, and staggered into the bathroom, dragging my hand along the wall for support. In the dim light, I could see a thin line trailing behind me.

When I got into the bathroom and fumbled for the light switch, I must have cried out because suddenly Paul was there, the landline in his hand, calling for a cab to the hospital. As he gave out the address for our building, I looked down to see my legs were covered in purple blood. Fresh pain hit me like a tidal wave.

Strangely, or perhaps not so strangely, during my pregnancy with Harry fresh flashes of what happened that night started coming back to me, unwanted and unshakeable.

Flashes of the pain and the apologies from the doctor as I writhed on the bed in the scanning room while they scanned me internally and pointed at things on the screen. I found the picture indecipherable but it seemed clear as a bell to them.

'Where's the blood coming from?' I eventually asked, feebly. 'Is it my stomach?'

'Oh, darling,' said one of the nurses, picking up my hand in hers. 'I'll let the doctor explain.'

The doctor was a no-nonsense-looking woman with clipped grey hair and small glasses but when she spoke, the gentle reassurance of her voice buckled me.

'Did you know you were pregnant, Kate?' she asked.

'Pregnant? Oh God,' I said, shaking my head. 'No.'

She reached to hold my hand, waited for the penny to drop.

'Am I having a miscarriage?' I said, trying to sit up, to crawl away from the shock and pain. 'Is this a miscarriage?'

She shook her head briefly. 'Please lie down, Kate,' she said and squeezed my hand. 'The foetus has implanted in one of your fallopian tubes,' she said, and pointed to a white blurry lump on the screen. 'It's called an ectopic pregnancy and it's very serious. The tube has ruptured and we need to get it all out as quickly as possible.'

'Get it all out of where? All of what?'

'The pregnancy tissues *and* the tube, I'm afraid.'

'My tube?' I sobbed, suddenly very protective of all these components of my body, elements I'd barely considered before.

'I'm afraid so. If we'd found out before the tube ruptured, we might have been able to make an incision to remove the blockage but it really is too late—'

'The blockage,' I repeated. A tiny little blockage. Did the blockage have toes yet?

Babies had been theoretical until this point, something other women were having, women like John's wife. Something that waited the other side of a hill I'd not started to climb.

And pregnancy was just something to avoid, something we briefly covered in biology in school. I'd been a B-grade pupil then, now I'd flunked the class entirely.

'If we leave a ruptured tube in place,' the doctor carried on, as I put one hand on my stomach and tried to understand how it related to the shape on the screen, 'the damage could cause big problems for you in the future.'

'Will removing it cause her any problems in the future though?' I heard Paul's voice from behind the pleated blue curtain that wrapped around the bed on which I was lying.

'Paul?' I said, embarrassed and comforted that he hadn't stayed in the waiting room.

'Hey,' he said. 'I'm here.'

'Removing one of Kate's tubes won't affect the other one detrimentally,' the doctor said, almost certainly assuming Paul was my boyfriend. 'But a rupture like this *is* life-threatening so we really need to get her into surgery.' She turned back to me and softened her voice until it sounded like honey. 'I know it's frightening but the other tube will do more of the heavy lifting in future, so it's not as bad as it might sound right now.' A pulse of pain made my leg involuntarily kick. 'We do need to get you into theatre, though,' she said.

Between the scan and the theatre doors, time was a blur. There were painful attempts to get drips in, sickening strip-lighting whizzing overhead as the trolley was rushed along corridors, two anaesthetists chatting chirpily over me. My countdown from a hundred only got to ninety-seven before all was black.

I woke up numb and saw Paul sitting upright on the visitor's chair next to me. It was morning, but that early, private time of the morning, when most people across the city were still in bed. Under my sheets and gown, my belly sat like a hill. I looked five months pregnant and my ribs hurt like hell.

'Why am I fat?' I asked, struggling to sit up.

'I'll get the nurse,' Paul said, practically running into the corridor. When he came back with a middle-aged woman in uniform, he avoided my eye.

'How are you feeling, Kate?' she asked in an accent I couldn't quite place. Somewhere in the north-east.

'What's wrong with my stomach?'

'Oh, that's from the surgery. They fill your tummy with gas to separate everything so they can work easier. It won't stay like that.'

I'd always thought keyhole surgery was precise like a sniper, but this felt more like a bomb had been set off inside me. Paul left to go home and change for work, hovering uneasily next to the bed before kissing me on my cheek. Up close he was pale, and looked exhausted.

'Thank you,' I said. 'I think you might have saved my life getting me here.'

He waved my thanks away and left the room, coming back a minute or so later and standing in the doorway.

'Hey again,' I said, my eyes filling with thick tears that overran my eyelashes and soaked hot into the pillow.

'Hey,' he said, and walked over to the bed, crouching down next to it and gingerly wrapping his arms around me. He was still wearing his pyjama T-shirt and jogging bottoms and smelled salty, a night of fevered sweating.

'Paul,' I cried, as he held me as tightly as he dared. 'There was a baby.'

We stayed like that until the tears ran out. When he pulled away from me, I saw his eyes were red-rimmed.

'Do you. . .' He paused, rubbed his eyes. 'Do you think you'd like to have a baby sometime?'

'Sometime,' I whispered.

'Then there'll be other babies. Okay?'

'Okay.' I said.

The main thing, I was told later that morning as they showed me an image that looked like a ghost was in a sewer, was that the 'obstruction' – the apparition in the picture – had been successfully removed, along with the tattered and torn tube. The other tube was in fine fettle, apparently. I didn't give a shit about the other tube right then. And I couldn't bear to look at the little ghost either.

I wanted my normal stomach back and for the pain to be gone. I wanted my memories wiped. I didn't want to feel like I'd lost something I never really had, I didn't want to be falling into a black pit of grief for something, someone, I never deserved. Another woman's husband's baby. Contraband biology. I deserved to feel shame, to feel punished, but I just felt loss. I didn't want to feel anything at all.

Paul came back on his lunch break. He sat on the chair next to my bed as I struggled to get comfortable, rubbing my bulbous empty stomach without meaning to. He'd called in sick for me, telling Janet that I'd been throwing up all night. Apparently, Janet hadn't been surprised after the incident with the tuna sandwich.

'Janet says to take it easy and cut back on the coffee,' Paul shrugged. 'She'll let John know.'

I hadn't even thought about work but flinched at John's name.

'You look a bit better already,' Paul said as he got up to return to the office. 'You're a tough old broad, Howarth. You'll be okay.'

'I hope so,' I said.

'I'll make sure of it.'

He kissed my cheek and this time left me with some magazines, a bag of my clothes and a tube of wine gums. It was this small gesture that made me cry. Again. I cried so much that when I was helped to the toilet, I saw a trail of misty salt marks under my eyes.

Every time I was helped to the toilet after that, my mesh pad would fall out of my paper knickers and need replacing. The nurse helping me the final time had audibly tutted at this and I'd wanted to cry, 'But this isn't my fault.' And yet it was. It all was. Everything that happened up until that point, and everything that happened afterwards. I hadn't even realised then how much I made my bed, but I was already lying in it.

The last lot of painkillers started to wear off and my belly felt raw, like I wanted to twist my body around and wring out the discomfort.

One of the doctors came to see me that afternoon. She checked my stitches and explained *again* what they'd taken out, told me *again* about how dangerous it had been, that silent assassin growing inside me. 'It may not feel like it now,' she said, 'but you were very lucky. Ectopic pregnancies can be fatal if they're not treated in time.'

'I know,' I said. 'I'll count my blessings.'

After work, Paul came back just as I'd finished pulling on the loose clothes he'd brought me, ready to be discharged. We got a cab home in silence. I managed to tip the contents of my handbag out while trying to find my purse to pay the fare. Paul scooped it up and gave it back to me, passed his own bank note to the driver.

I was woozy and exhausted, everything was in slow motion and my body felt twice its normal weight. He steered me into the flat, carrying my holdall and I remember being so grateful. So gulpingly, tearfully grateful.

The painkillers I'd been given were incredibly strong but didn't quite knock me out. Instead, they stole my ability to speak and made me punch drunk so I sat back in my own head and just watched what was happening outside of my eyes with no ability to engage with it.

I lay in a ball on the sofa under a fake-fur throw, trying not to think about the little ghost. Trying not to think about what I would have done if it had been growing in the right place. At what point I would have found out. Was I even sure when my last period was?

I knew, as much as I tried not to let myself know, that I wouldn't have been able to end the pregnancy. Despite the clandestine genes. Despite my own shoddy parental experiences. Or maybe because of them. Would I have really dared let myself be a mother? Risk the cycle continuing? Yes. I knew the answer was yes and I couldn't bear to even consider the question.

Paul made me dinner that first night home. A nursery tea of soft-boiled eggs and buttery soldiers. I watched him dumbly from my nest and ate without tasting. I stared at the television while Paul tried to talk about films and books and all sorts of nonsense that I think was designed to distract me. I just hung there, my face slack and my thoughts suspended.

Eventually I zombie-shuffled into bed and fell into a heavy, dreamless sleep.

———

I woke up at 10.30 in the morning and panicked for a few seconds. I hadn't woken up that late in years, even at the weekend. Outside, the weekday bubbled up and I drifted painfully around my flat feeling like something was missing. I tried very hard to deny what it was. And how could it have really been that? The blockage? The little ghost? Until it was tearing through me, I hadn't even known it was there. And yet thoughts of tiny toes, of the purest skin and an untainted heart whispered their way into every thread my mind took.

Had my mother seen me as a fresh start? Had my father clasped her hand and told her not to worry, everything would be better for me, better than it had been for either of them? Had she stroked her belly and sung to me? Had she planned me? Had she had dreams for me? Or had she drunk gin and taken hot baths and wished she still had her life ahead of her? I'll never know. I hope that she and my father hadn't had the best intentions. They'd certainly not seen them through if they did and that was somehow worse.

But I didn't need any best intentions. I wasn't allowed any intentions at all, and with one tube left, maybe the point was moot. I tried to focus on missing work instead.

And I definitely did miss my work. I wasn't used to being idle and I'd long forgotten how to stay still.

I made myself a cup of tea, taking so long to get the bag out and stir in the milk that it was sludgy and barely warm. I tipped it away and started again because I didn't have anything else to do.

The flat was so clean it shone, light bouncing off every surface. I had a cleaner, or maybe it was a team of cleaners, I didn't know because I was never there while the magic happened. I paid an agency to send around someone who they called a 'maid', although that was really over-egging it. Every Monday and Thursday the flat was vacuumed, bleached, wiped, polished and buffed. My favourite bit had always been that he/she/they – the 'maid' – folded the ends of the toilet roll into a little point.

I had returned to a glossy flat the night after the operation but I didn't really notice until I was alone in it the next day. I almost wished the place had been filthy so that I had something to do, a challenge to meet. Not that I had the energy, the pills I was taking made me feel seasick and heavy, and my stitches were on fire, but I needed something.

After drifting around the flat for another half an hour, I felt a sudden pain in my lower abdomen, like a sharp kick. But, I grimaced, there would be no kicks for me. I wondered if I'd lost my chance to ever feel kicks.

I took my pills and lay on the sofa in front of *This Morning*. It wasn't Richard and Judy presenting, which rocked me. When did that change? There was a phone-in discussion about incontinence after childbirth and I closed my eyes and sank my head into one of the turquoise John Rocha cushions that the 'maid' had plumped up the day before. When I woke up again, it was the lunchtime news.

I'd never been idle. I'd filled every day of my life, even as a lonely child. Now that I wanted a distraction from the little ghost that followed me, with little eyes that might have looked like my eyes, my world was emptier than ever. It was oppressively quiet. If I'd had the energy to go out, to run away from it, I would have.

My stomach throbbed and I felt agitated. In the end, I decided it would be better to scratch the work itch so that I could reassure myself all was well. I switched my phone on to check nothing urgent had happened and saw three missed calls and two messages from John. I slowly pulled myself up from lying to sitting, my feet on the floor and back hunched over, about to listen to my voicemail when John called again. I answered, robot that I am. He barely waited for a hello.

'Kate, I'm sorry to call when you're feeling rough but I need you to come in. George & Lili have called a crisis meeting, they don't like the campaign plans and they're threatening to pull out altogether and Pete, fucking Pete, didn't get the PO signed so they have us over a barrel. And I have to go. Jill's gone into labour.' He paused, for congratulation or well wishes, I think, but I didn't give any. 'Can you come in? Please?'

'You're having a baby today,' I managed to say.

'Can you come in?' He sounded irritated. 'Take some Imodium or something, yeah?'

I fell asleep in the cab to the office.

It's easy to look back now and say that I should have called John back and told him no, I can't, I'm too sick and they need to sort this out themselves. But I didn't. George & Lili had been a hard-won campaign. Finally fashion, of sorts. Children's fashion, high street meets designer, angora baby cardigans and slogan T-shirts for toddlers. It was as close to fashion as I ever got.

I won that account through sheer bloody-mindedness. Back then, George & Lili – G&L as we called them in house – had grown a huge presence in America but hadn't made a dent in the UK. The prices weren't designer but they were a far cry from Mothercare, and they saw themselves as couture for kids, which they weren't. G&L had wanted to go with a fashion agency for their campaign but I convinced them that we would get them in front of the people who actually bought children's clothes, whereas a fashion agency would push them into high-fashion mags with beautiful adverts that wouldn't shift 10 per cent of the numbers they wanted. More than anything, I sold them *me*.

And now I'd been away for one and a half days and the whole thing was falling to shit.

By the time I slowly shuffled into the office, the meeting had already started in the boardroom. I could see the bobbing heads of the assembled team (almost everyone that worked for TMC seemed to be there) and the marketing director and sales manager from G&L sitting together with their arms folded across their chests. Straight from the off, this had been badly handled. Don't assemble the whole team and act like it's a crisis, go one on one in a neutral place and talk openly and freely, be collaborative. Remind the client that it's a partnership, that you're deeply invested rather than acting like a bunch of gormless sycophants.

Furious and fatigued, I pushed through the glass doors, wincing with pain, and interrupted the senior account manager drafted in to perform a holding pattern until I got there.

'Maria, David, it's so good to see you, I'm glad I could make the meeting,' I tried to breeze.

Maria, the G&L marketing manager, and David, their sales manager, stood up to greet me. Out of the corner of my eye I saw the account manager mouth 'thank you'. 'I'll leave you to it,' she said, as she practically ran out of the room.

Maria was almost my height, a little older than me, with beautiful glossy brown hair. David was a lot smaller, with slick back hair and beady eyes. He wasn't a bad guy, he just looked an awful lot like Joseph Goebbels.

On the white board was layer upon layer of photographs of dimpled children in adorable knitwear and tufty-haired babies rolling in rompers and sucking their thumbs. I stood for a moment in front of it, my eye drawn to the rows of little toes.

The room was quiet, I felt a bubble of something in my throat and swallowed it down. I reached awkwardly across the boardroom table and pulled out the cord from the monitor so the images faded to black.

'Let's start from scratch,' I said, and turned to Maria. 'What are your concerns? Because obviously we're at the start of the process and we're still at the brainstorming stage.'

David opened his mouth to answer but I said, 'Maria?'

I'm not sure why I cut him off, I think I was trying to make a show of being in control, to try to counteract the woozy feeling from the pills and day-sleeping.

'I, um,' Maria started, 'I'll let David explain.'

I never really recovered ground after that. I smarted and floundered through the rest of the meeting. We kept the account by a thread, and with the kind of damaged relationship that would see us limping through the campaign rather than striding, unable to take bold ideas to them for risk of frightening them – and not delivering the best campaign as a result. I saw them out to reception, watched through the glass doors as they hailed a cab and then fell back into a waiting chair, exhausted. After a few minutes I heaved myself up. My stomach was hurting again and I swallowed my next lot of pills early, without water, so they stuck in my throat and made me gag. I made my way back into the boardroom slowly, to find one of the admin girls plugging the cord back into the monitor and collecting up the left-over paper. She was small and pretty with tiny wrists. I could smell her coconut shampoo and it turned my stomach a little. Apparently, the pregnancy hormones would take longer to drain away than the pregnancy.

'I'm going to get off now,' I said, reaching for the coat and bag I'd tossed on a chair. As I bent to pick them up, I was hit by a wave of nausea and dizziness. I reached behind me for a chair but didn't connect properly so the chair wobbled and I stumbled backwards.

'Shit, you okay?' she said. Her voice was like a child's. I hated it.

'I don't know,' I said, trying to stand up straight but buckling at the knees.

I felt warm, too warm and then hot. In the seconds it took the admin girl to reach over and grab my hand to pull me up, my palm had become slick with sweat.

'Sorry, I'm a bit dizzy. I haven't been able to eat so I'm a bit, I don't know, spaced out, I guess.'

'John said you hadn't been your usual self,' she said.

'John did?' Since when did John chat easily with admin girls? Oh. How many of us were there?

'Maybe you should take a proper break?' she said, turning to leave. She called over her shoulder in her baby voice, 'I'll hail you a cab.'

The flat felt like a held breath when I re-entered it that afternoon. It stank of my body, my sleepiness. I curled up on the sofa with a throw and cradled a cup of tea. When that didn't help, I opened a bottle of wine from the rack in the kitchen. I grabbed it indiscriminately, a heavy red, and fell asleep after half a glass. Fell was the right word, it was so fast I didn't have a chance to put my glass down and a trickle had made its way onto the carpet by the time I woke up hours later, still holding the stem.

I struggled to open my eyes and shake the heavy throw off my legs. After having a wee and taking the next clutch of tablets, I poured another glass of wine and turned the TV on. It was *The Weakest Link*, some kind of teatime game show where Anne

Robinson from *Watchdog* berated eager members of the public. I struggled to answer early round questions that were clearly supposed to be easy, and shifted myself around on the sofa to stop my legs going dead. I knew Paul wouldn't be home for a few hours and I didn't have the wherewithal to cook myself dinner so I opened a box of chocolates I'd been sent in a Christmas hamper months earlier and ate three.

The afternoon sleep clung to me and I felt headachy after the chocolate, falling in and out of sleep before Paul got back. He ordered us a Chinese take-away and I picked at it, eventually waking up again to find Paul had cleared up and gone to bed.

Because I'd dozed on and off earlier in the day, I struggled to catch the first thread of sleep that night and lay hot and sweating on the bed. The streetlights outside taunted me and thoughts of the George & Lili account whirled until I felt frantic. I made notes that seemed like gibberish in the light of the next day, when I found them scrunched into the bed.

I went back to work a few days later, despite being told I should take up to four weeks. I couldn't have explained such a long absence, and with John on a week's paternity leave, I was more needed than ever.

In truth, I couldn't face another day at home, trying not to think about ghosts and tattered tubes and lost futures I'd never worried about having. Trying not to imagine John holding his new baby and telling his wife how well she'd done.

And I didn't want anyone swooping George & Lili from under my nose. That's how it starts, one account in crisis is 'saved' by some keen, energetic rank-riser and then you're old news. I did it myself enough times, breezing in to established accounts with my youthful enthusiasm and stealing them from under the noses of more established account managers.

I couldn't face the morning Tube commute: the seasickness of standing in the crush, the lock-jawed determination needed to bash everyone out of the way. I got a cab and slept all the way again. I was so grateful that the driver had woken me (and not driven me around longer routes to bump up the fare) that I threw an extra note through the slot.

I just about held it together that day, despite my eyelids closing of their own volition and my head thumping. I nodded at the right times, gave the right answers – I thought – and listened as carefully as possible. The cogs of activity soothed me and I felt safer being in my little box, my glass lair. Paul had come to check in on me a couple of times but I shooed him away, embarrassed. I got to the end of the day and practically fell into a cab again without thinking to wait for him.

I struggled to sleep that night too. My lower belly, the scene of the crime, was aching and throbbing around a central pang that shot through me and made me sweat and shake. The site where the supposedly keyhole surgery had taken place was swollen and red, more like a letterbox than a keyhole. The join of skin seemed a little more frayed than it had been, and was oozing a little. A double dose of my painkillers was the only thing that helped me sleep and I woke up drenched with sweat, having slept through my alarm. It was John's first day back, my timing couldn't have been worse.

I showered and dressed in a hurry, make-up caked over my pale and clammy face. I staggered into the G&L creative meeting, half an hour after it had started. The direction they were taking was already wrong. It was my job to steer the art director and copywriters to the client's needs and wishes, to give them the context in which to create. But the ideas everyone was enthusing about were the polar opposites of the initial brief and it all needed a sharp swerve back on track.

'Hang on,' I said to Colm, the calm Irish art director who worked closely with Paul. 'This isn't what we talked about. Why the change?'

'John felt that we should go more personality and less utility, Kate. He briefed us from home and Paul's been working on the new creative.'

Paul nodded at me from his seat next to Colm. I felt anger rising up through my neck and glared at Paul. 'You didn't say anything to me,' I heard myself saying to him, as Colm's face grew pink under his sandy hair.

'If you think it's the wrong way to go, let's get John in here,' Colm said, his breezy tone almost hiding his irritation.

'This just isn't what G&L wanted, Colm,' I said. 'They've already rejected a lot of our ideas so I'm concerned that this'll really piss them off.' Colm gestured to the conference phone set into the big table and I dialled the familiar extension.

'Hello?'

'John, it's Kate.'

'Yes?'

'I'm in the G&L creative meeting and I've got some concerns.'

'Oh?'

'I know you've briefed the team but I think I'm missing some background on that because it's quite a change of direction—'

'It's a fix, Kate.' He cut me off. 'And I had to make that fucking fix while I was off with my newborn. Thanks for your congratulations, by the way.'

Paul audibly sucked the air and looked at me. I bit my lip and kept my face stony.

'Congratulations,' I said.

'The whole account was headed in the wrong direction and G&L were threatening to walk. I heard about your bullshit in the meeting with them. That certainly didn't help, so I think you need to sit back on this one and let the team work without interference, alright?'

The click as he disconnected cut through the room like a cough. I saw Paul looking at me uneasily, and no-one spoke until Colm said, 'Okay, well, if we maybe carry on with these ideas and see where they take us, yeah?'

I nodded, grateful to him for speaking. As I stood up, a surge of pain ran from my belly to my spine and I doubled over. Paul ran over to me and helped me sit down, a huge flower of blood spreading from my operation scar and through my blouse.

'Fuck,' I said.

'Everyone out,' Colm called. 'We'll come back in five.'

CHAPTER THIRTY-FOUR

1991

In the spring before we took our exams, Paul and I applied to university.

Paul applied to a few universities and a handful of polytechnics. He had been predicted better grades at A-level than me and had a glowing reference from his history tutor. He applied as far as Manchester and as close as Bristol. Like me, he applied for University College London and also King's College London but didn't get an offer from either. In the end, from the offers he got, he chose Bristol Polytechnic. It changed to a university in his second year, becoming the University of the West of England but he still has a hang-up about it. I've been bored to tears, figuratively anyway, from annual laments about his poly degree and hand-wringing over doing a master's.

The fact is, education for Paul was sullied by students. If he could take a prestigious MA in a sealed library in isolation, only then he might manage it with a smile on his face.

I always knew I'd apply to university in London. I was never clever enough to consider Oxford or Cambridge. I didn't really know anything about any other cities, didn't really have any interest in discovering them. Perhaps because, for so long, London was the place where my parents went. The city swallowed them up and spat them back out, but I never got to see inside that dangerous mouth.

I was deadly bored in Somerset and I wanted to live faster. I wanted to live in my own way, find new faces, new ideas, new music. To throw bloody paint everywhere like a YBA and get drunk on ridiculous kitsch drinks like Snowballs. To wear clothes out of magazines without ridicule. I wanted to become a butterfly, crushing my cocoon on the way out. In other words, I was just like every other eighteen-year-old preparing to leave home in 1991.

We both did well in our A-levels that summer. For me, well enough to meet the offer I'd been given by Central Saint Martins. In truth, having Sunnygrove on my application helped more than Yeovil College or my own abilities ever could. If I hadn't got in, I would have gone to the City of London Polytechnic. If I hadn't got in there, I would have gone to anywhere in the city that would have had me.

I'd outgrown Somerset but felt small in my dad's empty house. He was never home, flying between the newly unified Germany and the newly dismantled USSR. He hated the ideology of the Eastern Bloc but he'd made a fortune selling things to them, and was now salvaging rather than building.

I couldn't be bothered to salvage anything. I'd burned my bridges with everyone at college. Not dramatically, just a slow crackling flame that turned friendships to ember, eventually cooling to grey.

Paul and I were due to start at uni on the same date and could move into our respective halls in the days running up to it. Mick offered to take me to London first, with Paul and Viv in tow, and then take Paul and Viv to Bristol the next day. I knew the price of all that petrol, not to mention the hassle of so much driving, was a steep cost and a generous gift. I said yes, the kindness choking me a little as I thought of how easily I'd left the Loxtons to themselves after Will.

My father came to see me in my room while I was packing.

'So,' he said, making like he would sit on the edge of my bed but then changing his mind at the last minute. 'All packed?'

'No, not yet.'

'And are you feeling. . . are you, how do you feel?' he asked.

'Okay,' I said. 'I'm looking forward to getting out of Somerset,' I added, a little spitefully.

'Do you have enough—'

'Money? Yes,' I said, 'I have enough money.' My father looked down at his hands, so I added, 'But thank you.'

'I'll have Ted run us up there and then perhaps we could have dinner once you're settled?'

I sat up and looked at him, trying to understand. 'Do you mean in London? You'll come with me?'

'Well, of course. Unless, you don't—'

'Of course,' I said, so taken aback by the interest that thoughts of the Loxtons and our plans briefly faded away. 'If you're sure?'

My father had taken a brief look around the room, the piles of clothes and records ready to be bagged and boxed, the boxes of books and tapes. 'Yes,' he nodded, leaving the room.

The next day, I walked to Church Street and knocked on the front door. Through the living-room window, I could see Paul with his arm around Viv, her nodding as he spoke. She'd been so young when she had him, I think now, she'd never really been an adult without him. That day must have loomed like a bottomless pit. And I think he knew it too, more than I did. He and his mum always had that unspoken understanding.

'Katie,' Viv said, opening up. 'Stop knocking, what's got into you?'

'I'm sorry,' I said.

'I'm only teasing, love. All set for tomorrow? Mick'll come round here first and get me and Paul, and then we'll come and load up and—'

'Viv,' I said quietly, avoiding her eye. 'I'm really sorry but my dad wants to take me.'

'Your dad?'

Viv had always respected that, no matter how shabbily they treated me or how absent they were, my parents were always my parents. She'd taken them to task – more than I knew then – she'd questioned their decisions, but she'd never tried to step on their toes. But this one thing, this thing that really was small compared to everything else she'd shared with me, this was different. She crossed her arms over her chest and fixed her dazzling eyes on mine.

For a moment she didn't say anything, and I squirmed under the precision of her gaze.

'How come?' Paul said, eventually.

'I don't know, he just, he seems to think it's important,' I said.

'Well, it is important,' Viv said sharply. 'Just like all the other things he should have done, and *she* should—'

'Please don't talk about my mother like that,' I heard myself say, quietly.

Viv uncrossed her arms, looked briefly at Paul. 'I'm disappointed,' she said, as she went into the kitchen and started banging things around.

'Shall I leave?' I asked Paul.

'Yeah,' he said softly. 'You probably should.'

Ted had loaded the car when I got back from the Loxtons', while I nodded dumbly as he asked of each bag, 'And this one?'

The next day, the morning of the trip, I came downstairs and made toast. The house was quiet, no Mr or Mrs Baker bustling around. No footsteps in distant rooms, no telephone ringing. I took my plate and drink of orange juice to the kitchen table and sat down. In the middle of the rich antique wood was a cheque for £500 dated the previous day and signed by my father.

'Your dad's sorry,' Ted said, appearing from the pantry with an apple. 'He had to go early this morning, it couldn't be helped.'

'Go where?' I asked, although I had some idea. 'Will he be long?'

'He's on the Aeroflot to Moscow.' Ted seemed embarrassed, bit into the apple and looked away.

I ran full-speed, the toast lurching around in my stomach. I reached Church Street, head buzzing with my heart beat, dripping in sweat. The car wasn't there, so perhaps Mick hadn't arrived yet. Or perhaps he wasn't coming that day at all now, as there was no London trip planned. I hammered on the front door and peered in the window. Nobody came. I hammered again.

'Viv!' I shouted.

'You've missed her,' came Lorraine's voice from behind.

I turned around to see her standing in luminous yellow leggings and a bright pink top, glowing in front of the grey stone of The Swan.

She clattered across the road to me.

'They were all in here last night for a send-off and they've taken Paul to Bristol.'

'Bristol?'

'The poly,' Lorraine said, as if I was simple.

'I know but, they weren't going until tomorrow.'

She shrugged. 'Sorry, love. When are you off anyway?'

Before Ted and I left, I took a final look at the house and felt a sting of surprise as my lip wobbled. I slid in next to a box of records and buckled in, as Ted asked what I was going to read at university. 'Art and textiles,' I said.

'Very nice,' he said. He nodded his head and added, 'Very nice indeed,' as the smoked glass slid silently up between the front and the back. I heard the radio crackle on.

I later found out that some of the other students that had seen me pull up in a glossy black Jaguar XJ thought Ted was my dad. I also found out that someone started a rumour that I was Cilla Black's daughter. Because obviously a well-off redhead girl must be related to the only famous rich redhead at the time.

Ted and I wordlessly carried my stuff into my room, tag teaming. I wondered if he'd done this for his own daughters, whether they had gone to university and if he had sat in their empty bedrooms afterwards, wondering where the time had gone. Remembering how small their hands had once been when they reached for him. Sometimes I imagine Harry's room emptied out and chilly but I have to stop myself, the black hole in my chest is too much to bear.

When everything was settled in my room at the halls of residence, I thanked Ted.

'Good luck then, maid,' he said, giving my shoulder a squeeze. 'I'm sure your dad'll visit soon.'

———

My room was on the ground floor and there were bars on the windows. It looked out over Russell Square, incredibly central. God only knows how much that property would be worth now. In the basement there was a huge windowless refectory, where those who paid extra – as I did, or rather my father did – got breakfast and dinner provided.

I stayed in my room, pacing the few square foot of space between items of furniture. I organised my clothes, books, records and tapes. I hung up my David Bowie, Kate Bush and Patti Smith posters. I took them down again. *Too childish?* I stuck them back up in a different order. I laid my make-up out in front of a mirror and hung my new Christie's towels from hooks on the back door.

There wasn't a basin in this room. The shared toilet was down the hall and the showers were on the third floor. I put my toothbrush in a cup on the bookshelf. It looked weird.

Dinner was available from 6 p.m. so I waited until 6.30 p.m., unsure if 'better to be late' party rules applied to halls of residence dinnertimes, then made my way down.

The line for food was full of pale, wide-eyed faces. Many eyes were red and stained with wet mascara and there were frequent outbursts of nervous laughter. The strip-lighting and lack of windows made me feel giddy, I wanted to grab someone and shake them and say, 'Oh my God, we're all here, we've all escaped!' Instead, I shuffled slowly and then got flummoxed when faced with the options of macaroni cheese, cod and chips, egg salad or chicken curry. I stepped back from the food counter and out of the queue. Instead, I made my way to the corner where a large industrial toaster was rotating aimlessly. It took several tries to find the sweet spot between warm bread and burnt toast but I finally managed it and snuck the plate back up to my room, along with a carton of orange juice that said 'not for individual sale' and had a picture of a dancing fruit on it.

London was right outside the window as I nibbled cold toast and drank orange juice through a straw. It was dark already, the late September sun long hidden.

I felt uniquely old and new. And restless. I laid my pyjamas out on my single bed while the city blazed the other side of the window. I picked up my toothbrush and toothpaste from their hall-issued cup, then put them down again. I looked around and decided to leave. As I reached for the door handle, I actually said 'Fuck it' out loud.

The breeze whipped my nose and lips as I pushed out through the heavy wooden doors and into the night. Russell Square was dotted with taxis outside the various hotels and I pulled my scarf up over my face like a ninja and fumbled to do the rest of my coat buttons up with chilly fingers as I marched determinedly nowhere in particular because everywhere in London looks like somewhere.

I was in storybook London. Red buses and black taxis slid past me like film props. I had to remind myself that this was real life.

I walked down to Charing Cross Road and all I saw at first were bookshops. I walked over to gaze in the window of one, drawn by their stillness, their longevity. I thought of Paul. His birthday that year was to be the first I'd missed since our ninth. On my birthday, I'd gone to Viv's for a birthday tea and we'd had a cake, just the three of us. Then I'd gone home to be given a framed photo of my mum to take away to uni with me. The gesture had winded me, until my father told me – almost apologetically – that it was Mrs Baker's idea. I had taken the photo with me but I hadn't decided whether to put it out on show or not. Instead, I faffed around with my toothbrush.

And maybe it was feeling like a tiny dot in a huge place, or maybe it was the row upon row of old books, lit up like gems. Maybe it was guilt for dropping them for a crumb of attention from my father, but all I wanted right then was to hear Viv's voice.

I slipped into the nearest phone box, temporarily agog at the sheer quantity of tart cards offering spankings and pre-op experiences and almost nothing that sounded like common or garden sex. And then I dialled, pressing the cold square buttons, the sequence engraved in my mind.

'Hello?' Viv sounded wobbly, older than I remembered.

'You're home,' I said. 'It's Katie.'

'Mick just dropped me off,' she said, her voice curt.

'I came to say goodbye,' I said, 'this morning. I came to say goodbye before I left.'

'We decided to go this morning, love. No need to wait if we weren't fitting London in.'

I took a breath.

'I'm sorry,' I said. She held out longer than me and I started to cry into the silence until the pips went.

'I know you are,' she said finally. 'I was just disappointed.'

I pushed another coin in, took a breath and shook my tears away. 'How did it go in Bristol, then? Was Paul alright?'

She softened as she talked, telling me about Paul's halls of residence and the 'big bugger' in the room next to him. She complained about Mick driving too fast on the way home because he's 'a man and they don't know how to handle emotions'.

'Was he alright?'

'He'll live. I'm sure a few pints will be helping tonight.'

'And you?'

'I miss the bones of him, Katie. And you, love.'

'I miss you too. I miss you all.'

I gave her my address and said I'd call again. My money ran out fast, the pips going far sooner than they did with local calls. We hastily said goodbye, my eyes prickling with fresh tears, and I marched back up to Tottenham Court Road and then into Leicester Square, watched over by the looming cinemas.

I pushed against the wind, head down, and marched through Coventry Street into Piccadilly Circus. The iconic Fosters, TDK and Sanyo signs bigger and dirtier than they'd seemed on the TV. Back in 1991, I hadn't known what Sanyo was; a few years later my agency worked on their account.

There were crowds of people bustling about. Despite it being night-time, I felt like nothing bad could possibly happen somewhere so constantly illuminated. Maybe it was better that I hadn't spoken to Paul that morning, I decided. That the Loxtons didn't get to bring me here.

I wanted to look forward, in a place that was just mine. I hugged my coat tighter to me. I felt a sense of relief and contentment spreading underneath the sadness. This was it, yeah, I was finally here. Adulthood.

I had just turned nineteen, brave and free. I was ready to start living.

CHAPTER THIRTY-FIVE

November 2012 – Saturday morning

We decided before we came to Cornwall that we'd go to visit the Eden Project during our stay. Everyone who has ever been to Cornwall bangs on about it so much that going there is practically a legal requirement. Naturally averse to tourist attractions but beholden to the kids, we've been putting the trip off all week. It ends up being our ten-year wedding anniversary before we're agitated and sweating, wearing November clothes in a Mediterranean biome.

It took an hour and a half to get here, the last couple of miles a grumpy car crawl. It's easy to forget how vast Cornwall is.

I woke up this morning feeling harassed. There was tension in my bones and my muscles were twitchy. I couldn't shake the feeling that I just wanted to crawl somewhere quiet and lick my wounds. But at the same time, I'm agitated to just get on with it. *Rip the plaster off.*

'What animals are there?' Izzy had asked over and over on the drive here. In the end, after explaining the premise of the Eden Project ten thousand times, I snapped and said, 'It's not a fucking zoo, Izzy! How many times?'

There was a horrible cold silence in the car after that. Izzy was tearful and chastened, looking at the back of her dad's head for reassurance and solidarity. I could tell that Paul was unnerved by my mood, juddering the brakes once or twice but not saying anything directly. Meanwhile, Harry looked uneasy and fidgety. He was old enough to know that rips in the fabric of a family are often identified first through snapping and swearing. And he'd had more than one or two tense and tragic drives under his belt and those were to the south-west too.

We didn't hear about Viv's illness until it was too late. Two years ago, our household seemed to fold in on itself at the same time that she did. Izzy was two and far too little to understand, but Harry had watched Paul and me warily, his dark brown eyes tracking us as we kicked doors, snapped at each other and swore over the tiniest misdemeanours. And then, worse, we were silent.

We'd not seen Viv for a few months, not since Izzy's birthday where she'd sat down in a garden chair and nodded off. We'd not called, or Skyped, or really even thought of her much since then, which I hate to admit. Harry was particularly bombastic around then, pumped up with little kid testosterone, and Izzy was still essentially a baby koala, gripped to me for hours at a time. And I have more hollow excuses too. Paul had been recently promoted. He was working longer and longer hours and all we wanted to do when he got home was share a bottle of wine, bitch about our very different days and then watch whatever box set we were working through at the time. I was going through one of my yoga phases, and also spending hours a day pointlessly fretting over which distance-learning course I should take to make myself feel like a whole person. (I applied for none in the end.)

It wouldn't have taken much effort to just pick up the phone, but it was still easier not to.

And then the phone had rung just as Paul was coming in the door from work, earlier than usual. I had Izzy on my hip while

Harry ate chicken dinosaurs and veg at the kitchen table, firing green-pea bullets all over the floor. The clatter of the landline by the door was so unusual that Paul jumped and I came out of the kitchen and into the hall to investigate.

Paul lifted the receiver like he'd never seen it before and I danced from foot to foot trying to interpret the one-way conversation.

'Oh, hi Dad. How are you?'

'Oh, really, why?'

'What is it?'

And then his voice had grown small.

'What? Mum?'

Then he'd sagged like a dropped sack. 'When?' he'd whispered, strangulated, into the receiver.

'Why didn't you tell us?'

'But we could have—'

'But, Dad—'

'I know. I know. We'll be straight down.'

'Okay. Dad?'

'Tell her I love her too.'

He ended the call and stayed there like a droopy sunflower. He lifted his head and, as I approached, he reached out and swooped Izzy from me and onto his chest, spinning around on his heel and walking into the lounge with her, his face buried in her hair. I trailed after them.

'What's wrong?'

'It's Mum,' Paul said, cut off by a crash from the kitchen. 'I'll tell you when the kids are in bed.' I was stung by the arbitrary watershed and desperate to know. Instead I did as I was told, walking back to clear up after Harry, who had dropped his drink.

The kids were finally in their beds before Paul spoke to me. He'd spent the evening either chastising or negotiating with them and as I came down the stairs from tucking them in, nerves squirming in my belly, he'd already opened a bottle of red wine and was holding a glass ready for me.

'Mum has cancer,' he said.

'Cancer? Is she?'

'Stage four. Lungs. It's too late.'

We drove down the next day. I don't think Paul slept at all, he still hadn't cried and I'd spent the night creeping away from the bed and into the bathroom to gulp tears into balled-up toilet paper. I didn't get to cry first, that wasn't fair.

I offered to drive down but Paul wanted to; I think he needed to focus on the road and not the destination. I put the shared bottle of wine and his sleep deprivation out of my mind with gallows confidence. We were already living through The Bad Thing, we weren't going to crash and die as well. *I know, I know.*

The journey was slow and almost silent, even Harry – my fidgeting, chatty, sunny boy – knew to stay quiet. And Izzy had slept for hours in that dribbly, pink-cheeked toddler way. We'd got to the hospital mid-afternoon. The hospital in which Viv had worked her whole adult life. She was on the oncology ward, part of a new glass chunk on the side of the old building. She looked so tiny in the bed that I wanted to look away.

'My boy,' she croaked when Paul walked in. His knees buckled and he crumpled into the chair at her side and held her arm, sobbing. I hovered, Izzy in my arms and Harry huddled to my legs. Eventually, she looked up and searched my face with her violet eyes, 'Hello, my lovely girl,' she smiled. 'And who is this beautiful little lady you're carrying? This can't be my Isobel, she's huge!'

Viv insisted that Harry and Izzy should lie on the bed either side of her. She asked about our journey and clung to their robust little bodies like life rafts.

Harry brought her up to speed on his latest dinosaur information and Izzy sat on the en suite toilet with the door open to rapturous approval, then fell over, yanking up her training nappy and nearly sliced her forehead open.

Paul attended to her while Harry swung his legs on the visitor's chair. 'These new rooms are nice,' I said, unsure what the hell else to say.

'Better than the crumbling old corridors we had when I first started here,' she croaked. I reached over urgently and put my hand on hers, she closed her eyes and moved her other hand up to her chest, pressing it flat to her little gold necklace as brief tears scribbled out of her eyes.

Mick arrived just as the kids were getting too fractious to ignore.

'I'll take them for a walk,' I said to Paul but he looked panic-stricken.

'No, I will,' he said, scrambling up from the visitor's chair to wrestle Izzy into the stroller.

She'd writhed and twisted and turned and Mick had tried to entertain her by grabbing her toy cat, which was a disastrous idea. 'My cat!' she screamed, lurching back out of the stroller and onto the floor, while Harry jumped onto his knees to play with her. Viv tried to get out of bed to break everyone up so we left in a hurry, promising to be back tomorrow.

'I don't want to be a burden, love,' Viv had said. 'I know how long these things take, remember?'

We stayed in a Travelodge outside Yeovil, which had been a Happy Eater in our day. Paul had walked up to the reception desk with his credit card in his hand when we first arrived. 'How long would you like the room for?' the woman behind the desk had asked, smiling and polite, the familiar Somerset voice sounding pantomime-ish to our London ears.

'I don't know,' Paul said, suddenly looking at me. 'I don't know.'

I told him to sit down and he nodded dumbly, doing as he was told like a child. I held Harry's hand and plonked Izzy next to her dad, her head resting on his lap, thumb in her mouth. Her toy cat was tucked in the crook of her elbow, fluffy and clean back then. 'Can we book for three days at the moment, and see if we need more? Do you have space?' I asked, my voice low.

'We always have space,' she said – Rebecca, by her name tag – 'just let me know what you need.'

Viv died six days later, just after we'd left her for the day. We checked out of the motel and I drove us back to London in near silence.

Before we left Somerset, Paul handed Mick a blank cheque for the funeral directors and gave him permission to make every decision. Permission that was more of a request. Mick had stood there with the cheque still in his hand, watching us leave. 'Bye, Grandad,' Harry had said, waving. 'Bye, bye, bye,' Izzy had sung as we wrestled her whirly legs into her car seat.

Paul returned to work the next day and I was glad. I could cry and wail in secrecy, taking a subdued Harry to school, plonking Izzy in front of CBeebies, and just bawling my eyes out. I cried far more for Viv than I had for my own mum. Then in the afternoon, I cleaned myself up, made up my face and went to collect Harry from school. Paul worked until the kids had gone to bed. He returned home wild-eyed with commuter rage and grief, and then stared at the TV in silence.

Mick called to let us know the funeral would be the following Tuesday. We trudged through the weekend, agonising over the logistics of travel and whether the kids should go.

In the end, we left the kids with friends and drove down. We set off in the early hours, a cold black silence enveloping the car so totally that the sound of shutting the doors sounded like gunshots ringing through the street. We travelled in our funeral clothes, plunging down the M5 as the day grew blistering hot, the sky bright orange once the sun emerged.

We arrived stiff and creased with gritty headaches from the sun. Agitated and angry. At ourselves, each other, her, Mick. It made no sense. Funerals are there to help it all make sense, but the moment just before the service starts is the very apex of confusion.

Viv didn't have a will, but as the house had been Mick's all along, it just reverted to him. Viv had changed the locks after the storm of 1987 but she'd given him a new key long ago. We went there with him after the funeral. He wouldn't stop babbling about nothing and no-one until the key went in the lock, then he fell silent and took an audible breath. It was the first time he'd been inside since she was admitted onto the ward for the last time. A huge hospital-style bed in the small lounge made me jump.

It was Mick who'd taken Viv to hospital for the tests a few months earlier, Mick who'd been there when she got the news, holding her hand and asking questions for her. He barely left her side after that. His on-again/off-again girlfriend had left and he'd not really noticed. Said he didn't care.

Viv had found out she was ill earlier in the summer. Mick visited her daily, sitting and watching TV on the sofa in the lounge, later sitting on the edge of her divan upstairs and then next to the bed downstairs once she'd moved down there for good. He started staying over, telling the morning Macmillan nurse how Viv had been through the night. When the time came to move into the oncology care ward at the hospital one afternoon, Mick had carried her into the ambulance. And then he'd called Paul.

Until that point of no return, he'd spent their time together making endless cups of tea, washing her face and reminding her about her medicines. He even did her laundry. She'd tried to teach him how to use a washing machine decades earlier. It had been a running joke. 'When will I ever need to know that?' he'd mock-grumbled, continuing to dump his concrete-crusted work clothes on the floor in front of the machine. He'd never had a machine of his own after they broke up, he said. He just used a laundrette when he was between girlfriends.

The funeral Mick had planned and Paul had paid for was perfect. It was far better than if we had done it. Everyone had to wear something purple – Viv's favourite colour – and they played sixties songs instead of hymns and had brightly coloured flowers spilling out everywhere, where we would have had prissy lilies and tea lights. The church was packed with colleagues from the hospital, patients and people from the village. None of her gypsy family came. I was disappointed on her behalf but relieved for Paul. He wouldn't have been able to cope with an existential crisis on the same day that he buried his mother. To this day, he doesn't acknowledge his Romany blood. Afterwards, there were sandwiches, pickled onions and Scotch eggs in the pub. That time, it was perfect.

When the well-wishers and village nobility left, I helped collect up plates and made awkward small talk with Lorraine while Paul and Mick went to have a moment together by Viv's grave.

She was buried officially in her birth name, Vivian Priscilla Lee, but her gravestone, thanks to Mick, read: 'Viv Loxton, devoted wife, mother and granny, missed by all.'

If I can pinpoint a moment that things shifted between us, it was then. Unspoken questions formed in the back of my throat, which I swallowed back down to concentrate on being a perfect wife. A better mother. And still the questions remained. Perhaps I was looking for something when I found that letter after all. Perhaps way down in a secret part of me, I knew.

It's only just gone noon at the Eden Project but everyone's blood sugar is dangerously low and if we don't stuff the kids full of food soon, it'll be carnage. We go to the Eden Bakery and I see Paul's jaw jut at the sight of hundreds of people. But the food smells amazing and we all relax a bit once enough carbohydrates and dairy fats have been absorbed into our systems. I surprise myself by eating a huge doorstep sandwich and a scone.

'This is nice, Paul,' I say, trying to focus on the moment and not the evening that awaits.

'Yeah, it is quite nice,' he says, and fiddles with some salt packets.

'Happy anniversary,' I say, but it's almost a question.

He kisses me on the lips, still frowning. 'Happy anniversary, Kate.'

'Eurgh,' says Harry.

2002

In retrospect, I never recovered from the embarrassment of my bleeding belly derailing a creative meeting. And I never regained John's respect. I could never recreate the cut-glass demeanour I'd spent years chiselling in front of the more junior staff, either.

Paul promised that no-one outside of the room knew about my bleed but I didn't believe him. Why would anyone keep quiet about something like that? Illness and gross incidents are bread and butter in a gossipy office. And besides, it *must* have raised questions: why was I bleeding from my guts when I'd been supposedly off with a stomach bug? *I'd* have asked questions.

Once he bundled me out of the room that day, Paul helped me into a taxi and took me straight back to A&E. He called John on the way to let him know I was still ill and he was taking me home. I know full well that John must have heard all about the blood.

At the hospital, after a long, embarrassing wait during which I covered my lap with a magazine that kept slipping from my sweaty hands, I was told I had a nasty infection. I was given a prescription for another bag of pills and stronger painkillers and told to rest.

I had to take another week off, and actually take it off properly that time. The antibiotics and painkillers cleared up the bad flesh but I was feverish and struggled to sleep. Jugs of coffee and not much else got me through each day but it's fair to say I wasn't operating at full capacity.

The daytime is the preserve of mums. Every TV show I flipped to was either for children or about children. Earnest doctors on morning TV talking about vaccinations or nappy rash. Strollers jamming the pavement if I shuffled out to buy milk. Everywhere I looked, the little ghost.

For the first time in a long time, I felt motherless. Acutely aware of a black spot, darker than the others on my bare family tree. While Paul had been there almost throughout at the hospital, I found it impossible to talk about it with him. He'd borne witness to it all, but it was locked inside him. I wanted it to stay there. But I needed someone, and there was only one person I could ever have called.

I realised as the phone started to ring that she was probably at work. The burbling purr of the ring tone was strangely soothing. I could picture the same old phone ringing, the worn number three, 'Castle Cary 50235' carefully written in pencil under a protective window. I let it ring and ring – there was no answerphone on the line – picturing myself back on the little sofa under a lap tray with tea and toast.

'Hello?'

She sounded exhausted.

'Viv?' I said. 'I didn't think you were there.'

'Katie? Are you alright, maid?'

I managed to say 'no'. That's all I said for the next few minutes. Viv, having barely fallen asleep after a night shift at this point, listened to my sobs and soothed me wordlessly. Shushing and murmuring as decades of quiet compassion had taught her to do.

'I lost my baby,' I said, and gasped to hear that word from my mouth. Not pregnancy, not blockage. *My baby.* She barely said a word, cried a little with me. She told me she'd lost a baby too, many years ago, when Paul was tiny himself. I've carried that in silence ever since, Paul doesn't know.

In those moments, finding the words to describe, to fill out the situation, I allowed myself a sliver of time to grieve properly.

I cried, mother to mother, to Viv. For just one day at least, I took that name. A secret name, lost again before I ever really held it.

When I got back into the office a week later, I found out that G&L had been passed to Jenny, a new account manager triumphantly poached from Saatchi. Not only that, my newest booze accounts had been shared between the wider team and there was an email waiting from John asking me to come to see him when I arrived.

I went to the bathroom first and checked the mirror. My face looked puffy, my eyes wired from a week of over-caffeinating and under-sleeping. I'd had to undo my jeans button to avoid rubbing my still sore skin and my top hung from my bony shoulders. I looked like shit.

'How are you doing?' John asked, without looking up, as I slid into his office uneasily.

'I'm okay now, thanks,' I replied, still unsure at that point what John had worked out about my real condition.

'We missed you.'

I didn't reply so he carried on. 'You've seen that we've shared some of your accounts out and I think it was long overdue. You've been juggling too many clients for too long. You need to focus on guiding the team and helping to raise the next generation of little Kates, yeah?' He looked up for the first time.

'Do I?'

'Yes,' he said, he matey tone gone. 'I think it makes sense for you to keep hold of the clients that are ticking over in the background and have the young blood focus on the time-consuming new ones, with you in a more advisory role. What do you think?'

'I think that's overkill, John. I think everything was fine before I had to go off sick.'

'Well, I'm sorry you feel that way but it's done now.' He paused. 'And things weren't fine.'

'Why ask me what I think then?' I'd felt my eyes prickle with tears but had held his gaze since he looked up.

'Don't fucking push me, Kate. I had a lot of respect for you but that only carries you so far.'

I stormed out because I had nothing else to say and an overwhelming urge to cry. Rather than go back to my office, I went to find Paul. I had no-one else to confide in and needed to offload. When I got to Paul's bank of desks, he wasn't there. I asked around and was told he was in a meeting with Jenny. A meeting about G&L. I left a note on his desk. 'Gone to Pret, come and find me.' I sat in the Pret a Manger around the corner for over an hour, grinding my teeth and drinking yet more coffee, checking my phone for text messages. In the end, I gave up and went back to the office to find that Paul's chair was still empty. I swept my unseen note from his desk and shoved it into my pocket. And then I hid behind the glass of my office for the rest of the day.

10 Morrison House
St Katharine Docks
London
E1W

20th May, 2002

Dear Viv,

Thank you so much again for talking to me on the phone. I'm so sorry for waking you up after a shift, I can't imagine how tired you were.

Just chatting helped immensely and I'm so grateful. There's no-one I can talk to about what happened and I feel quite friendless at the moment. Paul's brilliant, of course, but that's different. And I'm certainly out on a limb at work.

I think this is the first time in years that I've felt vulnerable, to be honest. I really thought I'd made a go of things, y'know? I loved my job and my little flat. I thought that was enough but I'm starting to think that was short sighted. I don't feel like I have <u>anything</u> outside of my job and now, maybe, I never will. I know what you said about conceiving after losing a tube but I don't even have a boyfriend let alone someone to plan a family with! Maybe I lost my chance before I even knew I wanted to take it.

I know I'm on a big mope here, but I guess now that work feels wobbly, it shows me how alone I really am. My parents are dead, I have no female friends and my work colleagues don't even respect me any more. It feels like everyone's just waiting for me to make a mistake. I really don't know what to do. The only good thing in my life is my friendship with Paul. He's been amazing, he really takes after you.

I want to escape but there aren't any account director jobs around at the moment (believe me, I've looked on Monster daily). So, I'm stuck here. I'm trying to prove my worth and regain some composure but it's probably pointless. I think my card is marked. My boss keeps cancelling one-to-one meetings with me and doesn't want me involved in anything. I'm just so fed up.

I'd love to come down to see you soon. Maybe Paul and I could hire a car and drive down one weekend? I'd really like that.

All my love,
Katie xxx

CHAPTER THIRTY-SIX

November 2012 – Saturday afternoon

Paul is driving back from the Eden Project to Mousehole in silence. He seemed agitated in the biomes but now he looks calm, despite the gloomy weather. He even takes a hand off the wheel to pat me on the knee in a rallying, matey way and flashes me an unreadable smile. It takes me by surprise but I smile back. The children are noisy in the back, the heat of the car's radiator steaming up the windscreen and sweating them into a frenzy. They're not being naughty, they're just very 'present'.

Outside, the sky is rolling with blue and black shapes. There's a distant grumble that could be the beginning of thunder. Every few minutes, the clouds split and short bursts of rain send the car's windscreen wipers into a panic.

This time ten years ago, everything was quiet. The sky was clear, just a sheet of white-blue hanging there, passive. It was very cold though, a freezing blanket of air wrapping itself around my shoulders and face as soon as I opened the door. It was a beautiful, crisp day for a wedding.

We almost went abroad, but I like the snap of the cold and the glassiness of autumn. And I didn't want to wear a bikini, not then. It would have hung from me as if I was some kind of ghoul.

Izzy sometimes asks about our wedding day. She's that kind of child, all fairy tales and princess dresses. She likes to imagine herself there on the 'big day', playing a part. Flowergirl or bridesmaid. Harry doesn't care about the wedding, but he sometimes likes to hear about what we got up to when we were his age.

The life that your parents lived before your birth is a foreign land. Like most kids, our two are keen to explore it. They ask questions about 'before' so freely, as if the memories are easy. But their questions sound so strange to us. Paul always gets a little defensive, like they're trying to catch him out. I get watery-eyed, and spluttery, because what should flow comfortably gets censored and reconstructed, pixel by pixel. While Paul will tell the story of our vow to a rapt dinner party, it's very different telling the children, for whom all stories about their creation must officially start 'When a mummy and a daddy love each other very much. . .'

And when the kids delve further back – to the ancient times *before* Paul and I were friends – I'm even less comfortable. It's foggy, I'll claim. *I'm so old that my memory is bad.* They – crushingly – tend to accept my age as a defence. If I do start to pick my way through those earlier years, to find stories to tell them, I find I'm just feeling my way around a big, aching hole. It should sound so grand. I should be able to tell them staggering stories about Greenfinch Manor and the characters living between its walls. But now, as then, the truth is flat and disappointing.

I was bored and lonely until I met Daddy. That's not the truth that I'd like them to hear. The more they ask, the more I realise that I knew nothing about my parents. Even when I was Harry's age, I asked nothing. My mother was so young that her life was wild and half-formed. My father's longer life was less colourful and locked out of my view.

I know more about Viv's life than I do my mother's. And still not enough about her. But the parent I know most about is Mick. Thanks to those late-night car journeys coupled with his natural need to fill a silence. And, of course, there was all the chatting and joking that I was privy to just from being in the Loxtons' home. There were precious few truly private conversations because the house was too small. Paul and I would whisper upstairs in his bedroom and I still think Viv heard most of it from the kitchen.

Until Viv got ill, I convinced myself that perhaps she and Mick were right to break up. They certainly fought with increasing ferocity up until the night I drunkenly blundered into him. I tried to think that I did them a favour by sparking that split second of insurmountable mistrust. That it enabled Mick – forever scrabbling at the door – to get out and run free, so he could be chasing women and answering to no-one. That it forced Viv – long-suffering but no fool – to admit what she'd suspected for so long and to no longer live in perpetual suspicion.

But then Viv got ill. And the Loxtons had clung to each other with fierce dedication. And all those years apart seemed wasteful.

Mick still lives at 4 Church Street. The last time we took the kids to see him, which we don't do very often, he hadn't changed a thing. That last visit, he'd carefully used Viv's old egg slicer and salad spinner to make lunch and after watching him, I'd had to go to the bathroom to wipe my eyes and collect myself.

He didn't move a girlfriend in either. Didn't have one and wasn't interested. Didn't want someone messing with Viv's house, he said.

It's been about a year since that visit. As usual, he was content and chatty. He had his routines and rituals. Pub for lunch most days, throw some 'arrows', have a few pints and go home to watch the telly. He's also got a computer and his friend Rod has shown him how to use it. Two grey heads bobbing about in front of the screen, carefully typing with one finger each. Mick has now started using email (he sends Harry jokes sometimes, not all of them appropriate) and he orders his Tesco shopping online because he's given up driving now he has nowhere to go. 'How long until he orders a Thai bride?' Paul had asked me, semi-seriously.

'He wouldn't get married,' I said. 'He loved your mum too much.'

'Loxtons mate for life,' Paul said.

2002

I hadn't rested on my laurels after being sidelined, sorry 'realigned', at TMC. I may not have been given new accounts, but I got on the phone to all of the old faithfuls I'd been allowed to keep, and put lunches in the diary with each of them. I arranged one-to-one meetings with all of the account managers in my team, and listened to them whine about the clients whose accounts I'd lovingly cultivated.

Every day for two weeks solid, I was lunching with one client, and dining with another. Ordering their brand's booze with the food, trying to inspire them into extra ad spend, a refreshed campaign, branching out into burgeoning online ad space. I got home past midnight every night but still needed the sleeping pills to nod off, besieged by nightmares of John and my colleagues picking over my dead body, or turning up at meetings naked and empty.

At least I regained half a stone of the several I'd lost.

At the end of that fortnight of frenzied schmoozing, John's

PA asked me to see him urgently, just as I was about to go to yet another client lunch.

'Your expenses,' he said when I walked in, without preamble.

'What about them?' I asked, sitting down with a straight back.

'They're off the charts, Kate.'

'I've been re-engaging the clients you left me with, John, that's not cheap.'

'For God's sake, Kate, I told you to focus on advising and team-building.' He slapped his palm on the desk and glared at me.

I glared back but kept my voice steady. 'I've still got my older clients, John, and I'm getting them fired up to spend more. Isn't that my job?'

'Your job is whatever I tell you your job is. And I told you to stay away from the fucking clients and babysit the fucking team.'

'You know what?' I said, standing up. 'That *isn't* what you said. And perhaps if you had, we wouldn't be having this conversation.'

'Take a half-day, go home and cool off,' he'd called after me as I walked out of his office.

I wasn't going to take a half-day. I wasn't going to walk out of that office and let them think I'd given up.

I had a lunch with one of my longest-running clients scheduled at Nobu for one o'clock and it was ten past already. After a frustrating taxi ride, I blustered through the doors and into the restaurant. I had just opened my mouth to give my name to the maître d' when I saw Jenny, sitting with Graham Costa and Alan Fox from Ginseng Drinks.

I stood and watched. Jenny was good, clean and precise. She'd been a steal from Saatchi – a real bloodied nose for our rivals. She was seen as part of the new wave of tenacious young superstars that was going to keep TMC fresh and exciting. And she was a fucking snake.

Next to Jenny and her shiny blonde bob was Paul, smiling and laughing, effortless small talk dribbling out of his mouth in a way I'd never really seen before. He wore his dark-rimmed glasses and the same floppy Morrissey hair that he'd always had. He looked handsome and capable.

Next to Paul was Eva, a new hire for the design team, a smart and pretty urchin of a girl, barely five foot. They were opening a deck of ideas right there on the table. The waiter was only just bringing their drinks over and they were already looking at ideas? *Whose* ideas? Who even knew we had this lunch planned? I pursed my lips and walked over.

'Graham! Alan! Hi!' I reached my hand out to shake each of theirs as Jenny rose to her feet in surprise.

'Kate,' she smiled glassily. 'I've already made your apologies, I think we can handle this from here.'

'Nonsense,' I smiled back, 'you know how much I value this account. I wouldn't miss this lunch for the world.'

'Well, you've missed quite a bit of it already,' Graham said, grumpy bastard.

I looked at my wrist, which didn't have a watch on it.

'The meeting was moved forward,' Paul said softly to me, 'I thought you knew.'

'I didn't know, Paul,' I said in a voice that sounded more shrill than intended. 'I wish I had known,' I said pointedly to Jenny.

'Kate, can I have a word?' Jenny gestured back towards the foyer.

'No, let's not waste any more time,' I said briskly and pulled a chair from a nearby table, gesturing to the waiter to take my order. He came over and I ordered a Ginseng Fizz with Grey Goose.

'We're not drinking today,' Paul had said in a low voice.

'Let's talk through these ideas then,' I said to the table.

'Well,' Jenny looked flustered. 'As I was saying, the new team we've assembled has been looking at refreshing the assets to take you into next quarter.'

'Hang on,' said Alan, 'can you just clarify who will be leading this account?'

'Me,' Jenny and I both said at the same time.

'I will,' Jenny said, firmly.

'The fuck you will,' I growled.

In the end it was Paul who put a stop to it, apologising to Alan and Graham and ushering me out. Bundling, really.

'I get that you're pissed off but you're making a fool of yourself,' he said. 'It's not Jenny's fault. John gave her the account and obviously didn't tell you.'

'Who moved the fucking meeting?' I hissed.

'I don't know, Kate. Jenny told me the new time so I guess she must have rearranged it with the client. Look, I'll smooth things over here, you just go back to the office, okay?'

I paced around my office for most of the afternoon, copying names, phone numbers and email addresses from my Outlook account and into my leather address book. I don't know why, it felt like something. Safeguarding? Future-proofing? *Espionage?* In reality, it was nothing. I was due to have a one-to-one with a shiny new junior account exec that afternoon, but I cancelled. I didn't trust myself not to tell her to find another career and save herself before it was too late. I didn't fancy turning myself into the resident madwoman.

Towards the end of the day, I watched from my office as all the senior managers trooped into the boardroom. I'd not been invited in advance or called in so I stayed rooted to my leather chair, trying to ignore what I was seeing. My colleagues had studiously avoided walking past my office, even when that was the most direct route. I sat a little longer, tapping my foot up and down so my knee vibrated and my thigh shook.

After a few minutes, I stalked around my glass room, running my fingertips along every surface, closing, reopening and then half-closing the blinds. I saw Jenny talking to the creative team on their bank of desks near the boardroom. Colm and Paul shot looks my way then snapped their heads back when they saw my silhouette behind the semi-closed blinds. I cleaned out my email inbox, forwarding anything that incriminated John to my personal email. I noticed with a sinking heart that he'd never really said anything incriminating, it was always me. Everything had been verbal from him, untraceable. Did he plan that all along? To leave no trace? Does anyone plan anything that well? Not me, clearly.

I buzzed for Janet to bring me a coffee. She brought it in and placed it on the desk without meeting my eye. Chatty Janet, who normally had to be ushered out of the office mid-sentence.

'Leave the door open,' I called.

She left it open a crack and I slid into the doorway, leaning against the doorframe and sipping my machine-splurted pseudo-latte. I decided that if they were going to freeze me out, I wasn't going to make it easy for them by hiding. I glared at their heads through the window of the boardroom.

Not a single person looked my way.

As the last of my lukewarm drink drained away, I saw the boardroom open and Marian scuttling out, empty coffee pot swinging. She saw me watching from my corner, smiled apologetically, and hurried into the kitchen.

Ten minutes later, most of the senior managers left the meeting, avoiding my office again as they picked their ways through the desks and chairs. Deborah, the head of HR appeared, and started to walk towards me. I met her halfway.

'You want me in the boardroom, yeah?' I asked, blood pounding in my ears.

'Yes, Kate. Thank you.'

When I got in to the room, I saw John half-standing in a strange act of deference.

'Is this about *us*?' I said to him, knowing it wasn't.

'Sit down please, Kate,' said Deborah, ignoring the bait.

John's eyes blazed and he stared rigidly at Deborah rather than me.

My role was longer needed. I got a thank you for my years and a pay-off.

I'm pretty sure I only got the cash because I'd sat in on so many 'no minutes taken' sessions at similar meetings, and I knew what was often dished out to keep things simple. It wasn't much. A few months' salary. But it was more than they legally had to do, considering how I'd laid my own firing on a plate with my freak-out at lunch.

I didn't say goodbye to Paul in person. I didn't want to taint him by association so I just left the office on shaking legs and got into the nearest taxi. As the black cab coughed off down the road for the last time, I texted Paul. 'Just got sacked. See you at home.'

He replied within seconds: 'Shit. I'm so sorry, I'll bring wine.'

I got home at half-past four, took my antibiotics and half a sleeping pill and lay on the sofa under a throw taking long blinks and short naps while the TV burbled away in the background, the blinds closed. A decade later, it's easy to diagnose that I was in a deep shock that would eventually break like a tidal wave, but at the time I just felt numb.

Paul crept in around seven o'clock, peering around the door into the dark living room.

'It's okay, I'm awake,' I said, swinging my knees around to sit up in the blue glare of the screen.

'I brought wine,' he said, waving two bottles but seeming awkward and embarrassed.

'Thanks.'

He stood and stared at me for a while until I stood up, shook the throw to the floor and cried, 'What the fuck am I going to do, Paul?'

He walked towards me, balanced the bottles on the sofa and pulled me into a hug. My arms dangled limply by my sides as I cried, the shoulder on his light-blue shirt staining with wet mascara.

I should have left things well alone, of course I should. I should have taken a chunk of that 'goodwill' money and booked myself on a month-long holiday somewhere with white sand and free-flowing cocktails. But I didn't. I didn't know what to do because my whole adult life, I'd worked. I'd worked *there*.

I made endless lists of things I needed to do. I made lists of agencies to approach, lists of which of my clients I might be able to bring over with me. Thought about starting my own agency. Nearly threw up at the thought of all that paperwork. I made best-case scenario lists, and worst-case scenario lists. While I listed, I drank coffee, grinding beans and changing filter paper throughout the day like that was my new job. And on optimistic days, I made plans for alternative careers, courses I would take, hobbies I'd be able to try. By morning, the previous day's ideas looked cold and unappetising. I joined a gym but didn't turn up for my induction, feeling knackered just pulling on the workout clothes I'd ordered.

When Paul came home in the evenings, he'd bring back Marks and Spencer food from the Tottenham Court Road store near our – his – office. Or he cooked for us or ordered take-aways that I barely touched, knowing that I'd probably forgotten to eat that day despite having nothing else to do.

Maybe I should have gone out and got hammered every night, danced until my heels shattered, just let my hair down and caught up on the fun I'd not had for years. But I didn't know how any more.

Instead, I just kept filling my old TMC notepads with lists but I couldn't bring myself to act on them. I didn't know what had been said about my departure to clients or to competitors, but I did remember hundreds of gossipy conversations I'd had at industry dos about burnouts, tantrums and embarrassing firings. I wasn't an idiot, I knew that anyone who mattered must have known about my fall from grace.

Paul stepped up to the plate, bat swinging for me. He had a new purpose and poise. I'd ask him questions about TMC and he'd say, 'Don't ask, you don't want to know.' His protection stung me.

At night, we sat on the sofa and I watched television while he read. Sometimes he tried to read bits out to me, like he always had, but the endless lists running through my head meant I couldn't take the words in.

I finished my various courses of pills and didn't go back for more. The pain of the infection seeped away, but I hurt in other ways. I felt exhausted and useless. Paul brought me a coffee when he left in the mornings, and then I lay in bed until noon.

It amazes me, looking back, how I could spend the day doing absolutely nothing but feel so tired. It wasn't even like I filled the day with chores; I did a cursory clean of the flat just before Paul came home and the rest of the time I watched TV and read magazines. I told myself that I needed a makeover, a new haircut, a new wardrobe, and then I would have the confidence to go out there and hit the recruitment agencies in person. But taking a first step to even book a haircut seemed too demanding, too fraught with risk.

Every Saturday, Paul would go to the corner shop and get *The Times*, *Telegraph* and *Guardian* and then talk me out of applying for all the jobs I carefully circled. It didn't take much for me to cross them out again. I *was* opting for roles that I was wildly overqualified for because I thought that meant I stood more of a chance.

'They'll be suspicious straight away because it doesn't add up,' he said. 'What would you have done if a CV landed on your lap from an account director with nearly a decade of experience, and they were pleading to work as an account executive on a fraction of your old salary?'

He was right and this was advice I'd have given. But I wanted to slip under the radar. I hoped that for a lower-level job they might not bother to call for references, they'd just snap me up and hope the gamble paid off. Paul talked me out of testing the theory. It was a pretty shitty theory.

Two months to the day that I left TMC's shiny glass-front for good, I decided that to have any hope of moving on, of risking a call to a prospective new employer, I needed to know what had been said about me. To clients, to competitors and to my own staff. I needed to know what would be said in a reference, if I'd even get one, because I sure as hell needed to get another job.

Paul had started to give me rent money. I hated it but I needed it. My pay-off money was dwindling by then, I tried not to draw on it but I hadn't really noticed until then how much just got whisked out of my account each month for utilities and ground rent, for subscriptions to things I'd forgotten. Wine boxes and magazines. The unused gym.

After writing, deleting and rewriting numerous versions, I sent John a text message asking to meet at the hotel next to Paddington station. I knew the staff there were discreet and I needed to speak to him in person, to know for sure how badly my reputation had been damaged. Before we'd stupidly got intimate, he'd always been a mentor, and a fair boss. I hoped he still had reserves of that fairness to draw upon. God knows, I clearly needed some help.

I was surprised when he agreed to meet without an arm twist, surprised even further when he actually showed up, albeit late, rather than cancelling at the last moment. I was already in the dated bar when he arrived, perching on a bar stool and sipping my third gin and tonic as slowly as I could. I saw his stride falter just briefly when he saw me. I knew why. My thighs sat like sticks on the stool and my sweater, even though it was loose and expensive, couldn't hide my sharp collarbones. I'd worn a V-neck and hoiked my breasts up to try to draw eyes away from how angular I'd become.

'Thanks for coming,' I said. 'Can I get you a drink?'

'Just a still water, thanks,' he said to the bartender instead of me. 'I don't have long, Kate, but I'm glad you called.'

'How are things at TMC?' I asked.

'Yeah, yeah, going well, you're missed. How is life post-TMC?' he asked.

I stared at him. Did he really think that he could rewrite history, stamp a new version of events where I'd simply moved on? Despite my best intentions, I found it hard not to snap.

'It's not great, actually, John,' I said.

'Kate—'

'It's shit, to be honest. I miss the work, I miss the clients and I wish you hadn't sacked me because I think I could have carried on doing a good job.'

'You weren't sacked, it was a strategic realignment of team resources.' He sipped his water.

'Well, I'm pleased if you're telling people that, even if that's not how it felt.'

'Kate, if it's going to be like this then I need to go.'

'John, look, no. Please. I miss it. I need to work. There's no home for me at TMC, I get it. Maybe I should have left when Stephen Miller asked me years ago, but—'

'Don't be stupid, TMC were good to you. You'd never have got as far as you did at Elliot & Finch, they don't have the clients. You fucked this up, babe, it wasn't fucked up for you. Have some class about that.'

'So it wasn't a realignment of resources then, I *was* sacked.' I gulped the last of my drink. 'Another G&T here, please. Make it a double,' I called to the bartender, who was cutting up lemons and pretending not to listen to our conversation.

'What do you want me to say, Kate? You were good but you burned out, you got cocky. You thought you were bigger than the agency and then you shot yourself in the foot in front of clients and your team. What would you have done in my position?'

'I'd have remembered all the years of not putting a foot wrong. I made one mistake, John.' I said. 'One. After years of working my arse off.' I drained my drink and slammed the glass down harder than I intended. 'Another please,' I gestured. 'One for you? A proper drink?'

John frowned, I saw him look at the door, considering his

options. He leaned on the bar and his shoulders fell a bit. 'Yeah, go on. I'll have a Michelob.'

He turned to face me. 'Kate, wind your neck in. It wasn't just one mistake. Your hissy fit in front of clients was part of a bigger problem. You hadn't been firing on all cylinders for ages, you were knackered. You had too many clients, you weren't giving them all what they needed and you wouldn't let anyone else handle them so they all suffered.'

'That's not true and you know it. Look, I need another job. I'm not asking to come back, I just need to know what's been said. I need to know what a reference from you would look like.' I lowered my voice. 'How badly damaged is my reputation?'

He thought for a moment and then put his hand on my knee which, without me realising until then, had been jiggling up and down. 'Kate,' he said, 'it wasn't my decision, I wanted to keep you close.' I rolled my eyes. 'I really did,' he said. 'I thought there was life in the old dog yet but I couldn't be seen to fight unduly, you know that. Look, you won't get a bad reference from me, and no-one's been bad mouthing you, okay?'

'John, I need more than that. I need a good reference and I need some help. Please? For old times' sake?'

'Old times' sake,' he said, raising an eyebrow.

I wish I could say that he pleaded with me to go upstairs, that it was him who went to see the receptionist en route to the loo, slammed a credit card down and asked for a room. I wish I could say that I'd just stormed out of the hotel, reminding him loudly that he was married and that I was worth more than that.

But it wasn't him.

It was me who suggested we 'take the discussion somewhere

more private'. Maybe out of habit, residual desire or the need to feel that I still had a semblance of my old life. Whatever the reason, it was me who asked the bartender for the wine and the glasses. It was me who chose to ignore the 'old dog' remark, chose not to remind John that he said he couldn't stay long. Or that he'd already ended this once and then let TMC dismantle me.

Instead, it was him that balked at my flat chest and hollow stomach, struggled to keep his erection and threw back neat bourbon afterwards. By then, I was already drunk from the wine on top of the gin, but I unscrewed a tiny vodka bottle and sloshed the contents into a plastic beaker with a doll-sized can of Coke.

'Answer me one thing,' I said, unsure whether I should say it but buoyed on by drunken bravado. 'Did you want me to go because of what happened between us?'

'Don't do this, Kate.'

'I had as much to lose as you and no reason to tell anyone. So if you did get rid of me because of that, it was all for nothing.'

He laughed briefly and furrowed his eyebrows, pulling his boxer shorts up and sitting back on the bed. 'I'm a married father, and I was your boss. How did you have as much to lose as me?'

'Because all I had was my job,' I said, surprised by a sudden rush of tears. 'So I had everything to lose and I lost it.'

He stared at me for a moment, squinting. 'So if you had so much to lose, why weren't you more discreet?'

'What do you mean?' I asked, struggling to focus. 'I didn't tell a soul.' I sat up and pulled the duvet around me.

'You did though, didn't you?' He had a new edge to his voice. I couldn't think clearly and failed to form the words. The extra vodka had punched me unexpectedly. 'It was all around the office, Kate,' he said. 'If you'd just kept your mouth shut, we could have overlooked your tantrums.'

'That's not true and that's not fair.'

'Maybe all women go *Fatal Attraction* in the end, but I really thought you were different.' He sat heavily on the bed to pull his socks on. 'I really did.'

'I didn't breathe a word to anyone,' I said. 'I kept all your secrets, but you just binned me without giving me the benefit of the doubt.' I reached for his shirt to throw on like I always used to but he grabbed it. 'No,' he said. 'I need that.

'Kate, I'm not pissing about here. Jill had just had the baby and the stakes were too high. I don't expect you to understand yet because, like you said, all you had is your job so you don't have the first clue what it means to actually have a family to protect, a kid to think about.'

I opened my mouth but snapped it shut again.

He continued talking while he dressed himself, almost conversational like he was considering what to have for dinner.

'Look, I thought you were on a level but you started to act unhinged, didn't you?' He looked at me as if I was going to agree, raised an eyebrow when I didn't.

'I couldn't have you shooting your mouth off. This—' he pointed to the crumpled bed sheets '—was only supposed to be a bit of fun. The real deal was back at home and I wasn't going to let you risk all that.'

I dragged the sheets into my palms as I clenched my fists and stood up suddenly, pulling the bedding with me. 'You total bastard!' I seethed.

He marched to me, pointed at my chest and said, 'Unhinged. Like I said.'

I was so frustrated and drunk by then that instead of pulling together some actual words, I just made a kind of howling sound. Blind, drunken fury. He pointedly ignored me and fiddled with his watch. I pulled a towel around me and wobbled over to the minibar for another vodka, wincing as it hit my throat.

He was fully dressed by then. 'I didn't tell a soul,' I sobbed. 'I kept *all* your secrets, even when they hurt me. Even when they ripped me apart.' I think I was shouting then, tears falling hard.

'What do you mean?'

'I got pregnant, John. You got me pregnant and I didn't know until it ruptured in my tube.'

'You're lying.'

'I'm telling you the fucking truth, just like I always have. Just like I asked *you* to tell *me*.' I thumped my own chest and threw back the rest of the vodka, throwing the bottle at the wall which it bounced off and slid pathetically down to the floor.

'No doubt you heard about my stomach bleeding in the boardroom?' I shouted. I could see his expression change.

'Seriously?' he said.

'Yeah, and this is the thanks I get for it,' I shouted back. 'I dragged myself into work, drugged up and in pain, I showed my dedication and I got royally fucked over. You took everything from me.'

After thinking for a moment, he turned towards the door and kept his back to me, speaking flatly. 'You should have told me at the time, I wasn't a mind reader.'

'Is that it?' I said. 'No "Sorry Kate, turns out you *were* trustworthy and I just ruined your life for nothing?" No "Thanks for not telling my wife, thanks for nearly bleeding to death because of me?"'

He reached for the doorknob.

'Maybe I should have told your wife,' I spat. 'Maybe I should have told HR. They wouldn't have dismissed me so easily if they'd known my boss had taken advantage of me and I nearly died as a result.' I watched his shoulders tighten as he held the knob. His jaw clenched.

'Maybe I should tell your wife now,' I hissed.

Suddenly he was on me, dragging me by my hair into the dim bathroom and shoving my face up to the mirror. 'Stop, please,' I cried.

'Look at yourself,' he shouted. 'Look at who you are. A washed-up, jealous bitch!'

I tried to turn around but he forced my head to stay where it was until I kicked wildly to get free, bashing my knees and toes. He let go suddenly and I lost my balance, cracking my forehead on the sink as I slumped.

'Fuck you,' I whispered up at him from a dizzy pile on the floor.

'Fuck me? Fuck you. And if you ever so much as use my wife's name, I will fucking finish you. Do you understand?'

'You already finished me,' I said.

'If you think I've already done all I can, then you really are a naïve little tart.'

The door snapped shut behind him. I lay on the floor, touching my head and staring at the blood on my fingertips. I pulled myself up to sit on the loo. I picked up the phone by the toilet, eyes swimming, and dialled the number for my own flat.

I needed a friend.

I wanted Paul.

I woke up to someone hammering on the door of a room I didn't recognise, viewed from the bathroom floor where I lay.

'Come in!' I shouted, sitting myself up and touching my fingers to the dried blood on my head. A hotel manager in a badly fitting suit came into view, with Paul behind her.

'Oh,' I said.

'Are you okay, madam?' she asked, her voice sounding like a child's.

'I'm fine,' I said, 'I just had a fall.'

I realised then, as she flushed pink and Paul rushed forward with the eiderdown from the bed, that I was naked. The towel I'd been wearing was wrinkled next to me on the tiled floor.

'Fuck,' I said.

'It's okay, it's okay,' Paul said, studiously avoiding looking at my body as he covered it in puffed pastel fabric.

'Thank you so much for coming,' I said.

'Don't thank me,' he shook his head.

'I drank too much,' I added.

'Stop,' he said.

The taxi ride back to the flat was a blur. Closing my eyes made me feel sick, opening them made me feel worse. I went to bed wearing the jumper and knickers that Paul had helped wrestle me back into. I slept fitfully, writhing all night. When I finally dragged myself out and gagged my way through a mug of coffee, Paul had been at work for hours.

I took a long bath. Topping the water up with bursts from the hot tap, lying with a flannel over my eyes and trying to sort the order of the scenes playing through my head from the night before. Whichever way I shuffled them, the ending was the same.

I scrubbed myself clean, wrapped my hair in a towel and dwarfed my body in a dressing gown. I was still swathed when the front door opened and Paul walked in.

'Hey,' I said quietly. 'You're early.'

He nodded and clasped his hands together. He slipped off his shoes and trod carefully to the sofa and stood staring at me. I squirmed under his gaze.

'I'm mortified about last night,' I said.

He shook his head. 'I couldn't stay at work so I said I was ill.' He clenched his fists into tight balls. 'I had a meeting with that bastard,' he spat the word out.

'John?' I asked, my stomach churning. 'You had a meeting with John?'

'I hate him, I fucking hate him. He was there doing his greasy act, loudly laughing and pointing his crotch at some new account exec.' Paul stopped and I stood up gingerly and wrapped my arms around him. He hugged me back.

'Don't you dare let this fuck things up for you too,' I said.

He shook his head angrily. 'I can't stay after this, not after the way they treated you. I'm going to look for something else. I can't—'

I hugged him tighter, smelling a new aftershave over the same old scent of his skin that I used to wake up to as a kid in his tiny room.

'Please,' I said, 'I really don't want you to do that. I made my own bed, you shouldn't suffer for it. Seriously, please stay there. Okay?'

'I guess.'

'Anyway,' I said with faux gusto, 'I've done enough moping. I have a difficult call to make now but I think it'll be worth it.'

We broke away a little embarrassed. Paul went out to buy some food for dinner and I flipped open my phone and scrolled to M for Miller.

Stephen Miller hadn't seemed surprised to hear from me, which should have been a red flag. He agreed to meet the following week but when I'd suggested the Elliot & Finch office, he'd suggested Quaglino's. I'd suggested mid-afternoon and he'd said eight o'clock.

I spent the run-up to the interview bagging up old clothes for charity while I tried to find something to wear. Everything I tried was ill-fitting and ugly. I'd been living in loungewear and pyjamas, I hadn't seen a tailored waist in months and I no longer had much of a tailored waist myself – more like a shapeless tube. I spent hundreds in Selfridges, buying three different outfit options for the amount I used to spend on one dress.

On the night, I opted for a loosely fitted light grey Joseph dress, black LK Bennett shoes and a Louis Vuitton make-up bag that I used as a handbag and found myself gripping like a handrail without thinking.

Stephen looked good. He looked the same as the last time I'd seen him, after which I just stopped calling or replying to emails. I breathed deeply, counting in 'one, two, three' counting out 'one, two, three, four', a method that Paul had shown me. He'd read about it in *GQ*, it was a technique used by marines or something. I didn't really listen at the time but I found myself clinging to the memory on the Tube ride over. In the seconds before Stephen turned and noticed me, I dropped my shoulders back, lifted my chest and strode in.

'Hey, Red,' he said, standing and leaning to kiss both of my cheeks as I offered my hand. 'You look smart,' he said, 'have you come straight from work?'

'No,' I said, 'I'm not working right now. I thought you might have heard.' It was a question but he didn't answer it. 'You know I'm, y'know, trying to find the right position now. One where I can grow and—'

He cut me off, his eyebrows dipping for a second. 'I'm not interviewing you!' he laughed. 'It's not a test. I just thought you'd be on a contract somewhere. I know you left TMC.'

I sat down and tried to smile. 'So you're not interviewing?'

'Nah, Red. I'm not interviewing.' He smiled broadly and picked up a menu, fingering it for a minute and then putting it back down. He opened a pack of Marlboro and tapped one on the table like he was some kind of cowboy. Lighting it in a quick, practised move.

'Sorry,' he said. 'Want one?'

'I don't smoke.' The flimsy smile had already faded from my lips.

'So, you wanna eat?'

'I guess so. I mean, I mostly wanted to catch up and see how things are going at Elliot & Finch. I'm not going to lie, I've often wondered if I made the right decision and now that I'm a free agent, I thought perhaps—'

'You thought you'd tap me up for a job again, and then use it to get something better?'

'No, I—'

'Look, let's not talk shop, okay? Let's just have a nice night and catch up. Old friends, yeah?'

'Old friends.'

I wanted to cry. I wanted to excuse myself, go to the Ladies and cry. Sit on a toilet seat, ball up two handfuls of tissue and weep into them.

Instead I sat there, with a rictus smile, and I made small talk. I made small talk with this man who did not want to make small talk with me. He wanted to make me squirm. And obviously, he did 'talk shop'. He talked shop all night as he dolloped his thick grey ash into the Q-shaped ashtray. I hated Quaglino's.

Stephen asked me all the questions I did not want to be asked about TMC and I answered them. He asked me for information that I was still contractually not allowed to share, and I shared it. He asked me things about John and other managers that I should not have even known and I just opened myself up like a carcass. And he'd told me there was no job and I did it anyway because

I was already on the ropes when I arrived. All he needed to do was step into the ring.

I remember looking up and seeing the mirrored ceiling reflecting my scrappy white arms slapped to my side and my dull, faded hair. I looked up at that mirror image and I knew right then. That was it, it really was over.

CHAPTER THIRTY-SEVEN

November 2012 – Saturday evening

Ordinarily, it's me who pushes to go out to dinner while Paul will always opt to cook 'something special' at home. For him, eating in fancy restaurants is a busman's holiday. Except if he's taking our family rather than clients, he has to pay from our bank account rather than put it on his TMC card.

Tonight, I'd planned to give the kids an early tea, hustle them into bed, and then cook 'something special' together, in the beautiful white kitchen. I figured a little bit of small talk, maybe some quiet concentration while we chopped, would help me build up to it: The Conversation.

I've fretted all week about what we'll have, and agonised so much that I've managed to put Paul off. This afternoon he declared that we would go to a restaurant instead.

'Somewhere romantic, with kids?' I said, wrinkling up my nose.

'I'm sure we can find somewhere nice.'

I hadn't banked on the kids eating our ten-year anniversary meal with us, studying our faces and bickering over who could have the last bread roll. I spent the last half an hour of the journey back from the Eden Project begrudgingly searching the internet for restaurants. The signal was patchy, so it took three times as long and I barely managed to stop myself from lobbing the phone out of the window and listening for its innards popping as the tyres crunched over it. Of course, I didn't do anything like that. I kept my face as neutral as possible and diligently searched for somewhere that Paul would appreciate.

Back at the cottage I got ready slowly, looking at my scrubbed face in the mirror as I dried my hair. Studying it and trying to remember how it looked ten years ago. Wondering what Paul thought he was taking on.

Although we've had to drive half an hour to get here, the restaurant *is* idyllic. Under normal circumstances, I'd have been delighted. The front windows are lit by storm lanterns, candles dribble wax onto the weathered tables and an amazing chandelier hangs over the diners like great mythical feathers.

I nudge Paul. 'It looks like Bowie's hair in *Labyrinth.*'

He smiles. 'We should show that film to the kids,' he says.

I wonder if I can really do what I plan to do tonight.

After a salmon starter, the waiter brings over our chateaubriand with pearly oyster mushrooms, glazed bone marrow and fondant potatoes. We've let the kids have a bowl of chips each, fuck it. 'Are you sure I can't tempt you with the wine list, madam?' the smiling waiter asks, all twenty years and floppy surfer hair of him.

'You know what?' I say, 'he's driving but I'm not. Bring me a bottle of your best Argentinian red.'

'Yay!' says Izzy, not understanding any of it but seeing some potential spoils in the excitement.

Paul smiles thinly. 'I guess I can have one glass.'

My heart races.

We were raised to drink, to toast or commiserate, to open a bottle of something for no reason at all. Paul can put it away far more than me, but tonight he's driving back to Mousehole so he makes his glass last. He eyes me carefully, I know I'm a little off kilter, a little loud maybe.

Izzy is transfixed; I rarely drink anything stronger than Appletiser when they're still up but she's just about old enough to know that wine makes adults 'silly'.

We finish our main and the kids are droopy and fidgety.

'Let's get them back,' Paul says, and something twists in my gut.

'Maybe we should get pudding?' I say.

'You never have pudding,' Harry says, wrinkling his nose.

'I don't *never* have pudding,' I say. I hate that he's started monitoring my food too, just like his father.

I eat a big slice of cheesecake, even though I was full ages ago. The kids eat bowls of ice cream and now Paul picks at a cheese board, pulling at his hair with one hand like he does when he's looking over campaign plans he's not happy with.

I feel swollen and hot as we walk to the car. The black November night buffeting me, my brain whistling like an old kettle.

'Let's do gifts when we get this lot in bed?' I shout into the wind as we unlock the car.

'Okay,' Paul says, his unease clear even in the dark.

2002

I started to notice when Paul got home from work, then I started to wait for him. If it got past seven o'clock and he hadn't mentioned that he would be late, I'd feel a nervous twist in my gut. He got promoted just before our thirtieth birthdays, and without telling me he was going to do it, he upped the rent that he paid into my account.

Unfairly, his kindness infuriated me. I called it passive-aggressive, like he was dangling his good fortune in front of me, whistling nonchalantly and swinging his legs while he waited for me to notice and collapse in gratitude.

'I didn't ask you for extra money,' I barked, the second he came through the door after I opened my monthly bank statement.

'I know you didn't,' he said, frowning at me as I stood, hip cocked in my grey joggers, conscious of my bare breasts under an old Ginseng Drinks T-shirt. 'Why are you cross?'

'You're rubbing my nose in it,' I said, weakly.

'Were you rubbing my nose in it when you helped me?' he asked. I had no answer so I went for a bath.

He'd started to dress smarter, dressing for the job he wanted, not the job he had and all that guff you're told. He wore brogues and Ralph Lauren jeans, nice shirts.

He walked taller and prouder, the latent confidence he'd been nursing coming to the fore. He was senior copywriter by then, trusted and respected. He was good at what he did. He is good at what he does. He's earned it all.

'Look,' he said that night, pulling things out of the fridge and swirling olive oil into a pan as I watched dumbly with a towel still on my head. 'When I first came here I didn't have anything, I couldn't pay you any rent and I couldn't help you out and all I could do was leech off you.'

'You weren't a leech,' I said, bristling that now I was the one in apology mode when I'd been so fired up with irritation.

'And I vowed that as soon as I could pay you back, I would. And now it's you who needs a bit of help and I can help you. So that's what I'm trying to do.'

He was used to me being aggravated and twitchy when he came home and he'd learned how to diffuse it, even though that often wound me tighter initially. I could never be bothered to make lunch, so my blood sugar was generally argumentatively low by dinner. I spent the days watching television and making plans for things that never happened.

I drank too much caffeine still, making a pot of coffee as soon as I got up and then another when that one had drained away. These rituals that used to be for the weekend, now filling my weekdays because nothing else did.

I had registered with a few recruitment consultants who were all wildly optimistic about my chances by phone, but after calling around their contacts, stopped phoning me back.

'I like looking after you,' Paul had said one night while I was brushing my teeth while I paced around the flat. I stopped brushing for a second, and then carried on. I didn't acknowledge it but I couldn't stop thinking about it. The next day, he left for work without leaving me a coffee, and I cried. I missed that coffee, that moment of waking and seeing his hand placing it down in my room, next to my bed. That quick chat before he left. God, I missed it like a limb, carrying my stump around all day and waiting for him to come back. It was a Friday in September. As I was waiting for him to get home, watching the clock and checking my text messages, the buzzer to the flat shook through me.

'Hello?'

'Delivery!'

Two tin foil cartons from my favourite Chinese take-away. I texted Paul, 'Thank you! Are you coming home to share it?'

Seconds later: 'It's a little apology. Mum called and asked me to go down to Somerset tonight and I knew we didn't have anything in the flat. Hope you enjoy it.'

'Give Viv my love, Paul,' I replied.

'I will.'

I had no right to be cross or sad, but I felt so left out that I nearly tipped the food in the bin. I wasn't even upset with Paul, I was upset that Viv hadn't asked for me to go with him. But I didn't tip the food away. I was hungry and lonely so I washed it down with three-quarters of a bottle of cooking wine that had been left in the fridge. And then I texted Paul.

'I miss you,' I wrote.

'Have you been drinking?' he replied.

'Only a couple of glasses,' I lied.

He got a taxi home that Sunday. I watched it pull up to the road outside our flat and I watched him climb out backwards, with a smart holdall he hadn't had when he left on Friday. 'I went and got some clothes to take down after Mum called,' he explained later.

'Rather than come home?' I asked but he ignored me.

'Paul,' I said when he came through the door.

'Yes?'

'I meant it. I missed you.'

He placed his holdall down and took his brogues off, taking care over his shoelaces and not meeting my eye.

'Did you really?' he asked, his cheeks looking flushed.

'Really,' I said. He didn't say anything for a while.

'I've got you an early birthday present,' he finally said and I noticed that his shaking hands were holding a box. Right there in our hall, he got down on one knee and snapped it open.

'We took a vow, Howarth. We're both single. And we're both about to turn thirty. What do you think? Will you marry me?'

A shock ran up my spine at first, but was almost immediately replaced with something like déjà vu. Something that felt like 'well, of course'. Something that felt like warmth. Fractured images of the night of the storm twinkled into view, Church Street, Paul's bed. The feeling of coming home to something. The potential to feel good, to feel comfort. The Loxtons. To be a Loxton.

'Do you mean it?' I asked, finally.

'Yes.' He didn't look at me, he looked at his hands, at the ring sitting in its box. A tiny little diamond set into gold, simple and honest.

'It wasn't legally binding, you know.'

'I know,' he laughed nervously. 'But I love you, Kate.'

'You do?'

'Yes.'

'Has someone put you up to this?'

'No.'

I took a deep breath, looking at his hair and his glasses, his mouth set in an awkward half-smile. I watched as he stood up straighter, and I stooped down a little. I looked at his eyes, his nervous, open face. The face I knew better than any other, even then. And I said yes.

We went out for dinner. Our first date. Me wearing the engagement ring that I still wear next to my wedding band. We toasted our arrangement that night, and ordered champagne. I felt like I should call someone, like there was some kind of procedure I'd not fulfilled but there was no-one for me to call.

'We should call your mum and dad,' I said to Paul.

He looked unsure. 'I'll call tomorrow. I've had too much to drink now.'

Nerves silenced us on the taxi ride home. We got into the flat and brushed our teeth side-by-side in the bathroom. I went into my room and changed into my nightie, the nicest one I had, and called him in. 'Would you like to sleep in here tonight?' I asked.

He smiled, coyly, I thought, but then he took a deep breath and strode across the room.

He was wearing pyjamas I'd seen a million times, but seeing them that night, outlining his body, seemed almost comical. But I didn't laugh, I slid down so I was lying on the bed. He looked at me, avoiding my eye, and then pushed my legs apart with his knee and lay half on top of me, carefully.

'Am I too heavy?' he asked, 'I don't want to hurt you.'

'You're not too heavy,' I laughed, breaking the spell. I felt him kiss me, gently at first. I'd kissed his cheek many times. I'd kissed his lips very few. It felt clandestine.

He ran his hand up my thigh and I thought I caught him gasping. There was very little there to touch, a long narrow limb, a sharp knee.

He knew my body. He remembered it from fifteen years before and I remembered his. He'd changed a little. Broader, taller, hairier. My hips were sharper than they'd been at fifteen. My bones clinking against his as we found a rhythm together. It was not wild and passionate. It was careful and gentle, awkward at first but somehow smoothing out into a feeling close to ease.

Along with my body he knew my brain. He knew my plans, he knew my hopes, fears. My history, the future I'd had, the future I'd lost. From the simplest things like doctor's appointments and the date my council tax was due, to the big things, the date my tube burst, the anniversary of my mother, the fact I couldn't remember which day my dad died. He knew it all.

I woke up again a few hours after we'd gone to bed and noticed he was still awake, looking at me. We were both back in our night clothes. He leaned across and kissed me quickly on my nose.

'Okay,' he said, smiling. 'We can do this. We can make this work.'

CHAPTER THIRTY-EIGHT

November 2012 – Saturday evening

The kids buckle in clumsily, they're tired and droopy so I climb into the back and check they're properly secure. The wind is bitter and wild. It seems to have picked up bits of sand and wet leaves to hurl at anyone stupid enough to be outside. I reach into the boot and grab the big car blanket, shake it out and lay it over the children. Hopefully they'll sleep and we can just scoop them into their beds back at the cottage. I've delayed it enough, now I need us to get back so I can get on with it before I lose my nerve.

As I open my door to get in to the passenger seat, the wind pulls it out of my grasp and I have to lurch after it.

'This wind!' I say, to no-one in particular.

'Let's get going, eh,' Paul says urgently. As I slide into the seat and pull the door closed, the sudden quiet of the car disorients me. 'I think this storm's going to be a rough one,' Paul says, as a nearby tree swings with a whoosh from one side to the other. 'I want to get back as quickly as possible,' he adds in a whisper.

2002

The night before our ceremony, Paul, me, Viv and Mick had gone for dinner at Chapter Two in Blackheath, the suburb where Paul and I hoped to buy a house eventually. 'A family house,' Paul had said, gripping my hand and looking at Mick until the older man looked down at his food. Fussier food than he was used to.

'You left Tina at home then, Mick?' Viv had asked, eyes playful.

'She's not wedding-day material, love,' he'd answered.

When Paul went to settle the bill and Mick nipped to the gents, Viv had fixed her sapphire-blue eyes on mine and said, 'Are you sure about this? About the wedding?'

I froze. I didn't say, 'What else do I have to be sure about?'

I didn't throw my hands up to the sky and hang my head and cry.

I didn't ask her if she thought people could start again from scratch, when they have nothing left to try.

After a second or two I simply nodded and smiled. 'Deadly,' I said.

She smiled broadly then, relief, I now think.

We held the wedding in Chelsea's Old Town Hall. We opted for the tiny Register Office, room for the two of us and our witnesses – Viv and Mick. Both Paul and I got ready at the flat, but Viv insisted that Paul leave before I put the dress on. He and Mick got a taxi ahead of us and had a pint in The Churchill Arms near the Town Hall.

Viv helped me into my dress and I heard her take a sharp breath when she saw my back, the individual vertebrae peeking through thin white skin.

'We need to get you fed up,' she muttered as she popped in the final button.

We'd ordered a cream vintage Bentley MK VI for the wedding car. It picked its way through the east-to-west traffic, standing out like a black-and-white photograph in a box of garish Polaroids. Throughout the stop-start ride, Viv and I talked about the wedding, the logistics, the car, the dress, the traffic. . . but nothing about the marriage. Nothing about what would happen after the wedding. The 'from this day forward and as long as we both shall live' part. I was grateful for that, and perhaps she was too.

As the Bentley pulled up outside the elegant stone steps of the Old Town Hall, Viv picked up my hands in hers and told me I looked beautiful, and that my mum would have been so proud. I remembered my mum's last words and I wasn't so sure, but I loved Viv for the gesture.

Our wedding song was 'Heroes' by David Bowie. Mick walked me into the little room, and down the almost-aisle between the two witness chairs, both of us stepping carefully like we were picking our way through nettles. I wore pretty rose-red ballet pumps, this was before they were worn by every woman everywhere, and a pale lemon dress with a false waist just under my bust leading to a full, petticoated skirt.

I'd had my hair dyed back to its postal red, but the new salon I'd gone to near my flat hadn't quite got it right. If I look at the photos now, I can see it. I doubt anyone else can tell the difference but I know now that everything was slightly off-colour.

Mick wore a new grey suit that his girlfriend Tina had helped him to choose from the Great Universal catalogue. He proudly told us he was paying it off weekly, that our big day was worth it.

Viv wore heels, which was something I'd never seen before, and a smart navy skirt suit. She had on a lilac blouse and a purple and gold butterfly brooch that I recognised from years before. Around her neck hung the gold-plated necklace Paul had bought her as a kid, now a slight green shade despite regular polishing and careful cleaning.

Paul stood at the register desk, turning to watch as I entered on Mick's arm. My husband-to-be looked clammy and white, wringing his hands. He'd had a haircut and wore a black suit and pale lemon shirt that we picked out together. He looked smart, and handsome. But seeing the outfit in situ, it reminded me of his old school uniform, and his first nervous days, and I nearly fled.

As I got to him, he smiled. And I smiled. We all smiled. We could do this.

CHAPTER THIRTY-NINE

November 2012 – Saturday night

Paul drives carefully along the pitch-black country lanes that hadn't seemed half as windy and perilous on the way to the restaurant. We're still about twenty minutes away from the cottage, and for the last ten neither of us has said a word. The kids are sleeping in the back, sticky under their coats and blanket. Izzy's hair has stuck to her forehead and I reach back to lower the blanket a little, always worrying about them overheating – a hangover from the baby years.

The car surges on, Paul frowning with concentration as he steers against gusts of wind and bursts of sideways rain. The low rumbles of thunder and occasional lightning have picked up apace, pulling themselves together into a proper pattern. The gathering storm reminds me of giving birth. The terror as the scattergun and sporadic contractions stabilise and the pain starts to feel like an organised assault. Building to something.

Ahead of us, the sky lights up blue, purple and white and the loudest thunderclap yet makes us both jump in our seats, snapping from our journey trance.

'Fuck,' Paul says, and we look at each other very briefly.

'Should we be driving in this?' I say.

'I don't know.' His uncertainty throws me. Paul is never uncertain. 'I don't know if there's anywhere safe to stop though,' he adds.

I look at the satnav for answers.

'It's only fifteen minutes now,' I say, trying to be positive but feeling nauseous from the wine and the buffeting wind. 'I guess it's worth driving for fifteen more minutes to get into the warm.'

Paul doesn't argue.

As the lightning throws another huge firework into the sky, I notice that the hedge all along the other side of the road has been knocked on its side. A huge, thick bush just crushed like a paper cup. I look at Paul's frown but say nothing.

We're about ten minutes away from Mousehole when I realise that I've not heard thunder for a little while. 'I think we've passed through the worst of it,' I say.

'God, don't tempt fate,' Paul says, but he seems a bit more relaxed.

'Ten years,' I say.

'Ten years,' Paul agrees.

'Ten years,' I say again, and realise I'm crying.

'Hey,' he says softly, and puts his hand on my knee. 'We'll be okay.'

I don't know what happens first.

All at once I hear the near-deafening creak above us, see the sky light up ultra-white and feel the weight as a huge tree is struck by a fork of lightning and crunches onto the roof of our car.

Everything shifts, we skid and then stop sharply, held in place by the chunk of charred wood like some malevolent giant teasing us with his thumb.

The engine is dead, the sky is black now and I have no idea which way we're facing.

I can't move my head, I can't turn around or see Paul. I can feel the roof above me dipping and catching strands of my hair in its jagged metal. I can feel wind and damp air inside the car, and for a moment I can't hear anything over the roar of my heartbeat in my ears. And then pain. Waves of pain from above, from my left side and finally radiating out from my chest. I struggle for breath.

I can see more lightning shooting out of the sky ahead and dancing across the sky towards us, like a drunk ballerina. The car has completely spun around and we're facing away from the hill, lying across the road, nose towards the sea.

I can hear the growl of the thunder, building itself up to bellow again.

'The kids!' I cry, and finally manage to turn my head a little to see the side of Paul's face. In the dark, I can make out the silhouette of his chin, the sharpness of his nose. His glasses are gone and he's perfectly still, his hands still gripped around the wheel. Lightning bursts the sky open again and I see his eyes wide in the brilliance of the brief light.

I try to turn in my seat but it's no use. I can't move, I can't look back and I can't see the children.

'Mummy?' Harry murmurs.

'Oh Harry! Harry! Are you okay?'

'I'm okay, what happened? Did we crash?'

'I don't know, is Izzy okay? Can you see if your sister's okay?'

This seems to shake Paul out of his shock. 'Oh God,' he says, trying to move in his seat to look behind at Izzy. 'I don't see her! I can't get out of my seat! Izzy!'

Harry unclips from his seat belt and climbs across to his sister and tugs at the blanket. There she is. Still curled up in her seat, breathing heavily, asleep, toy cat in the crook of her elbow.

'Oh, that girl,' Paul says. And then he exhales a rattling breath and closes his eyes. He thinks for a moment while I stare dumbly.

'Stay in your seat, Harry, we're going to call for some help,' Paul says.

'Okay, Daddy.' He sounds so little. He is still so little, really.

Paul manages to turn the key once; the engine is dead but we can at least see each other now, illuminated by flickering dashboard lights telling us that many things are wrong with the car. Both of us are pinned in place by airbags. We have some kind of powder on us that exploded like a flour bomb when the airbags deployed. I'm fairly sure that mine has broken some of my ribs, but I breathe slowly and the pain becomes more like a stitch as adrenaline kicks in.

I try to stay calm, try to ignore how close we are to the edge of the cliff. It can't be more than ten metres. The thought of the sea below, black and furious, sends a chill down my spine.

'I can't find my phone,' Paul says quickly. 'Can you see it anywhere?'

I can feel something in the footwell with my shoe but I can't reach down to get it. I can't even unbuckle. I gasp for air that's never enough.

'I can't reach it, Paul,' I pant. 'Can you reach my handbag? My phone's in there.'

Paul manages to free his left hand and reaches up to turn the overhead light on. I can see the strap of my handbag, can touch its corner with my knee if I move carefully. But neither of us can reach it.

'Let me get it,' I hear Harry say in the back, his voice startling me.

'No, baby,' I say, 'you can't come up here, there's no space.'

'I can go around the outside.'

'No!' Paul and I say at the same time.

The wind has picked up again and is dancing all around us, bits of debris, grit and sand hitting the sides of the car like waves. Right ahead of us, the lightning spikes down and nearly hits our windscreen as the thunder roars overhead.

'Daddy,' Harry says. 'Daddy, please. I can get it. I can hold on to the car and I can open Mummy's door and I can get your phones. Please, Daddy,' he pleads.

'No, Harry,' Paul says, abrasively and then softens. 'You can't, darling. It's not safe. Someone will see us soon and call for help.'

I can feel blood trickling down my left temple from somewhere under my hair but decide not to say anything. I don't want to scare Harry, I just want him to go back to sleep and stay warm. Suddenly, without warning, Harry has opened his door and the freezing wind rushes in, waking Izzy who shrieks, 'Daddy!'

'No, Harry!' Paul and I both call but it's too late. All we can do is watch as he tentatively feels his way around to the front of the car, along the bonnet and round to my door. I can see the wind rippling his coat. I watch his face tighten with concentration, so like his father as he grips my door handle and starts to pull. The door opens a crack, groans a bit but doesn't budge. Harry yanks and yanks and all we can do is watch and wait.

It doesn't move.

The lightning just ahead illuminates my boy's face and we can see the tears of frustration contorting him, his hair soaking onto his head as rain appears and is torrential in seconds.

'Please, Harry,' I call through the tiny gap he's opened. 'Please get back into the car.'

He keeps yanking, crying and yelling with exertion and won't stop until Paul yells across at him: 'Please, Harry, we need you back in the car, we need you to stay safe.' Beaten, he inches back and climbs in next to Izzy.

We try flashing our headlights, on and off, on and off. We think we can remember Morse code, we certainly knew SOS when we were in full storm mode as kids.

Dot, dot, dot. Dash, dash, dash. Dot, dot, dot.

'Or was it. . .' Paul says to himself.

Dash, dash, dash. Dot, dot, dot. Dash, dash, dash.

No-one appears. We can see the distant lights of Mousehole, but have no hope of reaching them.

Izzy goes back to sleep but Harry fights it until he can't hang on any longer and we see his head droop onto his shoulder. The car is still and quiet, just our little family tucked up under a broken tree, hidden. The crack in my door is freezing my left side and my teeth start to chatter.

'I hope they're warm enough,' I say to Paul.

'They'll be okay,' he says, more to himself than to me.

I know he's not sure if that's true but we have to believe it.

We give up with the headlights and put the overhead light on in lieu of a better plan. I feel my eyelids tugging downward, and marvel at the body's ability to prioritise sleep even in the eye of an emergency. I'm still struggling for air.

I shake my head awake and look across at Paul, studying his face in the white light. We both have crow's feet now, but not as deeply as our parents did at our age. Paul's parents, I should say, my mother never reached my age.

We're younger at forty than they were, healthier too. I look at Paul's hair, a shorter, smarter, greyer version of the style he's had since he was thirteen. He's not bad-looking, my husband. He has thinned out around his neck in the last few years, his belly sticks out a bit but nothing like many of our contemporaries.

My hair is very grey under the dye, but I'm not sure that Paul knows that. My hands show my age more than my face. My body has looked far worse, so that's something.

'I guess it's fitting that we're stuck in a storm,' Paul says after a while.

'Do you ever wonder,' I say falteringly, 'if things would have been different if it hadn't been for that other storm?'

'I think about that all the time,' he says.

I concentrate on breathing in and out, building up strength.

'Have you told her about the storm?' I say eventually, quietly.

'Her? Her who?' If there's a tremor in his voice, it's lost to the wind. He's a better liar than I thought.

'Paul,' I say quietly. 'It wasn't legally binding. We were fifteen.'

He says nothing, I gulp in some more air. 'You *can* leave,' I say.

'What are you talking about?' I hear him try to shift in his seat, feel the car move a little as he tries to touch me but can't move enough.

'You've been distracted, you've been working late, you've been less interested in sex, in me, in everything,' I say. It comes out flat, robotic. There's silence for a long moment.

'You think I'm having an affair?' he says.

'Aren't you?'

'How can you ask me that?'

I don't know what to say so I close my eyes for a moment and wake up to Paul nudging me.

'Kate? Are you okay?' he says. 'Are you hurt?'

'Have you fallen in love with someone?' I ask. I can't waste words, it hurts to talk.

'Not since you,' he says.

I think about the people I've loved. Who have I loved? The children, that's the purest and most unequivocal answer. I could have loved Will, back in college. I loved my mum, even if she didn't deserve it. I loved Mick and Viv. I loved The Loxtons.

'Kate,' he says more urgently. 'Are you hurt?'

I think about lying, about telling him I'm fine so that he doesn't worry but I'm getting colder and more afraid and a selfish need for comfort overtakes me.

'I'm a little hurt,' I say, 'and I'm a bit scared,' I whisper, just in case Harry is faking his sleep.

'Don't be scared,' Paul says back.

'Okay,' I say, and we both laugh briefly at the absurdity of it. *I might die*, I think. That's a turn up for the books. I wasn't expecting that when I woke up this morning, thoughts of tonight's plan bleeding into the dying embers of my dreams before I'd even come-to.

My greatest fear has always been something happening to both of us and there being no-one to look after the kids. Them landing in the care system, floating away.

'Are *you* okay?' I ask. 'One of us needs to be okay.'

'I'm fine. I'm stuck but I'm fine,' Paul says determinedly and I don't know if he's saying it to make it true or if it is true. 'And you will be too.'

I think about the three of them back at the cottage without me. I imagine him calling someone, a woman, telling her that things have changed. That there's a vacancy.

'Kate,' he says. 'I'm not having an affair. I have never, through our whole marriage, ever even considered having an affair.'

'You're always on the phone.' It sounds so small and inconsequential when I say it out loud.

'Everyone's always on the phone. There's no escape, work is. . .'

he sighs. 'Work is horrible. It's fucking horrible and I hate it and I have to—' He stops. 'I'm not having an affair.'

'I'm sorry.' What else can I say?

'Do you believe me?'

Paul would handle my dying better than my dad handled my mother's passing, I tell myself. It becomes a mantra for a little while in my head. Amazing how your own mortality can be reduced to a logistical panic when you have children to consider.

'I don't think it matters now,' I say.

'Stop thinking that,' Paul says suddenly.

'How do you know what I'm thinking?' I say a little snappily, my chest hurting with the sudden expulsion of air.

'I know exactly what you're thinking and you don't need to. It's not going to happen, we're all going to be fine.'

I feel the warmth running down from my temple. I feel the skin numbing under my hair, my stomach grows nauseous.

I think about them letting themselves into the cottage. Paul packing up my things, taking them back to London, even though they're no longer needed. I think about him finding the letter. He'd find the copy of *Under Milk Wood* and that might even make him smile whimsically, and then he'd be buoyed on to keep looking at my things. *Oh fuck.* Despite my worries, I feel my eyelids growing heavy until Paul starts to talk again.

'Soon we'll be back at the cottage and everything will be the same as it always was,' he says, but there's an edge to his voice.

'You want everything to stay the same?' I ask, my voice quivering through my chill-shaken jaw. Does he think I'm dying? *Do you think I'm dying, Paul?*

He's quiet for a long time and then he starts to wince and I realise he's trying again to release his seat belt.

'What are you doing?' I whisper hard. 'You can't go anywhere.'

I hear the buckle spring eventually and see him struggling to get his hand into his pocket.

'Kate, I've not been distracted by a fucking affair. I don't want an affair, I, it's not that at all. I've been trying to work out if I have the nerve to go through with something.'

'What?' I say, left eye blinking away the blood that's trickling onto its lashes.

'Look, there's something I need to give you,' he says with a new urgency. 'It's something of yours.'

The airbag has started to sink and shrivel and Paul manages to put something on top of it, in my eye line. I can hear the effort it takes.

Of course, I know immediately what it is as soon as I focus my right eye. The original letter. I recognise it just from the colour of the paper and the way it's folded, the same creases it had when it was tucked in its hidey-hole. 'You should have had this a long time ago,' he says quietly.

I don't know what to say, I just squint at the paper.

'I was going to give it to you later. I was trying to force myself to give it to you later, anyway. It doesn't make sense on its own, but here we are. It's the most important thing I have to give you, but if I tell you there's a beautiful platinum bracelet at home with emeralds in it, would you believe me?'

I laugh a little, despite myself. 'I believe you.'

'It's true,' he laughs too. Gallows humour.

He stretches and unfolds the letter with two fingers.

'It's two years too late,' he says. 'And I know that.'

'Oh fuck, Paul,' I say. I read the familiar words as if it's the first time.

Dear Katie,

By the time you read this, I'll have passed. You've always been like a daughter to me and I'm so sorry that you've lost two mums now. I hope you know that I've always been proud of you. I'm delighted with the wife and mother you've become and I couldn't want for more for my son. But Katie, I want more for you. If you want or need more, that is.

My girl, there's something I need to tell you. Something I should have told you eight years ago. I've thought about this so many times over the years but Paul begged me not to say anything. He's always looked out for you and always will.

Katie, I talked Paul into marrying you. It wasn't his idea and he didn't think it was the right thing to do. He didn't think you loved him, not like that. He thought you were in a rough spot and that you'd bounce back and find someone new. But I knew how you felt, I knew how lonely you were, how much the loss of your baby hit you. I knew that you wanted a family, and that no-one had shown you how to make one.

He's loved you since you were little. And he told me about your promise to each other and I told him that he had to honour it. That together you'd be stronger. He thought you'd say no and it would ruin your friendship. He wanted to wait for someone who really loved him, but I knew that deep down, you could be that person. I didn't let up. Every time we talked on the phone, every time he text messaged me and in person.

He turned up unannounced, you know. Just before he proposed. I know he told you something different, that I'd asked him to come down at short notice. But he turned up, he needed advice he said, he was beside himself about how to help you.

Over that weekend I convinced him.

I know it will hurt you to know this, but I should never have played God like that.

I didn't really know your mum but we did talk sometimes, while she was on my ward. I've been thinking about her a lot recently, after my diagnosis and especially when I came here. She told me that her greatest fear was you keeping yourself small, settling for less than you really wanted. I should have listened but I didn't really understand it until now.

After you and Paul got married, I watched and waited for you to become yourself again. But I'm still waiting. I worry that all I did was give you a placebo, and I don't want either of you to live like that. I was selfish to meddle. I'm not superstitious but maybe this is my punishment.

I love you like my own, Katie, you know that. You know there's nothing I wouldn't do for you but remember what I always say: nothing is ungetoutofable. If either of you regret this, if this is holding either of you back, it's not too late.

I'm sorry.

All my love,

Viv

In my heart, I'd suspected that things happened too conveniently. As soon as I could look in the mirror and take stock a little. I could see too many planets that were knocked into alignment by the big fucking snooker cue in the sky.

Paul changed towards his mum after the wedding. At the time I thought it was because he was busy, or maybe that the apron strings just slacken for everyone in their thirties – I had no personal experience to draw on. But I looked back with fresh eyes after I found the letter. Did he change because he was angry for the life she pushed him into? The life with me. Our family.

There was a strained Christmas visit a few months after we got married, which Paul cut short early to go into the office for an apparent emergency. I clung to Viv as we left, feeling guilty as her face had dropped when Paul said we had to go.

We drove down for her birthday the year after. We talked about visiting during my pregnancy with Harry the year after that. Paul was a fretful father-to-be, worrying about the effect the journey would have on me and my sickness, then worrying about the effect it would have on my back and then worrying about premature labour in the countryside miles from our nominated hospital.

And then Harry was born and we were immersed in him, holed up at home.

I was upstairs when the doorbell rang, feeding as usual. Harry was two weeks old and we'd found a kind of rhythm, a kind of path through each day, which wound around feeds and nappies and cups of cooling tea. I heard Mick's voice first, Paul shushing him and his voice lowering. I heard Viv's apologies and Paul's restrained manners, offering tea and showing them around the downstairs of our new house.

They couldn't wait any longer for an invitation, they said. They were sorry but they just had to meet him. Viv, of course, was the ringleader, Mick the designated driver.

When they held Harry, my son, their grandson, I saw them smile in a way I'd not seen since Paul was a kid. They were totally smitten.

After they'd left a few hours later to drive all the way back to Somerset that same day, Paul was quiet. Then he started to pace and fume. He complained about the imposition, the lack of respect for our bonding time as a new family.

Looking back through the lens of the letter, I wonder now if he was terrified. Terrified that his mum would give away what thin ice our family was built on. Terrified that we'd made a huge mistake, the consequences of which were deepening.

I'd been glad to see them and moved by their determination to meet our little boy. Because that's what grandparents should want to do and that's what they did and wasn't Harry lucky?

After that, the visits got further and further apart. Christmas and birthday cards were always sent, calls were always promised. I sent flowers from both of us every Mother's Day, I sent thank-you cards from Harry and Izzy, after Christmas and birthdays. But Paul would quieten at the mention of his mother's name in a way he didn't when I mentioned Mick. With Mick it was more of a sigh, an 'Oh well, that's Dad.' With Viv, it was a scrunching of the shoulders, a furrowing of the brow, a silence.

Angry at the life she'd nudged him towards or anxious that she might burst my bubble by confessing my husband had never really wanted me? I'd planned to find out tonight. And to set him free, if he wanted. But not like this.

'I don't understand,' I say eventually.

'I had the best intentions, Kate. You have to know that. And my mum did too, she just. . . you know what Mum was like. She fretted.'

'How did you know I'd found the letter?' I say, flatly. This is not how this was supposed to go. Not any of it. He's stolen my anger, just like he stole Viv's last words from me.

'You already found this letter? What? When? Why didn't you

say anything?' He looks genuinely shocked, the colour draining from his cheeks in thin light.

'I saw it and you know what I thought?' I wheezed, furious that he can keep secrets for years but I'm supposed to have admitted finding the letter immediately.

'I thought *there it is*. Proof. Proof that none of this is real. That you just wanted to claim a prize and your mum just wanted to save a waif and stray. Proof that the two people I trusted above all else manipulated everything. That you didn't fall in love with me, you didn't make a romantic snap decision, you were ground down and eventually just did what your mother told you.'

'Manipulated?' Paul sounds aghast. 'No, Kate.' I can hear him shaking his head against the headrest.

'And,' I hiss, 'I think it's proof that you were jealous. That you didn't want me to share your mother's love. How could you keep this from me otherwise?'

'You make it sound like I trapped you.' He sounds close to tears. 'Like I locked you up and threw away the key. You wanted us to get engaged, Kate. Don't forget that. You were desperate to be saved.'

'Why did you start this conversation now, like this; do you want me to die knowing you never really loved me?' I say. 'We could have kept this pretence up for a few more hours. It's all a bit pointless if I'm not here anyway.'

'You are *not* going to die,' he says, quietly and urgently. 'But what you're suggesting isn't true and it's not fair, Kate.' The airbag slackens a little more and I can turn slightly. He looks older than he did earlier this evening.

'You act like you were this amazing career girl but it was a house of cards,' he says. 'And when it was already crumbling you set fire to it for good measure. Look, this isn't what I wanted to say, I don't want this to be a row, that's not what this—'

'And every step of the way you were there in the background, Paul, helping it along.' I whisper hard, panting, my teeth still chattering. 'You got rid of Lucy so I had no hope of rekindling that friendship and having someone on my side, you—'

'What are you saying? That I dismantled your life? How, just, I just, fuck. I can't get my words out, how can you say that to me? Here, like this? You and Lucy were barely on speaking terms. How and why would I get rid of Lucy?'

'The pictures. And because you wanted me isolated. You wanted to take advantage.'

'You were already isolated! You isolated yourself!'

Harry stirs in the back and Paul takes a deep breath then lowers his voice.

'She showed those pictures to everyone. I'd seen them! And so had one of the juniors she went out with for a couple of weeks. He stole them after she dumped him. Everyone knew that.'

'I didn't know that.'

'Of course not, you didn't talk to anyone to find out. I was the only friend you had in that place, and I was your friend because I knew how decent you were underneath all those clothes and heels and attitude. You were a mess after the ectopic, that wasn't me!' He thumps his chest and tears spring in his eyes again. 'I just wanted to look after you. And before you say it, I didn't take advantage of you. Sleeping together was your idea.'

'Sleeping together,' I pant, quietly.

'Making love. We made love, and *I* meant it, even though you were a total mess.'

'I'm sorry it was so awful for you,' I say.

'No, it wasn't awful, that's not what I mean. I made love to you because I loved you. I loved you at your worst and your best. And I finally had a chance to believe that you loved me back, a chance to make you happy, I couldn't walk away. I was too weak, I had to take it.'

'I wanted to make you happy, too,' I hear myself say quietly. 'All I do is try to make you happy. Try to create the world you expect, the house, the kids, all of it.'

'Exactly. My mum was right.'

'You're angry with me for trying to be a good wife?'

'I'm not angry with you for anything, it just upsets me. Even after all this time, it's an effort, it's not natural. You're not yourself, not really. Still.'

'And that's why you're giving me the letter? To get yourself out of this?'

'Oh God, Kate. That's not it at all. I want you to know everything. I want you to know what went into my decision to propose, and I want you to know that I loved you so much that I hid that letter when Dad gave it to me. I didn't want you to leave me on Mum's encouragement. It was selfish, I know. I know it wasn't mine to keep but—'

'Your dad?'

Paul exhales. In the back, I can hear Izzy snoring and Harry breathing loudly through his mouth. Our babies.

'It was after the funeral, when Dad and I went to see her. . .' he falters. 'Went to see her grave. Mum had written us both a letter each and I think Dad was supposed to give them to us separately, but you know Dad.'

I smile despite myself. Who fucks up a dying wish?

'What did yours say?' I ask, my eyes sliding closed again.

'Pretty much the same. That she loved me and was proud of me but that she was sorry for playing God. Hey, don't go to sleep. Don't give in to it.'

I breathe in raggedly, feeling icily sober but desperately tired.

'Which book did you keep your letter in?'

I didn't stay awake for the answer.

Paul shakes me awake, I don't know how much time has passed. It could be seconds or hours.

'It was *Emma*,' he says. 'Jane Austen.'

'Huh,' I say. 'Right.'

I reach up to touch my head. The blood has stopped dripping but it's sticky and makes my stomach flip. I'm so cold I can no longer feel the pain in my ribs.

The airbag sags even more and I turn awkwardly in my seat. Something tears in my chest and I gasp.

'Oh God, Kate, your head.'

Paul can see the blood dripping down my face now. I nod, carefully, my left eye closed shut with crusted blood.

'Kate, don't worry,' he says, but he's saying it to himself, not me. I've made my peace with this. I just want to sleep. 'Someone will be along soon,' he says. His own airbag has loosened a little and I can see him desperately trying to find his phone.

'Where the fuck is it?!' he cries.

'Paul?'

'Yes?' he says but he's still desperately feeling for his phone, trying to reach my bag, checking on the kids. He's wild with panic.

'I don't know if I'm going to be okay.'

'You are,' he says, with fake jollity. 'Of course you are! You're going to be absolutely fine but after this holiday, things need to be different.'

I open my mouth but don't know what to say. Eventually, I whisper, 'You mean you'll leave me?'

'Leave you?' He stops searching and looks at me. 'Is that what you want?'

I don't know what I want. I want to sleep again, I know that.

'Don't go to sleep,' he pleads, shaking my shoulder until I cry in pain. 'Sorry, but please, stay awake. We need you. They need you.'

I sob quietly; I'm so tired but I know he's right. Children need their mother alive.

'You're going to be fine!' he announces loudly. 'But we should have been honest with each other. I need to be honest with you. About everything.'

I force myself to open my eyes and look across at him, unsure if this is a trick.

'I need to tell you something about your mum too,' he says. 'It wasn't cancer.'

My heart beats faster but I have to close my eyes again.

'She caught HIV and she died of AIDS,' Paul whispers. 'And I shouldn't have known that and you should.'

'I know she died of AIDS, Paul,' I whisper back. He's unburdening himself before the end, and I want him to stop. I want to sleep now. I want someone to tuck me in.

I hear him breathe big, slow breaths.

'You never said.'

'Nor did you,' I say, my eyes still closed.

'But how did you know?' he asks. 'Everyone told you it was cancer. *You* always tell people it was cancer.'

'Viv told me when I turned eighteen.' I feel another prickle of anger. At him, at her, at all of them.

'Why didn't you tell me you knew? At the time, I mean.'

'Because I didn't want to,' I say. It's the truth, but it's obviously not enough. 'And I didn't want it to be true. I asked her not to tell you either.'

'She'd already told me by then.'

'When did she tell you?'

'At the time.'

'So everyone knew except me. Why? Did they think I couldn't handle it? That I was too weak?'

'Your dad refused to let anyone at the hospital tell you but I always wanted to. And then after Will. . . The way you fell apart, how quickly you unravelled, I thought maybe they were right. Your mum didn't even know how she got it, Kate. There were men – men plural, Kate – and there were drugs. Your dad didn't have it, she caught it after they got married and had you.'

'And?' I say, quietly. 'I don't care how many guys she slept with.'

'No, I'm sorry, I didn't mean—' I heard him trying to twist in his seat.

'She was just unlucky,' I say. 'She was so young and all alone in a loveless marriage. She just wanted some fun. It wasn't her fault.'

'I'm not saying it was her fault, I'm sorry. I'm not blaming her, I was just—'

'You were though, and your mum did too. That's why I don't tell people, I don't want to give them the chance to judge her. She was a shit mum but she loved me, she just didn't know how to do it and then she didn't get the chance to put it right because she got unlucky. That's all.'

It still sits on me, this realisation. It's lain heavy and cold over my chest ever since I was a teenager, but mostly I've been able to lock it away. I had no idea that Paul had too.

I hear him exhale. 'It was probably wrong to keep it from you but what would you have done?'

I don't answer. Instead I think of my mum's friends at her funeral. The skinny man trying to apologise to me. I've thought about him a lot over the years, wondering if it was him that gave it to her or the other way around.

'Your dad tried to buy my mum's silence, you know. It would have ruined him, apparently. His foreign contacts wouldn't have dealt with him if they knew he was an AIDS widower.'

'You should have told me as soon as you knew, Paul,' I mumble, the words hard to form. 'It wasn't your secret to keep. I trusted you.'

'I trusted you,' he says. 'I lost my virginity to you, for God's sake.'

'I lost my virginity to you too,' I murmur.

'And then you just left, you just left me not knowing what had changed or what it meant.'

'And you've stayed angry with me all this time.' It wasn't a question.

'I'm not angry with you, Kate.' I feel his free hand on my arm. My eyes close again.

'How did Viv know about our vow to get married?' I ask, coming to abruptly, the whistling cold wind waking me.

'How?' he repeats, and I can hear him trying to move more in his seat. 'Because I told her.'

'When?'

'Just before your father's funeral.'

'Huh,' I say. 'And that's why she invited you down?'

'Maybe. Probably.' I prise my eyes open and I think I see tears forming again in the corner of Paul's eye but I can't keep mine open long enough to focus.

'I was visiting a few weeks before and I was having such a shit time. I got really down and Mum and I had some wine. I was feeling really maudlin and. . .' he snorts a little laugh '. . .at the same time dangerously nostalgic. I told her about that night. About our vow, about the fact that nobody I had ever met in my life had more of an effect on me, that I couldn't bear the thought of anyone else by my side. And bear in mind, Kate. . .' I hear him shift around uncomfortably in his seat. 'Bear in mind that you were gone from my life, you were not by my side, you were off doing whatever it was that you were doing and I don't think you thought about me once.'

'Not true.'

'That's not an accusation. You didn't owe me anything. And even when Mum meddled and invited me down to see you after your father's funeral, you still didn't owe me anything. I ended up owing you something. I've worked so fucking hard, Kate. For you, for those kids, for us. But it was built on a debt and that debt started that weekend. When you lay down in that bedroom and changed my life. Again.'

I realise that I haven't heard thunder for a while and the little hairs of lightning have moved further away. In their place, fat raindrops start falling onto the car and I imagine them collecting in a big puddle in the dip of the roof, it helps to calm me. I listen to Paul's voice and it seems to wave in and out in time with the drips and drops overhead.

'When it all started to crumble for you, Mum was desperate for me to honour our agreement, to propose, to prop you up, to pay you back. To give you the stability you needed and contain the explosion. But I couldn't do it. What was I going to do, walk in waving a contract around on your thirtieth birthday demanding you come good on our deal? I wasn't going to mention it at all. I was just going to let it lie and just try to be there for you while you patched yourself back up but you just kept spinning your wheels spraying mud everywhere and making things harder and harder for yourself. And then when you'd really fucked everything up, you brought up the vow.'

This wakes me up a little. 'I didn't,' I say indignantly, and try to sit up in outrage but the pain in my ribs pushes me back down and I wince, my breath reedy.

'Don't move, Kate, please.'

'I said I missed you, Paul. I didn't say anything about our promise.'

'You did,' he says firmly. 'You brought it up that night we were listening to old music at the table, remember? We were drinking red wine and you started dancing around and mucking about and asked if I remembered the night of the storms. And I said that of course I did.'

'I don't remember that, that's not how I remember it at all,' I say but even as I'm protesting, I can feel the memory of the night he's talking about appearing in a dark corner of my mind.

'It was you, Kate. And it was you who texted me to say you missed me. It was you who made that step. Not me. Never me. And fool that I am, I couldn't resist. I walked in to a marriage with my eyes wide open knowing that you didn't love me. I couldn't even pretend that it was one of those "well, we've been together three years and we want to settle down so we may as well" marriages. No, this really was a loveless marriage of convenience from the start for you.' He's ranting, nervous and filled with adrenaline. The rain drums relentlessly on.

'But it wasn't convenience for me,' he says. 'For me, it was everything I ever wanted, and it was broken from the beginning.'

'Paul,' I say, trying to grasp a handle on my thoughts. 'I'm so sorry that I haven't been the wife that you deserved but I'm so cold. And I'm so tired and scared but I need you to promise me that you will love our children with everything that you have. That you'll love Harry like I love him and that you'll—' My voice is raspy and it takes longer than I expect to make the sounds I'm trying to make. Paul cuts me off.

'Nope,' he says. 'Nope. I'm not doing this. This isn't what this is. We're all going to be fine. And when we're back, and everything's okay, I want to, things need to—' He stops and takes a deep breath. I hear him breathe it out one, two, three, four.

'Be my friend, Kate. I wasn't joking about the bracelet, it really is back at the cottage and you can see it when you get there. You'll get there.'

I start to cry and the tears sting in the cold.

'I bought you a friendship bracelet. That's my ten-year gift to you and I know that's not tin and I know that's not romantic but when we got married, I gained a wife but I lost my friend. And it's been ten years now, and you're still not my friend again, you're just my wife. My bored, small, resentful wife.'

I sob and shiver. Not because he's wrong, but because he's right. I am resentful and I am small. I don't see him as a friend, I see him as benefactor, boss and co-parent.

'We have to try so hard to be married but we didn't have to try to be friends. I'd rather you risk upsetting me, risk making me angry, than pussyfoot around me.'

'I don't—' I start to deny, start to follow my usual line and then, maybe it's the cold or the pain, I just stop. 'Yeah, you're right,' I say. 'I still don't know how to do this, not really. And it's not enough. It's not enough at all.'

'I know,' Paul says. 'Kate, I love you. I've loved you since we were eight years old but I miss you. We were best friends. And maybe finding someone you love that much, finding a best friend for life, a true "other half", maybe that's what it's all about. Maybe that's the vow we should have made.

'So here it is,' he says, taking a deep breath. 'I'm not my dad, I'm not going to storm off and flit in and out of Harry and Izzy's lives. We'll always be their parents but if you want to be free, you're free, but I can't lose you as a friend. I need you to take the piss out of me, to love me like you used to, not like you tried to.

'Fucking stamp all over the eggshells you walk on around me. Piss me off, I'll still love you. Say no to me, stand up to me, get a job, if that's what you want. Or don't. Get fat, get old, laugh, take risks, have adventures. Let the kids see us argue and the kids see us joke. Let them see what love looks like *for us*.' His voice breaks as he speaks. 'So what about it, Kate? Will you be my friend?'

'Paul,' I stumble on his name as I feel myself slip into an icy sleep.

When I open my eyes, there are lights shining in them. A gloved hand on my temple, my door off its hinges. How did they get that off without me hearing? I turn my head and cry out to get away from the sudden light, which hurts my eyes. I can hear beeps of machinery, see the blue light of the ambulance pulsing pointlessly in the corner of my eye.

They help the children out first, leading them carefully to the ambulance, Harry calling for me and Izzy dumbstruck in the green uniformed arms of a paramedic.

The rain has died down and the air lies heavily all around the car. Paul is watching the children helplessly from the driver's seat as they're placed in the ambulance like precious heirlooms. In the distance, I hear more sirens. Police, maybe. Now I know the kids are safe, I can feel my eyes closing again.

They're trying to get Paul out and are preparing a stretcher for him. He's protesting but I can't make out what he's saying over the sound of machinery cutting through his door.

As he's helped out, I reach for his hand.

Our fingertips touch and I manage to open my eyes properly one last time. His face is a mask of worry.

'It was always you,' I say, my voice barely there. 'It was always you.'

CHAPTER FORTY

November 2017

I take the stairs carefully; the timed light has already clicked off and I have to use the banister to steady myself, my other hand struggling to grip the suitcase. I still get a little breathless. It's pretty unedifying. The big brass key opens the room and I step into the sunlit room.

It's a disquieting feeling to be able to slip, alone and free, into this new place. No kids trying to burst through before me, no noise, no chaos.

And the room is lovely. Far nicer than I would have predicted when I first knew this building, when my life was so very different.

There's a big bed bursting with bright white linen, two tiny folded towels on top which, maybe because of their size and maybe because emotions bubble up unbidden so much more for me now, make me tearful.

The bed takes up most of the room and there are two cottage windows cut out of the deep walls with wooden shutters over them.

I place my suitcase down and step into the bathroom. It's surprisingly large with a walk-in shower and huge designer basin. I catch my breath for a moment and step back out into the main bedroom.

Outside, there are children playing in the beer garden. I peek out and see the small clutch of kids, their parents drinking nearby.

A bang on the door makes me jump and I pull it open cautiously.

Once inside, he passes me the other case in silence. I line them up like little soldiers.

I think of the kids. There's no way to ignore it, they're being looked after by a man who has never had to look after children by himself, not really.

'Do you really think they're okay?' I say, trying to sound light but not managing it, obviously.

He steps forward, puts his hands on my waist and yanks me to him like a rag doll. I look down but I can't help but smile. He presses his mouth onto mine, I move my hands up to his hair, weave my fingers into it and tug just a little. He releases me, just briefly and says, 'No, I don't think they're okay. I think they're probably having to listen to the Barron Knights and put up with my dad's jokes.' Paul grimaces. 'Which are probably pretty blue.'

I laugh.

'They'll be fine, won't they?' I ask, but instead of answering, he pushes me so I fall onto the bed.

'Happy anniversary,' he says, pulling his jumper over his head.

We drove down after work yesterday, our colleagues waving us off as we skipped out early to collect the kids from their schools, a little giddy with it. I started there first, a bijou agency literally called The Bijou Agency. But I'm jumping ahead.

When I woke up after the crash, the first face I saw was Paul's. True to form, he'd not left my side. The kids were dusted off and treated for shock but then Mick had been brought down to Cornwall by Tina, a particularly understanding old girlfriend, and the two of them had kept the children occupied at the Mousehole cottage, which was luckily still available for another few weeks.

I was transferred up to the Queen Elizabeth Hospital in Woolwich when I was strong enough to handle the long ambulance transfer. While the kids were at school, Paul would come and sit with me, nominally checking in with work on his phone but mostly reading with me, playing Shit Head with rules we found online and a deck of cards from the hospital shop.

We talked. About the crash, of course, he told me that he'd been breathalysed while I was unconscious, and nearly hit one of the police officers for keeping him away from the kids and me for those minutes. I couldn't imagine that. He told me that Harry had pleaded to ride in my ambulance. Actually on his knees, in the lashing rain. My boy. But we talked more about the ten-year journey leading up to the crash. And then we stopped talking about that and just started to talk. About nothing really, we just chewed the cud like we used to. After school, Paul brought the kids to see me and we watched TV in the private room that was costing more than I dared to ask. And I am wearing five years' worth of rose-tinted spectacles, because I nearly died. Not just in the crash but during surgery afterwards. And my body hurt like hell and I had an excruciating headache for weeks and I couldn't reach to shave my legs so I was both itchy and mortified, but once I was over the worst of it, once I believed I wasn't going to die, those weeks were strangely wonderful. And then finally I was home.

After weeks of caring for me and looking after the kids, Paul cried before he went back to work one Monday and we knew by Wednesday that his card was marked.

Whether they'd decided to manage him out while he was off or after he returned without any of the hunger of before, we'll never know. He stalked his corner office as colleagues avoided his eye and was called into a meeting on Friday afternoon.

We took a long holiday. Renting a *gite* in France and getting fat on cheese while ignoring the emails from school about fines for unauthorised absences. We talked about what we wanted. Surprising each other and ourselves.

A few weeks after we returned to Blackheath, I found a job at The Bijou Agency running their training academy. I mentor the juniors, I run workshops for women, I help tease out talent. I love it. My agency specialises in charities and socially responsible business, which is why I suggested Paul ignore the two job offers from corporate agencies that gave him an anxiety stomach and instead meet my new boss for a coffee.

Even with our combined salaries, we earn half what Paul used to bring home alone. We travel in to work together most days. Sometimes we have lunch in the small cobbled garden behind the office. I've made new friends too, women who make me laugh until I'm close to wetting myself. Paul works to help organisations he cares about advertise themselves. And he reads again.

We're happy.

Unaccustomed to afternoon sex, we fall asleep and when I shake myself awake, the sky outside is dark blue. The chatter of smokers gathering outside bubbles up to our window.

I reach for my phone and look at the time. It's past six. I slide over to Paul, put my head on his chest. There's still that old ghost of a feeling, that maybe I'm crossing a boundary, that familiarity and sexuality are getting all messed up. But it's an old feeling, a facsimile of the truth and I have let it go. I kiss his chest and he stirs.

'Hey,' he says and reaches for his glasses, neatly placed on the little bedside table.

'Do you want to get dinner downstairs?' I say.

'It's lovely here now, isn't it?' he replies. 'I never would have imagined The Swan turning into something like this.'

'It is lovely.'

I sit up and run my fingers through my hair. 'I could do with a shower.'

'Yeah,' he smiles, 'we probably both could.'

'You know what I really want to do though?' I say.

'What?'

'Put my jeans back on and go out and get some chips.'

We split a bag of fat, vinegary chips. The portion is smaller than I remember from our childhood. Or maybe we're just so much bigger. I lean on him just a little as we walk, noticing all the changes in the village.

We walk past the church and fall silent for a moment. But we don't walk into the graveyard where Viv lies, buried in a purple dress and her necklace from Paul. Instead, we turn left into the recreation ground, which used to have a couple of rusty swings and a climbing frame. It now has some kind of arty wooden jungle gym. A few metres away, a teenager with floppy dark hair stands awkwardly next to a blonde teenage girl who is sitting on a bench looking at her mobile phone.

'Oh shit,' I say, 'isn't that the girl we met last time we came down?'

Harry scratches his head and leans over to say something to her. He's so tall I almost don't recognise him.

'What's he doing out at this time?' Paul says.

'Were we indoors at seven o'clock on a Saturday when we were thirteen?'

'You know we were!'

We stand and watch for a moment. The girl stands up, as if it's causing her some inconvenience but she supposes she'll make the effort. Harry smiles, offers her his hand and she takes it. He leans in to kiss her.

'Oh my God,' I say, stifling a laugh.

'Bloody hell,' Paul whispers, squeezing my hand, 'he's a lot more efficient than we were.'

We sneak back out of the park and dump the greasy chip wrappers in the bin.

'We've done alright, haven't we?' Paul says.

'We've done alright,' I say. As we walk back to The Swan, we stop just a moment outside 4 Church Street. The curtains are closed but we listen at the door. The faint sound of Status Quo seeps through.

'I love you,' I whisper to Paul.

'I know,' he whispers back. 'I know.'

Acknowledgements

Thank you for reading *Love Will Tear Us Apart*. It is the most personal book I've written to date, and I really hope you liked it because it means an awful lot to me.

Love comes in many forms. We may grow up thinking about it in binary terms, but then we meet friends who we love like siblings and partners who we love like friends. I am a very lucky woman. I have a lot of people I love and there's not much more I could hope for than that. But of course, above all others are my husband James and my children, Mia, Alfie, Elliot and Finch. I love them fiercely.

When I started writing this book, I had been happily married just over seven years. It's pure coincidence that it has been published in the tenth year of my (still very happy) marriage!

I am definitely not Kate (I'm five foot three, for a start, and my parents are lovely) nor is my husband anything like Paul, but we do have one thing in common: friendship. No-one's opinion matters more to me than his, no-one makes me laugh harder and I've never had a bigger champion. But unlike Kate, I fell head over heels without prior arrangement and my life with this man has been the most awesome adventure. Every year together is a privilege; I love the bones of him.

I spent many childhood years living in the Somerset town of Castle Cary, and it holds a huge place in my heart. I hope its residents will forgive the fictionalised version of the place, and the surrounding villages. Little Babcombe itself does not exist but is an amalgam of various homes I've had. I also hope that anyone who works in advertising will forgive the massive massaging of truth. . .

Special thanks to Sarah Fletcher and Kate Diamond who read an early draft and were so encouraging, even though I've now accidentally stolen both of their names for characters across my last book and this one.

Finally, becoming an author has brought me many wonderful things, but perhaps the most wonderful of all things are the friendships it's gifted me with other writers. Gilly McAllister and Hayley Webster, I'm especially looking at you two.

As ever, I have to thank my amazing agent Nicola Barr. Right from the first few chapters that I nervously sent over, Nicola was so very supportive and I'm forever grateful to have her on my side.

My brilliant editor, Sara O'Keeffe, understood instinctively what I was trying to do, who the Loxtons were and how their story should be told. Both Sara and Susannah Hamilton from Corvus have helped immeasurably; their suggestions and edits were always spot-on and the whole team there is just such a pleasure to work with. Thank you all.